The Luck of Ginger Coffey

The Great Victorian Collection

BOOKS BY
BRIAN MOORE

The Lonely Passion of Judith Hearne
The Feast of Lupercal
The Luck of Ginger Coffey
An Answer from Limbo
Canada (with the editors of *Life*)
The Emperor of Ice-Cream
I Am Mary Dunne
Fergus
The Revolution Script
Catholics
The Great Victorian Collection

BRIAN MOORE

The Luck
of Ginger Coffey

The Great
Victorian Collection

The Luck of Ginger Coffey

A Novel by Brian Moore

An Atlantic Monthly Press Book

Little, Brown and Company · Boston Toronto

To Jacqueline

LIBRARY OF CONGRESS CATALOG CARD NO. 60–6533

ATLANTIC–LITTLE, BROWN BOOKS
ARE PUBLISHED BY
LITTLE, BROWN AND COMPANY
IN ASSOCIATION WITH
THE ATLANTIC MONTHLY PRESS

*Published simultaneously in Canada
by Little, Brown & Company (Canada) Limited*

PRINTED IN THE UNITED STATES OF AMERICA

One   Fifteen dollars and three cents. He counted it and put it in his trouser-pocket. Then picked his Tyrolean hat off the dresser, wondering if the two Alpine buttons and the little brush dingus in the hatband weren't a shade jaunty for the place he was going. Still, they might be lucky to him. And it was a lovely morning, clear and crisp and clean. Maybe that was a good augury. Maybe today his ship would come in.

James Francis (Ginger) Coffey then risked it into the kitchen. His wife was at the stove. His daughter Paulie sat listless over Corn Flakes. He said "Good morning," but his only answer came from Michel, the landlady's little boy, who was looking out the window.

"What's up, lad?" Coffey asked, joining Michel. Together, man and boy, they watched a Montreal Roads Department tractor clambering on and off the pavement as it shunted last night's snowfall into the street.

"Sit down, Ginger, you're as bad as the child," his wife said, laying his breakfast on the kitchen table.

He tried her again. "Good morning, Veronica."

"*His* mother was just in," said she, pointing to Michel. "Wanting to know how long we were going to keep the place on. I told her you'd speak to her. So don't forget to pop upstairs and give our notice the minute you have the tickets."

3

"Yes, dear." Flute! Couldn't a man get a bite of breakfast into him before she started that nattering? He knew about telling Madame Beaulieu. *All right.*

A boiled egg, one slice of toast and his tea. It was not enough. Breakfast was his best meal; she knew that. But in the crying poverty mood that was on her these last weeks, he supposed she'd take his head off altogether if he asked her for a second egg. Still, he tried.

"Would you make us another egg?" he said.

"Make it yourself," she said.

He turned to Paulie. "Pet, would you shove an egg on for me?"

"Daddy, I'm late."

Ah, well. If it was to be a choice between food and begging them to do the least thing, then give him hunger any day. He ate his egg and toast, drank a second cup of tea and went out into the hall to put his coat on. Sheepskin-lined it was, his pride and joy; thirty guineas it had cost him at Aquascutum.

But she came after him before he could flee the coop. "Now, remember to phone me the minute you pick up the tickets," she said. "And ask them about the connection from Southampton with the boat train for Dublin. Because I want to put that into my letter to Mother this afternoon."

"Right, dear."

"And, by the way, Gerry Grosvenor's coming in at five. So don't you be stravaging in at six, do you hear?"

What did she have to ask Gerry Grosvenor up here for? They could have said good-by to Gerry downtown. Didn't she know damn well he didn't want people seeing the inside of this place? Flute! His eyes assessed their present surroundings as Gerry Grosvenor's would. The lower half of a duplex apartment on a shabby Montreal street, dark as limbo, jerry-built fifty years ago and going off keel

4

ever since. The doors did not close, the floors buckled and warped, the walls had been repapered and repainted until they bulged. And would bulge more, for it was a place that people on their way up tried to improve, people on their way down to disguise: all in vain. The hegira of tenants would continue.

Still, what was the use in talking? She had asked Gerry: the harm was done. "All right," he said. "Give us a kiss now. I'm off."

She kissed him the way she would a child. "Not that I know what I'm going to give Gerry to drink," she said. "With only beer in the house."

"Sure, never mind," he said and kissed her quick again to shut her up. "So long, now. I'll be home before five."

And got away clean.

Outside in the refrigerated air, snow fine as salt drifted off the tops of sidewalk snowbanks, spiraling up and over to the intersection where a policeman raised his white mitt paw, halting traffic to let Coffey cross. Coffey wagged the policeman the old salute in passing. By J, they were like Russkis in their black fur hats. It amused him now to think that, before he came out here, he had expected Montreal would be a sort of Frenchy place. French my foot! It was a cross between America and Russia. The cars, the supermarkets, the hoardings; they were just as you saw them in the Hollywood films. But the people and the snows and the cold — that woman passing, her head tied up in a babushka, feet in big bloothers of boots, and her dragging the child along behind her on a little sled — wasn't that the real Siberian stuff?

"M'sieur?"

The other people at the bus stop noticed that the little boy was not wearing his snow suit. But Coffey did not. "Well, Michel," he said. "Come to see me off?"

"Come for candy."

"Now, there's a straight answer, at least," Coffey said, putting his arm around the boy's shoulders and marching him off to the candy store on the corner. "Which sort takes your fancy, Michel?"

The child picked out a big plastic package of sourballs. "This one, *M'sieur?*"

"Gob stoppers," Coffey said. "The exact same thing I used to pick when I was your age. Fair enough." He handed the package over and asked the storeman how much.

"Fifty cents."

By J, it was not cheap. Still, he couldn't disappoint the kid, so he paid, led his friend outside, waited for the policeman to halt traffic, then sent Michel on his way. "Remember," he said, "that's a secret. Don't tell anybody I bought them."

"Okay. *Merci, M'sieur.*"

Coffey watched him run, then rejoined the bus queue. He hoped Veronica wouldn't find out about those sweets, for it would mean another lecture about wasting his money on outsiders. But ah! Coffey remembered his boyhood, the joys of a penny paper twist of bullseyes. He smiled at the memory and discovered that the girl next to him in the queue thought he was smiling at her. She smiled back and he gave her the eye. For there was life in the old carcass yet. Yes, when the good Lord was handing out looks, Coffey considered he had not been last in line. Now, in his prime, he considered himself a fine big fellow with a soldierly straightness to him, his red hair thick as ever and a fine mustache to boot. And another thing. He believed that clothes made the man and the man he had made of himself was a Dublin squire. Sports clothes took years off him, he thought, and he always bought the very best of stuff. As he rode downtown on the bus that morning there wasn't a soul in Montreal who would say There goes a man who's out of work. . . . Not on your earthly. Not even when he went through the doorway of the Unemployment Insurance Commission and marched right up to *Executive & Professional*, which seemed the right place for him.

"Fill it out at the table over there, Mr. Coffey," said the counter clerk. Nice young fellow, no hint of condescension in his tone, very helpful and natural as though this sort of thing happened to everyone. Still, pen in hand, *write in block letters or type*, Coffey was faced once again with the misleading facts of a life. In block letters, he began:

Born: May 14, 1916, DUBLIN, IRELAND.

Education: PLUNKETT SCHOOL, DUBLIN. NATIONAL UNIVERSITY OF IRELAND, UNIVERSITY COLLEGE, DUBLIN.

Specify degrees, honors, other accomplishments: [He had not finished his B.A., but never mind.] BACHELOR OF ARTS . . . [Pass.] 1938.

List former positions, giving dates, names of employers, etc.: [Flute! Here we go.]

IRISH ARMY. 1939-1945. ASST. TO PRESS OFFICER, G.H.Q. COMMISSIONED 2ND LIEUT. 1940; 1ST LIEUT. 1942.

KYLEMORE DISTILLERIES, DUBLIN. 1946-1948, SPECIAL ASSISTANT TO MANAGING DIRECTOR; 1949-1953, ASSISTANT IN ADVERTISING DEPARTMENT.

COOMB-NA-BAUN KNITWEAR, CORK. 1953-1955, SPECIAL ASSISTANT.

COOTEHILL DISTILLERIES, DUBLIN.
COOMB-NA-BAUN KNITWEAR, DUBLIN.
DROMORE TWEEDS, CARRICK-ON-SHANNON.
} AUGUST 1955-DECEMBER 1955. SPECIAL REPRESENTATIVE FOR CANADA.

List Present Position:

[His position as of this morning, January 2, 1956, was null and bloody void, wasn't it? So he put a line through that one. Then read it all over, absent-mindedly brushing the ends of his mustache with the pen. He signed with a large, much-practiced signature.]

The wooden plaque in front of the young man who looked over his application bore the name J. DONNELLY. And naturally J. Donnelly, like all Irish Canadians, noticed Coffey's brogue and came out with a couple of introductory jokes about the Ould Sod. But the jokes weren't half as painful as what came after them.

"I see you have your B.A., Mr. Coffey. Have you ever considered teaching as a profession? We're very short of teachers here in Canada."

"Holy smoke," said Coffey, giving J. Donnelly an honest grin. "That was years ago. Sure, I've forgotten every stitch."

"I see," J. Donnelly said. "But I'm not quite clear why you've put down for a public relations job? Apart from your — ah — Army experience, that is?"

"Well now," Coffey explained. "My work over here as Canadian representative for those three firms you see there, why that was all promotion. Public relations, you might call it."

"I see. . . . But, frankly, Mr. Coffey, I'm afraid that experience would hardly qualify you for a public relations position. I mean, a senior one."

There was a silence. Coffey fiddled with the little brush dingus in his hat. "Well now, look here," he began. "I'll put my cards on the table, Mr. Donnelly. These firms that sent me out here wanted me to come back to Ireland when they gave up the North American market. But I said no. And the reason I said no is because I thought

8

Canada was the land of opportunity. Now, because of that, because I want to stay, no matter what, well, perhaps I'll have to accept a more junior position here than what I was used to at home. Now, supposing you make me an offer, as the girl said to the sailor?"

But J. Donnelly offered only a polite smile.

"Or — or perhaps if there's nothing in public relations, you might have some clerical job going?"

"Clerical, Mr. Coffey?"

"Right."

"Clerical isn't handled in this department, sir. This is for executives. Clerical is one floor down."

"Oh."

"And at the moment, sir, ordinary clerical help is hard to place. However, if you want me to transfer you?"

"No, don't bother," Coffey said. "There's nothing in public relations, is there?"

J. Donnelly stood up. "Well, if you'll just wait, I'll check our files. Excuse me."

He went out. After a few minutes a typewriter began to clacket in the outer office. Coffey shuffled his little green hat and deerskin gauntlets until J. Donnelly returned. "You might be in luck, Mr. Coffey," he said. "There's a job just come in this morning for assistant editor on the house organ of a large nickel company. Not your line exactly, but you might try it?"

What could Coffey say? He was no hand at writing. Still, needs must and he had written a few Army releases in his day. He accepted the slip of paper and thanked the man.

"I'll phone them and tell them you'll be on deck at eleven," J. Donnelly said. "Strike while the iron's hot, eh? And here's another possibility, if the editor job doesn't work out." He handed over a second slip of paper. "Now, if nothing comes of either of those," he said, "come back here and I'll transfer you to clerical, okay?"

Coffey put the second slip in his doeskin waistcoat and thanked the man again.

"Good luck," J. Donnelly said. "The luck of the Irish, eh, Mr. Coffey?"

"Ha, ha," Coffey said, putting on his little hat. Luck of the Canadians would suit him better, he thought. Still, it was a start. Chin up! Off he sloped into the cold morning and pulled out the first slip to check on the address. On Beaver Hall Hill, it was. Up went his hand to signal a taxi, but down it came when he remembered the fourteen dollars left in his pocket. If he hurried, he could walk it.

Or shanks' mare it, as his mother used to say. Ah, what's the sense giving Ginger any money for his tram, she'd say; he'll never use it. Doesn't he spend every penny on some foolishness the minute you put it in his pocket? And it was true, then as now. He was no great hand with money. He thought of himself in those far-off days, hurrying to school, the twopence already spent in some shop, whirling the satchel of schoolbooks around his head, stopping at Stephen's Green to take out his ruler and let it go *tickety, tak, tak* among the railings of the park. Dreaming then of being grown up; free of school and catechism; free from exams and orders; free to go out into a great world and find adventures. Shanks' mare now along Notre Dame Street, remembering: the snow beginning to fall, a melting frost changing gray fieldstone office fronts to the color of a dead man's skin, hurrying as once he had hurried to school. But this was not school. School was thirty years ago and three thousand miles away, across half a frozen continent and the whole Atlantic Ocean. Why, even the time of day was different from at home. Here it was not yet midmorning and there, in Dublin, the pubs would be closing after lunch. It made him homesick to think of those pubs, so he must

10

not think. No, for wasn't this the chance he had always wanted? Wasn't he at long last an adventurer, a man who had gambled all on one horse, a horse colored Canada, which now by hook or crook would carry him to fame and fortune? Right, then!

So shanks' mare he went across Place d'Armes under the statue of Maisonneuve, an adventurer and a gambler too, who had sailed out in sixteen forty-one to discover this promised land, and shanks' mare past the Grecian columns of a bank and do not think what's left in there, but shanks' mare alone up Craig Street, remembering that he was far away now from that wireless network of friends and relations who, never mind, they would not let you starve so long as you were one of them but who, if you left home, struck out on your own, crossed the seas, well, that was the end of you as far as they were concerned.

And shanks' mare up Beaver Hall Hill, last lap, all on his onlie-oh, remembering that any man who ever amounted to anything was the man who took a chance, struck out, *et cetera*.

But oh! he was close to the line today. Only he knew how close.

And at last, shanks'-maring it into a big office building, riding up in an express elevator to the fifteenth floor, he was let out into a very grand reception hall. Up he went to a modern desk that was all glass and wooden legs which let you see the legs of the smashing blond receptionist behind it. Who smiled at him but lost her smile when he said his name and in aid of what Ginger Coffey had blown in. She was sorry but Mr. Beauchemin was presently in conference and would you just sit over there for a moment, sir? And would he just fill in this form while he was waiting? In block letters, please. In block letters he pondered once again the misleading facts of a life.

When he had set them down, he handed back the form, and the girl read it over in front of him. Which mortified him. There were so few things you could write down when faced with the facts of a life. "Fine, sir," she said in a schoolmistressy voice. "Now, perhaps while you're waiting you'd like to familiarize yourself with our house organ. Here's our latest issue."

That was very kind of her, he said. He took the glossy little magazine and went back to the banquette to study it. The *Nickelodeon* was the name of the house organ. He wondered if that was funny on purpose but decided not. Canadians saw nothing comical in the words "house organ." He flipped through the glossy pages. Pictures of old codgers getting gold watches for twenty-five years of well-done-thou-good-and-faithful. Wasn't it to avoid the like of that that he had emigrated? He skipped through the column of employee gossip called *Nickel Nuggets* but looked long at the photos on the *Distaff Doings* page. Some of the distaffers were very passable pieces indeed. Well now, enough of that. He turned to the main article which was entitled J. C. Furniss, *Vice-Pres. (Traffic): A Profile*. It seemed that even J. C. himself had started in humble circs as a chainman (whatever that was). Which was the rags to riches rise the New World was famous for. Which cheered a fellow up, because at home it was not like that. At home it was Chinese boxes, one inside the other, and whatever you started off as, you would probably end up as. Which was why he had come here. Which was why, this morning, he had been stumped when faced with the facts of a life.

12

For the true facts you could not put on an application form, now could you? For instance, when Ginger got out of the Army, Veronica's relatives had influence at Kylemore Distilleries and the job they offered him was a real plum, they said: Special Assistant to the Managing Director. Plum! Two years as a glorified office boy. Get me two tickets for the jumping at the Horse Show, Ginger. Book me a seat on the six o'clock plane to London. Go down to customs and see if you can square that stuff away, Ginger. Orders, orders . . . And, after two years, when Ginger asked for a raise and more responsibility, the Managing Director gave him a sour look and kicked him downstairs into the Advertising Department. Where, when he tried some new ideas, the Advertising Manager, a Neanderthal bloody man, name of Cleery, called him in and said: "Where do you think you are, Coffey? New York? Remember, the thing that sells whiskey in this country is being on good terms with the publicans. Now, get back to your desk at once."

Orders. Taking guff from powers that be. So, the minute Ginger heard of an opening in a place called Coomb-Na-Baun Knitwear in Cork, he resigned and over Veroncia's protests moved his family down there. But Cork was not New York either. Ah, no. Orders, orders . . . Fifty years behind the times. Taking guff. Never free.

In fact, he might never have got free if his father (R.I.P.) hadn't died, leaving two thousand quid to Ginger, enough to pay their debts and start them off again. Again, he did it over Veronica's protests; but this time, by J, he decided to get right out of the country. Far too late now to do the things he once had dreamed of: paddling down the Amazon with four Indian companions, climbing a peak in Tibet or sailing a raft from Galway to the West Indies. But not too late to head off for the New

World in search of fame and fortune. So he went up to Dublin and took his old boss out to lunch. Filled the Managing Director of Kylemore Distilleries with Jammet's best duck *à l'orange* and asked him point-blank if Kylemore would be interested in opening up a North American market. They would not, said the Managing Director. "All right then," Coffey said. "You'll be the sorry ones, not me." And went straight across the street to Cootehill Distilleries, Kylemore's chief competitor. But flute! At Cootehill they told him they already had a man in New York. "Well," said Coffey. "Well . . . what about Canada, then?" No, they did not have anyone there. And yes, they were willing to let him have a crack at selling their whiskey in Canada. Seeing he was paying his own way out there, why not? A small retainer? Yes, they might manage that.

Right, then! Before he sailed, he lined up two side lines. A North American agency for Coomb-Na-Baun Knitwear, which the Dublin office gave him over the Cork office's objections. And a little side line as American representative for Dromore Tweeds of Carrick-on-Shannon, which was part-owned by an old school pal of his. And so, six months ago, after a round of good-bys forever, he, Veronica and Paulie sailed out to Montreal, taking the great gamble. His own boss at last.

Except that now, six months later, he was his own boss no longer. And so, at a quarter to twelve, the *Nickelodeon* read from cover to cover, he smiled at the receptionist, still hoping. She came over. "I'm afraid Mr. Beauchemin will be tied up until after lunch. Do you think you could come back at two-thirty?"

Coffey thought of Mr. Beauchemin trussed-up on his office carpet. He said yes, he thought he could.

Down he went in the express elevator, across the lobby and out into the street. The noon crowd scurried along icy pavements from central heat to central heat. Six office girls, arms linked, high voices half lost in the wind, edged past him in a tottering chorus line. Bundled against the wind, no telling what they looked like. He followed them for a while, playing an old game of his. That very instant a genie had told him they were all houris awaiting his pleasure, but only one must he choose and he must not look on any of their faces. He must choose from the rear view. All right, then, he decided on the tall one in the middle. His choice made, he followed them to the intersection of Peel and Ste. Catherine Streets, and as they paused for the traffic light he came level and inspected their faces. She had a long neb. He should have picked the little one on the outside right. Anyway, none of them was half as pretty as his own wife. He turned away.

Businessmen clutching hat brims butted impatiently past his aimless, strolling figure. A taxi, its tire chains rattling in the brown-sugar slush, pulled up beside him to disgorge six Rotarians who ran up the steps of a hotel, their snow-filthy rubbers tracking the wine-colored carpet. A bundle of newspapers, hurled from the tailgate of a truck by a leather-jacketed leprechaun, fell by his feet. He paused, read the headline on top, as a news vendor rushed from a kiosk to retrieve.

WIFE, LOVER SLAY CRIPPLE MATE

Which reminded him. He had not phoned Veronica.

Slow stroll across Dominion Square, everyone hurrying save he, every face fixed in a grimace by the painful wind, eyes narrowed, mouths pursed, driven by this cruel climate to an abnormal, head-bent helter-skelter. He passed a statue of Robert Burns, reflecting that this snow-drifted square was an odd place for that kiltie to wind up. And that reminded him of failures: Burns's brew was called for a lot more often on this continent than usquebaugh. "Usquebaugh is the name of it, Mr. Montrose; yes, we Irish invented it, quite different from rye or Scotch. I have a booklet here, Irish coffee recipe . . ." Promotion, they called it. You had to promote before you could sell. But, to those thicks back in Ireland, promotion was not work.

Dear Coffey:
Yours of the 6th to hand. Before we approve these expenses, which seem very high to us, our directors would like to know how many suppliers you can guarantee. So far, in our opinion, you have not . . .

That was in the beginning of October. He should have seen the writing on the wall. But instead, he started to use his own savings to keep the ship afloat. He had to. Those thicks refused to pay the half of his expenses. And then, a month later, three letters with Irish postmarks arrived in the same week, as though, behind his back, the whole of Ireland had ganged up on him:

Dear Coffey:
I regret to inform you that at the last meeting of our board of directors it was decided that in view of current dollar restrictions and the heavy "promotion" expenses you have incurred, we feel unable at this time to continue our arrangement with you. Therefore, we are no longer prepared to pay your office rent or to continue your retainer after this month. . . .

Dear Coffey:
Four orders from department stores and single orders from six other shops which have not been repeated do not justify the money you are charging us. And advertising at the rates you quote is quite out of the question. Coomb-Na-Baun Knitwear has always enjoyed a modest sale on your side of the water without any special promotion, and

*so we feel at this time that it is wiser all around for us to
cancel our arrangement with you. . . .*

Dear Ginger:
*Hartigan says we would be better off sending an out-
and-out traveler to cities like Boston, New York and Toronto to show samples and take orders as the British tailor-
ing firms do. High-power American methods do not go
over in Carrick-on-Shannon, so if you will kindly let us
have back the swatches. . . .*

He burned those letters. He economized by giving up
their flat and moving to this cheap dump of a duplex.
But he did not tell Veronica. For two weeks he sat in
his rented office, searching the want ads in the newspapers, dodging out from time to time for half-hearted
inquiries about jobs. But the trouble was what his trouble
always was. He had not finished his B.A., the Army years
were wasted years, the jobs at Kylemore and Coomb-Na-
Baun had not qualified him for any others. In six months
he would be forty. He thought of Father Cogley's warning.

The pulpit was on the right of the school chapel.
Ginger Coffey, aged fifteen, sat under it while Father
Cogley, a Redemptorist Missioner, preached the retreat.
There's always one boy — Father Cogley said — always
one boy who doesn't want to settle down like the rest of
us. He's different, he thinks. He wants to go out into the
great wide world and find adventures. He's different, you
see. Aye, well, Lucifer thought he was different. He did.
Now, this boy who thinks he's different, he's the lad
who never wants to finish his studies. Ireland isn't good
enough for him, it's got to be England or America or Rio-
dee-Janeero or some place like that. So, what does he do?
He burns his books and off he runs. And what happens?

17

Well, I'll tell you. Nine times out of ten that fellow winds up as a pick-and-shovel laborer or at best a twopenny pen-pusher in some hell on earth, some place of sun and rot or snow and ice that no sensible man would be seen dead in. And why? Because that class of boy is unable to accept his God-given limitations, because that class of boy has no love of God in him, because that class of boy is an ordinary, lazy lump and his talk of finding adventures is only wanting an excuse to get away and commit mortal sins — Father Cogley looked down: he looked into the eyes of Ginger Coffey, who had been to confess to him only half an hour ago. And let me tell that boy one thing — Father Cogley said — If you burn your books, you burn your boats. And if you burn your boats, you'll sink. You'll sink in this world and you'll sink in the next . . .

And woe betide you then . . .

It was all missionary malarkey, of course. But although he had forgotten all else that was ever preached to him, Coffey had not forgotten that sermon. He had thought of it often; had thought of it that third week of December when Veronica found out. She wept. She said she had seen this coming for a long time. (It was the sort of thing she *would* say.) She said if he did not land a job by Christmas, they must go home the first ship in the New Year. She said they had six hundred dollars put aside for their passages home, and he had promised her they would go back if it did not work. It had not worked. And so, look at us — she said — we know no one here. No one would lift a finger if we froze to solid ice in the streets. You promised me. Let's get out before we have to sing for our passage. At home, there's people know you. You can always find something. Now, there's a ship leaving Halifax on the tenth of January. I'm reserving our tickets —

But it's not even Christmas yet, he said. What's the hurry? I'll find something. Chin up!

Christmas came and went, but the snow was their only present. They saw the New Year in, with Veronica starting to pack as soon as the radio played "Auld Lang Syne," while he, alone in the dun-colored duplex living room, decided that on January second, as soon as the offices were open again, he would humble himself and go down to the Unemployment Commission. Because he would have to find *some* job. Because, you see, there was one thing he still hadn't told her. He no longer had the money for the tickets. In fact, all that was left was — never mind — it was a frightener to think how little.

And today was D-day. The wind was stronger now. The snow had stopped and his ears began to hurt as if someone had boxed them. He looked into a restaurant, saw people lined three-deep beside the hostess rope, the waitresses stacking dishes, placing paper place mats and fresh glasses of water before anyone who dared to dawdle: no, there was no shelter in Childs. But he must phone Veronica — start preparing her. So in he went.

"That you, Kitten?"

"Did you get the tickets, Ginger?"

"Well, no, not yet, dear. That's what I'm phoning you about. You see, dear, right out of a clear blue sky I met a man on my way downtown who told me about a job. So I'm going for an interview."

"What man?"

"You wouldn't know him, dear. The point is, I have an interview arranged for half past two this afternoon."

"Today's the last day to pick up those tickets," she said. "If you don't get them they'll sell them to someone else."

"I know, dear. The point is, I'm going to wait until

after I've had this interview. I should be finished by three. That leaves lashings of time to pick up the tickets, if nothing comes of it."

"But what job *is* this?"

Flute! He reached in his waistcoat and pulled out a slip of paper. It was the second slip which Donnelly had given him but he had started reading it out before he realized his mistake. "*Wanted,*" he read. "*Aggressive publicity man for professional fund-raising group, province-wide cancer research campaign. Apply H. E. Kahn, Room 200, Doxley Building, Sherbrooke Street.*"

"But that doesn't sound permanent at all?" she said.

"Well, never mind, dear. It would tide us over."

"If we're going to stay," she said. "You've got to get something permanent, Ginger. At your age, you can't afford to be chopping and changing any more. You know that."

"Yes, dear. We — we'll talk about it later. Good-b—"

"Wait! Ginger, listen to me. If this job is only a few weeks' stopgap, don't you take it. Get those tickets."

"Yes, dear. Bye-bye, now."

He replaced the receiver and stepped out of the booth. There must be a law of averages in life as well as in cards. And surely if anyone's luck was due for a change, his was?

A Childs hostess beckoned with her sheaf of menus but he thought of the fourteen lonely dollars left in his pocket. He went outside but it was too cold to hang about the square. Then where? He looked across the snowy park; three old dears were going up the steps of the Basilica. Warm it was in God's house. How long was it since he'd been in a church? Not since he'd left home, not that he'd missed it, either. Maybe . . . ? Well, it wouldn't hurt him, now would it?

The interior darkness was familiar. He listened to the

20

murmur of water pipes, located a bench near a radiator and moved in. Catholic churches were all the same. The pulpit on the right (shades of Father Cogley!) and on the left the Altar to Our Lady (Distaff Doings) with a bank of votive candles underneath. He remembered how, as a boy during the boredom of mass, he used to count the candles, sixpence a big one, threepence a little one and try to estimate the profit to the priests.

Coffey's father, a solicitor, had been buried in the brown habit of a Dominican Tertiary. Enough said. His elder brother Tom was a missionary priest in Africa. And yet neither Coffey nor Veronica were what Dublin people called pi-odious. Far from it. In fact one of his secret reasons for wanting to get away to the New World was that, in Ireland, church attendance was not a matter of choice. Bloody well go, or else, tinker, tailor, soldier, sailor, rich man, poor man, you were made to suffer in a worldly sense. Here, he was free. . . .

And yet . . . Staring now at the altar, he remembered the missioner's warning. Supposing it were not all nonsense? Suppose his brother Tom, worrying about the Moslems stealing his African converts, was right after all? Just suppose. Suppose all the prayers, the penances, the promises were true? Suppose the poor in spirit would inherit the kingdom of heaven? And not he.

For he was not poor in spirit. He was just poor. Well, what about him? If he did not believe all this stuff about an afterlife then what *did* he believe? What was his aim in life? Well . . . well, he supposed it was to be his own master, to provide for Vera and Paulie, to . . . to what? Damned if he could put it into words. To make something of himself, he supposed. Well, was that enough? And would he? Maybe he was one of those people who get the best of neither world, one of those people the Lord had no time for, neither fish nor fowl, great sinner nor saint? And maybe because he had never been poor in spirit, had never been one for pleading and penances, maybe God had lain in wait for him all these years, doling him out a little bad luck here, a little hope there, dampening his dreams, letting him drift further from the time and tide that led on to fortune until now, at the halfway mark in his life, he was stranded in this land of ice and snow? If there was a God above, was that what God wanted? To make him poor in spirit? To make him call pax, to make him give up, to herd him back with the other sheep in the fold?

He looked at the tabernacle. His large ruddy face set in a scowl as though someone had struck it. His lips shut tight under his ginger mustache. I never could abide a bully, he said to the tabernacle. Listen to me, now. I came in here to maybe say a prayer and I'll be the first to admit I had a hell of a nerve on me, seeing the way I've ignored you these long years. But now I cannot pray, because to pray to you, if you're punishing me, would be downright cowardly. If it's cowards you want in heaven, then good luck to you. You're welcome.

He picked up his little green hat and left the church.

At two-thirty Mona Prentiss, receptionist, went into the office of Georges Paul-Emile Beauchemin, Public Relations Director of Canada Nickel, and handed him Coffey's application form. Yes, the man was outside and had been waiting since this morning. Would Mr. Beauchemin care to see him?

Mr. Beauchemin had time to kill. He had just finished buying someone a very good lunch in exchange for two hockey tickets. In half an hour, at the midweek meeting, he planned to hand the tickets over to Mr. Mansard. Mr. Mansard was a vice-president and a hockey fan. So Mr.

Beauchemin was in a good mood. He said to show the guy in.

Miss Prentiss came back up the corridor. "Will you follow me please, sir?" And Coffey followed, suddenly wishing he'd worn his blue suit, although it was shiny in the seat, watching her seat — melon buttocks rubbing under gray flannel skirt, high heels' *tic-tac,* cashmere sweater, blond curls. A pleasant rear view, yes, but he did not enjoy it. Sick apprehension filled him because, well, what were his qualifications for *this* job? What indeed?

"This is Mr. Coffey, sir," she said, shutting the door on them. And hooray! The face that fits. Because, by some miracle, Coffey had met Mr. Beauchemin, had met him last November at a party in the Press Club where the Coffeys had been Gerry Grosvenor's guests.

"Hello there," Coffey said, jovially advancing with his large hand outstretched, the ends of his mustache lifting in a smile. And Beauchemin took the proffered hand, his mind running back, trying to place this guy. He could not recall him at all. A limey type and, like most limey types, sort of queer. Look at this one with his tiny green hat, short bulky car coat and suède boots. A man that age should know better than to dress like a college boy, Beauchemin thought. He looked at Coffey's red face and large military mustache. Georges Paul-Emile Beauchemin had not served. That mustache did not win him. Oh no.

"I don't suppose you remember me?" Coffey said. "Ginger Coffey. Was with Cootehill Distilleries here. Met you at a Press Club do once with Gerry Grosvenor, the cartoonist."

"Oh yes, eh?" Beauchemin said vaguely. "Old Gerry, eh? You're — ah — you're Irish, eh?"

"Yes," Coffey said.

"Good old Paddy's Day, eh?"

23

"Yes."

"Lots of Irish out here, you know. Last year I took my little girl out to see the Paddy's Day parade on Sherbrooke Street. Lot of fun, eh?"

"Yes, isn't it?" Coffey said.

"So you're not with — ah —" Beauchemin glanced at the application form — "not with Distillery any more?"

"Well, no. We had a change of top brass at home, and they wanted me to come back. But I like it here, we were more or less settled, kiddy in school and so on. Hard changing schools in mid-term, so I decided to chance my luck and stay on."

"Sure," Beauchemin said. "Cigarette?" Perhaps this guy had been sent by someone from upstairs. It was wise to check. "How did you know we were looking for an editorial assistant, eh?"

Coffey looked at his little green hat. "Well, it was the — ah — the Unemployment Commission people. They mentioned it."

Reassured (for if it had been a brass recommendation he would have had to send a memo), Beauchemin leaned back, openly picked up the application form. A nobody. Seventeen from fifty-six is thirty-nine. Let him out on age.

"Well, that's too bad," he said. "Because — what did you say your first name was again?"

"Ginger. Had it since I was a boy. Red hair, you see."

"Well, Gin-ger, I'm afraid this job's not for you. We want a junior."

"Oh?"

"Yes, some kid who's maybe worked a couple of years on a suburban weekly, someone we can train, bring along, promote him if he works out."

"I see," Coffey said. He sat for a moment, eying his hat. Fool! Stupid blundering fool! Why didn't you wait to see if he remembered you? He doesn't know you from a

24

hole in the wall, coming in with your hand out! Oh God! Get up, say thank you and go away.

But he could not. In his mind, a ship's siren blew, all visitors ashore. He and Veronica and Paulie, tears in their eyes, stood on the steerage deck waving good-by to this promised land. This was no time for pride. Try? Ask?

"Well," Coffey said, "as a matter of fact, my experience has all been on the other side of the water. I imagine it's quite different here. Maybe — maybe I'd need to start lower on the scale? Learn the ropes as I go along?"

Beauchemin looked at the man's ruddy face, the embarrassed eyes. Worked for a distillery, did he? Maybe they let him go because he was too sold on the product? "Frankly, Gin-ger," he said, "you wouldn't fit into the pension plan. You know it's a union-management deal. The older a man comes in, the more expensive for the others in the plan. You know how these things work."

"But I wouldn't mind if you left me out of the pension plan?"

"Sorry."

"But — but we New Canadians," Coffey began. "I mean, we can't all be boys of twenty, can we? We have to start somewhere? I mean" — he said, dropping his eyes to his hat once more — "I'll put it to you straight. I'd appreciate it if you'd make an exception."

"Sorry," Beauchemin said. He stood up. "I tell you what, Gin-ger. You leave your name and address with Mona, outside. If we think of anything we'll get in touch with you, okay? But don't pass up any other offers, meantime. All right? Glad to have met you again. Give my regards to Gerry, will you? And good luck."

Beauchemin shook hands and watched Coffey put on his silly little hat. Saw him walk to the door, then turn, and raise his right hand in a quick jerky movement of farewell, a kind of joke salute. A vet, Beauchemin thought. I was right. They do okay, free hospitals, pensions, mortgages, educations; the hell with those guys. "Be seeing you," he said. "And shut the door, will you?"

In Room 200 of the Doxley Building, Sherbrooke Street, an aggressive publicity man for professional fund-raising group, province-wide cancer research campaign, put his little green hat between his feet and stared at H. E. Kahn, to whom application must be made.

H. E. Kahn wore a blue suit with narrow lapels which curved up to the points of his tight, white, tab-collared shirt. His black tie knot was the size of a grape and the tie itself was narrow as a ruler. The mouth above it was also narrow; narrow the needle nose, the eyes which now inspected the form on which, for the third time that day, the applicant had set down the misleading facts of a life. H. E. Kahn was a swift reader. He turned the form over, read the other side, his young, convict-shaven head bent, showing a small monkish tonsure at the crown. Yet for all that hint of baldness, Coffey estimated that H. E. Kahn could not be more than thirty years old. Which was older than the three other young men he had noticed at work in the outer office, older than the two pretty stenographers who sat facing each other, transcribing from dictating belts behind Coffey's back, and older certainly than the other applicant who had filled up a form as Coffey did and now waited his turn outside.

H. E. Kahn finished his reading and leaned back in his swivel chair until the tonsure on his head touched the wall. "You speak French?"

"No, I'm afraid not."

"French might have helped."

"I suppose so."

"Not essential, mind you, but I see you're not a local man. Not a Canadian, are you?"

"No, I'm Irish."

"Irish, eh? That so? I've been in Ireland. Shannon Airport. Got a wonderful camera deal there coming back from Paris last summer."

H. E. Kahn's chair jacknifed to desk level, his hand crumpling the application form. Balled, the form accurately described a parabola over Coffey's left shoulder, holed into a secretary's wastepaper basket. "Sorry, Mr. Cee. You wouldn't suit us."

Coffey stood up. "Well, thanks for seeing me, anyway."

"My pleasure. Hey, Marge, hey, send that other guy in, will you? And Jack? JACK? Shoot me over that special names list. Nice meeting you, Mr. Coffey. See you."

"See you," Coffey repeated mechanically. In hell, he hoped.

But afterwards, out in the street, he wondered if that had been fair. After all, Kahn had been polite enough. Was it because Kahn seemed to be a Jew? No, he hoped that wasn't it. Coffey did not agree with many of his countrymen in their attitude to Jews. None of his best friends were Jews, but that was no reason to dislike Jews, was it? Besides, he had not particularly liked Beauchemin either and that wasn't because Beauchemin was French-Canadian. Of course not. So, what was it, apart from the fact that neither man had wanted to employ him? *They were younger than he.* That was the first thing he had thought about both of them. And Donnelly too, the man in the Unemployment Commission. Younger. All day he had been going hat in hand to younger men. And yet — Suffering J, I'm not old, Coffey thought. Thirty-nine isn't old!

Walking, he turned the corner of Ste. Catherine Street and saw again this morning's tabloid headline: *WIFE, LOVER SLAY CRIPPLE MATE.* He remembered the

27

unbought steamship tickets. Flute! Better stay downtown awhile.

At a quarter to five he arrived in the street where he lived. Dawdling still, walking a little off the track of other pedestrians, watching his abominable snowfeet mark the white, new-fallen snow, waiting until five when Gerry Grosvenor would come because, with Gerry on hand, the dreaded scene about the tickets would be staved off for another hour or so. But, as he reached the lane running alongside his place, he saw, with relief, that Gerry's sporty little car was here and had been here for some time because there were no tracks on the snow where it had driven in. Which was peculiar.

Gerry Grosvenor, a political cartoonist on a big magazine called *Canada's Own,* was, Coffey supposed, their only real pal in Canada. Someone in Dublin who had known Gerry during the war had given Ginger a letter of introduction to Gerry and from the first go-off Gerry had taken to them like first cousins and favorites. Which was all well and good, but awkward because, when Coffey moved from his other flat and the cash started running out, he had to duck Gerry Grosvenor. For dammit, Gerry was a social sort and popular, and the last thing in the world Coffey wanted was for Gerry to start looking down on him. So, as he unlocked the door of the duplex, he was shocked to hear Gerry's voice say: "There now, there now. Cheer up. It won't be so bad as you think."

What was that? Veronica was sniffling, that was what. What was she sniffling about? Had she found out about the tickets? How? Lord blessus and saveus. Bloody females! Sobbing out her private affairs to some outsider, had she no dignity, the woman? He hesitated, dreading his entrance, wanting to hide.

28

There was one safe place. Paulie was not at home, and Veronica would never expect to find him there. He slipped into Paulie's tiny nest, cluttered as all her other rooms had been, and sat on the bed for a breather.

Three-quarter-profiled in their tin-finish frames, Paulie's favorite singers, film heroes and guitar players smiled on Daddy in autographed contempt. He avoided their glossy stares and picked up Bunkie, his daughter's oldest plaything, a wooden-headed pajama-case doll. Other talismen, less favored, lined her dressing table: a copy of *Little Women*, a worn beaded purse which had once been used by Coffey's mother at a Viceregal Ball, a glass snowflake paperweight, a pencil case Coffey had made for her in a woodworking shop. The pencil case, now chipped and broken, was filled with bobby pins and head combs. Paulie was growing up.

He looked again at the doll's wooden head, its painted features half-obliterated by childish kisses, childish tears. Ah, Paulie . . . what happened to us? Once, I wasn't able to stir without you running after me, oops-a-daisy, come to Daddy, whirling you up in the air, my Goldilocks and me the Big Bear. The games we played, the childish shrieks of fun . . . But now you never look at me. What happened? If only you were a boy?

But they had never had a boy. And whose fault was that? Not his, although she sometimes tried to make it seem so. You see, she got pregnant the month he married her. At the time, he had just been commissioned and everyone expected Ireland to go into the war. So they waited and waited. About the time Paulie was born, the thicks in the government announced that Ireland would stay neutral. And Veronica blew up when Coffey wanted to desert and move to the British side. He wanted to see some action but she said his duty was with his family. Family! He wanted adventure, not diapers. So he sulked for a month or so and she got the priest after him for practicing birth control. He said he was damned if any priest would dictate whether or not he'd have another child. The priest then threatened to refuse Veronica the sacraments and if there was one thing Coffey would not stand for, it was being threatened. They would not have another child, he said. Not yet. Not until he was good and ready. When would that be, she asked. Soon? Yes, soon. He promised her. Soon.

But they never had one. The years had passed: he no longer knew if she even wanted one. Ah, children . . . children . . . His large hand caressed Bunkie's head. He put the doll on the coverlet and awkwardly tidied the bed. He was acting like a child himself, come to think of it. Hiding like this. He went out, listened in the corridor, but heard no further weeps. So he risked it into the living room.

"Hello there, Ginger," Gerry Grosvenor said, getting up. He was tall, and so neat he reminded Coffey of a dummy in a men's furnishings window. Yet for all his height and neatness, for all his thirty years, his Gillette-blue chin and black-haired hands, adolescence, like an incurable disease, had never quite left him.

"Hello, Gerry lad," Coffey said jovially. "Hello there, Kitten."

Yes, she had been sniffling.

"So you never picked up the tickets?" she said.

"What was that, Kitten?"

"I phoned at quarter to five," she said. "You hadn't picked them up then, and they were closing in a few minutes. Does that mean you got a job?"

Coffey did not answer her at once. Instead, he winked at Gerry. Sure, women are always starting a barney over nothing, eh, Gerry lad? But Grosvenor did not return the wink; left Coffey in the field, alone. "No," Coffey said, turning back to her. "I did not get a job."

"Then why didn't you buy those tickets?"

"Look, we'll talk about that later, Kitten? Now, what about a beer? Are there any beers in this place, by any chance?"

"In the kitchen," she said.

"Gerry, will you have another?" Coffey asked.

But Grosvenor shook his head. His round brown stare, which reminded Coffey of a heifer watching you cross a field, was now fixed and glassy. He was ploothered, Coffey decided.

"No, I have to run," Grosvenor said. "I have another appointment. Now, don't worry, Vera and Ginger. I'm going to see what I can do, okay?"

"Listen. Have a short one for the road, won't you?" Coffey said, knowing that, the minute Gerry left, the roof would fall in.

"No, I'm late now," Gerry said. " 'By, Ginger. 'By, Veronica."

Veronica did not move out of her seat, did not even say good-by. Which mortified Coffey, for, no matter, she might at least be polite to visitors. Angry, Coffey followed Gerry out into the hall. "I'm sorry I was late home, old man," he said. "I hope Veronica hasn't been bothering you with our troubles."

Grosvenor bent his head to drape a long woolen scarf about his neck, then looked at Coffey with round, brown cow-eyes. "But I'm your friend," he said. "I mean to say, I didn't know you were having trouble. I mean, your troubles are my troubles, right? That's the essence of any relationship, isn't it?"

"I suppose it is," Coffey agreed. Canadians were terribly slabbery, he'd noticed. Even the men were always telling you how much they liked you. Shocking way to

31

carry on, especially when you'd be daft to heed one word of it. Still, there was an excuse for old Gerry. He was drunk. "There we are," Coffey said, helping Gerry on with his overcoat. "Steady as she goes."

"I mean, I thought you *wanted* to go home," Grosvenor said. "But now that you don't — well, I'll see what I can dig up. Right?"

"Right," Coffey said, guiding him to the front door. "And thanks very much, Gerry."

"Listen," Grosvenor said, stopping, fixing Coffey once more in his drunken stare. "Going to look into a possibility right now. Call you tonight, okay?"

"Fair enough. I'll be at home."

" 'Kay," Grosvenor said. He stumbled on the step, went down the path to the street in a shambling, head-heavy walk. It occurred to Coffey that Gerry was not fit to drive.

"Gerry?" he called — because if he drove Gerry home it would put off Judgment Day a while longer . . .

" 'By," Grosvenor shouted back. "See you, Ginger."

Ah well. Slowly, Coffey shut the front door. Slowly he made his way back into the living room. She had not moved from her chair. She sat, her dark hair framing her pallor, her long fingers laced over one knee, the leg drawn up, her large, dark eyes looking up at him, implacable and waiting.

"Well," he said, sitting on the arm of the sofa. "Pal Gerry certainly has a skinful in him this afternoon, wouldn't you say?"

She did not answer. He smiled at her, still trying to jolly her. "Do you know, I could have sworn for a moment he was going to kiss me, out there in the hall," he said.

"Kiss who?"

"Me," he said, trying to smile at her.

"Why didn't you get those tickets, Ginger?"

"Now . . ." he said. "Look, dear," he said. "Listen, do you know where I went today?"

No answer.

"First thing this morning," he said. "I went down to the Unemployment Commission. You know, the labor exchange? And do you know, right off they gave me two jobs to look into. They were very decent. So, I spent the whole day at interviews and — and listen, Vera, I admit I didn't get anything. But it was just a start and tomorrow they're going to have another try at placing me —"

"Tomorrow you're going to get those tickets," she said.

"Ah now, look here, Kitten. Sure you don't want to go home to Ireland any more than I do. Now, why not wait awhile —"

"No. We've waited too long already."

"But just another week wouldn't kill us?"

"Ginger," she said. "I'm doing this for your sake, if you only knew it. We're getting those tickets tomorrow, and that's all's about it."

"For *my* sake?" he said. "Am I the one who wants to go home?"

"We're buying those tickets," she said. "That's final!"

"It is not final," he said, suddenly losing his temper. "We can't buy the tickets, so shut up about it, will you?"

"*What?*"

"How the hell do you think I've carried on this last while?" he said. "It costs a fortune, this country."

"You spent the money? *You-spent-the-money?*"

"I couldn't help it, Kitten. There were expenses — at the office — things you never knew —"

"One," she said, "two —"

"All kinds of bills —"

33

"Three-four —"

"Ah, now, cut it out, Kitten. I'm sorry. I'm not a good manager, I never was. I'm sorry."

"Five-six-seven —"

"I said I was sorry, Kitten. God knows it's not just my fault. Those thicks at home, not paying my expenses. I skimped on lunches, even."

"Eight-nine-ten!" She took a long breath. "I am not going to lose my temper," she recited. "I-am-not-going-to-lose-my-temper."

"Good, that's the girl. Now, cheer up, sure, listen, I'll get a job soon and it'll be all for the best. You'll see."

"Go away," she said. "What on earth good does saying you're sorry do?"

"Vera?"

"If you just knew what you've done," she said, beginning to cry. "If you had just the *faintest* idea. You've torn it, this time. You really have."

"Ah, now, Kitten —"

"Go away. Eat your supper."

"Aren't you eating, dear?"

"*Get out!*"

Ah, well. Women were peculiar cusses. They had nervous troubles men knew nothing about. Ah, she had been acting very peculiar this last while, cold and fed up and so on. That was nervous trouble, he was sure. If you read medical books, it was all explained in there. So, leave her be. She'd come around.

He went into the kitchen and found sausages and potatoes warm in the oven. A little mental arithmetic indicated three for him, three for her, and two for Paulie. He took his portion and settled down at the kitchen table. The sink tap dripped onto stacked pots and pans. Upstairs, someone knocked on a radiator and a moment later the basement furnace whirred and coughed into life.

Lordsaveus, what a dump this was, was it any wonder Vera hated it? Coffey was hungry. He ate his sausages and helped himself to more gravy and potatoes. Fork halfway to his mouth, he noticed her standing in the door, her face pale, her eyes bright. Still in a rage. He put the forkful in his mouth and winked at her.

"How much *do* we have left?" she said.

He smiled, gesturing that his mouth was full.

"Answer me. The truth, mind!"

Eighty and fourteen — well, make it an even — "About a hundred dollars," he said.

"Oh my God!" She went away.

He finished the spuds and wiped his plate with a bit of bread. What did Vera know about money anyway? An only child, brought up by a doting mother, pretty, with plenty of beaux, until she met and married him. And, even so, in all those years of marriage, the Army years, the years at Kylemore and in Cork, had she ever bloody starved? Had she? Give him credit for something. And remember, Vera, you married me for better or for worse. This is the worse. Ah, but supposing she won't put up with the worse?

Now that was nonsense. She loved him in her way and despite her temper. And she had Paulie. He could hear the two of them talking now in the living room. Paulie, home from her dance practice, had gone straight in to see Vera. And, as usual, not even hello for Daddy. They were like sisters, those two, always gossiping away about womany wee things he knew nothing about.

There was the phone. He got up to answer, because Vera hated the phone.

"Ginger?" It was Gerry Grosvenor. "Listen, how would you react to a hundred and ten a week?"

"Get away with you!"

"No, seriously, there's a job going as deskman on the

Tribune. And the Managing Editor happens to be a friend of mine."

"Deskman?" Coffey said. "But Gerry lad, what's that? What does a deskman do? Make desks?"

"Copy editor," Grosvenor said. "Easy. This is on the international desk, all wire copy, very clean. It's just writing heads and putting in punctuation. Nothing to it."

"But I have no experience on a newspaper. I never wrote a headline in my life."

"Never mind that. Would you take the job?"

"Would a duck swim!"

"Okay. Wait. I'll call you back."

Coffey replaced the receiver and looked down the long railroad corridor hallway. Total silence from the living room, which meant she and Paulie had been listening. So he went in. "Hello, Apple," he said to Paulie. "Had a good day in school?"

"Was that Gerry?" Veronica asked in an angry voice.

"Yes, dear. He says he can get me a job. Hundred and ten dollars a week to start."

"What job?"

"On the *Tribune.* It's an editing job. I pointed out that I'd no experience, but he said not to worry."

"I'd worry," Veronica said, "if I were you. This isn't acting the glorified office boy, or playing poker and drinking pints in barracks."

He gave her a look intended to turn her into Lot's wife there on the sofa. Imagine saying that in front of Paulie!

"Go and have your supper, Apple," he told Paulie. He waited as, unwillingly, Paulie trailed out of the room. "Now, why did you say that in front of the child, Vera?"

"She might as well know."

"Know what?"

"What sort of a selfish brute she has for a father."

Suffering J! No sense talking, was there? He went out

and, while he was in the bathroom, the phone rang again. He hurried up the corridor.

"Yes," she said to the phone. "Yes — wait, I want to explain something. I mean apropos of this afternoon. Ginger doesn't *have* our passage money home. He spent it. . . . Yes. . . . So that leaves me no choice, does it? . . . Yes . . . yes, here's Ginger. I'll let you tell him yourself."

"Ginger?" Gerry's voice said. "It's all set. I've given you a good build-up and old MacGregor wants to see you in his office at three tomorrow afternoon."

"Thanks a million, Gerry. But what did you tell him?"

"I told him you'd worked on a Dublin newspaper for two years and said, after that, you'd been a press officer in the Army, and then that you were a public relations man for Irish whiskey out here. It sounded good, believe me."

"But, Holy God!" Coffey said. "It's not true. I never worked on a newspaper."

At the other end of the line there was a Remembrance Day hush. Then Grosvenor said: "Ginger, the point is, do you want this job or don't you?"

"Of course I do, but —"

"But nothing. Everybody bullshits out here. Every employer expects it. The point is to get in. After that, doing the job is up to you."

"But maybe I can't do it," Coffey said.

"Beggars can't be choosers," said Vera's voice. She reached out, took the receiver from him and said: "Thanks, Gerry, you're an angel. Thanks very much. . . . Yes. . . . Yes, I know. . . . Good night." She replaced the receiver, turned away, walked down the hall and went into their bedroom. He followed her but she shut the door. When he tried the door, it was locked.

"Vera? I want to talk to you?"

"Go away," she said. She sounded as if she were crying again.

"Listen," he said. "Don't you want any supper?"

"No. And go away, will you? Please! Sleep on the living-room sofa. I want to be alone."

Ah, well. What was the use? He went back to the kitchen where Paulie was at table, reading some trashy magazine. He got out Vera's sausages and offered Paulie one but she shook her head and, still reading, carried her dishes to the sink.

"Stay and have a chat with me, Apple?"

"I have to study, Daddy."

"Just a minute, miss," he said, surprised at the anger in his voice. He saw she was surprised too. It wasn't like him to be cross. "Sit down," he said. "I want to ask you something."

"Yes, Daddy?"

"Apple, do you want to go back to Ireland?"

"Jeepers, no. I like it here."

"Why?"

"Well, the kids are more grown-up here. And school's more — oh, it's just nicer, that's all. Besides, I said good-by to everybody at home. I'm going to look silly going back now. I wish we weren't going back, Daddy."

"Well, we're not," he said. "It's much better here. You're right. I wish your mother could see that, though."

"But Mummy's never wanted to go home."

"Is that so?" he said. "That's not the way I hear it."

"She likes it here, Daddy. Honestly she does. She's just afraid you won't find a job, that's all."

"I'll get a job," he said. "No need to panic."

"Sure. Of course," Paulie said. "Can I go now, Daddy?"

"All right, Pet." You'd think he was a leper or something, she was that anxious to run away from him. Children . . . children . . .

He ate the remaining three sausages and lit a smoke. If Veronica really wanted to stay over here, why the blazes couldn't she say so? No bloody faith in him, that was it. Suffering J!

He went into the living room with the *Montreal Star* but he was too upset to read it. He went back into the kitchen and brought out two quarts of beer. Last of the last. He poured himself a glass, lay down on the sofa and switched the radio on, trying to salvage something out of this miserable bloody evening. He searched for music, for music hath charms and had better have, because, looking back on the day, he had a savage bloody breast on him, all right. Hat in hand to younger men, wife sniveling to strangers, asked to lie his way into some job he'd be caught out in, and what else? Oh, a savage bloody breast!

And all there was to drink was this gassy Canuck beer that gave him heartburn. And to sleep on, this bloody sofa that was too short. No faith. If your nearest and dearest had no faith in you, then how could a man give his all? Where would he be unless he still could hope? Without hope, he'd be done for. Aye, a savage bloody breast.

"Daddy? Dad-eee?"

"Yes, Apple," he said, sitting up in hope.

"Daddy, I can't hear to study with all that noise. Could you turn the radio off?"

"Right, Pet."

Not even able to enjoy a bit of music. Bloody females! He lay back, entering a world where no earthly women were. In that world soft houris moved, small women of a Japanese submissiveness, administering large doubles and sweet embraces in rooms filled with comfortable club sofas and beds. In that world, men of thirty-nine were Elder Brothers, prized over any Greek stripling. In that world, a man no longer spent his life running uphill, his hope in his mouth, his shins kicked by people with no faith in him. In that world, all men had reached the top of the hill; there were no dull jobs, no humiliating interviews, no turndowns; no man was saddled with girning wives and ungrateful daughters, there were unlimited funds to spend, the food was plentiful and nonfattening, there were no Father Cogleys handing out warnings, no newspapers worrying you with atom bombs, no sneerers and mockers waiting to see you fail, no rents to pay, no clothes to buy, no bank managers. In that world you could travel into beautiful jungles with four Indian companions, climb a dozen distant mountain peaks, sail rafts in endless tropic seas. You were free. By flicking your fingers in a secret sign, you could move backwards or forwards in time and space, spending a day in any age that took your fancy, but as a leader of that age, the happiest man of that day. In that free world . . .

In that world, both quarts finished, Ginger Coffey fell asleep.

Two   He came to consciousness, aware of a telephone ringing. Sunlight struck down on him from the window in a white column filled with tiny, floating feathers of dust. He turned his eyes from that light and, as in a frame from a film, saw his wife pass by in the corridor. The ringing stopped.

He had lain all night in his clothes. Mother of God, she would think he'd been drunk. Up with him now! He undressed, dropping clothes in a heap, found blankets and sheet in the cupboard, made up the sofa as a bed and hopped back in his underpants, closing his eyes as she passed back to the bedroom. Yes, that was a little victory.

Relaxed, he lay for a while, listening to the voice of a French-Canadian radio announcer upstairs, listening to the thump and shuffle of Madame Beaulieu's feet on the ceiling, remembering that last night he had been supposed to tell Madame whether or not they would keep this apartment for another month. Oh, well. Tell her tonight, when he knew about the new job. The job. That started him thinking of the day ahead, remembering that Veronica now knew the worst about the tickets, remembering that she would want to know how he had spent the money and what they were going to do. Ah, dear God!

He exhaled noisily, feathering up the ends of his mustache. As usual, you must balance the good with the bad. And if there was no good at the moment, then think of the important things. Health and strength and a wife and daughter. And here you are in a foreign land listening to French on the radio and you a man who has cut loose from all the old codology and cant at home, a man who struck out alone in search of fame and fortune. So, you're not dead yet. Now, raise your big carcass out of this excuse for a bed. Lift it. One, two, three, and up! And up he got, feeling a touch of heartburn after last night's beer, a twinge in his knee as he went heavily down the dark corridor to knock on her door. "Veronica?"

He went in. Nobody there. She had already made up the bed. He put on his dressing gown and slippers and wandered back up the corridor to the bathroom. When he came out, he saw the pair of them in the kitchen. Paulie, her head in pincurls, eternal book propped up against the milk jug as she finished her Corn Flakes. That child didn't eat enough and Veronica didn't seem to care. But when he looked at Veronica, he forgot to be angry. She was in her dressing gown, her dark hair down about her shoulders. She smiled at him. "Did you sleep all right?" she asked.

"Like a top," he said, kissing the end of her nose.

"I'm sorry about last night," she said. "I had a terrible headache. It made me grumpy."

He looked to see that Paulie was not watching, then ran his hand down his wife's back, giving her buttocks a little slap. "Sure, that's all right," he said. "Was that the phone I heard earlier?"

"Yes, Gerry rang. He wants us to have lunch with him today before you go for your interview. His treat, he said."

"Isn't he the decent skin, though?" Coffey said. "You told him yes, I hope."

"Of course. Now, eat your breakfast."

There must be at least two eggs in the helping of scrambled eggs she ladled out to him. He peppered and salted it, warmed by the sunlight, by this matutinal kindness; sure that it was a good omen somehow. He thought of J. F. Coffey, Journalist. He liked the sound of that. Or better, Coffey, the Editor; Coffey of the *Tribune* . . . Yes, it was a grand morning, right enough. Maybe today his ship would come in.

"Was Madame Beaulieu around yet?" he asked.

"Not yet."

"Well, we'll tell her about the place tomorrow," he said. "Although, if I get this job, I don't fancy staying on in this hole."

"I've been thinking," Veronica said. "If we're really going to stay I'm going to get a job as well. Paulie's out until after three, five days a week. There's no need for me to sit at home, is there?"

No need for her to get a job either, was there? He could take care of his own. Ah, this was old stuff, her wanting a job, wanting to slave away in some shop. Ah, for God's sake! But he held his whist: let her dream, the woman. He finished his eggs, ate four pieces of toast and sat idle over his third cup of tea while Paulie rushed off to school and Veronica washed the breakfast dishes. And after, following Veronica down the corridor in the morning sunlight, everything quiet, everyone else off to work, he stood in the bedroom door watching her as she took off her dressing gown and stood in her pink slip. His Dark Rosaleen.

"Lay out my old blue suit, will you?" he said. "I'd better wear it today. They're shocking conservative in their clothes over here."

Obediently she leaned into the closet to get the suit and at that moment the sight of a fold of her slip caught between the cleft of her buttocks aroused him to a sluggish, familiar desire. Married as long as they were, desire was not something a man could waste. He dropped his own dressing gown and pulled her down on the bed. He kissed her, fumbled her slip off her, then remembered. He looked at her, and, obedient, she went to the bathroom. He shut his eyes, carefully nursing his desire until she came back. Then, forgetting her years of complaints about his roughness, his selfishness, he took her, tumbling her naked beneath him. Animal, his breathing harsh in the morning silence, he labored towards that moment of release and fulfillment. And afterwards, fell down beside her, pulling her on top of him, crushing her face against the reddish, graying hair on his chest. He exhaled in contentment; dozed off to sleep.

Ten minutes later, he awoke to find her sitting up in bed beside him, smoking a cigarette, her cheek reddened by contact with his unshaven chin. He was in good form, this morning: her body, familiar as his own, still could rouse him to another round. He reached up, taking hold of her breasts, smiling at her, his mustache ends curling upwards in anticipation —

"No, Ginger." She drew back, put her cigarette in his mouth, slipped off the bed and went into the bathroom. That was women for you, they never enjoyed anything. He heard her begin to run a bath.

"Ginger?"

"Yes?"

"Ginger, promise you'll tell me the truth?"

"Promise."

"Who do you love more? Paulie or me?"

"Love both of you, Kitten."

"But if anything happened to Paulie that would be worse for you than if anything happened to me, wouldn't it?"

44

"Nothing's going to happen to anyone," he said. "Oh, Kitten, I feel it in my bones. Today is going to be the day that counts. There's a law of averages in life. You just have to wait for your chance to come up."

"But, supposing you had to decide in a matter of life or death? I mean between Paulie and me. You know, one of those things about save the mother or save the child. Which would you save?"

"Will you, for the love of Mike, shut up and get on with your bath?" he said contentedly.

"No, answer me. Which one would you save?"

"Well, I suppose if a ship was sinking, I'd save Paulie. I mean, she'd have all her life before her. Kids of her own and so forth."

"And what makes you think I can't have any more kids?" she said. "Good grief, it's not my fault we hadn't any more kids. And I still can have them, otherwise why did you send me off to the bathroom this morning? What do you think I am — a grandmother? Most men — let me tell you — most men still find me *very* attractive, do you hear?"

"Listen, Kitten," he said. "I didn't mean that. I was only saying that Paulie has her whole life before her. We haven't."

"Maybe *you* haven't," she said. The bath water began to run again. "But *I* have," she said. "God, you're selfish!"

After her bath, she cheered up. She put on her best black suit for lunch because they both knew Gerry would take them to some posh place. Yes, he was the soul of generosity, Gerry, always lending them his car for a run up north, inviting them out to parties and for lunch. Not that Ginger hadn't held their end up, when he could. Matter of fact — although Vera didn't know it — that was where some of the return passage money went. Although, even in these last days when Coffey had to cut his entertaining to a duck egg for lack of spondulicks, Gerry never let that make one bit of difference. None of your eyes right and cross the street for him when a pal was down on his luck. Ah, no. Dead on, Gerry was. A heart of oak.

Still, for all his decency, Gerry could be a strain at times. Talk? A phonograph. And, being a political cartoonist, he fancied himself as in the know. He was always up in Ottawa, and to hear him talk about the place it was the hub of the bloody universe. He referred to the two head men in the Canadian Government as Lester and Louie. He had once had tea with Madame Pandit, and when he talked politics he let slip names like Joe Enlee or J. F. Dee or Rab or Mac or Matsy Dong or Mick O'Yan as if he was related to all of them.

But today, for a change, Gerry talked about Ireland. He said he was glad they were not going back there. He said until he had met the Coffeys he had considered Irish people bigoted, untrustworthy and conventional. Although he had some very good Irish friends, he said. But he had been relieved to find that the Coffeys were not nationalists or religious. Although he admired people who believed in something; didn't they? Of course, none of *his* Catholic friends ever went to church, he said. Which was a relief to him. Yes, the Irish were wonderful people, imaginative, romantic and creative. Wonderful people.

Coffey winked at Veronica.

Then Gerry talked about the interview that was coming up: "Confidence," Gerry said. "That's the important thing in an interview. Now, in Canada, we don't go in for the hard sell. On the contrary" — and his face loosened in that self-satisfied smile peculiar to him when discussing his country — "I like to think that Canadians combine the best facets of British reticence with a touch

46

of good old American down-to-earthness. And that's the tone I took when I sold you to MacGregor. I made him feel I was doing *him* a favor."

This time, it was Veronica who winked. Ah, God knows, Coffey thought, when you come right down to it, she's a darling. Not that Gerry would notice that, he was so wrapped up in himself. But she was a darling.

After the lunch with Gerry, the Coffeys walked over to the *Tribune* building and just the fact of having her with him made Coffey less nervous about the interview to come. Into the lobby they went and she stopped to straighten his tie. "I'll wait for you here," she said.

"But there's no need, Kitten. I mean, even when you have an appointment in this country, they often keep you hanging around for hours on end."

"Doesn't matter," she said. "I'll be nervous no matter where I wait. Oh, Ginger. What if they find out you've no experience?"

"Steady the Buffs," he said, smiling at her. But the sickness came suddenly upon him. No faith, she had. No faith. "Don't worry," he said. "Why, I'll bet you a —"

"I know," she said. "A brand-new frock. I could run a dress shop if I collected on half your bets. Now go on, and good luck."

So, into the elevator he went, sick with nerves, praying that . . .

"Fourth floor. Editorial," the elevator man said. Funny, whenever you were in no hurry to get somewhere, elevators, buses, taxis all went like the wind. Coffey stepped out, hearing the elevator door shut behind him, feeling shabby and ill at ease in his old blue suit, pausing to stare at his image in the brass plaque in the corridor. The plaque said City Room and in it he seemed all squeegeed up, head tiny, eyes aslant like a Chinaman. Exactly how he felt. But you'll do, he told himself. Keep your chin up and someday you can buy yourself a brass plaque like this to remind yourself of the day your luck changed and you started in a whole new career. Right, then! He went in.

On the fourth floor of the *Tribune*, the night's business was just beginning. Under fluorescent lights, lit all year round, a few reporters studied the afternoon papers. A police radio blared routine calls in a corner and in the nearby teletype room a jammed machine tintinnabulated incessantly, calling for attention. In the center slot of a large horseshoe desk a fat man in a woolen cardigan sliced open the afternoon's crop of wire service photographs. He looked up as Coffey approached. "Yes?"

"May I speak to Mr. MacGregor, please?"

"Boy! Take this man to Mr. Mac."

An indolent adolescent shoved a rubber cylinder down a communications tube, then hooked a beckoning finger. Across the City Room he led and down a corridor to a partitioned-off office on the opened door of which a small brass plaque announced MANAGING EDITOR. The boy pointed to the plaque, then went away, wordless. Inside, Coffey saw three young men in shirt sleeves looking over the shoulders of an old man who was seated at a large, scarred desk. He was a thin old man with a pale, bony face, a pumping blue vein in his forehead and eyebrows thick and crumbling as cigar ash. His voice, a Low Church Scottish rumble, could be heard clearly in the corridor. For once, Coffey was not comforted by the fact that he faced an older man.

"Dorrothy Dix? Where's Dorrothy Dix?"

"Here, Mr. Mac."

"O.K. Now, where's the funnies?"

"Here, Mr. Mac."

"Make sure that Blondie is up top and then Mutt and Jeff and *then* Moon Mullins. *Not* Rex Morrgan, M.D. Some bleddy rascal in the composing room changed the order in the Early last night."

"Right, Mr. Mac."

"O.K. Now, away with ye."

The three young men clutched up page proofs and galleys and rushed out, jostling Coffey in the doorway. For the love of J, how was he going to tell this sulphur-breathing Scottish Beelzebub that he was an experienced subeditor? Grosvenor must be daft.

The old man spiked a scrap of paper, like Calvin downing sin. His eye picked out Coffey in the doorway.

"Come in. State your business."

"My — my name is Coffey. I believe Gerry Grosvenor spoke to you about me?"

"Grrosvenor? Och, aye, the cartoonist. Come in, come in, sit you down. Where's my notes? Aye, here we are. Deskman, aren't you?"

"Yes, sir."

"What paper did you wurrk for in the Old Country?"

Confidence, Grosvenor had said. The time and tide that leads on to fortune. One good lie and — But as Coffey opened his mouth he was taken with a sort of aphasia. The old man waited, becoming suspicious. "I — ah — I worked on the *Irish Times,* sir."

"*Times,* eh? Good paper."

"Yes. Yes, isn't it?"

"Grrosvenor said you were in the Army?"

"Yes, sir."

"Officer weren't you? Serve overseas?"

"I — I was in the Irish Army, sir. We were neutral during the war."

"Indeed?"

"I — I was a press officer in the Irish Army," Coffey

added, trying to correct the hostility in that "Indeed?"

"Press officer," the old man said. "Trying to keep the facts from the public, that is the services' job. However, I need a man who has some knowledge of wurrld events. Most Canadians have none. What about you?"

"I — ah — I try to keep up, sir."

"Grrosvenor tells me you were a publicity man for a whussky company?"

"Yes, sir."

"Scotch whussky?"

"No, sir. Irish."

"No wonder you're out of a job, then. Did you wurrk on the foreign desk at the *Times?*"

"Yes, sir. Ah — part-time."

"What do you mean, part-time?"

"Well, ah — summer holidays and so on. Filling in."

The old man nodded and consulted his notes again. Coffey fingered his mustache. A good touch that summer holidays. He was pleased with himself for thinking of it.

"When was it you wurrked for the *Times?*"

"Oh — after I got out of the Army. About — ah — six years ago."

"How long did you wurrk there?"

"About" — what had Grosvenor said? — "about eighteen months."

"I see." The old man picked up one of the phones on his desk. "Give me Fanshaw," he said. "Ted? When you were in Dublin, did you ever hear tell of a subbie on the *Times* by the name of Coffey? . . . Aye, about five years ago. . . . Hold on." He covered the mouthpiece and turned to Coffey. "What was the name of the foreign editor?"

Coffey sat, his eyes on his little green hat.

"Well?"

He raised his eyes and read a title on the bookshelf behind MacGregor. *Holy Bible.*

"Right, Ted," the old man told the telephone. "Disna' matter." He put the phone down and glowered at Coffey under the crumbling ash of his eyebrows. "If you'd been a Scot," he said. "You'd have come in here wi' references in your hand. But you carry nothing besides your hat and a lot of cheek. Och, aye. You may fool the likes of Gerry Grrosvenor, but there isn't an Irishman born that I'd trust to pull the wuul o'er *my* eyes!"

Coffey, his face hot, stood up and put his hat on.

"Where are you going?" MacGregor said.

"I'm sorry I took up your ti—"

"Sit down! Are you hard up for a job? Tell me the truth."

"Yes, sir."

"O.K. Can you spell? Spell me parallel."

Coffey spelled.

"Correct. Are you married?"

"Yes, sir."

"Children?"

"One daughter, sir."

"*Hmm.* . . . Have you a vice?"

"Advice, sir?"

"Are you deef? I mean, have you a weakness? Booze or horses or wimmin? Own up now, for I'll find out, anyway."

"No, sir."

"O.K. You say ye've been a P.R. That may be. But what a P.R. knows about the wurrkings of a newspaper could be written twice over on the back of a tomtit's arse and still leave room for the Lorrd's Prayer. So you'd best start at the bottom. Do you agree?"

Coffey took a deep breath. He was too old to start at the bottom.

"Well? Don't stand there gawking."

"Well, sir, it depends. I'm not a boy of twenty."

"I'm proposing to start you off in the proofroom," the old man said. "So that you can acquaint yourself with the rudiments of our style. That's the best training there is."

"A — a p-p-proofreader, did you say, sir?"

"I did. My readers are not unionized, thank the Lord. And I happen to be shorthanded there at the moment. If you wurrk well, I might try you out on the floor as a reporter. You might even wind up as a deskman if you play your cards right. What do you say?"

"Well I — I'd have to think about that, sir. How much — how much would that pay?"

"Fifty dollars a week, which is more than you're wurrth. Start at six tonight. Go and think it over now, but let me know no later than half-past four, if you want the job."

"Thank you —"

"Clarence?" Mr. MacGregor shouted. "Where's Clarence?"

A fat man rushed in, notebook at the ready.

"What's the last two paras of Norrman Vincent Peale doing in the overset, Clarence?"

"Don't know, Mr. Mac."

"Bleddy well find out, then."

The fat man rushed out. Mr. MacGregor spiked another galley. "All right, Coffey. Good day to you."

Coffey went away. Fifty dollars a week, reading galleys. A galley slave . . . He passed along a corridor lined with rolls of newsprint, wandered across the wide desert of the city room and out past the brass plaque to the elevator. The red light flashed above the elevator door. Going down. Down, down, all his high hopes failed; with Veronica waiting below, Veronica who wanted to know that the bad days were over, that they could move to a better place . . .

"Ground floor," the elevator man said. "Ground floor. Out."

There she was under the big clock, the nervous beginnings of a smile on her face. Poor Kitten, it was not fair to her, not fair at all, she'd be in such a state —

Maybe, through Gerry Grosvenor, maybe he might just manage? Maybe. And so, he went towards her, his mind made up. Don't tell her now. Smile instead, be the jolly Ginger she used to love. He kissed her, squeezed her and said: "Steady as she goes."

"Did you get it, Ginger?"

"I did, indeed."

"Oh, thank God."

"Now, now," he said. "What's that? Sniffles? Come on, come on, it's laughing you should be. Listen — let's — let's go and have a cup of tea. How would you like to sail into the Ritz, just like the old days?"

"Oh, Ginger, I'm so glad for you."

"Glad for *me*? And aren't you glad for yourself, Kitten? Ah, it's going to be super. Just super. Come on now. We'll take a taxi."

"But we can't afford it, Ginger."

"Come on, come on," he said, out in the street now, signaling a cab. "Let me be the judge of that. In with you. Driver? The Ritz-Carlton Hotel, on the double!"

He leaned back in the taxi, put his arm around her shoulders and hugged her, watching the city rush past: pretending. Making her feel as she did in the first weeks they landed, two people in a new and exciting country, him with three good agencies to make his fortune and all the old fogeys at home confounded. Sweeping her off to the Ritz for tea, happy as sandboys, the pair of them.

"But, how did the interview go?" she said. "What did he ask you?"

53

"Why, first rate, first rate," said he. "The old fellow took to me like a long-lost relative. He's going to show me over the different stages of the job, let me work awhile in each department until I get my hand in."

"Isn't that marvelous?" she said. "We must phone Gerry and thank him."

"Plenty of time. Tea first."

"Ginger, how much are they going to pay you?"

"Hundred and ten, but that's only a start. There's no telling how far I can go in a job like this. You may be looking at an important citizen, Kitten. J. F. Coffey, the editor."

"But Ginger, do you think you can do it?"

"Didn't Gerry say I could?"

"Yes, but —"

"Gerry has perfect faith in me," Coffey said, "and you have none. Isn't that a nice thing?"

"No, I didn't mean that," she said, contrite. "It's just that I hope nothing goes wrong this time."

"What would go wrong, would you tell me? Now, come on. Here we are."

He helped her out of the taxi under the brass carriage lanterns of the hotel, already lit in the gray winter afternoon. Up the steps they went, past the black wood panels of the entrance hall, and into the heat of the lobby. He took her coat and removed his own, dodging off to the cloakroom. He had to get a hold of Gerry. For one thing Gerry might be able to tell him how long he'd have to wait before they made him a reporter. And, for another, Gerry would have to help him because this was Gerry's fault after all. They would just have to keep mum, Gerry and he, and try to get through the weeks until he was made a reporter. Wasn't that the best plan? Well, if it wasn't, it was the only plan he could think of at the moment.

So when he checked the coats, he hurried down the back stairs to the row of public telephones in the basement. He called *Canada's Own*.

"How did it go, Ginger?"

"Disaster. Listen, Gerry, he caught me red-handed. Now listen — I haven't had the heart to tell Veronica the truth. And listen — he's offered me a job and I have until half-past four to make up my mind. It's in the proofroom, but that's only temporary. He's promised to promote me to reporter. Now, if I take it, maybe I can last out a few weeks without Vera being any the wiser. Until they make me a reporter, you see?"

"But did MacGregor give you a definite date for this promotion?" Gerry asked.

"No, he didn't. I think it won't be long though."

"How do you know? I wouldn't put it past that old bastard to con you into this, just so's he can get himself a nonunion proofreader on the cheap."

"But dammit, what's the use in talking, I'll have to take it," Coffey said. "I've told Vera I have a job."

"It's up to you," Gerry said. "But if you start small, you'll wind up small."

"Yes, but beggars can't be choosers —" Coffey began. Then he stopped. In the little mirror in front of the telephone, he saw Veronica's face. He turned around.

"Let me speak to Gerry," she said.

At once, Coffey hung up.

"Why did you do that? You're too late, anyway. I heard you."

He took her arm. "Now, listen — listen, Kitten, it's not as bad as you think. Let's — let's go up and have a cup of tea. I want to talk to you."

Carefully he led her up the stairs. They went into the Palm Court, a room that reminded Coffey more of a drawing room in some big house than a place where you could buy a cup of tea. He guided her to a sofa in a corner and at once called a waiter, ordering tea and crumpets from the waiter, taking as long as he could, postponing the inevitable. But at last the waiter went away. "Now listen, Kitten," Coffey said. "It's a sort of apprenticeship, that's all—"

She was sniffling. He passed her his handkerchief, then looked anxiously around at the other people in the room. "Vera, please?" he said. "People are watching."

"Go and sit by yourself, then."

"Vera, I didn't mean that. Now, cheer up."

"Why?"

"Well, this thing is only temporary, just for a week or so."

"Does Gerry think it's temporary?"

"Of course he does."

"Word of honor, Ginger?"

"Word of honor. It's just a training period —"

"Proofreading, isn't that what it is?" she said. "How much are they going to pay you during this 'training' period?"

"Ah — seventy dollars a week. We can manage on that."

"How much? Do you want me to phone Mr. Mac-Gregor and check?"

Nervously, Coffey touched the parting in his mustache. "All right," he said. "Fifty is what it is. But that's only for a week or so."

"Oh? How many weeks? Ginger, for once in your life, why can't you tell me the truth?"

"Well . . ." he said. "Well, anyway, this is Grosvenor's fault, not mine. Bloody daft caper, asking me to tell this old codger I had experience. Sure he trapped me in no time, made me look like a bloody idjit. God, wait till I see Mr. Gerry Grosvenor. Him and his bloody schemes."

"It's Gerry's fault," she said. "Not your fault, of course. Oh, it's never your fault, is it, Ginger?"

"Well, it wasn't my idea to pretend I was something I'm not."

"A proofreader," she said. "That's what you are. That's all you are. How are the three of us going to live on fifty dollars a week?"

"But he promised to make me a reporter. And then an editor, he said. Now, that's true, Kitten. Here — have a crumpet."

"You can't *afford* a crumpet," she said, weeping.

"Ah now, for the love of Mike, will you give over that boohooing, Vera? What sort of way is that to carry on?"

"Listen to me," she said. "Li-listen to me. I'm not going to put up with this any more, do you hear? God knows," she said, her tears now coming uncontrollably, "I've tried. You'll never know how hard I've tried. I was even ready to go home, even though I hated to go home. But I thought it was the only way to save us. That wasn't easy. No, it wasn't easy, believe you me."

"I know, Kitten. I know."

"And then — then last night you walked in and admitted that you'd been lying to me for weeks. Letting me pack and write Mother and make plans and everything. After you'd promised on your word of honor you'd never touch a penny of that passage money."

"I know," he said. "I should have told you. I'm sorry, Kitten."

"You're sorry. That makes it all right, I suppose? What good does saying you're 'sorry' do? Is that supposed to make me stay with you?"

"What do you mean, *stay* with me?"

"You heard me," she said. "I'm going to get away before it's too late."

"Is that so?" he said, with all the sarcasm he could

manage in his sudden fright. "And what about Paulie? Did you ever think of Paulie?"

"Oh, who's talking! Don't you know the only thing that's kept us together, this past while, is Paulie?"

She doesn't mean that, he thought. Ah no, she doesn't mean that. He looked at her.

"Not that you care about Paulie," she said. "Not that you care about any of us except yourself. If you did care, we'd never be in this mess."

"Now, is that fair, Vera? Just because I happen to be between jobs —"

"Ginger, Ginger," she said, shaking her head, "aren't you always between jobs?"

"What do you mean?"

"Isn't the job you're in always a burden to you, isn't it always no good, according to you? And isn't there always a crock of gold waiting for you in the next job you're going to get? Ginger, will you never learn anything? Will you never face the facts?"

"*What* facts?"

"That they let you go in nearly every job you've had. Why do you think Mr. Pierce sent you down to the advertising department? Why do you think Mr. Cleery in the advertising let you go? I'll tell you why. Because you're a glorified secretary, that's all you are, that's all you can ever hope to be. But you can't see that, you had to tell them how to run their business, you that knew nothing about it."

"Glorified secretary, my foot," he said. "Those old codgers were living in the dark ages," he said. "Fifty years behind the times."

"Yes," she said. "Everybody's out of step except our Ginger. Same thing when we were in Cork, wasn't it? And then you were coming over here to Canada, setting yourself up to do a job you never did in your life, a job you had no experience in. How could you sell whiskey or tweeds or anything, you that had no experience?"

"If it wasn't for those thicks at home —"

"Oh yes. Blame them. Blame anybody except yourself. And today — walking in, bold as you please, asking to be made an editor. You that knows nothing about it."

"That was Gerry's idea."

"But you went along with it, didn't you?" she said. "Oh yes, it's Gerry's fault. . . . Do you know the thing I can't stick about you? It's never your fault. *Never*. You've never had the guts to admit you were wrong."

"That's nonsense," he said.

"Is it? Then is it my fault you spent the ticket money home? Is it, Ginger?"

"Ah, what's the sense in raking all that up again, Vera? Former history."

"Former history! It happened yesterday!"

"*Shh*," he said, looking around the room.

"Yes, shush," she said. "People are watching. And you care more about people than you do about me. Playing the big fellow, spending our passage money."

He looked at his hands. He joined his fingers in the childhood game. A game between him and all harm. *Here's the church* . . .

"Well, from now on, don't bother to tell me anything," she said. "Not even lies. Because I don't want to hear. I'm sick of lies and dreams and schemes that founder as soon as *you* put your hand to them. I'm sick of your self-ishness and your alibis. You can go to hell for all I care."

And here's the steeple. Open the gates . . .

"Tomorrow morning," she said, "I'm going to look for a job of my own. And when I get it, I'm moving out."

"What about Paulie?"

"I'll take Paulie," she said. "Then you won't have to worry about anybody except yourself. Which will suit you down to the ground."

. . . and let in the people. And here is the minister coming upstairs . . .

"In the meantime," she said, "I'd advise you to take this proofreading job. Come down off your high horse, Ginger. It's just about what you're fit for. A proofreader."

And here is the minister saying his prayers.

He separated his hands, looked at her at last. "For better or for worse," he said. "For richer or for poorer. Ah," he said bitterly. "You could sing that, if you had an air to it."

"You'd better go," she said. "You have to let MacGregor know at half past four, don't you?"

"There's plenty of time. It's not even four. Besides —"

"Oh, God's teeth, Jim, why are you so dense? Don't you understand *anything?*"

She never called him Jim except when things were desperate. She wanted rid of him, this minute, that was what she wanted. All right. *All right.* He stood up and took the bill. "I'll have to wait for change," he told her.

She took a ten-dollar bill out of her bag. Where did she get that, he wondered. "Go on," she said. "I'll pay the bill."

But he could not move. Suffering J, they weren't going to leave things like this, were they? Ah, Vera —

"Are you leaving, or must I?" she said.

He tried to grin. "Just looking for the cloakroom tickets, dear. I have yours in my pocket somewhere."

He fumbled for a while.

"Breast pocket," she said.

"Oh, yes. Silly. I always put it there and then forget. Vera — listen to me —"

"No," she said. "And stop standing there like a dog waiting for a pat on the head. You're not getting any pat. Not any more. Now, go away."

He saw her hands tremble on the catch of her purse. Listen, listen, listen, he cried silently, for God's sake don't let this happen. But he had said listen so many times, in so many rows, for so many years. And she had said listen, as often. Listen to me, they cried to each other. Listen! Because neither listened any longer. She stared at him. Her face was pale, her eyes were fixed and bright, and, now that it had been said, he saw that all her irritations, all the fits of temper he had discounted, all that was hate. She hated him.

Still, as he went away across the room, he turned back to her once more. Tried to smile, hoping that somehow she . . . sure that she . . . Wouldn't she signal, call him back?

But she did not. She sat watching him, willing him to go. Go away, Doggy.

So he went.

Three   It was twenty past four. For several minutes he had been standing in the lobby of the *Tribune* building wondering whether he should go upstairs. After all, Mac-Gregor had said it would only be a short while until he was made a reporter. And you wouldn't heed Gerry, would you? Why should Gerry know whether MacGregor was tricking him or not?

But he had heeded her. That was why he was here. Ah, sure that was a lot of malarkey, that stuff about them letting him go in those other jobs he had. A lot of malarkey too about him being selfish and putting the blame on other people — all nonsense — sure, what did she know, the woman? But it was not nonsense that she said she wanted to leave him. Not nonsense that he had seen a hatred in her look. She would get over it. Sure, she would. She had just been letting off, as women do, with the first hurtful thing that came into her head, hadn't she? She didn't hate him; not Vera. Not his Dark Rosaleen?

He was troubled as he had rarely been. It was hard to find something to be cheerful about in what she had said and the way she had looked at him. And so, he had to think of something else. He thought of J. F. Coffey, Journalist. There was some good in that thought. Say what you like, he had a foot in the door there. Maybe Mac-

Gregor would promote him in a week or so? Probably would. All right, then. Take the job. Show her she's wrong.

At twenty-five past four he went in, took the elevator up and once again presented himself at the open doorway of the Managing Editor's office. "Excuse me, sir?"

"Aye?"

"I — ah — I would like to take the job, sir."

Mr. MacGregor pulled out a sheet of paper. "Right," he said. "Full name?"

"James Francis Coffey."

MacGregor wrote it down. "Hours, six to one, five nights a week. Except when you take the late trick, until two. Saturdays off, and one rotating day a week. If sick, report to me pairsonally by phone before three in the afternoon. Okay?"

"Yes, sir."

"One more thing, Coffey. I have fifty gurrls wurrking in the mailroom, one floor down, Dinna interfere with them, d'you hear?"

"Yes, sir."

"Now go to the composing room and ask for a man called Hickey. He'll give you a stylebook. Study it before you start wurrk tonight."

Galley slave. Suffering J, that was apt. Coffey went back down the corridor and asked directions of a man in shirt sleeves. He followed the directions and after several turnings entered a large room, loud with noise. In even rows, like children in some strange classroom, the linotypers threaded their little tines of words. Men with wooden mallets hammered leads into place; others, wearing long blue aprons and green eyeshades, plucked strips of lead from a table, fitting them in, tossing the rejects backwards to crash into large tin hellboxes. A foreman in stiff white

63

collar and black knitted tie moved with ecclesiastic tread up the aisle. As he drew level with Coffey, he leaned over, hand to his ear, in smiling dumbshow inquiry as to the visitor's business.

"Mr. Hickey?" Coffey shouted, over the machine roar.

The foreman showed comprehension by a nod and led Coffey across the room to a small, cleared area, surrounded by rows of linotype machines. There, in Dickensian concentration, sat three old men, each facing a pigeonhole desk, each scanning a galley of proof. At once their strange apartheid, combined with the extreme shabbiness of their clothing, reminded Coffey of MacGregor's remark. These were outcasts in a union sea. As he drew near he saw that each desk was double, with seats for two men.

"Hickey?" he shouted.

Without looking up from his work one old man elbowed the next, who rapped on his neighbor's desk with a pencil, who, hearing the rapping, turned slowly in his stool. His eyes, huge and shifting under lenses thick as an aquarium window, floated up to find the interrupter. Then he stood, buttoning about him a darned, many-stained cardigan of navy blue wool.

"Mr. Hickey?"

The red face nodded, the shifting eyes indicated that Ginger must follow. The old man's large, gently sliding posteriors moved between rows of linotypes, leading Coffey into the comparative quiet of the locker room. There Mr. Hickey paused, his distorted eyes searching for enemies, his raw, red hands knitting together a homemade cigarette.

"Yes?" he said. "New man?"

"How did you know?" Coffey said, surprised.

"Gets so you can tell," Mr. Hickey said. "Hitler send you?"

64

"Who?"

"Hitler. The boss."

"Oh! You mean Mr. MacGregor. Yes, he told me to ask you for a stylebook."

Mr. Hickey wheezed like an ancient organ. "Mac-Gregor," he said. "Never call him by that name, son. Hitler's his name. Because he's —"

And then came a slow, enjoyed recital — noun, adjective, verb — of fourteen well-rehearsed obscenities. When he had finished, Mr. Hickey reached into his darned cardigan to produce a small red booklet. "Stylebook," he said. "Now, go on down the street, one block to the left of here. In the tavern on the corner you'll find the night men. Look for a fellow with a crutch. That's Fox, head of the shift. It's pay night, so they all like to come in together. Better come in with them, okay?"

"Okay," Coffey said. "And thanks very much."

"Thanks?" Mr. Hickey seemed surprised. "For what, fella? This job, you don't have much to be thankful for. God bless, fella. Be seeing you."

"Going down," the elevator man shouted. "Going down."

He went down.

The tavern described by Mr. Hickey was unnamed. Above its door was an electric sign: *Verres Sterilisés —Sterilized Glasses,* a sign which no one read but which conveyed to the passing eye that here was a place to drink, a place which shut late or never, a place unlikely to be well-frequented. This last was its deception, Coffey found. Forgotten, faded, off the main streets, in a downtown limbo where property owners allowed buildings to live out a feeble charade of occupation until the glorious day when all would be expropriated in a city slum clearance drive, the tavern, instead of dying, had burgeoned in a new and steady prosperity. As Coffey pushed open its doors he was met by a beer stench and a blast of shouted talk. Two waiters in long white aprons, each balancing a tray containing a dozen full glasses of draught beer, whirled in and out among the scarred wooden tables, answering thirsty signals. Slowly Coffey moved up the room, searching for the man with a crutch. The customers put him in mind of old Wild West films: they wore fur caps, peaked caps, tuques. They wore checked shirts, lumber jackets, windbreakers. They wore logging boots, cattle boots, flying boots. They talked in roars, but they numbered also their solitaries. These sat alone at smaller tables, staring at the full and empty bottles in front of them as though studying the moves in some intricate game.

No one heeded Coffey as he moved on. At the far end of the room a huge jukebox, filled with moving colors and shifting lights, brooded in silence amid the roar of voices. Near it, disfigured with initials, an empty phone booth — symbol of the wives and worries the tavern's customers bought beer to forget. Coffey paused by the phone. What if she were sitting in the duplex this minute, already sorry for what she'd said? She could be. Yes, she might be.

He went into the booth and shut the door on the noise. He dialed, and Paulie answered.

"Is that you, Bruno?" she said.

"Who's Bruno, Pet?"

"Oh, it's you, Daddy."

"Is your mother home yet?"

"She was in but she went out again."

"Where?"

"She didn't say, Daddy."

"And she left you all alone, Pet?"

"Oh, that's all right, Daddy. I'm going to supper at a

girl friend's house and her mother's giving me a lift home in their car."

"Oh."

"I must go now, Daddy. I'm late already."

"Wait a minute, Pet. Did Mummy tell you I've got a job?"

"No."

"Well, I have. A — an editing job on a newspaper. Isn't that good?"

"Yes, Daddy."

"Well — well, tell your mother I phoned her, will you, Apple?"

"Okay, Daddy."

"And listen, Apple — don't be too late getting home, will you?"

But Paulie had already hung up. Who the blazes was selfish — he or a woman who would go out of the house and leave her little girl all alone? Suffering J! Ah well — let's have a beer. Where's this man I'm supposed to meet? Fox with a crutch.

He came out of the phone booth and stood solitary among the shouting drinkers searching for the cripple's sign. On the top of a radiator by the far wall, he saw an aluminum cane with a rubber-covered elbow grip. Nearby, sticking out into the aisle, a built-up boot. Its owner was a tall, vaguely professorial man with fairish hair and a gray stubbled chin. Coffey went over.

"Mr. Fox?"

The cripple ignored him. "First million," he said to his companions. "That's the caste mark. As long as they made it long enough ago for people to forget what it was made in, they become one of Canada's first families."

One of the men at the table, a bald, sweating person in a navy blue shirt and a vermilion tie, looked up, saw Coffey. "Fu-Fox," he said. "Wu-wanted."

"Oh?" The cripple sprawled backwards in his chair, letting his gaze travel slowly from Coffey's brown suède boots to the tiny Tyrolean hat. "New man, eh?"

"Yes. How did you know?"

"How did I know? Hear that, Harry?"

Both Fox and the stammerer were seized with a laughing fit. Fox cleared glasses and bottles from in front of him in a rash sweep of his arm, laying his laughing face on the beer-wet table top. He was, Coffey realized, half-seas over.

"Sit down," said a third reader, pulling out a chair for Coffey. He was very old, strangely dressed in a duck-billed fawn cap, fawn windbreaker and high, elastic-sided boots. A feathery white goatee grew precariously on his caved-in jaws, and as he reached forward to shake hands, Coffey was put in mind of the recruiting poster's Uncle Sam. "My name's Billy Davis," he said. "And this here is Kenny."

Kenny was little more than a boy. His face, tortured by eczema, looked up at Coffey in a lost, posed smile. His right hand clutched the neck of a beer bottle. He sat primly on the edge of his chair.

"Drink up, Paddy," Fox said, signaling a waiter. "You're behind."

A waiter came and Fox paid for four glasses of draught beer which he at once lined up in front of Coffey. His companion, Harry, seemed to consider this a further occasion for laughter. "Now, Paddy," Fox said. "Let's see you sink these. Go ahead."

"Thanks very much," Coffey said. "That's very decent of you. My treat next, I hope?"

"Drink!" Fox shouted. "One, two, three, four. Go ahead."

Lord knows, Coffey liked a wet as well as the next man.

But there was something lunatic about this. He began on the first beer. Bald Harry's upper lip dripped sweat. The boy widened his fixed smile a fraction, in encouragement. The old man nodded his goatlike chin. Glass empty, Coffey put it down and reached for a second.

"Good man," Fox said. "Away you go. One swallow."

It took two swallows.

"Number three, now," Fox said.

But as he raised the third glass to his lips, Coffey paused. Wasn't this daft? What was he doing, drinking himself stocious for a clatter of strangers?

"What's up?" Fox said.

"Nothing. Only that it's against nature, guzzling like this. What's the rush?"

Fox and Harry exchanged glances. "A good question, Paddy," Fox said. "And it answers mine. Booze is not your problem, right?"

They must be joking. It must be some sort of joke, this chat?

"Never mind him," the girlish boy said. "Say, that's a dandy overcoat you have. Sharp." He touched Coffey's sleeve.

"Wu-women?" Harry said. "Du-do you think that's his pu-problem, Foxy?"

"Why must I have a problem?" Coffey said. "What are you talking about?"

"Every proofreader has," Fox said. "All ye who enter here. Look at Kenny." He leaned over as he spoke and put his arm around the boy's shoulders. "You know what Kenny's problem is, I suppose?"

"Shut up," the boy said. "Lousy gimp."

"Hostility to the father figure," Fox shouted. "Classic!"

Feathery fingers plucked at Coffey's wrist. The old man thrust his Uncle Sam visage close. His mouth opened, showing gaps of gums policed by ancient dental survivors. "Could be money," he said. "That's everybody's problem, am I right, fellow?"

"That's right," Coffey said, uneasily jovial. "It's the root of all evil, they tell me."

"Wrong!" Fox shouted. "Why, money is not evil, Paddy my boy. Money is the Canadian way to immortality."

"Cu-christ, here he gu-goes again," Harry said.

"Quiet now," Fox shouted. "I have to explain the facts of life to our immigrant brother. Do you want to be remembered, Paddy? Of course you do. Then you must bear in mind that in this great country of ours the surest way to immortality is to have a hospital wing called after you. Or better still, a bridge. We're just a clutch of little Ozymandiases in this great land. Nobody here but us builders. This is Canada's century, they tell us. Not America's, mind you. Not even Russia's. The twentieth century belongs to Canada. And if it does, then you had better know our values. Remember that in this fair city of Montreal the owner of a department store is a more important citizen than any judge of the Superior Court. Never forget that, Paddy boy. Money is the root of all good here. One nation, indivisible, under Mammon that's our heritage. Now drink up."

Coffey reached for his fourth glass of beer. Might as well. She didn't bloody well love him any more so what did it matter if he got drunk. Today was enough to drive any man to drink.

"Tonight, Coffey, you will become a proofreader. You will read all the news. War in China, peace in our time. Mere finger exercises. Later, Coffey, if you show promise, we may let you read something more important. The Quebec Society News, for instance. Or the Governor-General's speech to the Crippled Deaf Mute Division of the

United Sons of Scotland. And if you continue to show promise — if you make no mistake, allow no errors typographic or orthographic to slip into print, then we may even let you read an advertisement. And some day, you may become a senior man, a man who reads *only* advertisements. Because, Coffey, news is cheap. Here today and gone tomorrow. But advertisements cost money. They count. So you must get them right, do you hear? Compree?"

"Compree," Coffey said, raising his hand to signal the waiter.

The old man nodded and smiled. "It's money that counts, all right," he said. "Ten men run this country, did you know that? Ten big fineenceers. And did you know there's a book tells you who they are and how they made it? You'll want to read that book, being a New Canadian. Yes, you will. You can borrow my copy, if you like."

Yes, Coffey said, he must dip into that sometime. He paid for another round of beers.

"Are you just pu-passing through?" Harry asked him. "Or du-do you pu-plan to stay for a while?"

Coffey took a long pull of his beer. "Passing through," he said. "Matter of fact, I'm just in the proofroom so's I can pick up the *Tribune* style. MacGregor's going to make me a reporter."

As he said this, he saw Fox screw up his left eye in a large drunken wink. Harry collapsed in a fresh rush of laughter. The old man shook his head. "Big fineenceers," he mumbled. "Scab labor, that's what we are."

"But — but what's the matter?" Coffey asked. "I mean, what's funny about it?"

Again Fox winked at the others. "Nothing funny," he said. "I just hope you succeed, that's all."

Coffey stared at their knowing faces. What did they

mean? Had he been tricked? "Look, fellows," he said. "Tell me. I want to know. Do you think he *will* make me a reporter?"

"Stranger things have happened," Fox said. "Drink up."

"Big finenceers," the old man mumbled. "I remember one time —"

But Coffey no longer listened. He sat dumb, drowsy with beer, the glasses multiplying in front of him, the stylebook forgotten in his pocket. Were they making a joke of him? Was MacGregor tricking him? What was going on? Was it for this he had traveled across half a frozen continent and the whole Atlantic Ocean? To finish up as a galley slave among the lame, the odd, the halt, the old?

"Money," Fox was saying. "Oh, let me tell you, you can be a four-letter bastard all your life but never mind. If you die with enough money in the bank, the *Tribune* will write you a fine editorial eulogy —"

Had he been wrong to bet his all on Canada? Would he have been better to stick in those dead-end jobs at home, plodding along, day in and day out, until he dropped? Canada — listen to these fellows — they seem to think Canada is the back of beyond. . . .

"Nu-nother depression," Harry said. "You just wu-watch it. They sneeze in the States and we get pneumonia here."

Was that true? Was it a backwater, like the land he had fled? Had he made the mistake of his life, landing himself up here among these people, either smug like old Gerry, or full of gloomy prophecies like these fellows? Bloody Canada! Bloody Canadians!

"Just a poor clutch of Arctic-bound sods —" Fox was saying.

For if Veronica was going to leave him, then hadn't this been the greatest mistake ever?

"Greatest mistake this country ever made was not joining the United States," Fox said.

There was always Paulie. I've got a job, Pet, he'd told her. Yes, Daddy. Daddies are supposed to get jobs. Not very great to have a job, is it? Not this job. Yes, if he lost Veronica, he would lose Paulie too. And would have no one.

"Drink up," Fox said. "Last call, boys."

"Must phone," he said, standing up. "Just a moment."

Because, ah, Vera didn't mean it, did she? She was just upset, she would say she was sorry now. Never mind, dear, he'd say. My fault. I love you, Kitten. I love you too, Ginger. Yes . . . she'd be over it now. . . .

He dialed. "Vera?"

"It's me. Paulie."

"Oh, Paulie," Coffey said, closing his eyes, leaning his forehead against the cool glass of the booth. "Is your mother there, Pet?"

"I told you she went out."

"Out?"

"Daddy, are you drinking?"

"No, no, that's a way to speak to your Daddy! Listen, Apple. Give her a message. Tell her to phone me. All right?"

"Where?"

"The *Tribune.* It's a newspaper. All right?"

"Okay. I'll leave a note for her," Paulie said.

"Listen — Paulie?"

"What is it?" Paulie asked crossly.

"Paulie . . . You don't think I'm selfish, do you? I mean — listen, Apple. You're still my own little Apple, hmm?"

"Oh, stop it, Daddy!"

"Not cross at me . . . I mean . . . listen, Pet. I mean, Paulie . . . Daddy's not bad, is he? *Mmm?* . . . Paulie?"

Dizzy, all that beer in a hurry, but the pane of glass was so cool against his forehead . . .

"Listen, Pet . . . won't be home. Want to speak to Mummy . . . tell her . . . Apple . . . Tell her, Daddy's sorry —"

Fox banged on the door of the booth. "Saddle up," he shouted. "Come on, galley slave. Hitler's Legion rides again."

"Paulie — Paulie?"

Brr-brr-brr-brr the phone went. He shoveled the receiver back on to its cradle, and looked at it dully. No, Paulie didn't care. . . .

He stepped out of the booth and stumbled. "I'm drunk," he said. "I'm ploothered."

"Never mind," Fox said. "So are we all, all honorable men. Take his arm there. Hurry! Hurry!"

Into the men's washroom behind the composing room, Old Billy Davis led Coffey, fumbling drunk. Stood him beside the basins, took hold of Coffey's jaws, forcing them open as though he would administer a pill, but instead darted his finger into Coffey's mouth, pulled it out again and forced Coffey's head down towards the washbasin. Then waited, placid and fragile in his fawn windbreaker, as his victim, hands gripping the basin, retched wildly, flooding the bowl.

"Once more?"

"No . . . no," Coffey moaned, coughing until the tears came.

"Better now? All right. Follow me."

Out of the men's locker room in a trembling run, past the compositors' lockers, through the lanes of linotype machines to the row of steel desks . . . Hands reached past, claiming galleys, shuffling copy, spiking galleys; busy, everyone busy, no voices heard above the chattering mumble of machines. Drained, but still ill, Coffey made a cradle of his arms and rested his head on the dirty steel desk top. J. F. Coffey, Editor; J. F. Coffey, Journalist. In a weak moment he felt the tears come: she did not love him; she hated him and why shouldn't she, rotten with drink, he was, great drunken lump, J. F. Coffey, Journalist, ploothered his first night on the job. Ah God! He hated this great lump, blowing into his thick red mustache, self-pitying fool. . . .

"Hey, hey," Fox said, shaking him. "Wake up, Paddy. Hitler's coming. Here you are."

A half-finished galley appeared in front of Coffey's face. And just in time.

Mr. MacGregor was coming through. Bony old arms hanging naked from shirt sleeves, blue vein pumping in his pale forehead, fanatic eye starved for trouble. As he swept out on his nightly visitation, office boys, delinquent deskmen, guilty reporters, all avoided his eye, practiced the immobility of small animals as a hawk moves over a forest. But on the instant MacGregor entered the composing room, some of the ferocity drained from his walk. Here, old battles had been fought, old forts abandoned. Here, the enemy was in full command, camped permanently within MacGregor's walls. Strikes, scabs, shutouts; all had failed. Hedged around by clause and contract, the Managing Editor was forbidden to lay a finger on one stick of type, denied the right to speak one word of direct command. The composing room foreman waited his nightly sortie with the amused contempt of a Roman general dealing with the chieftain of a small hill tribe. Here, each night, MacGregor relived his defeat.

And so, as was his custom, his impotence sought its

revenge. Alone in that union camp, the proofreaders were still his servants.

"Who let this pass?" he shouted, shaking a galley high above the dirty steel desks. "Who let this pass?"

Fox raised his gray stubbled chin, took the galley, consulted the penciled initials. "Day man," he said.

"Jesuschrist! Got this name wrong, see? Friend of the publisher. Jesuschrist!"

Fox looked at the ceiling as though engaged in mental arithmetic. His fellow workers read proof with awful intensity.

"Not our shift, sir," Fox said. "And we're late, sir. Still short of men."

"I gave you a new man tonight. Where is he? New man — aye — let's see . . ."

As he spoke, MacGregor ran around the desks and snatched up the half-finished galley. "Well, Coffey, let's see your wurrk?" He spread the galley on the desk top, scanning it, block-reading not for sense but for typographical errors. Years of practice gave him an unerring eye for flaw, but tonight he saw no flaw. Four errors on the galley, four caught, so far. A new man? He did not believe it. He turned on Fox. "These aren't his marks. They're yours."

It was a guess, but once he had made it, MacGregor snatched some of Fox's galleys off the spike and compared. "Aye, these are your marks," he said in triumph. "Coffey?"

"Yes, sir."

"Show me your other galleys."

Behind his high desk, the composing room foreman had been watching. He saw the new man's face, red, confused, turn upwards towards his tormentor. Poor sod. The foreman stepped down from his desk, approached, stopping MacGregor in mid-shriek. "Your men are behind here, Mr. Mac," he said. "All this talk is holding up the work. You're short-staffed here, as usual. And we're late."

"We're doing our best, damn ye!"

But MacGregor turned away, spiked the galleys and made off without another word, fearful of a new defeat, a new infestation of mediators, arbitrators, international representatives and similar union incubi and succubi. The foreman winked at Coffey's bewildered face and returned to his desk. The linotypers, prim and efficient on their little stools, smiled as at an old and favorite joke and — monks performing a rite of exorcism — the proofreaders downed galleys and intoned a short chant of MacGregorian abuse. Then, the obscenities observed, Fox leaned across the desk and fed Coffey his first galley of the night. "All right," he said. "Coast's clear. Do your best."

At ten the bell rang for supper break. At ten-fifteen it rang again and they went on to work until one. Sober now, Coffey found that he could do the job. Soon he was reading galleys only seconds slower than old Billy and half as quick as Fox. He was surprised, and pleased, because, all his life, do you see, he had been in jobs whose only purpose seemed to be to convince some higher-up that you were worth the money he was paying you. But in this job, you read your galley and made your corrections and, if you looked across the room, you could see the make-up men going on with the next step in the process. Within an hour or two, a newspaper would come off the press and tomorrow morning people would buy it, would read it over breakfast. You made something. There was no coming the old soldier, either. You signed your initials at the foot of each galley and if you let something slip, it could be traced back to you.

It was a new and satisfying feeling.

And so, at one in the morning, when Coffey rode home on the bus, a newly printed newspaper on his lap, he had, by his habitual processes of ratiocination, convinced himself that the day was not a defeat but a victory. A little victory. He had a job: he was working alongside a bunch of Canadians in a far-off country, pulling his weight with the best of them. As for Vera, she would be over her bad temper by now. He would make a cup of cocoa for her, bring her into the kitchen and tell her all about his evening. He would kiss her and they would say they were sorry, both of them. Hard-working Ginger. Not selfish, no. Doing the best he could.

There were no lights on in the duplex when he let himself in. In the outer hall, he listened for signs of life as he emptied snow out of the turnups of his trousers. Quietly, he passed by Paulie's room and, in the darkened master bedroom, fumbled for the curtain drawstrings. The curtains screeched on their runners, opening with a quick flounce. Moonlight fell on his wife's slender body, wrapped like a furled sail in all the bed-sheets.

"Veronica?" he whispered.

But she slept. Ah well, let her sleep: he would make up with her tomorrow. He undressed in the moonlight, looking out of the window. Snow, dead and thick and white, shaded the arms of the tree opposite; wedged itself in clefts of branches; cake-iced the roofs of houses across the street. The city was quiet, its traffic noises muted by the snowfall. He yawned and reached for the curtain drawstrings, sending the rings screeching on their runners, closing the room to blackness again. He slipped into bed and lay, listening to her breathe. How strange life was! Only this morning he had lain here beside her, happy after joy, not knowing what the day would bring. Only this afternoon he had walked away across the Palm

Court, in dread of her leaving him. Only a few hours ago he had sat in a room full of machines, doing something he had never done before. How could people say life was dull? Ah, look at her now, asleep and at peace. If only there had been no bitterness, if only those things had not been said. If only he could take that part of the day away, erase it with a kiss.

And why not? He snuggled against her. She was tall, but his chin touched the top of her head, his feet slipped under her soles, a pedestal for her feet. Oh, how warm and soft she was, her nightgown rucked about her waist. Warm she was. And warm he loved her.

"Don't," she mumbled. "No."

He smiled in the darkness and moved his hand up to cup her breast.

"Stop it. Please, Gerry, stop."

He lay very quiet. He could hear his own heart. She must hear it too; it was thumping like an engine. Slowly, he reached out and fondled her breasts, his loins cold, his heart hammering.

"No, Gerry. Please. Not now."

He took his hand away. Slowly, careful not to wake her, he turned his back to her and lay, eyes open in the dark, his large body still as a statue on the lid of a tomb. He listened to her breathe. The intake was regular, yet irregular in the way of sleep. She was asleep. Yes, she was dreaming a dream.

Do you remember that summer you were stationed at the Curragh and you got a great crush on an eighteen-year-old girl who never even knew you fancied her? Didn't you dream about her many's a night that summer, and did that mean that you slept with her? Or even kissed her? Haven't you been unfaithful to Veronica a thousand times in dreams?

Still, she only knows one Gerry. That long drink of

79

water? Besides, she's thirty-five, five years older than he is. But he's a bachelor, he has a sports car and he's free with his money. And she wept her troubles to him the other day. *He's* why she wants to leave you. It's plain as the nose on your face.

But was it? It could be a dream. One sentence in her sleep after fifteen years of marriage didn't make a whore of her, did it?

He lay, his eyes open in the darkness. He blinked his eyes and felt something wet touch the corner of his mouth, seeping through the edges of his mustache. He was not going to boohoo like a baby, was he? Was he? No.

But, suffering J! It was hard to hold on to his hopes.

Four   Next morning, after she had fed him breakfast, she said she was going downtown to see about a job.

"What job?"

"It's a millinery place that's run by a friend of Gerry Grosvenor's. They need a saleslady."

"Oh."

"I won't be back for lunch," she said. "And if you go out, you'd better buy something to put in your sandwiches tonight."

"All right." He looked down at his plate. He had noticed she was wearing her good black suit.

"Paulie?" she called. "Get a move on, you'll be late for school. Good-by, Ginger. Are you going to be at home all day?"

"I suppose so."

"I'll phone you later on, then."

He heard the front door close. No kiss good-by. He sat, his tea growing cold, hardly noticing Paulie, who rushed in, ate, and fled late to school. Let her go. Let them all go.

A ruler went *tickety-tak-tak* down the staircase which connected his apartment with the landlady's upstairs.

"*M'sieur?* Want to play with me?"

He looked up, met eyes lonelier than his. "Come on in, Michel," he said. "Let's have a game, the pair of us."

The little boy had brought his building blocks. Coffey cleared a space at the kitchen table and gravely, thirty-nine and five years old, they built a house with a long sugar-lump chimney. They played at building for more than an hour until Michel's grandmother called from upstairs.

Alone again, Coffey sucked a sugar lump. . . . Maybe if he went down to Grosvenor's office, ostensibly to discuss the proofreading job, and somehow brought the conversation around to Veronica? If he had any gumption at all, wouldn't he see in Grosvenor's eyes the guilt or innocence of last night's phrase?

All right. He shaved, dressed himself in his suit of Dromore tweed, and took a bus to the financial district. It was a quarter to twelve when he got off the bus. He went into a drugstore, already crowded with typists on their lunch hour, and in a phone booth at the rear, surrounded by display cards showing smiling girls half-naked under sun lamps, he phoned Gerry Grosvenor.

No, Mr. Grosvenor had just stepped out for a moment. Would he mind calling back, please? And what was his name, again? Coffey. Yes, he would call back. He hung up; stared at the display cards of pretty, half-naked girls. There were so many pretty girls in the world. Why couldn't that long drink of water find one, instead of coming after a friend's wife, a woman of thirty-five who was not *that* pretty? Suffering J!

At five minutes to twelve he phoned again, this time from the lobby of Grosvenor's building. Oh, she was very sorry but the other girl had just told her that Mr. Grosvenor had stepped out to lunch. Would he care to phone after lunch? He would? Fine, then.

Flute! He stepped out of the phone booth and was immediately jostled and pushed into a corner by the flow of people hurrying from the elevators. Everybody was in such a hurry here! Everybody shoving and pushing you aside! Canadians had no manners! Raw, cold country with its greedy, pushy people, grabbing what didn't belong to them, shoving you aside! Land of opportunity, my eye!

Now stop that, he told himself. Don't blame the whole country for one twister of a cartoonist. Stop it. So he stopped it. He went over to the newsstand in the lobby and bought a package of cigarettes. No sense behaving like a lunatic because of one little word in a woman's dream. Ah, why didn't he go back to the house and forget all this nonsense of waiting for Grosvenor. For it *was* all nonsense. In the noon rush of people, it seemed incredible. He had imagined the whole thing.

Someone caught at his sleeve. "Ginger. Hello there."

"Oh, hello, Gerry," he said guiltily.

"What are you doing in this part of the forest?"

"Well — ah — I just dropped by to have a word with you. I mean about that proofreading job. I took it, you know."

People were passing, bumping against them as they stood, stuck driftwood, in the current towards the revolving doors.

"Look, we can't talk here," Grosvenor said. "Let me give you a lift uptown."

Coffey followed Grosvenor's tall thin back into the merry-go-round of the doors. A cold wind met them as they stepped out into the cavern of the street, and as Coffey paused to put up his overcoat collar, Grosvernor jumped boyishly out into the traffic, snapping his fingers for a cab. A cab careened out of the traffic lane and drew up, inches away from Grosvenor's body. But, flute! He was unharmed.

"Come on, Ginger, hop in. Okay, driver, go on up Beaver Hall Hill. I'll let you know where, later."

They settled in the back seat, side by side. "Well, Ginger," Grovenor said. "Lucky day, eh?"

"What?"

"Veronica's new job, of course. Didn't she tell you?"

Coffey's ruddy face stared straight ahead. "No," he said.

"Well, she was hired this morning at Modelli. It's a chi-chi sort of hatshop. The pay is forty a week and a sales bonus, which should bring it up to fifty-five most weeks. Not bad for a start, eh?"

"Not bad," Coffey said. Five dollars a week more than me, that's not bad.

"Well now, and what about you?" Grosvenor said. "So you took the proofreading job, did you?"

In the side panel of the cab, enshrined under a tiny light, was a police permit photograph of the driver. *Marcel Parent: 58452.* Coffey looked at this photograph, then at the back of the driver's head. God, it was mortifying trying to talk in private while *Marcel Parent: 58452* listened in on every syllable.

"I gather Vera knows the truth about the job," Grosvenor said. "Too bad. I wonder is there anything I could do, I mean about getting you promoted?"

Coffey shook his head. What did he care about jobs now? What did it matter?

"I might phone old Mac and try to find out how long he intends to keep you in that sweatshop?"

"No," Coffey said. "Don't bother."

"Look, there's no sense in your staying on there if it's a dead end," Grosvenor said. "After all, don't forget, that's the lowest job in the newspaper business. You can do better than that."

Thank you, Marcel Parent, for looking into your driving

84

mirror to see what sort of specimen would accept the lowest job in the newspaper business.

"So what else is new?" Grosvenor asked.

You tell me, Coffey thought. But he said: "Nothing. Are you having lunch with anyone?"

For the first time, he saw a flicker of uneasiness in Grosvenor's eyes. "Well, yes, as a matter of fact I am," Grosvenor said. "It's a business lunch. I'd like to have you join us, but it would bore you stiff."

"No, I didn't mean that," Coffey said. "I was just wondering where — where you could drop me off."

"Anywhere you say, Ginger."

"Well, just drop me anywhere that suits you. Where are you going?"

"The Pavillon," Grosvenor said. "So I'll drop you on the corner of Ste. Catherine and Drummond, okay?"

"Fair enough."

When the taxi stopped at the corner of Drummond Street, Grosvenor refused Coffey's share of the fare. "I'm loaded," he said. "Lots of expense account money these days. Be seeing you."

"Be seeing you," Coffey echoed. He watched the cab move away. Seeing you, yes; and, seeing you, aren't you one of the drippiest drinks of water I've ever laid eyes on? Expense account or not, artist or not, what could she see in you, you self-satisfied sausage?

Still, Veronica had phoned Grosvenor this morning. Not him. And wasn't Grosvenor just the boy who would invite a person to lunch to celebrate anything under the sun? He was indeed.

Ah, nonsense.

But he turned around, hurried down Drummond Street and went into the Pavillon. At the entrance to the dining room, he hesitated, wanting to turn back. A headwaiter came from behind a stand-up desk, tapping a sheaf of

menus against his stiff shirt-front. "Have you a reserva-
tion, sir?"

"No. I'm just looking for a friend of mine."

"What name, sir?"

"A Mr. Grosvenor."

"Oh yes, sir. This way please."

The headwaiter sailed out among the tables like a
ship's figurehead, turning to make sure that Coffey followed. Halfway across the room, he stopped and
pointed. "Over here, sir. This way."

"Never mind. I — I see he's busy."

Busy he was. In a corner, at a tiny table behind a pillar,
the pair of them deep in chat over Martinis. Out of the
dining room Coffey fled, running down the steps into the
street, a boy escaping a pair of bullies. But wasn't it them
who should have run from him? He stopped on the street
corner, out of breath. Why had he ever gone in there?
And why had he bolted? He should have faced them, but
how could he start a row in front of a roomful of people?
To fight or not to fight. To run or stand. What did it matter? He crossed the street and stood in line for a bus.
Every hour of last night had moved as slowly as a sun
crossing the midsummer sky. And yet he had managed
to get up this morning with a reasonable amount of
doubt. But now . . .

Now, it made sense. Even her anger when he told her
he had spent the ticket money. She had been prepared to
go home to Ireland with him, that was the worst of all.
She had been willing to stick with him.

He stopped off on the way back and bought some boloney for sandwiches. He bought two pears for Paulie. Poor
Paulie. No wonder Veronica didn't care if the child ate
properly. No wonder she let Paulie run around with ink
spots on her school tunic. Why shouldn't she, when her

mind wasn't on her family at all? Ah, a lot of things made sense now.

When he entered the outer hall of their apartment, little Michel was sitting on the staircase, waiting for him. "Hey, *M'sieur.* See what I got?"

"Yes, just a minute, Michel." He unlocked the door of his apartment and put the grocery bag inside. A toy made a noise behind him. It was a small robot, battery-operated: its cubed legs moved with a slow grinding of cogs, its eyes lit red and there were little antennae coming out of its head. As Coffey watched, the toy fell. The legs had not gained purchase on the slippery linoleum.

"It's too slidey here," the child complained.

"Oh. Well — bring him in, why don't you? There's a carpet in the hall."

They went into Coffey's place. The boy placed the toy on the worn carpet runner. "Watch now, *M'sieur.* I press this button."

Coffey squatted to watch. Robot cogs ground, robot eyes glowed. The manikin, stiff-legged, rocked slowly forward. "By the holy," Coffey said. "That's a grand toy. Where'd you get it?"

"My Mama give it to me."

"See this little door in his back?" Coffey said. "That's where the battery is."

"Don't touch him. He's *my* toy!"

"Sorry," Coffey said. "Here you are."

But the child handed the toy back at once. "*Montrez — montrez?*"

"Now hold on, old son," Coffey said. "You know I don't parley-voo. Wish I did, though. . . . There you are. See that little thing in there? That's what makes him work."

"What?"

"Well, it keeps him alive. It's his juice."

"Why does juice make him walk?"

"Well, if you have no juice — Look here, Michel, why don't you go on upstairs now? I feel tired."

"But there's nobody upstairs," Michel said.

"Where's your Mama?"

"Mama's out. *Grand'mère* is sleeping. Please, *M'sieur.* Play with me?"

Coffey sighed. "All right," he said. "Let's take it in the kitchen."

They went into the kitchen. Coffey unloosened his tie and sat down. For fifteen minutes Michel played with the robot while he, with a pretended show of interest, answered the childish questions. He looked at Michel's ragged little head bent over the toy. Was it because he had never given her a son that she had done this to him? Was that far-fetched? But oh! What reason could be stranger than the strangeness of the fact.

"He's broke, *M'sieur.* He's broke, he don't work."

"Wait a sec. Let's see." Coffey took the robot, opened the back and fiddled with the wires. Probably a bad connection. He straightened the contacts.

"Will he work now?"

"Let's see. Put him on the floor, Michel."

"For the love of Mike, why didn't you close the front door?" Veronica's voice shouted down the corridor. "You'll freeze the place."

Man and child exchanged glances, strangely united in apprehension. Coffey stood up as she came into the kitchen. "Did you have lunch?" he said.

"You know damn well I had lunch. Why did you run off like that?"

"*M'sieur,* he still won't work."

"Go home, Michel," Veronica said.

"Now, just a moment, dear," Coffey said. "Michel's been keeping me company, haven't you, Michel?"

"I want to talk to you, Ginger. Gerry's outside."

"Look, Michel, push the button like this. See? Now, I'll bet you he'll even walk upstairs with you. Try? All right? Off you go, lad."

Michel rubbed the tears from his fat little cheeks. He took the robot, which was now moving and grinding perfectly. "Oh, thanks, *M'sieur*," he said. "Thanks, thanks."

And ran off down the hall, the robot in his hand. Slowly, Coffey stood up. Oh, to be a boy . . . tears one moment, all wiped away the next. A world of toys. Nothing so terrible a kindness would not change it. Oh, to be a boy. . . .

Too old for toys, he turned to face her; waited for what new bead she would string on her rosary of lies.

"Gerry's here," she repeated. "I didn't want him to come, but he insisted. He wants to talk to you alone. And, Ginger?"

"What?"

"Ginger, I don't want you to fight with Gerry. It won't do any good, do you hear?"

He turned away without answering and went down the hall.

He opened the front door, and there was Grosvenor.

"May I come in a moment?" Grosvenor asked and came in, walking as though he entered a house where someone was ill. Together, with Coffey leading the way, they went back along the railroad corridor passageway to the living room. Coffey opened the door and, out of habit, stood back to let his visitor pass. As he did, he saw Veronica sitting in the kitchen, shoulders bent as though anticipating a blow. Irrationally, he wanted to go to her and tell her everything would be all right. But how could he tell her, he who did not know how wrong things were? And why should he, he thought, in sudden anger. This was not *his* fault.

He went in after Grosvenor and carefully shut the door. He looked at Grosvenor as though seeing him for the first time. Grosvenor was nine years younger than he; taller too. Yet Coffey knew he could win. One good clout and Grosvenor would burst like a paper bag. He waited as Grosvenor took off his overcoat and laid it on a chair. Then Grosvenor produced cigarettes, and a lighter initialed G.G. He offered both. Coffey shook his head. They stood back, fighters after the traditional handshake.

"I saw you go out of the restaurant," Grosvenor said. "I called after you, but you didn't hear me. So I thought, under the circumstances, I'd better come up here and explain. I'm not the sort of man who hides behind a woman's skirts, Ginger."

Only go up them, Coffey thought.

"I'm not going to lie to you, Ginger. I've been in love with Veronica ever since I met her. At first, I thought there was no hope for me. Now I realize there is. I'm going to fight for her, Ginger."

Grosvenor waited but Coffey did not speak. "I'm sorry this has happened, Ginger. Believe me, no matter what, I think of you as a friend."

"Do you, now?" Coffey said. "Trying to stuff another man's wife, is that your idea of being a friend?"

"Now, wait, Ginger. I know you're angry and you have every right to make ugly remarks about me. But not about Veronica. Veronica's a wonderful girl and she's been terribly loyal to you."

"She's my wife," Coffey said. "I don't need you to tell me what she's like."

"You don't?" Grosvenor said. "I'm not sure about that. If you knew her, you wouldn't have spent your ticket money home. And I'd have lost her."

90

"You haven't got her yet. Nor will you."

"Maybe not, Ginger. But she wants to leave you. You know that."

"Will you shut your gob!" Coffey shouted. "This is a private matter between me and Veronica —"

"Now wait. I'm nearly finished, Ginger. I've told Veronica that any time she's ready, I'll take care of her. I've promised to give her all the things she needs: love and consideration. And security."

"You louser," Coffey said. "What the hell do you know about love? All you want is to get up some woman's skirts, you skinny bastard you."

"I knew you'd say that," Grosvenor said. "But let me set you straight on one thing. This is love, not lust. What Veronica and I feel for each other is precious. I know that sounds corny, Ginger, but it happens to be the truth. We're in love, and we intend to stay in love until we die."

"Get out," Coffey said. "Get out before I flatten you."

"Wait a minute, Ginger, I'm not finished yet. I came here to settle this —"

"Right, then. Put up your dukes!"

"I don't mean fighting, Ginger. Fighting isn't going to settle anything. Now — wait a minute —"

But Coffey hit him, his fist thudding against Grosvenor's cheek. Grosvenor's head cracked back; his knees joined ludicrously like an opened scissors. He stood, holding his face with both hands as Coffey hit him again, first on the side of the head, then, with all his strength, in the body. Grosvenor stumbled. His hands went to protect his stomach. Immediately, Coffey finished him with a blow in the mouth, then stood back, his knuckles skinned on Grosvenor's teeth. Grosvenor fell against a sofa and sat down on the floor, his mouth widening in a trickle of blood like a sad clown's grin.

"Get up," Coffey said, waiting.

"Go on," Grosvenor said, thickly. "Hit me. Hit me if it does you any good."

"Get up."

"No," Grosvenor said.

Coffey stood sucking his knuckles, staring at Grosvenor. He had never met one like this before.

"Hit me if you want," Grosvenor said, still sitting on the floor. "But the fact is, I didn't come to fight, I came to talk. Veronica tells me she doesn't think you'd have any religious objections to getting a divorce. Is that true?"

Coffey ignored him. He opened the living room door and called: "Veronica?"

She came, from the kitchen.

"Is it true you want a divorce, Vera?"

But she had seen Grosvenor sitting on the floor. She went to him, bent over him. "Oh, Gerry," she said. "What happened? What did he do to you?" She turned to Coffey. "How could you?" she said. "He was only trying to help."

How could he? He looked at her, looking at her face which he knew so well and did not know at all; saw the thing he had seen yesterday. Hate. He could not bear that hate. He lowered his gaze to the worn pattern of the carpet, the fleur-de-lis, blue and gold. "Paulie's coming with me," he said.

"You have no money, Ginger. You can't look after her."

"I have some," he said.

"No, Ginger. I went to the bank yesterday. I took all that was left."

He remembered the ten-dollar bill she had paid the tea with. So that was it. "Paulie's coming with me," he repeated.

"Look, Ginger," Grosvenor said. "In case you're worrying about the effect this might have on Paulie, I give you my word to keep out of things until this is settled between you —"

"*Your* word of honor?" Coffey said. "You specimen!"

"You're a nice one to talk," Veronica began. "You that —"

But he could not bear to hear her. He left the room, went into the bedroom and shut the door. Confused, he began to open closets and drawers, throwing shirts, socks and underwear in a heap on the bed. No, she wasn't going to get Paulie. She wasn't going to leave him all alone now, with nobody, with nothing. He and Paulie, just the two of them —

But where? And on what?

He sat down on the bed, in large, trembling dignity. His image in the dresser mirror looked at him: large, trembling. Look at him, would you, sitting there with his great big ginger mustache, in the hacking jacket he spent hours picking out in Grafton Street, with the tie to match. When, what matter, ties will not make the man, no, nor throwing her across this bed yesterday morning, pleased with yourself for being the great stud, when all the time she was dreaming of Grosvenor. Look at yourself, would you. Take a good look.

He looked at him. A stupid man, dressed up like a Dublin squire. Looked at the frightened, childish face frozen now in a military man's disguise. He hated that man in the mirror, hated him. Oh, God, there was a useless bloody man, coming up to forty and still full of a boy's dreams of ships coming in; of adventures and escapes and glories still to be. When, what were the true facts of that big idjit's life? FACTS: James Francis Coffey, failed B.A.; former glorified secretary to the Managing Director of a distillery; former joeboy in the advertising department, after he was kicked downstairs; former glorified secretary to the Manager of a knitwear factory;

93

failed sales representative of three concerns in this new and promised land. FACTS: Husband of a woman who wanted out before it was too late; father of a fourteen-year-old girl who ignored him. . . . Fathead! Great Lump! With nine solitary dollars between him and all harm.

The mirror man looked sad. Yes, he hated that man, that man he had made in the mirror, that mirror man who had unmade him. No one honored that foolish sad impostor, no one loved him. Except him: for only he knew that the big idjit had meant no harm, had suffered many's a hurt. Ah, poor fraud, he thought. You're all I have. Yet, even I don't like you.

Quiet footsteps passed in the corridor. Whispers. The front door shut. That was Grosvenor leaving, he supposed. He looked at his face and his face looked at him. Well now, you, what are you going to do?

Speak to Paulie when she comes in? Ask her —

What good will that do? She's her mother's girl.

No, no, I'll explain. I'll show her how we can manage, just the two of us.

Yes, the mirror man said. You've managed rightly, until now, haven't you? Judging by today.

Now, wait — I'll get a job, I'll get two jobs, I'll work day and night if need be. . . .

But the front door had opened. Paulie's voice called: "Mummy? Are you there, Mummy?"

He stood up, pulled down the peaks of his doeskin waistcoat and went into the hall. "Paulie?" he said. "Would you come into the kitchen for a second?" He waited as she removed her duffel coat and overshoes and followed him down the corridor. As they passed the living room, he saw that the door was shut. They went into the kitchen.

94

"Sit down, Pet," he said. "I want to have a word with you."

"What about?"

She was tall for her age, Paulie. Her hair was reddish, like his own. She had his large hands and something of him in her pale, placid face. As he drew out a chair for her, he noticed again the patch of ink on the shoulder strap of her jumper.

"I was wondering," he said. "How would you like to move to a new flat, Pet?"

"Anything would be better than this dump. Are we going to move, Daddy?"

"Well, I mean just you and me," he said.

"What about Mummy?" Paulie asked, her pale blue eyes worrying at him. "What happened? Did you have a row?"

"No — it's just that — Well, Mummy's got a job. It would suit her better if she stayed on here for a while. I mean, alone."

"I can't see any sense in that, Daddy. You *did* have a row, isn't that it?"

"Look, Pet," he said. "It's just that — well, I need you more than Mummy does."

"I'd have to do the cooking, you mean. And make the beds and stuff?"

"Oh, I'd help you, Apple. It's not for that. It's for company I'm asking you."

Paulie picked at her fingernail. The sink tap dripped on a plate. "I want to stay here," she said. "Let's both stay here, Daddy. All right?"

He nodded, uncomfortably. To get her to come he would have to tell the truth, and how could he? No matter what, as his mother used to say, a child has only one mother. And Paulie, tall and fourteen, was still her mother's child.

"All right," he said. "We'll talk about it later. Listen, Pet. I have some boloney in the fridge. Would you make me three sandwiches for my supper tonight? And I left two pears there for you, as a present."

"Oh thanks," she said, offhand. "Do you want mustard in your sandwiches?"

"Yes, please." Mustard, no I don't want mustard, I want you. He watched her at the refrigerator and, after a moment's hesitation, turned and left the kitchen. He went to the living room and knocked on the door. Veronica was sitting on the sofa.

"Did you tell her?" Veronica asked.

"What do you mean, tell her? It's pretty hard to tell a child that her mother is some class of whore."

"What are you talking about?" she said. "How dare you?"

Hope, sudden and joyful, made him raise his eyes from the carpet, blue fleur-de-lis on gold. "You mean there's been nothing between you and Pal Gerry?"

"Of course not. Who do you think I am?"

"What did you expect me to think, Vera?"

"I wouldn't know. Did you try to get Paulie to go with you?"

He nodded, eyes on the carpet once more.

"Well?"

He shook his head.

"Good for her," Veronica said. "She has some sense."

"Has she? I wonder."

"She knows if she stays with me, I'll look after her," Veronica said.

"So would I. Don't sneer. So would I!"

"I'm not sneering, Ginger. I'm sorry for you."

"Sorry?" He looked at her. He'd sorry her. "I'm going to work now," he said. He left the room, calling to Paulie. "Apple? Are those sandwiches ready yet?"

"Hold your horses, Daddy. I'm making them."

He went to the hall, put on his coat and hat. Paulie came out with the sandwiches in a brown-paper bag. She gave them to him and he took her by the shoulders, kissing her pale cheek. "Daddy," she said. "Could I have a dollar? I want to go to a movie with some girls tonight."

He took out his wallet. He had nine dollars left. Nine between him and all harm. He gave one to his Paulie. Now there were eight.

He went out, closing the apartment door behind him, and in the common hallway put on his overshoes. Money, oh those proofreaders were right. Money made this world go round. If he had enough money Veronica wouldn't be leaving him. If he had enough money he could have wooed Paulie to come with him, promised a housekeeper, promised her treats. Money, that was Our Savior. Not love, mind you, not good intentions, not honesty nor truth. Because if you couldn't make money, they would leave you, wife, child, friends, everyone. It looked that way, didn't it? It did. It did indeed.

"*M'sieur?*"

Jesus, there he was again, sitting on the stairs, the robot on the step beside him.

"*M'sieur,* you want to play a game?"

"No, Michel. I have to go to work now. Play with your toy. Your little man there. Tell him a story, maybe?"

"What will I tell him, *M'sieur?*"

"Tell him your name and all about you. All about where he's going to live and who he's going to meet. Tell him some of the stories I told you."

"*Bien,*" the child said. He picked up the robot and put it on his knee. Coffey bent over, rumpled the boy's ragged crop of hair. "Good man yourself," he said. "So long, now."

"Wait. Let's play the wish."

97

"All right," Coffey said. "But hurry up."

As he had done many times before, he leaned over and put his ear close to Michel's mouth. The little boy put his arm around Coffey's neck. "What do you wish for?" he whispered.

The wish game. Wish, if he could wish, what would he wish for? Not for adventures now, not for travels, not for fame. For love? Was it any use to wish for love?

"You wish first," he said to the boy. "You first."

"I wish," the childish voice breathed in his ear, "I wish we had a whole lot of toys and you and me could play with them all the time. Because I love you, *M'sieur*."

Awkwardly, Coffey disengaged himself and stood up. He looked down at Michel's head, big and vulnerable on the slender, childish neck. Oh, to be a boy. . . .

But children must grow up. "Good-by, Michel," he said.

He went to work. There was no time for the facts of his situation, the disasters of his day. All the world's news waited: it must be read, corrected, initialed, sent back to linotype, rechecked, cleared. The presses waited. The edition was running late. And yet, at eight o'clock, in the midst of it all, a copy boy came through the aisles of linotype machines towards the dirty steel desks where proofreaders helter-skeltered among galleys, late, all late. Linotype gremlins, double line, transpose, insert, delete, new lead, add front, all had to go, no time for talk now, hurry, hurry. Late.

"Phone for Coffey?" the copy boy shouted. "Got a Coffey here?" Coffey looked up, waiting Fox's permission to go; but Fox was too busy, they were all too busy, and so, a man leaving the sinking ship, Coffey stood, ran guiltily to the corridor where the phone was, passing the service elevator which waited to rush plates down to the presses. Late, late.

"Ginger?" It was Veronica on the line.

Above the phone stand was a printed card:

No Personal Calls During Working Hours
G. E. MacGregor
Man. Ed.

"Yes, what is it?" Coffey said.

"Madame Beaulieu's just been in here raising the roof. You were supposed to tell her whether we were keeping the place on or not."

"Look," he said. "I've no time to talk now, I'm in a hurry —"

"Well, hold on. Because I told her we weren't going to stay and she says in that case we have to move out by tomorrow morning at the latest. She has another tenant —"

"But that's impossible, Vera. Why —"

"No, it's not. I've already made arrangements about Paulie and me. We're moving to a ladies' boardinghouse tonight."

"But that's not fair —"

"Paulie wants to go with me," she interrupted. "And I have to move tonight because I'm starting work tomorrow morning. Gerry's coming to take our stuff in an hour or so. That's why I called you. We won't be here when you get back."

"Ah now, wait a minute — where are you going?"

"I'm not telling you the address," she said. "I'll be in touch with you. And listen, I've left ten dollars for you on the dresser under the mirror —"

"You skunk!" he shouted. "Waiting until I was out of the house —"

"Ten dollars is all I can afford, Ginger. I'll need the rest to get Paulie settled."

"I'm not talking about money — Vera? Listen, Vera, wait until tomorrow, at least —"

But as he spoke, he saw young Kenny running towards him along the corridor, gesticulating. "Hitler," Kenny whispered. "Hurry."

MacGregor. Involuntarily, and at once, Coffey hung up. In a winding rush, he followed young Kenny back to the proofroom. Late, late. No PERSONAL CALLS. He rushed back to reading and read in a daze, not even thinking of what had happened, mesmerized by MacGregor's imminent arrival, afraid to do anything which would incur that ancient's wrath. It was only later, during supper break, that he realized the enormous consequences of her telephone call and the strangeness of his own behavior. Even then, he could not believe it had happened. She and Paulie would be there when he got home. They *must* be there.

But that night, when he arrived back at the duplex, they were gone. Even their clothes were gone. He went to the dresser mirror, found the ten dollars and looked for a note. But there was no note.

At eight o'clock the following morning, Madame Athanase Hector Beaulieu knocked on the door. When he opened, she bent down, picked up a pailful of soaps and rags and marched in.

"The rent was only paid until yesterday," she said. "Today, you should not be here. I have to clean this place, my husband's bringing a tenant to see it in his lunch hour."

"Fair enough," Coffey said. "Carry on."

Madame Beaulieu opened the hall closet. Coffey's raincoat and little hat hung forlorn on the long rack. "All this stuff," she said. "I want it out." She shut the closet and marched down the corridor into the kitchen, sniffing and

100

peering like a social worker in a tenement. "My husband warn me," she said. "He told me: Bernadette, he said, these people come from the other side, they have no references, you don't know who they are. And I told my husband, don't worry, I said, they're nice people, you don't have to worry. But, look what happened. You never told me you weren't keeping the place on. You should have told me."

"I'm sorry, yes, I know I should," Coffey said. "Very sorry indeed. Look — perhaps I can give you a hand to clear up in here?"

"No."

He went back into the bedroom and dressed himself. He must pack. He was not used to packing for himself. It seemed impossible that at any moment Veronica and Paulie wouldn't come in and help him. It seemed impossible that he did not know where they were. Or what to do now. Or where to go.

An hour later, he carried two clumsily stuffed suitcases into the outer hallway which connected his apartment with the one upstairs. Beside the suitcases he placed the overflow: three paper bags full of socks and handkerchiefs and a lamp which, for some reason, Veronica had not bothered to take. Then, carrying his raincoat, a cloth cap and a package of books tied with string, he went down the railroad corridor of that dismal place for the last time. He put his key on the kitchen table. "I just came to give you this and say all the best, Madame. And to thank you for everything."

Madame Beaulieu was scouring the kitchen floor. She did not answer; did not look up. Ah well . . . there was a lady he never cared to see again.

He went outside and sat islanded by his possessions in the common hallway, waiting for the taxi he had ordered. He thought of Michel. Quietly, so that Madame would not hear him, he ascended the flight of stairs to his landlady's place. Quietly, he knocked on the door. "Michel?" he whispered.

The little boy opened, all joy. Coffey squatted on his heels, grinned at Michel and in a sudden sadness pulled the child towards him, planting a bristly mustache kiss on the soft childish cheek. Michel, tickled, snatched off Coffey's hat and placed it on his own head, laughing.

"Looks grand on you," Coffey said. "Now, wait a sec." He took the hat from Michel's head, removed the two Alpine buttons and the little brush dingus and handed them to the boy. "And here," he said, closing Michel's plump little paw around a dollar bill. "That's to buy the car I promised for your birthday. Now, be a good boy, won't you, son? I have to go."

"Please. Stay and play?"

"Must go. Bye-bye." Gently, he pushed Michel back into the apartment, closed the door, and ran downstairs, his chest tight and hurting. What's this world coming to, he wondered, when at my age I've just said good-by forever to the only person in the world who seems to love me? Michel: what will become of him? What will become of me?

"Where to?" the taxi driver asked.

He tried to grin. "By the holy, I have no notion. I'm looking for a cheap room downtown. Some place clean."

"What about the Y?" the driver said.

"Fair enough. The Y it is, then."

Five   At the Y.M.C.A., they rented him a basement locker for his possessions and asked for a week's room rent in advance. That was nine fifty in all, which left him exactly seven dollars and forty-five cents until his first payday. And while he put that worry out of his mind as not his greatest, still it occurred to him that his new life would not be easy.

The room was furnished with a bed, a Bible, a chair and dresser. When he sat in the chair, his knees touched the bed. When he lay on the bed he could reach out and open the door, pull down the window blind, open the dresser drawers and get at the Bible, without ever putting his feet on the ground. So, bed it was then. He removed his shoes and jacket and lay down. Opposite his window a forty-foot neon sign flashed on and off every eight seconds.

BUBBLE BATH CAR WASH
DAY & NIGHT

Did it flash on and off all night? He pulled the window blind down and the sign light beat like a hot, red wave against the dun darkness which resulted. He shut his eyes.

He was alone: for the first time in fifteen years no one in the world knew where Ginger Coffey was. For the first time in fifteen years, he had stopped running. He exhaled, stroking the ends of his large mustache. Yes, it was good to rest.

Of course, there were things he should do. He should find his wife's hidey-hole, for one. He could hang around outside Paulie's school and shadow her home to wherever they were staying. But why should he? Hadn't he been far too soft with the pair of them? Wouldn't it serve them right if he never tried to find them, if he just disappeared altogether and settled in here like a mole gone to ground? Not a bad life either: sleeping late every morning, eating his breakfast in some cafeteria, going for walks, seeing the odd film, having a daily swim in the pool downstairs and then each night, to work at six. No ties, no responsibilities, no ambitions. By the holy, that would be a grand gesture. To retire from the struggle, live like a hermit, unknown and unloved in this faraway land.

Hermit, eh? No sex?

No sex. Wasn't that the height of freedom, to be able to tell any woman to go to hell? Any woman, no matter how beautiful, no matter how much she begs. Sending them all away, spurning all ambitions, content to be a proofreader to the end of his days.

But wouldn't that be ruining his whole life, out of pure revenge?

Well, and supposing it was, wasn't it a grand revenge? Because, God! he knew her; she'd be expecting him to run after her, to plead and beg and argue and shout. Well, to hell with her. Let her try to be the breadwinner, she'd find it wasn't so easy. No, the good doggy wouldn't beg any more. As of this morning, Good Doggy was Lone Wolf.

Yes, but wasn't it a crime to abandon your wife and child?

Who abandoned who, anyway? Didn't they throw me over?

But you'd be lonely, you'd have no friends?

Well — well, he would talk to the fellows at work. And now and then pass the time of day with a waitress or a fellow lodger here. He would be a mystery man, the hermit of the Y.M.C.A. After thirty years or so, he would die in his sleep and people would say, Didn't notice Mr. Coffey around lately. Wonder what happened to him? Never knew much about him, dignified man, lived all alone, kept to himself, probably had some shocking tragedy in his life. A quiet, mysterious man. . . . Wouldn't that be a grand way to go? Nobody with a word against you, nobody judging whether you were good, or bad. Your secrets interred with your bones.

In the day-darkness, he began to daydream of that future life. A hermit in the city, his tongue cracked from unuse, he lay on his narrow pallet in that tiny cell listening to a radio down the hall. A woman's voice sang:

> Don't you be mean to Baby —
> 'Cause Baby needs lovin' too!
> Embrace me —

From now on, all the world would be like that faraway woman, singing without him, not knowing if he lived or died. He thought of all the rich and beautiful women in the world; of how many thousands of rich and beautiful women must be in this city, this minute. To hell with them. He had turned his back on them. They could be as rich and lovely as they liked. What were they to him, or he to them? Why, if he dropped dead here this instant, that woman would go on singing. Which was shocking, the bloody inhumanity of it. Singing over a dead man.

Of course, to be fair, the only reason that woman would

go on singing was because she did not know him. After all, he could make himself known; could ring her up on the telephone if he wanted to. But if he did, would she even speak to him? Supposing he waited for her as she came out of the radio station and stepped up to her, his tongue cracked with unuse: "Madam, for years now, yours has been the only woman's voice heard in my hermit's cell." Would she pause, the tears coming to her eyes, would she put out her gloved hand, leading him towards her limousine, saying Take me to your room and tell me all about yourself? What is your name? Why is a handsome, intelligent man like yourself living this hermit's life? Why? Ah, it was criminal of that wife and daughter to abandon you. You gave them up? Why? Because you had your pride, you refused to stay where you were no longer wanted. Ah, you are a saint, James Francis Coffey. A saint to have put up with them so long.

But he would never meet her, that unknown singer. And if he never met her, if he never met anyone from now on, nobody would know about his renunciation of all ties, all ambitions. What good was it, doing something, if nobody in the whole world knew you were doing it? What was more terrible than being alone all your life, nobody caring if you lived or died? Why, if he went on being a proofreader for the rest of his days, living in a place like this, he might never have another intimate conversation with a living soul. What sort of man was he that he could even consider such a thing? Look at yourself, would you? Lying in this dump, all alone. And that damned singing woman. Ah, shut your gob, woman!

"Turn that bloody thing off," he shouted.

But the singing continued. Nobody heard. Holy God, nobody heard him, shut up in this cell. He could die this instant, call for help — suffocate — and nobody would hear!

106

He got off the bed, put on his shoes and went out into the corridor. The doors to the other rooms were open. Nobody there. He was alone here, he could die here, that was what Vera and Paulie had done to him. He went down the corridor. One door was shut. One door, behind which that bloody woman caterwauled her song. In a sudden mindless rage, he ran towards that door, thumped on it, shouting: "Turn that off. Turn it down, do you hear?"

Nobody answered. The horrible endearments went on.

> 'Cause Baby needs lovin', yes
> Baby needs lovin' — to-oo!

He grabbed the door handle and the door opened inwards, spilling him into pitch-blackness.

A light snapped on. One of the thinnest men Coffey had ever seen stood on the bed in his undershorts, his long hair rumpled like a coxcomb. The horrible woman sang from a miniature radio dangling like a camera around the thin man's neck. The tiny room, twin to Coffey's, was jammed with developing trays, film packs, muscle-building equipment, a stripped-down radio transmitter, a judo mat, a tape recorder and a huge pile of men's magazines.

"You bastard," the man said. "Look what you done. You just ruined five bucks' worth of color film."

"I'm sorry."

"Sorry isn't enough. Come on in. Let's get a little natural light on the subject."

The stranger ripped a blanket from his window, switched off the overhead light, shut off the radio, and sank down on the bed, crosslegged, like an Indian holy man, sweeping the pile of men's magazines to the floor. "Sit down," he said. "Know what you done? You ruined my entry for the Popular Photography Contest, that's

107

what. Two hours I spent in the cab of a crane to get this shot and now it's ruined. The least you can do is pay me for the film. Five bucks."

"But I — well, I'm very short of money," Coffey said. "I can't afford to pay you. I'm sorry."

"Now, wait a minute; let's discuss it," the thin man said. "This is a problem in human relations. My name is Warren K. Wilson, by the way. What's your name?"

"Ginger Coffey."

"Okay, Ginger. Now, you've got a job, right?"

"Yes. But I'm just a proofreader. I don't earn much —"

"Well, get another job, why don't you?"

"It's not so easy," Coffey said. "I've been trying."

"What do you mean, it's not easy? There's plenty of work in this country if you know how to go after it. You live here in the Y?"

"Yes."

"Single?"

"No — ah — my wife's not with me just now."

"Oh-oh," Wilson said. "You got a wife, have you? Not so good. I happen to know about a couple of jobs that's going up North this week. I'm heading up to Blind River myself, Monday morning. Of course, you married guys are screwed. Now, let's see. What are your hours on this proofreading job?"

"Six at night until one in the morning."

"Perfect. Can you drive a truck?"

"As a matter of fact, I can. At least, I drove one in the Army."

"Right. How'd you like a job making deliveries, here in Montreal? Eight to four, six days a week, and it pays sixty bucks."

Coffey stared at the judo mat on the floor. Driving a truck? Was that what he had come to Canada for?

"See, I just quit this job yesterday," Wilson said. "Tiny

ONES — it's a diaper service outfit. Suppose I get you taken on there? That worth five bucks to you? You owe me the dough anyways."

"Diapers?" Coffey said. "Isn't that sort of a — sort of a dirty job?"

Wilson bent forward, his body half-disappearing under the bed, his knobbly backbone curved like Charlie Chaplin's walking stick. Up he came with a package of cigarettes. He lit one and blew a smoke ring. "I done the job for two months," he said, staring at Coffey through the ring. "Do I stink?"

"Sorry. No, of course not, I just meant —"

"Disinfectant," Wilson said. "Every sack of returns smells like perfume. And anyways, if you want to get somewhere in this world, you've got to push. Now, look at me. I'll go anywhere and work at any job that pays. And you know why? Because I'm studying. Look at this." He pointed to the radio transmitter. "Now, this is on loan to me from the American Home Radio and Television Engineers College. That's a low-power broadcasting transmitter. I bet you didn't know that radio and TV repairs is one of the fastest-growing industries on this whole continent?"

"No, I didn't."

"Well, it's a fact. Now, once I get my diploma as a graduate of the A.H.R. and T., I can pick up fifty a week in my spare time. At least, that's what the ad says."

"It sounds very good."

Wilson put his finger into a second smoke ring. "Right. But when I make that extra jack, know what I'm going to do? Invest in German cameras. And then I start studying another course. How to be a magazine photographer. Now, there's the life! Movie stars posing for you, flying in planes all around the world, meeting all kinds of personalities. How do you like that?"

109

"Yes," Coffey said. "That sounds interesting, I suppose."

"You *suppose?* I'm telling you. Now, you take me, that's why I can move anywheres I want. I'm mobile, see. And I don't miss my fun. Any time I feel like it, I just check into a hotel, buy a quart of liquor and ask the bellboy to send a pig up."

"A pig?"

"Right. Why jump in the ocean, eh? I mean, look at you, you're tied down, you can't go no place unless you bring the wife along. And because you're tied down you got no ambitions, right?"

"My wife just left me," Coffey said.

"Well then, what are you worrying about? Big guy like you, whyn't you come up North with me, you'll get hired right away. Look —" Wilson bounded up from his crouch on the bed and struck a strong-man pose. Large knobbly muscles lumped out all over his back. "I had to work to get like you are," he said. "I done it on a home gym set in Toronto. Built myself up from a runt to a Mr. Junior Honorable Mention. That's what I mean about getting ahead. You see, I was doing this home study course. There's a place in Chicago gives you a diploma that guarantees you a job as a private investigator any place in the States. Well, I done fine in the test, but I failed the physical. So I took this body-building course and, like I say, I built myself up to a Mr. Junior Honorable Mention. That's something, eh?"

"But why didn't you become a private detective?"

"Bad timing," Wilson said. "When I wrote back to the college in Chicago they said I was too late. All the private eye licenses was given out for that year and they want me to do the course over again. Well, eff that, I said. So I started this TV course, instead. I mean" — and he leaned over and gripped Coffey's arm — "I mean . . . Say, your

110

deltoids are like dead mice, you want to build them up. . . . Anyways, as I was saying, you got to keep moving, do whatever comes along. Now, how about coming up North with me next week?"

"Well, I — I — what was this truck-driving job you mentioned earlier?"

"Oh, *that* job. You want to take that instead? You could make more money up North, you know."

"Yes. . . . But my wife . . . I have a little girl here. Perhaps I'd better stay here."

"Okay, suit yourself. Now, let's see. . . ." Wilson scrambled around under the bed once more and came up with a writing pad and a ball-point pen. "He-ere we are." Busily he began to write, his lips moving as he formed large childish letters on the paper.

Coffey looked at him. Here was a single man, a free man who next Monday would head up to Elind River; a man who could still dream youth's dreams, who could see himself as a magazine photographer traveling over the world, meeting beautiful girls, living life's adventures. It was an old dream of Coffey's; one he'd started to dream at the age of fifteen. And the men's magazines, the mail-order courses, the talk of women as an inanimate pleasure to be enjoyed as you would enjoy a drink, the room jammed with evidences of boyish schemes, boyish pursuits — yes, it was familiar. A world of toys.

Yet Wilson was no longer a boy. The thin neck was clawed with age; there were gray streaks in the long untidy locks of hair; the hands were veiny, stippled with telltale brown moles. Was manhood what Wilson had missed?

"There we are," Wilson said, folding the paper. "Now you take this over to the bossman this aft. And write me out an IOU for five bucks, right?"

Coffey took the pen and wrote that he owed you, Warren K. Wilson, the sum of five dollars, signed J. F. COFFEY. They exchanged slips of paper.

"See?" Wilson said. "I knew we could make a deal if we talked things over. That's human relations for you. Now, here's my address up North. I'm trusting you to send me the dough, okay?"

"Fair enough."

They shook hands on it; boys crossing their hearts. In the corridor, alone again, Coffey looked at the slip of paper.

Mr. Mountain,
TINY ONES *Depot,*
1904 St. Donat Street.

Dear Mr. Mountain:
Here is a friend of mine, very relible driver who has lots of experince in driving trucks and making deliveres and has part time night job which would suit you if you take him on 8 to 4 on my old shift.

Sincerly,
W. K. Wilson

He put the piece of paper in his pocket. At least it was true that he could drive a truck. It was worth a try. With two jobs, he'd have enough money to support her and Paulie. And that was what mattered now. For after a morning's freedom, one thing was clear. It was too late to begin again, alone.

The small office at the rear of the TINY ONES depot was decorated with a large lumber products calendar showing a young woman, her skirts entangled in a fly-fisherman's cast. Her hands had gone up to shield the O of horror her pretty mouth made, instead of readjusting the

112

resultant deshabille. It seemed to Coffey as he stood beneath this calendar that the pretty girl's embarrassment perfectly mirrored his own.

Underneath the calendar sat Mr. Stanley Mountain, his enormous weight severely testing a stout swivel chair. His most noticeable moving part was a stomach, large as a regulation basketball, which bobbed regularly up and down, straining against his very clean white shirt and his yellow felt braces. His head of hair, white as detergent, bent in perusal of Wilson's note.

"Show me your driver's license," he said.

Coffey showed it.

"You a vet?"

"Yes," Coffey said. It was so bloody hard to explain about the Irish Army.

"R.C.A.F. transport officer myself," Mr. Mountain said. "And let me tell you I still run things by the book. . . . Corp?"

A small man in white overalls put his head around the office doorway.

"Corp, take this man out to the yard, give him a truck. Test him."

"Right now, sir?"

"Right now."

So Coffey followed Corp out into the snow and was introduced to a small closed van which bore a picture of Winston Churchill, neatly diapered, and the legend: TINY ONES. "Drive her across the yard and park her between the two vans on the far side," Corp said.

Coffey did this without difficulty, then waited as Corp joined him. "Have a smoke, Paddy," Corp said. "Never mind about the rest of it. I just passed you."

"Thanks very much."

"I mean," Corp said — "I mean, I don't go for this service bull. Who does he think he is? The war's over, you know.

I mean, you got to help other people," he went on, becoming, Coffey thought, quite upset. "I mean, you're out of work, Paddy, right? Probably got a wife and kids to support, right? Well then, good luck to you. Now here — give him this card. Finish your smoke. Then go on back."

Coffey finished his cigarette as told, crossed the yard again and gave the card to Mr. Mountain. Unconsciously, he assumed atten-shun! as he waited to hear Mr. Mountain's verdict.

"Check," said Mr. Mountain. "You're assigned, then, on a three-week trial. Terms of duty — Monday to Saturday. Hours of duty — o-eight hundred hours to sixteen hundred hours. Truck to be checked and presented to your relief at sixteen-ten. Morning check-out inspection o-seven-fifty hours. Now, double on back to Corp and get your uniform."

"Right, sir," Coffey said. "Thank you, sir." Involuntarily, he wagged Mr. Mountain the old salute. Mr. Mountain seemed pleased.

"Carry on, Coffey," he said.

A battle-dress jacket; a military cap with a badge which read TINY ONES; a machine for making change; a pair of sky-blue trousers and a pair of knee-length rubber boots. He signed for all, followed Corp into the locker room and began to try them on. Off went his Tyrolean hat, his hacking jacket, his gray tweed trousers and brown suède boots. On the bench they lay, the last remains of Ginger Coffey. On went the uniform, anonymous and humiliating. He thought of the first time he had worn a uniform, as a private in the Regiment of Pearse; still a boy, still dreaming of wars, battles and decorations. And of the last time he took off his uniform on the day of his discharge. Of the

114

relief he had felt then, knowing that it had all been a waste, that never again would he willingly become a number, a rank, a less than a man.

The uniform fitted him perfectly.

"Okay," Corp said. "You'll do. Take them off and stow them in your locker. Now you're a regular member of the shit brigade."

Six   The Tɪɴʏ Oɴᴇs depot was in the east end of the city. To return to the *Tribune* he must walk a long way. As he started off, the sun moved west, unadmitted by the pall clouds which all day had curtained the frozen river and the city islanded within it. Thermometers outside banks and filling stations began to fall. Four forty-five. Office workers, waiting release as the minute hand moved slowly towards the hour, looked at the darkness beyond their windows and saw edges of frosting begin to mist the panes. While below, approaching the financial district, saving the price of a bus, Coffey hurried on.

Five o'clock. In the financial district the street lights flared. Down came the office workers, spilling out into the streets, released, facing the freezing bus terminal waits, the long, slow-stopping journey home. Uptown they turned in their hundreds while down he went, down, still hurrying, no sandwiches in his pocket for the night's break, his night's work not yet begun.

Five-thirty. It grew colder. A policeman in fur hat and black greatcoat shuffled like a dancing bear under the harsh arena light of a traffic intersection. White mitt paw invited Coffey to cross. Crossing, Coffey scurried along

116

the outer rim of light, raising his right hand to the police-man, giving the old salute.

Five-forty. On a corner, three blocks from the *Tribune* building, the red traffic light called: halt. Winded, Coffey waited, knowing he would be in time. In a newspaper kiosk an old woman, squatting on her kerosene heater, rose to serve a commuter, red-raw fingers fumbling in woolen mitts as she made change. The newspaper passing to the commuter's hurried clutch headlined a vaguely familiar word, which made Coffey — crossing on amber — half-stop in the darkness, then walk close to the commuter, trying to read what it said. On the opposite pavement the commuter, unfurling the newspaper, shook it out. Coffey read, and moved away; last lap, going through the *Tribune*'s revolving doors . . .

Cripple Mate Case:
WIFE TELLS COURT
"I DID IT FOR LOVE"

The elevator came and he rode up, thinking it should be Cripple Mate who told court he did it for love: Cripple Mate who tomorrow would climb into a fancy dress uniform and go out to collect dirty nappies in proof of his love. Cripple Mate who, in one day on his onlie-oh, had more than doubled his earning power and who, no matter what she might have done with long drinks of water called Grosvenor, still loved her enough to want her back. Oh, he'd make her eat her words, so he would. She would never call him selfish again.

"Fourth floor. Editorial."

Seven minutes to six. Coffey hurried into the *Tribune* cafeteria, rejecting supper in favor of a phone call. He called Grosvenor's flat, for Grosvenor would know where to find her. The number was busy. He waited, then dialed again. Still busy. At one minute to six it was still busy;

117

still busy when the composing room bell rang, forcing him once again to abandon the facts of his life for the facts of the world.

When the ten o 'clock supper break came, he hurried to the cafeteria booth, still unfed, still trying. He spent the fifteen-minute break trying to reach Grosvenor in his flat, at the Press Club, and at three other places he remembered as Grosvenor's haunts. No luck. The bell rang. Back to work. And still, oh God! he had not reached her, had not told her his news, had not been able to show what Cripple Mate could do.

At one A.M., the work over, he took the elevator down to the lobby, waited until Fox and the others had gone, then entered a pay phone booth under the *Tribune* clock. The lobby was quiet. Outside the phone booth an old night cleaner swabbed the terrazzo floors with a wet mop as Coffey, for the umpteenth time that evening, inserted his dime and dialed the number of Grosvenor's apartment. The number was busy. Hooray! Grosvenor was on the phone to someone — maybe to her? Giving her a lover's good-night chat; sleep well, my lovely. Meantime, until the lovey-dovey chat was over, Cripple Mate must cool his heels.

Steady as she goes, Coffey warned himself. Wait a full five minutes so you won't be disappointed. And wait he did, smoking the last of his fags, watching the old cleaner slop the slimy, sudsy mop over the terrazzo flooring, wetting the inlaid letters: THE MONTREAL TRIBUNE.

At one-ten he watched the jerky minute hand complete its last revolution and again inserted his dime. Brrp-brrp-brr-brrp — Oh, rot your blabbering liver-lipped gob! By the holy, it was time someone put a stop to this. He replaced the receiver, dialed the operator and asked if FEnrose 2921 was out of order.

"Just one moment, sir, I'll check."

Another wait. "I'm afraid the receiver has been left off the stand, sir."

And why would the phone be off the hook? So that a certain Gerry Grosvenor would not be disturbed. Well, any man — *any man* — was justified in disturbing *that*, no matter how late it was. Out he ran into the icy streets, down one block, down another and there — little interior lights lit, drivers slumped over newspapers — a black snake of taxis lay in wait for nightbirds near the entrance to a hotel. No time for economy now. In went Cripple Mate and gave the address, sitting forward, silently willing the driver to hurry as the cab moved off, its tire chains rattling on the hard-packed snow, going up the mountain to Grosvenor's place.

Gerald Grosvenor lived in an apartment development opposite a large cemetery. Ten times as many people were located in the apartment development as in the graveyard, which was very much larger in area. Therefore, slithering and twisting in the snowy drives among a huddle of enormous neo-Georgian buildings, Coffey's driver twice lost his way. It was five minutes to two when, his cab finally dismissed, Coffey found himself in the foyer of Grosvenor's building. To enter he must ring a bell beside Grosvenor's name plate. Grosvenor, alerted, must press a buzzer which electrically opened the foyer door. But if Coffey rang the bell, he would give Grosvenor a chance to slip Veronica out by the back way. And if Veronica were not there he would waken Grosvenor and would seem to Grosvenor a blithering fool. So he stood, irresolute. Maybe he should go away. Flute! He didn't *want* to find Vera there. And besides, she wasn't that sort of woman; she'd never leave Paulie alone in some boardinghouse while she . . . or would she? What did he know about her, after all?

Just then a late-returning tenant came up behind him

and unlocked the foyer door. Coffey grabbed the door, met the tenant's suspicious stare with an apologetic smile and slipped in behind him, beginning the long climb to the fourth floor, remembering that curiosity killed the cat. And that if he were wrong he would look like an id-jit.

But on he went in a curious mixture of wrath and shame. Went on, forcing himself into doing something his whole nature cried out against. Making a fuss, acting the loony, exposing himself to a stranger's scorn. On the fourth floor he paused, looking at the numbers: 81, 83, 85. He turned to the other side: 84. There were no over-shoes or rubbers outside the door, though it was the custom for visitors to leave them in the corridor. Ah, she wasn't there at all: he was imagining things. Turn around now and go home. Ring Grosvenor in the morning. You'll find her tomorrow.

But just then a small man in a dressing gown came out of Number 80 carrying an empty gin bottle and the wreckage of a box of potato chips. The man went to the incinerator slot at the end of the hall, passing Coffey with a suspicious stare, a stare which implied that Coffey might be up to no good; that Coffey had no business in the corridor; that he was loitering with some thievish intent.

And that stare, from a total stranger, made Coffey turn around and ring the bell of Number 84. Reassured, the small man turned and went back into his own apartment. Someone stirred inside Number 84. Someone was coming. Someone fiddled with a chain. Veronica's voice whispered: "Who's that?"

Coffey had rung the bell out of funk, out of fear of a stranger. Now, he drew back as though he had been slapped, his lips tight under the curve of his mustache. Again her voice whispered: "Who's that?"

120

But Grosvenor — for it was Grosvenor who stood there with her, it must be! — Grosvenor waited behind that door, probably holding his finger to his lips, cautioning her to silence.

A loud buzzer noise sounded behind the door. Down four floors in the night silence of the hall the buzzer rang again, repeating the sound. They thought he was downstairs; that was it. Now they would open the door and Grosvenor would peep out, trying to see who was coming up.

The door did not open. Again, they pressed the buzzer, shaking in their shoes, the pair of them. Oh, he would bloody well kill them!

But in that moment, waiting there, he remembered why he had rung the bell. He remembered that he would have gone away. Oh, God, was it any wonder his wife was behind that door with another man? What was the matter with him that he wanted to avoid a scene? What was the matter?

But what's the matter with *her*, he thought. Why is it always me that's in the wrong? Oh, for God's sake, woman, what are you doing in there? Come home, for God's sake, you fool; how could you do this to me and Paulie? You were mine, you swore it, for richer or for poorer, for better or for worse, until death. Until death, do you hear?

And as though she heard, she opened the door.

"Ginger!" she said. "Do you realize what time of night it is?"

Did he *what?* Well now, didn't that beat the band? In her dressing gown and nightie, her feet bare, the brazen bloody nerve of her!

He pushed past her. "Where's Grosvenor?" he asked. "Hiding in the kitchen?"

"Gerry's not here. And *shh!* You'll wake Paulie."

"Paulie?"

"*Shh,*" she said again. She followed him into Grosvenor's living room, a bare, bachelor place with white walls, prints of Chinese horses and a long low bench of high fidelity equipment. She motioned to a wicker and iron chair. "Sit down. *Shh.* Gerry lent us his place. He's staying with a friend. The room I booked for us wasn't ready. Now, for goodness' sake, take that look off your face."

"Where's Paulie?" he said. "Where is she?"

"In there. Don't wake her."

But he walked out of the living room and opened the door she had indicated. He switched on the light. In a strange bed, clutching Bunkie, her nightdress-case doll, his daughter slept. He bent over her, saw her twitch, wake, and sit up.

"Daddy? What are you doing here?"

"I told you not to wake her," Veronica said.

He stared at his daughter's face, still drowsy with sleep, at her fair reddish hair in tiny steel clips, at her breasts pulling tight against the buttoned pajama top. Soon she too would be a woman. She too would leave for a stranger's bed.

"Are you satisfied?" Veronica said. "Go back to sleep, Paulie."

She switched out the light and shut Paulie's door. "Do you realize it's three in the morning, and that I have to go to work at nine?"

He followed her back into the living room. So *she* had to work, had she? Wait till she heard how *he* was working.

"Vera, there's something I want to tell you."

"It's the middle of the night, Ginger. I want to go back to bed."

"Vera, I have two jobs now. I'm earning a total of a

hundred and ten dollars a week. And Vera — are you listening to me?"

"What?" she said crossly.

"I said I have two jobs. I can well afford to support us now."

She sighed, in swift exasperation.

"And I've left the apartment and I'm bunked in at the Y."

"That's nice for you. Now, I really want to go to sleep, Ginger."

"But wait — wait till I tell you. I'll give you both pay checks next Friday. Every penny, mind you. You could make any conditions you like. I won't even ask you to sleep in the same room."

She began to cry. He got up, went over, put out his hand to touch her shoulder. She moved away, leaving his hand hovering.

"Listen to me," he said. "I may have been selfish in the past and I may not have made the best fist of things. But listen — even though I'm not the best husband in the world, I know this much. Nobody loves you more than I do, Kitten. Nobody. No matter what you may think, or no matter what Grosvenor tells you, he couldn't love you the way I do."

"You say you love me," she said. "Just because you miss me. Well, you'd miss a servant if she'd been looking after you for fifteen years. That's not love."

"Isn't it? Ah, for God's sake, woman, what do you know about it? Love isn't going to bed with the likes of Gerry Grosvenor, either."

"Then what is it, Ginger? Tell me. You're the expert, it seems."

"Well . . . Well — dammit, Veronica, we're a family, you and me and Paulie. That's why we have to stick together, no matter what."

123

He saw her bow her head. Her hand went up to her face; long fingers shielded her eyes, as though she prayed. Oh, Vera, he thought. How and under what mortal sky could you ever believe that you and Grosvenor will be as you and I have been? How could you have forgotten that life agreement we made fifteen years ago in Saint Pat's in Dalkey, me in a rented morning suit, a stiff collar choking me, praying to God Tom Clarke hadn't mislaid the ring, and you in white, your head bowed as now, kneeling before the altar — Love — oh, come on home now, and let's stop all this nonsense!

She removed the shield of her hand and he saw her eyes: bright; fixed in hate. "So love is staying together for Paulie's sake?" she said. "No thanks, Ginger."

"Ah now, wait. I've changed, honest to God I have. Listen — do you know what this new job is? It's putting on a uniform and going about delivering babies' nappies and bringing back the messy ones. Now, if I was as self-ish as you say, would I do the like of that? Would I, Vera?"

"I'm not going to listen to you. Oh, I knew you'd come back with some story. I knew it. It's not fair."

"But it's no story. It's the truth."

"All right," she said. "So it's true. Well, I'm sorry. And that's the trouble."

"Vera, would you for the love of God give over talking in riddles?"

"I mean I'm sorry for you, Ginger. But that's all. You're not going to catch me again. You're too late with this, just as you've been too late with everything else."

"Too late am I?" Coffey said. "Maybe you're too late. Grosvenor's five years younger than you. We'll see how long this lasts."

"Yes, he is five years younger. You've used up the best years of my life, that's why."

"What about my best years, Vera? Suffering J! What about my best years?"

"All right. Then why don't we try to save the years we have left? Why don't we get a divorce?"

"Divorce?" He felt his heart pull and thump in his chest. "You're a Catholic," he said. "What's your mother going to say about the sin of divorce?"

"Don't you preach religion at me, Ginger Coffey, you that haven't darkened a church door since you came out here. Don't you talk about Catholics. What's wrong with you is that you never *were* a Catholic; you were too selfish to give God or anyone else the time of day. Oh, you may think I'm like you now, and I am. I never pray. But once I did. Once I was very holy, do you remember? I cried, Ginger. I cried when Father Delaney said that unless we stopped practicing birth control he'd refuse us the sacraments. Do you remember that? No, you never think of that any more, do you? But I do. You changed me, Ginger. What I am now has a lot to do with what you made me. So don't you talk sin to me, don't you dare! Sins — Oh, let me tell you. Once your soul is dirty, then what difference in the shade of black?"

Trembling, she took one of Grosvenor's cigarettes out of a jar and, in a gesture familiar as one of his own, tapped it on the back of her hand before picking up a lighter off the table. The lighter was initialed G.G.

"Daddy?" a voice said at the door. Paulie, her pajama trousers crumpled like accordion pleats around her calves, her sleepy eyes blinking in the bright light, came into the room.

"Paulie," Veronica said, "you go back to bed this instant, do you hear?"

"No."

"Did you *hear* me, miss?" Veronica said.

"I'm not an infant, Mummy," Paulie said. "I've got a right to be here."

"Go to bed!"

"No, I want to talk to Daddy."

"Yes, Pet," Coffey said. "What is it?"

Paulie began to cry. "I don't want to stay here. I don't want to stay with them."

"With who?" Coffey said. "With who, Pet?"

But Paulie, still weeping, turned to her mother, woman to woman, bitter, betrayed. "You said it would be just the two of us. Just you and me. You said I was grown-up now. I'm not going to be sent to bed every night like an *infant*, just because you want to let Gerry in the back door."

"You little sneak," Veronica said. "That's enough. You'll do what you're told."

"You're not in charge of me!" Paulie screamed. "Daddy is. Daddy's in charge of me, not you. I want to go with Daddy."

"Do you now?" Veronica said. "Well, Daddy's living at the Y.M.C.A., aren't you, Daddy? No girls allowed, isn't that right, Daddy?"

Coffey did not look at her. He went to his daughter, taking her by the wrists. "Oh, Pet," he said. "Do you really want to come with me?"

She was trembling. She did not seem to see him, to feel his hands. "I can choose whoever I like," she said, wildly. "You're my father, not Gerry Grosvenor. I'm not going to be sent to bed just because she wants to see Gerry. It's not fair!"

"Of course it's not," Coffey said. "Now listen, Pet. If you want to come, I'll find us a place tomorrow. I promise you. I'll find us a place, don't you worry."

"Will you, Ginger?" Veronica said.

"Yes, I will. Don't laugh. I will!"

But she was not laughing. She turned to Paulie. "You

126

say I broke my promise to you," she said. "But what about your father's promises? This promise he's making now, he'll break it. Ask him. Go on, ask him. How is he going to get a place for you tomorrow?"

"I don't have to listen to you," Paulie said. "Daddy's going to take me, aren't you, Daddy?"

He looked at the carpet, his thumb absently grooving the part in his mustache, hating that stupid foolish man who once again had shown him his own true image. Vera was right: his promises were worthless currency. How could he make Paulie know that this time he meant it?

"Listen, Pet," he said. "What your mother says is true, in a way. But I have two jobs and as soon as they pay me, I'll have plenty of money, plenty! Now, listen — if you can wait until next Friday, I swear to you on my word of honor that I'll find a place for us. A nice place. If you'll wait, Apple?"

"Of course I'll wait," Paulie said. But she did not look at him; proud of her rebellion, she stared at Veronica.

"Thank you, Pet," he said. "Now, would you go into your room for a while? I want to talk to your mother."

Paulie went away: they heard her bedroom door shut. He looked at Veronica, thinking that, after all, this was a crush Vera had, it was — well, it was a sort of illness. It was up to him to try to make her see sense before it was too late. "Listen to me," he said. "If I were you I'd put on my thinking cap tonight and wonder what's going to happen if you go through with this lunatic performance. Remember, if you change your mind, you can come back tomorrow. I promise you there'll be no questions asked and no recriminations. We'd just forget this ever happened."

"Oh, go away," she said. "Go away."

He picked up his little hat from between his feet, went unsteadily into the hall and knocked on Paulie's door. When Paulie answered, he took her arm and led her to the front door. As he passed a table with a telephone on it, he saw that the receiver jarred slightly on its cradle. That was why the phone had not answered. He replaced the receiver, then said in a whisper: "All right, Apple. I'll come for you next week."

"Wait," Paulie said. "Here's the address and phone number of the place we're going to. When you're ready to come and get me, phone and leave a message. And Daddy?"

"What, Pet?"

"Daddy, promise you won't let me down."

He took her in his arms and crushed her against him. There, in the living room, his wife sat alone, sick with some madness he could not understand. He held Paulie and she put her pale cheek up to be kissed. "Word of honor, Pet," he whispered. "Word of honor."

Seven   First, park the truck, making sure that you are not beside a fire hydrant or in a no-parking area. Then check your book, Mrs. What'shername, how many dozen last week, how many this week. Then find her parcel, hop down in the morning cold, ring the doorbell, smile as she opens, and make change from your leather sporran. Thank you, Madam. Receiving in turn her apologetic smile as she hands over the long string sack containing her offspring's soilings. Then down the path, sky the sack into the back of the van and on to the next customer.

That first morning was a Saturday. So, although he was slow on the deliveries and late back at the TINY ONES depot, there was no panic. No proofreading that night. And the following day, Sunday, there was proofreading, but no TINY ONES. Monday now, that was another matter.

To begin with, by Monday morning he was stony-broke. So when he arrived at the depot to pick up his truck, he put out a feeler to Corp. But Corp, the soul of friendliness until then, said: "Why should I lend you five bucks, Paddy? After all, I don't know you from a hole in the wall. No dice."

No dice. Coffey had twenty cents left in his pocket. He had not had any breakfast. And to cap it all, the first call on that morning's run, he ran into trouble. An apartment building it was: modern, with a plate glass door and a sign outside which said AMBASSADOR HOUSE. Four dozen, the order. He hopped down, hefting his brown paper parcel, and went in through the glass doors to check the apartment number on the board.

"Looking for something?"

A doorman in a green coat and peaked green cap tapped a white-gloved finger against Coffey's chest.

"Number twenty-four?" Coffey said. "A Mrs. Clapper?"

Anger came like a sickness on the commissionaire's wintry features. "You blind or somethin', Tiny? Service entrance at the side. What's the matter with you?"

"I'm sorry, I didn't notice."

"C'mon, c'mon, you're blockin' up the hall. Take your fuggin' dipers up the back stairs."

Outside once more, Coffey tried Veronica's trick of counting ten. All that pushing and shoving: no need for that, was there? After all, people only saw things when they were on the lookout for them. He remembered when Veronica was pregnant, he used to see dozens of pregnant women on the streets. But not since. Well, service entrances were like that. Unless you were on the lookout . . .

Calming himself with these reflections, he found the service entrance, climbed four flights of stairs and rang the bell at the back door of Apartment 25. A uniformed maid opened to him. "TINY ONES," he said. "Good morning."

The maid took the package.

"That'll be two twenty, please," he said.

"Just a moment," she said. "The mistress wants to see you."

He stepped into the kitchen.

"Take your overshoes off," the maid said. "My floors!"

"That's all right, Anna," a woman's voice said. A well-dressed woman, she was, too old to need TINY ONES by the look of her. "Does your firm rent cribs?" she asked. And flute! She was from Dublin.

"No, Madam."

"Do they rent any other baby things, could you tell me?"

He felt his face grow hot. Not only was she Dublin, but Stillorgan Road, Dublin, as stuck-up as all get out. "Well no, Madam. They don't."

"Are you Irish?" she said.

"Yes."

"I thought I caught a Dublin accent," said she. "Have you been over here long?"

"Ah — about six months."

At that moment a younger woman (the nappy user's Mum, he guessed) came into the room. A blonde she was, in a tweed suit, all the latest style. Who took one look at Coffey, her eyes getting bigger. "Oh!" she said. "Oh, I could have sworn — Excuse me staring like that. But you're the spitting image of someone I know."

"But this man is from Dublin, Eileen," the mother said. "Isn't that a coincidence?"

"Oh? And what's your name?" the daughter asked Coffey, who wouldn't have had to ask hers. If floors could rise up and swallow a person — by the Holy, that wasn't just a figure of speech, for she was Colonel Kerrigan's daughter, the same girl he had danced with last winter at the Plunkett Old Boys' Dance in the Shelbourne Hotel. And had served under her old man in the Army.

"My name is — Cu-Crosby," he said.

"If I had a camera I'd take your picture and send a copy to this friend of mine," she said. "You're his double, right down to the mustache."

"Whose double?" her mother asked.

"Veronica Shannon's husband, Mother. Ginger Coffey. Do you remember him?"

"Oh, of course," the mother said. "Didn't he soldier with your Daddy once upon a time? And afterwards was in a distillery or something?"

"Yes, Mother."

"But they went to Canada," the mother said. "I remember Mrs. Vesey said something to me about looking Veronica up —"

As the mother talked, Eileen Kerrigan's eyes met Coffey's. Now, she knew. "Anyway, we mustn't keep this gentleman here all day," she said, cutting her mother short. "Anna, would you get the bag?"

"Here you are," the maid said and — Suffering J, let me out! — Coffey took it and backed out of the kitchen.

"Wait. Your money."

He had to make change for a five-dollar bill, aware that Eileen Clapper, née Kerrigan, had informed her mother with a look. The maid shut the door on him. Now, the telling would begin — Oh yes, Mother, it could be and it is. I'm positive — Now the Air Mail letters would fly. Now it could be told in Gath and embroidered in the Wicklow Lounge, chuckled over in the offices at Kylemore, dissected in Veronica's mother's flat. And how glorious a comeuppance it would seem to all the voices he had fled; how joyously they would savor each detail, the changing of his name, the absurd uniform with TINY ONES on the cap, the menial nature of his employment, the net result of all his hopes. They didn't even need to embellish it: though they would; like all Dublin stories it would lose nothing in the telling. Yes, the whole country could laugh at him now. He stood on the stairs and saw the whole country laugh.

Ha, ha! cried all the countrified young thicks he had gone to school with, who now, ordained and Roman-collared, regularly lectured the laity on politics and love. Ha, ha! cried the politicians, North and South, united as always in fostering that ignorance which alone made possible their separate powers. Hah! cried the archbishops, raising their purple skull-capped heads from the endless composition of pastoral letters on the dangers of foreign dances and summer frocks. Hah! cried the smug old businessmen, proud of being far behind the times. Ha, ha, ha! Emigrate, would you? *We told you so.*

Their laughter died. What did it matter? What did they matter, so long as he was not going home? And in that moment he knew that, sink or swim, Canada was home now, for better or for worse, for richer or for poorer, until death.

He went down the stairs, climbed into his truck and drove off, his tire chains rattling in the freezing slush. What did anything matter now except his word to Paulie?

For lunch he had a ten-cent bag of peanuts and a glass of milk. After eating it, he felt like a starving man. Money he must have to last out until Friday. His proofreading pals? Ah, weren't they all boozers, counting their ha'pence from one payday binge to the next? To last until Friday he would need more than the dollar loan they might afford. He would need at least ten dollars. Ten dollars required nerve. So, at the end of the day, he went to see Mr. Mountain and nervously requested an advance on wages.

"Advance?" Mr. Mountain's stomach heaved upwards in alarm. "That's got to be done through channels, Coffey. I don't handle payroll, that's G.H.Q. stuff. Top man deals with that. And I might as well warn you that Mr. Brott doesn't favor that procedure."

"I'm afraid I'll have to chance that, Mr. Mountain. I have to have the money."

"Well, it's your funeral," Mr. Mountain said. "It's

133

strictly against standing orders. However —" he reached for one of the many forms he designed personally in the depot. "Here's one of my unit identification check slips," he said. "It shows your rank, length of service and record in my outfit. If you want to try this, you'd better hurry. Head Office closes at five."

Hurry was right. The office was ten streets away and he had to shanks' mare it. So, chit in hand, with twenty minutes to get there, he set off through the darkening streets, wondering if he didn't win Mr. Brott's clemency would he be able to pawn the lamp in his locker or sell some of his clothing secondhand? How did you go about pawning something here? Or selling clothes? But do not worry about that yet, he told himself. Cross that bridge when you come to it.

Shanks'-maring it at five to five, pelting down an old street in the dock area past faded stores and warehouses stenciled with the names of unknown and unimportant enterprises: Pimlico Novelties; H. Lavalee Productions; Weiss & Schnee Imports; Wasserman Furs Ltd. And now, at one minute to five, he shanks'-mared it into a building, rode up in an ancient latticed elevator, came out on the third floor and hurried down a corridor which smelled overpoweringly of Jeyes Fluid, towards a frosted glass doorway stenciled:

TINY ONES INC.
Ring & Enter.

He rang and entered. Behind the counter which protected the office staff from the public, the desks were empty, the typewriters hooded, the file cabinets locked. He was late.

Still, someone must be here, he reasoned. The place was

not shut. He rapped his knuckles on the counter, noticing a cubicle at the far end of the room in which a light still burned. He knocked again.

A small man appeared at the cubicle's doorway. "Closed," he said. "Sorry."

"But . . ." Coffey began. But what? What the hell could he say?

The small man gave him a warning look, then shut the cubicle door. There was a name stenciled on the shut door, and, reading it, Coffey felt his heart pull and jump. For wasn't this the very man he was supposed to see? A. K. Brott, Pres. Again, he knocked his knuckles on the counter. The door reopened. The small man came out, angry now.

"Mr. Brott?"

"I said we're closed."

"I — ah — I work at the depot, sir," Coffey said. "Could I see you a moment?"

"What about?"

"About — ah —"

"Come in, come in. I can't hear you," the small man said, going back into his cubicle.

Coffey lifted the counterleaf and advanced among the empty desks. Inside the cubicle were several photographs in black frames, ex-voto scenes from the life of A. K. Brott. Brott with wife; Brott with children; Brott with first Tiny Ones van; Brott with first automatic washer; Brott with office staff; Brott with Chamber of Commerce outing. Coffey had plenty of time to study them as A. K. Brott, his shoulders hunched, whipped through the pages of a ledger. Brott with books.

At last, he raised his small gray head. Wary eyes studied Coffey. "Well now. What's *your* trouble?"

"I've just started work for you as a driver, sir. I was wondering if I might have an advance on wages?"

Driver? Unbelievingly, A. K. Brott's small eyes traveled from the big fellow's florid mustache to his woolly-lined coat, his tweedy legs and suède boots. What sort of people was Mountain hiring these days? Looks like a burleycue comedian. And that red face: a rummy? "No," said A. K. Brott.

"But it's only ten dollars, sir."

A. K. Brott's finger found a column, ran it down to a total. "*Only* ten dollars?" he said. "Look at this. Off 30 per cent from last year. And that's not because the birth rate is down. It's not down. It's up."

He turned the pages, found another total, contorted his small gray features as though he had been seized with a sudden attack of indigestion. "Look at this one," he said. "Worse. And *you* want ten dollars. You know what's going to happen here in TINY ONES?"

"No, sir."

"You're all going to be out of a job, that's what. Fifteen years I took to build up this business, and look what's happened. Everywhere the same. Down 20, 30, even 50 per cent on some routes. All right; you're driving a route. Now, what is it? What's wrong?"

"What — ah — what do you mean?" Coffey asked.

"Disposable diapers, that's what I mean. Paper, that's what. I mean it's a goddamn crime. There should be a law. There *is* a law, forest conservation, why don't they enforce it? And it gives the kids a rash, let me tell you, no matter what they say, paper skins a baby's ass raw. Ask any doctor, if you don't believe me. But it's new, and that's what people want, something new. Something easy. Now, you meet the customers on your route. Admit it. They're asking you for paper diapers, aren't they?"

"No, sir."

"You're a liar."

Coffey felt as though his face had been slapped. "I'm not a liar," he said.

"No? Well, come on then, wise guy. What *do* they want?"

What indeed? Coffey wondered. But if he was to get his advance, he must talk to this loony. Say something. What was it Eileen Kerrigan's mother had asked him for this morning?

"Well, as a matter of fact," Coffey said. "What most mothers want is to rent other things besides diapers."

"What things?"

"Cribs and — and bassinets and — and prams and so on."

"Sit down," Mr. Brott said. "What's your name?"

"Coffey, sir."

"Well, go on. Let's hear it. If it's good, you won't be sorry, I promise you that."

Coffey stared at Mr. Brott, then exhaled in astonishment, his breath feathering up the ends of his large mustache. *Someone had asked his opinion.* Memories of former years, of the District Manager of Coomb-Na-Baun Knitwear's unpleasant smile, of Old Cleery in Kylemore Distilleries shaking his Neanderthal skull — ah, so many head men all unwilling to hear his ideas. Yet now, when he'd least expected it, here was a head man waiting. What could he say? He began to speak, making it up as he went. "Well, sir," he said. "A lot of families are small nowadays. I mean, they have one or two children, and buying prams and bassinets and cribs is an expensive proposition for them. I remember in my own case, we only have one girl, and so we had to give all that stuff away when she was finished with it. Even the pram, which was in tiptop condition. I just think if we could have rented those things, we'd have saved money."

"*Mnn . . . hmm . . .*" Mr. Brott said. "Go on."

"So — ah — If you rented those things, sir? Rent a crib, for instance —"

"Rent-a-Crib!" Mr. Brott said. "You think of that name yourself?"

"Ah — yes, sir." What name was he talking about?

"Rent-a-Crib. . . ." Mr. Brott closed his eyes and sat for a long moment, as though trying to solve some problem in mental arithmetic. "I don't say it's without merit," he said. "What's your name again?"

"Coffey, sir."

"And you're a driver? You don't look like a driver."

"I'm a New Canadian, sir. This is just a temporary job. I have a night job as well. But the trouble is, sir, I've just started in both jobs, and haven't received any salary as yet. So that's why I came to see you about the advance, sir."

"Advance?"

"Ten dollars, sir. If possible."

Mr. Brott shook his head.

"I mean, I could sign a receipt. I've earned more than ten dollars already. Couldn't you manage . . . ?"

Still headshaking, Brott took out his wallet and handed Coffey a ten-dollar bill. "Advance nothing," he said. "You take it as a bonus. So you work at two jobs, eh? You know that reminds me of me when I was a young fellow. Ambitious, I was. How do you like Canada, Coffey?"

"I like it, sir. Very go-ahead country."

"And you'll do well here, Coffey, you know that? You're a go-ahead fellow yourself. New Canadian, are you? Bet you never went to college, eh?"

"Yes, sir, I did, sir."

"You *did?* Yet you're working as a delivery man. That's the spirit. Kids nowadays, they go to college, they think the world owes them a living. But it doesn't. I tell my Sammy that. I say to him, Sammy, you can have all the degrees in the world, they're no substitute for one good idea. What do you think, Coffey? Am I right?"

Coffey thought that A. K. Brott was not such a bad old geezer, after all.

"Yes, you're the kind we need over here," Mr. Brott said. "Of course, this particular idea might not work. Might fail. Probably *would* fail. Lots of overhead on maintenance, that's one problem. Disinfecting the equipment; repainting; repairs; eh?"

"Yes, sir," Coffey said. "I suppose there would."

"And then the pads, baby blankets, sheets, all that stuff? You figure on renting that too?"

"Well, why not, sir? You have a laundry. It would be just like diapers, wouldn't it?"

"That's right," Mr. Brott said. "Cleaning tie-in. Yes, you're all right, Coffey, you know that? If you've got any more ideas, why you just come right up here and we'll talk it over. Okay? Nice meeting you."

Pleased, confused, hungry for some supper, late because it was five-thirty now and he must rush, Coffey stood up, smiled at Mr. Brott and wagged him the old salute. "Good-by, sir," he said. "And thank you, sir."

"Don't mention it," Mr. Brott said. "And you just keep that ten bucks, that's a bonus. Now, turn off the lights in the main office and shut the door when you go out."

He switched off the lights, he shut the door. He hurried downstairs, hungry but content. Nice old geezer. It renewed your faith in Canada, meeting a man like that, a man who thought you were a go-ahead fellow. And he was a go-ahead fellow, dammit; he was no glorified secretary, no joeboy. He had been right to emigrate, no matter what. Tomorrow, he would find some place for Paulie and him to live, and at the end of the week he would ask Mac-Gregor for a raise. In a week or two he would be promoted. There was always a bright side: you just had to look for it, that was all. It was still uphill, but, with a little victory now and then, you could keep on running. As long as you had hopes. And he still had hopes.

Eight   "Miss Pauline Coffey?" said the girl at the
desk. "Yes, if you'll just take a seat over there, sir. Won't
be a moment."

"Thank you," Coffey said. He sat in the strange lobby
and watched the girl — a nice little piece in a pony-tail
hairdo and a pink angora sweater — go upstairs in search
of his daughter. He read a sign over the staircase: RESI-
DENTS ONLY: NO GENTLEMEN ALLOWED. Which meant
that Grosvenor was barred too. He was glad of that.

Still, it was strange to think that his wife and daughter
were living upstairs in this place and that he, their legal
husband and father, could not go up. Not that Veronica
would be up there at the moment. Oh no. Because, you
see, Veronica never came back from work until half past
five. No, it was not unfair, or sneaky. Hadn't Veronica
taken Paulie away from him in just that way? It was
only tit for tat.

He had promised Paulie. He had kept his promise. Friday it was; here he was, a taxi at the door, a little flat
rented, everything as planned. And now, as he watched
the staircase, he saw the girl in the fuzzy pink sweater
start down again, carrying two untidy bundles of possessions. Behind the pretty girl, his own Paulie, wearing

141

sloppy white socks and saddle shoes, her winter overcoat a bit shrunken at the wrists and hems. He made a note to buy her a new coat. He went to her and kissed her pale cheek. "Hello, Apple."

"Be careful, Daddy, you'll make me spill this stuff."

"I'll take it," he said. "I have a taxi outside."

"Wait, Daddy." She put her things down in the hall. "We can't go yet."

"Oh?"

"Mummy came home. She found out, I don't know how. She's upstairs pressing my good dress. She'll be down with it in a minute."

"Oh?" he said.

"I'll put this stuff in the taxi, Daddy. You stay here. I think she wants to talk to you."

"All right, Apple." She was not going to take his Apple from him now: not after he had worked like a dog all week to get things ready. Just let her try.

He walked towards the stairs, ready to repel the enemy, and as he did the enemy appeared on the landing above, carrying Paulie's party dress over her arm. He watched her come down, seeing not his wife but a stranger: a stranger who was more exciting to him than the woman who had been his wife. She had changed her hair style, and her dark hair, now cut short, fitted her face like a helmet. She wore more make-up and a dress he had never seen. He tried to imagine the familiar body beneath that dress; the full breasts with their large bruised nipples, the full thighs which swelled out of her slender waist, the familiar small mole beneath her ribcage. But it did not work: how could he imagine the body of this total stranger who now came towards him, smelling of an unfamiliar perfume? Was this what falling in love with Grosvenor had done to her — changed her from wife to a beauty he would have envied any man's possessing? With

142

shame, he realized that were she not his wife, he would preen and think of flirting with her; might even fall in love himself.

But when she spoke, she was Vera; no change. "Hello, Ginger," she said. "Could we go into the lounge a moment? I want to speak to you."

Yes. She was Vera and yet she was not. Again a stranger, as he followed her into the small lounge and shut the door so that they might be alone. But Vera once more as she handed him Paulie's dress, saying: "I've just pressed this. Mind you don't crush it."

He took the dress. He noticed that she was carrying her overcoat. She swung the overcoat out as a bullfighter tests a cape, whirling it on over her shoulders in a most un-Vera-ish manner. She pulled a new black beret out of the pocket and began fitting it on in front of the mirror over the fake fireplace. Was that what a crush could do to a person, make her exciting, a bit of a whore? What would she say if he were to kiss her this minute?

"What sort of place have you got, anyway?" she said, still adjusting her beret.

"It's a nice little place," he said. "Two bedrooms, a kitchenette and a living room. Reasonable too. Seventy a month."

"Does that include bedding?"

"Well, I — ah — I have the sheets and pillow cases from our old beds."

"Yes, so you have." Her beret now adjusted to her satisfaction, she began to powder her nose.

"Listen, I — ah — I was just wondering . . . You — you wouldn't think of coming with us?"

"No," she said, still powdering. "If Paulie had been going to stay here, I'd have stayed. As it is, I'm moving."

"Where?" The moment he'd said it, he knew it was a mistake.

143

"I've taken a cheap room," she said. "Not that it matters, as I don't suppose I'll be in it much."

She looked in the mirror to see how he had taken this. "Matter of fact, my things are outside now. Gerry's giving me a lift."

Again, she looked at him through the mirror. "Of course, I'd be willing to stay on here, if you'd leave Paulie with me?"

"Isn't that the height of you," he said, bitterly. "You trickster."

"It's no trick, Ginger. I still feel responsible for Paulie. She's not a child any more and frankly, I don't think you'll be able to supervise her properly."

"Who's talking," he said. "You have a bloody nerve talking of supervising a child."

She turned from him, her face flushed, and went to the door. She opened the door. "There's Paulie. I must say good-by to her."

He watched her through the opened doorway of the lounge as, impersonating his wife and Paulie's mother, she went up to Paulie, took her by the arms, and stood back looking the child over, as she had done a thousand times before, sending Paulie off to a party.

"You'll have to let that hem down soon," he heard her say. How could she say things like that, this brazen stranger who was going off with another man? "Good-by, darling," he heard her say. "I'll be over to see you in a day or two. And if there's anything you need or if there's any trouble, you know where to find me."

Her hands reached out, took Paulie's shoulders and she put her lips forward to kiss the child's pale cheek. (Oh, if those stranger lips would only kiss him!) But he, standing in the doorway of the lounge, saw Paulie look at him as she drew back, suffering but not returning her mother's kiss. Poor bloody lamb, he thought. The pair of us wolves

144

fighting over your body. Ah, Apple, Apple, I'll make all this up to you; from now on you'll be the only one that matters. Let her go; let that stranger go.

"Are you ready, Daddy?" Paulie called.

"Yes, Pet." He went up to them. "Good-by, Vera."

"Wait," she said. "I don't have your new address."

He begged a sheet of paper from the girl at the desk and wrote the address down. Paulie went out to the waiting taxi. He handed the sheet to Veronica, who folded it and slipped it in her purse. "I'm leaving too, Miss Henson," she said to the girl at the desk. "You'll forward my mail, won't you?"

"Yes, Mrs. Coffey."

"Ready, Ginger?"

Silently he went ahead and held the door open for her. In silence they descended the steps to the street. There, its rear door open and Paulie inside, the taxi waited. Farther up the street, on the opposite side, Coffey saw Grosvenor's sporty little car. So she was not bluffing.

"Well?" she said. "Sure you won't reconsider?"

He saw that she was afraid. Until now, this had been a threat. But now, she must cross the street and get into Grosvenor's car, cross the boundary into deed. She was afraid: she wanted to unpack and go upstairs, to go back with Paulie to the no man's land of the last week. And Coffey knew this: he, who so rarely knew what her motives were, knew she was begging him to yield. But wasn't she putting him in the wrong again, making it seem as if he were forcing her into infidelity by his stubbornness? He didn't want her to go, he didn't want her in Grosvenor's bed. But dammit, he was sick of this womanly blackmail.

"No," he said. "Go on, if you want to."

"All right. Good-by, Ginger."

And yes, by the holy, she was doing it, walking away

145

straight as a sword towards that bastard's car. Mad bloody woman, crossing the street in full view of her husband and daughter, to go off with another man. And why? Even now, she's sure that if only she goes through with it, I'll call her back, give her Paulie, admit she's won. Mad bloody woman.

She reached the car. Grosvenor opened the little red door and she settled in with a show of legs. A hot lust ran through Coffey as the little red door shut on that view of rucked-up skirts. There was still time to call her back, time to bring that strange woman to his bed this very night, time to strip those stranger clothes off her and find beneath them a body which miraculously was his by law. Ah dear God! Wasn't it lust that made him want to stop her going off now? Wasn't it jealousy at Grosvenor's getting her? Wasn't it? For it was not pity, it was not love. No, it was not love.

He did not call. He stood watching, an oddly ridiculous figure in his bulky car coat and tiny hat. The engine of Grosvenor's car coughed to life.

"Daddy? Are you coming, Daddy?" Paulie called.

He looked at the taxi: there was one who loved him, one on whom he had no designs. He climbed into the taxi, shutting the door with a slam. He put his hand on Paulie's knee and tried to manage a Big Bear smile. It was starting to snow. Soft blobs of snow fell like molting down on the cab windows as the little red sports car, its engine roaring, shot out and past them. Coffey and his daughter watched it go, their gaze following it as their taxi driver set his windshield wipers in motion. *Chig-chik* went the windshield wipers, wiping all out.

Nine   And so, in his fortieth year, Ginger Coffey began playing house with a fourteen-year-old girl. It reminded him of his first days with Veronica. Getting used
to each other took time. Keep her happy, that was it.
Promise her little treats. And soon, when things improved,
when he would have one good job instead of two poor
ones, when he was not exhausted running from pillar to
post, when he could sleep at night and not dream about
that woman — soon, it would be plain sailing.

But, in the meantime, he was unsure. What did Paulie
need in the way of clothes, for instance? If he gave her
money to buy things, she was likely to go out and get
something grown-up and unsuitable. He noticed she had
taken to wearing nail polish. He mentioned it: she said all
the other kids used it. What did he know? It was wrong,
he felt, but he must not be cross. She was much alone in
the flat, so it was only natural she'd want to ask her
school friends in. But he was away day and night. What
sort of children were these friends of hers? He worried
that she was not studying enough. It was hard to scold
her; he wanted to be friends.

And so, each day on his route, he tried to think of
things that would interest her. He made plans. In a week

147

or two when he'd be a reporter, they'd have much more time together. And then: "Listen, Apple, how would you like it if we took up skiing? Wouldn't you like to ski, Pet? And maybe this summer we'll take a little cottage on a lake, just the two of us. We might rent a sailboat. I've always wanted to sail a boat, ever since I was a little boy. What about you, Apple? Wouldn't you like to sail a boat?"

Ah, if she only were a boy. Or even younger. Remember when she was a tiny girl the fun we used to have playing games like snakes and ladders —

"I was thinking I might buy a draughts board, Apple. Give you a game on my night off, perhaps?"

But she was going to a skating party. Never mind, he would go to a movie. Ages since he'd seen a film. Or perhaps he would just have an early night. Two jobs could be tiring, you know.

How tiring, he could not tell her. Each night when he shut the door of his bedroom and undressed, he stared at his solitary bed in an act of exorcism, telling himself he was sleepy, dead tired, couldn't wait to hit the hay. Exhausted, he would stretch out; exhausted he would attempt to sleep. But he did not sleep.

An elegant, familiar stranger followed a man into the foyer of an apartment house, followed him up four flights of stairs, waited as he unlocked the door of Number 84, smiling familiarly as she stepped across the threshold into a room with bare white walls, prints of Chinese horses and a long low bench of high-fidelity equipment. The man drew the blinds. Music was switched on and that elegant stranger began to remove her skirt, her blouse; walked in garter belt and black stockings to a bar, bending over the bottles, her new short hairdo no longer hiding the white nape of her neck. Sick, Coffey watched as the man went towards her. Sick, he saw the man begin to undress. . . .

148

Then, never mind, no, no; count sheep, dead tired, think of Paulie, think of your promotion next week: J. F. Coffey of the *Tribune* . . . Think of your brother Tom in Africa; where is he at this minute? Think of little Michel and his robot toy, wonder how the little tyke's getting along. No one to play with. Think . . .

But who would ever have thought this long drink of water would be such a Casanova? Look at him now, naked, laughing, bending his long knobbly backbone to press a button, releasing the couch bed which shoots out from the wall, standing up, turning to her with the face of that man in the Y.M.C.A. — Wilson, who talked of women as pigs. Oh God, don't watch now what Wilson is doing as he lays her down. Who is she, anyway? Some woman you don't know, someone you never knew, so go to sleep! Of course she's a stranger: Vera never did the like of that with you. You never saw the real Vera excited like that, a Bacchante kissing his hairy flanks. No, that's not Vera, that's some stranger with a beautiful body, a whore in black stockings, abasing herself with that man, letting him pour wine over her breasts, laughing like a lunatic . . .

But she is not laughing. See? She is crying. Do you see that brown mole on her ribcage? Do you see that white nape, her long hair? Familiar, aren't they? Your Dark Rosaleen.

No chance to sleep, for now he must watch it all, must hear it all, must wait through the laughing, the music, the loud animal cries of fear and pleasure until, in the last hours of darkness, her voice starts to tell the man who she is, tell him how, for love, she crossed the street to get into his little red car, how, because of her husband's foolishness, the ticket money was spent, leaving her no choice. Telling on and on until the first winter light grayed the ceiling of his room, a false dawn which those two in that other room

149

greeted with cries of drunken delight, becoming faceless, rolling and rolling there as he lay still, hearing them cry love, love, love until, exhausted, they fell asleep in each other's arms. Then he too would sleep, a short sleep, murdered by the shrilling of his alarm clock. He would rise, put on the coffee, make the toast and waken his daughter. To sit haggard in the true dawn of his tiny kitchenette, the lights still lit in the winter darkness, a darkness presaging the night to come, the visions still in wait.

"Daddy, have you got a cold? You look pale."

"No, Pet. Just tired."

"Well, no wonder, working day and ni—"

"Won't be long, Pet. Matter of fact I'm doing very well down at the *Tribune*. I know they're pleased with my work there. I'm almost certain that old MacGregor's going to promote me to reporter any day now. Then I'll be able to drop the other job and spend more time at home. Tell you what. As soon as I get my promotion I'll take you out and stand you a bang-up dinner. Dress up in your best —"

"Yes, but Daddy, you'd better hurry now. It's after seven."

No faith. Her voice, like Vera's, cutting him off. Well, she'd see. On Friday. On Friday, his ship might come in.

On Friday he hurried to the *Tribune* office as soon as he had completed his delivery rounds. His pay check contained no notice of changed status. So . . . So, as he had learned the *Tribune* style and had spent two weeks as a galley slave, wasn't it time MacGregor was reminded about that promotion? It was, it was indeed. He went to MacGregor's office. As usual, the door was open. Clarence, the fat man, stood on the right of MacGregor's desk, notebook at the ready. MacGregor himself was holding a telephone conference with the *Tribune*'s publisher.

"Right, Mr. Hound . . . Yes, sir . . . Right away, Mr. Hound. Good-by, sir."

He replaced the receiver. His eye picked out Coffey in the doorway. "Come in. State your business."

"Well, sir, I've been in the proofroom two weeks, as of today."

"Yes?"

"You see, sir, you said that I should learn the *Tribune* style. I think, sir, that I've got the hang of it now."

"Well," said Mr. MacGregor. "Nice to know somebody's wurrking in this loafers' paradise. Good day to you, Coffey."

"But — but I came to see you, sir, to see if perhaps there'd be an opening as a reporter."

"We're still short-staffed in the proofroom, aren't we, Clarence?"

"Yes, chief."

"Very short-staffed, eh, Clarence?"

"Yes, sir. Very short."

Mr. MacGregor looked at Coffey. "We're short-staffed."

"But, sir . . . I've been counting on this promotion."

"Tell him how many men want to become *Tribune* reporters, Clarence."

"Dozens," Clarence said. "Literally dozens, Mr. Mac."

"So, we're not short of reporters at the moment, Coffey. You'll have to hang on."

"But, I —" Coffey felt his face hot. "But, I have a family, sir. I mean, I can't support my family indefinitely on a proofreader's wages."

"What are you getting now?"

"Fifty dollars a week, sir."

"I'll gi' you fifty-five. Now, go back to your wurrk."

"Thank you, sir. I'd rather have the promotion, sir. I mean, fifty-five dollars a week is still very little."

"Did you ever hear such cheek?" Mr. MacGregor asked

Clarence, turning. "Did you ever, in your mortal life?"

Clarence looked at Coffey with shock, reproach and disgust. But Coffey did not budge. There was a time and a tide. "Well, sir. I . . ."

"Well, *what?*"

"I'd still like to know definitely when I may hope to be made a reporter, sir."

"How the hell do I know?" MacGregor shouted. "When I get a replacement for you, that's when. Maybe in a week or two."

"In two weeks, sir? I mean, is that a promise? Because otherwise I don't see much point in my staying on."

"All right, two weeks," MacGregor said. "You have my wurrd."

"Thank you, sir."

"Now, take your arse out of here. I have wurrk to do."

"Yes, sir. And thank you, sir."

Two more weeks. Still, it was better than a kick in the pants, wasn't it? A little victory. He hurried off to the *Tribune* cafeteria, had a quick sandwich, then phoned Paulie to tell her his good news.

"Listen, Pet. That promotion I was telling you about. We've only got a fortnight to go."

"That's   good," she said, in an unbelieving voice. "Daddy — Mummy was here today."

"Was she?" He had been wondering when *that* would start.

"Yes, she took me out shopping," Paulie said. "She put down ten dollars on a new parka for me."

"But I could have bought you one, Pet. Why didn't you tell me you needed it?"

Paulie ignored this. "Anyway, Mummy wants to come and visit me tomorrow. She wants to see you too."

152

"I hope you told her we're getting along like a house on fire, Apple? Did you?"

"Yes, Daddy. Daddy — I have to hang up now. Kettle's boiling."

He fumbled, replacing the receiver. All the good had gone out of his news with that mention of Veronica. Ah, hadn't he been the fool to think she would let them alone? Now she would start sneaking around to the flat behind his back, buying Paulie presents with Grosvenor's money, turning the child against him.

Tiny lights appeared before his eyes. He fumbled, feeling for the phone booth door. For a moment he blacked out, felt like falling. Oh, dear Lord, if anything happened to him, what would become of Paulie? No insurance, nothing. His child would have to go and live with those two; would have to watch those things.

Steady as she goes, he warned himself. Steady now. If you go on like this they'll come for you in a little blue van and lock you up, so they will. Steady the Buffs. Put that woman out of your mind once and for all. You'll have to get rid of her.

But how? She was still his wife, the mother of his child. Divorce her. Get custody. Divorce her!

"Paddy?" a voice said. "What's the matter?"

Uncomprehendingly, Coffey looked up, saw Fox buying cigarettes at the cafeteria counter.

"Are you sick?" Fox said. "You look funny."

"No," he said. He joined Fox at the counter, knitting his hands in the steeple game. *Here is the church* . . . He had been sick, that was it. Sick because he somehow believed he would get her back; sick because he had wanted her back. The cure was plain: divorce her.

"Come and have a beer," Fox said. "Pay night. It'll make you feel better."

"No," he said. "I'll be better soon. Very soon."

That night he went to bed in peace: he would sleep, he was sure. But the elegant stranger smiled. She sat in a restaurant, cigarette smoke stippling upwards in a thin spiral past her smiling face. Coffey, watching, saw her hold out a glass. That was not his ring on her finger. The ring with which he had wed her was a gold ring: it had belonged to his mother. This was a thin platinum circle, third finger, left hand, with these presents, kiss a new bride. Friends surrounded the newlyweds. An older woman leaned forward across the wedding feast and said: "Didn't he soldier with my husband once? And was something in a distillery?" And the stranger who was once Veronica replied: "No, he was just a Good Doggy." Someone said: "Uniform, would you believe it, with TINY ONES on the cap? Diapers, it was. He delivers them to us every week. Of course, after that first week, I always made sure it was the maid who received him. Not to embarrass him, the creature." The wedding guests shook their heads in sympathy and congratulated the bride on her fortunate escape. They thought her a nice woman: they had not seen her as he had, naked and frenzied with all those men in all those rooms. They had not seen her walk across the street in full view of her child and husband, showing her legs as she stepped into her lover's little red car. In their eyes she was a woman who had wasted her best years as wife to a glorified secretary; a woman who had saved herself before it was too late. She and her new husband would take tea with Madame Pandit. They would be invited to dinner by Louie, the Prime Minister of Canada. The Prime Minister would ask for the signed original of a G.G. cartoon. There would be a good little doggy in the border of that cartoon.

He lay in the darkness waiting for that first false light which would banish her and bring him sleep. He would divorce her and then he would rest in peace. Do you hear me, Vera? Don't laugh! I'm going to divorce you.

Yet, on Saturday, when the doorbell rang and Paulie went to answer it, Coffey waited in the living room of their little flat, his lips dry, his mouth betraying him in a hopeful smile. And when she came in, wearing a new and unfamiliar hat, he was gripped once more with a painful sense of loss. Look how strange we are to each other, all of us. Even Paulie, Paulie who takes her mother's coat to hang in the closet and now, formal hostess, asks if we would like some tea.

"Yes, that would be lovely," Veronica said. And Paulie withdrew, the mistress of the house, while Veronica, a guest, waited to be entertained.

"Small, isn't it?" she said, looking around.

He did not answer.

"And how are you getting along, Ginger? I mean at your work?"

He said stiffly that he had received a raise; that in two weeks he would be a reporter. Everything was grand, thank you.

"But in the meantime these jobs must leave you very little time to spend with Paulie?"

"We manage," he said. "And it won't be for long. How are *you* getting on, Veronica?"

"Oh, I like my job very much. The woman who owns the shop speaks French but her English is poor. So we complement each other. As a matter of fact I made over sixty dollars with commissions last week. That's why I'm buying Paulie a new coat."

"*I* could have bought it."

"Ah, but you didn't, did you? And besides, I like doing

things with my own money, Ginger. After all these years it's such a marvelous feeling to be solvent."

He did not reply because, at that moment, Paulie came in with the tea tray. He noticed a box of assorted biscuits beside the teapot. Vera's favorites. In the time he and Paulie had been together, had she ever bought one of Daddy's favorite treats? No, she had not; and, watching the pair of them, listening to their womany voices, he felt alone, shut out, the heavy-fingered male. Listen to them, would you, chatting away like two old pals at a charity bazaar; Veronica going on about this bloody hatshop she worked in and Paulie regaling her with tales about the teachers at school, not seeming to know or care that her mother was a stranger who now had no mortal interest in Paulie and her school. Whereas he — all week he had hoped that Paulie would tell him about her little doings. He would have loved to hear her chat.

"More tea, Mummy? Daddy, would you get us some more hot water?"

He went into the kitchen and put the kettle back on the boil. The watched pot boiled all too fast for him. When he took the hot water back into the living room, they were still at it, heads close, hens clucking. He sat across the room from them unnoticed, wishing she would go.

But no. After two more cups of tea, Veronica settled back comfortably on the sofa, showing her long, slim legs. He had always hated her carelessness in showing herself. Careless? It had been deliberate, probably. She blew a reed of smoke and said to Paulie: "Look, darling, I wonder if you'd let your father and me have a little chat? Just for a few minutes?"

"All right," Paulie said. "I have to run down to the store for a moment. I'll see you when I come back."

Paulie got her coat and went out, no secret look at him,

nothing. And as soon as she had gone, the stranger sat up straight on the sofa, took her knee in her laced hands, letting her skirt fall away distractingly, and said: "I've been thinking about Paulie. You and I must come to some arrangement about her."

"What arrangement?" he said.

"Well, first of all, the expense; her school things and clothes and so on. And then there's this question of her being left alone so much. I could come in the evenings?"

"Could you?" he said sourly, watching that slim leg swing.

"Yes. I could be here at a quarter to six most evenings and I'd make supper and stay awhile and —"

She talked. He watched her lips move; those lips which at night kissed a stanger's hairy flanks. Talking, making noises of motherhood, that mouth which each night he heard cry out in desire. He felt his own mouth open. To kiss those lips, to bite into that white neck, to take her now, tumble her back, tear the clothes from that stranger body which all week he had not been able to touch.

"So, what do you say, Ginger? Are you listening?"

. . . .

"Ginger? What's the matter?"

The tea tray clattered, a cup fell sideways on its saucer. He lumbered across the room, his hands gripping her shoulders, his heavy body tumbling her backwards on the sofa. He tried to kiss her, his hands pulling up her skirt, quieting her hands as they tried to push him away. He felt her breasts come free within her dress as a shoulder strap snapped and heard his own breathing as he tried to control her kicking, struggling body.

A sudden pain made his eyes water. He let her go. She had caught both ends of his mustache and was pulling upwards by the short hairs. She wrenched up cruelly, then pulled down, bringing him stumbling off the sofa onto his knees beside her. His hands caught her wrists, stopping the pain.

"Let go, Vera. Let go!"

She let go. He stared at her, tears of hurt in his eyes, his lust lost at last in foolish pain.

"Are you out of your mind?" she said. "You've torn my dress and my bra. My God, Ginger, what's the matter with you? How dare you?"

How dare he? Slowly, he got up off his knees. She had unbuttoned the front of her dress and now, one white shoulder out of it, was searching inside for the strap of her bra. Her hair had fallen over her eyes and there was a red mark on her neck as though she had been scratched. With an effort he looked at the carpet as, her dress fully open, she lifted one breast up, fitting on the ripped brassiere. And all the time, scolding him. "Getting me up here and leaping on me like a lunatic. What if Paulie had seen you? For goodness' sake control yourself."

"I'm sorry," he said.

"You should be. Look at that. You've torn the dress too. And I haven't even paid for it yet."

"Grosvenor will pay for it," he shouted. "Let him pay for it."

"That's enough, Ginger. I came here to see what I could do for Paulie. That doesn't give you any right to attack me."

"No right? I'm your husband."

"You *were*. You dirty rotten pig, trying to — just trying to — just your own dirty desires!"

She was crying: wouldn't you know? "Ah, stop your whinging," he said. "I'll bet that's nothing to what your fancy man does to you every night in the week."

She stood up, buttoning her dress, distractedly trying to tidy her hair. "I'm not going to stay here and listen to you.

158

I want to help Paulie. I'm her mother, just remember that. I've got a right to help her."

"You've got no right," he said. "Go on back to Mister Canadian Viewpoint. You deserted Paulie and you deserted me. I'm going to divorce you, do you hear? And when I do, I'm getting custody of Paulie."

She sat still. Only her eyes moved in her face as she looked him up and down. Eyes bright with what he had once thought to be her bad temper, but which now he knew as her hate. "Divorce?" she said. "That's fine. I want one as much as you do. More."

"Do you, Vera? Then you can help me pay for it."

"Gerry will pay for it," she said. "I'll tell him to get in touch with you."

"Why should Gerry pay for it?"

"Because he wants to marry me."

He looked at his hands, joined them in the steeple game. Was that true? Would Grosvenor marry her? As they sat there in silence a key turned in the front door and Paulie came in with a bag of groceries and the afternoon paper.

He stood up, protecting Paulie, afraid of losing her. "You're just in time, Pet," he said. "Your mother's leaving."

"So soon?" Paulie turned towards him and, suddenly, winked.

Veronica saw the wink. She stood up, walked to the hall closet and put on her overcoat. Then turned, trying to save her dignity, trying to smile and say the things a guest might say. "Paulie, dear, you're turning into a very good housekeeper. Everything's so neat and tidy. Well, good-by, Ginger. Good-by, Paulie. And thanks for the tea."

This time, she did not try to kiss Paulie. She opened the front door herself and looked at him, meaningfully. "I'll have Gerry get in touch with you about that other thing on Monday. All right?"

"All right," he said. The door shut. He looked around the living room, smelling once again that unfamiliar scent, seeing the crumbs of biscuit on her plate, her lipsticked butts in an ash tray. He picked them up and carried them into the kitchen to dump them in the garbage can. He went back into the living room and opened the door to dissipate the scented smell. He saw his face in the windowpane. That sad impostor considered him: he considered the lack of dignity in the actions of that graceless fool. Look at you. Had you no pride, no self-respect, jumping on her, letting her humiliate you?

He stood, staring at his image. Was that man really he?

"Daddy? What was that she said about Gerry Grosvenor getting in touch with you?"

The mirror man watched from the windowpane as he went to the sofa, sat down and absently bit into one of his wife's favorite sandwich creams. Tiny crumbs powdered his red mustache. "Come here a minute, Pet," he said. He waited until Paulie sat on the sofa beside him. "Your mother and I are going to get a divorce."

"But Catholics aren't allowed to get a divorce, Daddy."

He sighed. "Your mother and I aren't real Catholics any more. You know that."

"Oh."

"You see," he said. "Grosvenor wants to marry your mother. And she wants to marry him."

In a gesture so rare that he had no courage to tell her he did not deserve it, Paulie slid off the sofa and sat at his feet, hugging his ankles. "Never mind, Daddy," she said. "I'll look after you."

Awkwardly, his hand stroked her head. "You won't mind?"

"Of course I won't mind, Daddy."

160

He touched her pale cheek. She loved him, yes, she loved him. She was his, not Vera's; his own and only child. Wasn't that enough for any man, wasn't that a victory? He must prove worthy of that love. But as he decided this, he became afraid. How could he keep her love without a promise or two? Afraid, that foolish sad impostor spoke up. "Oh, Pet," the impostor said. "We'll have a grand time, I promise you. You'll see, Pet, you'll see."

"Yes, Daddy." But why did she move her head away from his touch? Ah, dear God. She, too, was tired of promises.

Ten   On Monday Veronica would have Grosvenor get in touch with him. He took that to mean that Grosvenor would telephone. But at four that afternoon as he returned his TINY ONES truck to the depot, Grosvenor's little red midget car was parked outside Mr. Mountain's office. His first thought was that Grosvenor must not see him in uniform. Skirting the little car, he drove his truck to the far end of the depot yard. He got out on the side away from the little car and began to double back towards the locker room, under cover of the line of parked vehicles.

About twenty yards from the locker room, he ran out of cover. He was crouched behind a truck, trying to plan his next move, when a footstep from behind made him turn.

"Hello, Ginger. Thought I saw you."

His face hot with rage and humiliation, Coffey went through the useless pretense of fixing his boot buckle. Then, unable to look Grosvenor in the face, he straightened up and turned towards the locker room. "I'm in a hurry," he said. "I have to change."

"I'll come with you, if I may?" Without waiting for permission, Grosvenor followed Coffey across the yard and into the locker room where several other drivers were changing into street clothes. "I came here because I wasn't sure how I could catch you," Grosvenor said. "You're a hard man to see, these days."

Coffey, unable to think of a reply, stripped off his uniform and stood in his shirt, his legs oddly conspicuous in the heavy red underdrawers issued to drivers. "I came to talk about the divorce," Grosvenor said. "Veronica says you're willing to go through with it. I think that's wise of you."

The other drivers were listening. "Would you mind shutting your face about my private affairs until we get out of here?" Coffey said in an angry whisper.

"Oh — sorry."

In awkward fury Coffey unbuttoned the underwear and stood naked before his enemy; remembered that naked was how he imagined Grosvenor each night. Hurriedly, he began to dress in his own clothes.

"Maybe when you're through, Ginger, we can go and have a drink someplace?"

"You can drive me down to the *Tribune,*" Coffey said. "But I'll not drink with you."

"I'm sorry you feel that way, Ginger."

Coffey did not answer. He finished dressing and set off across the yard to check out his day's receipts. When he had finished, Grosvenor was waiting in the little red car, its door open to receive him as passenger. He got in, his knees rising uncomfortably to meet his chest, thinking of her show of legs as she got into this car that awful day. It had not been deliberate. In this car, she could not help showing her legs. He had been wrong.

Wrong. Grosvenor started the car with a loud throttling roar. They shot through the TINY ONES gate and into the street.

"The thing to settle is who's going to act as guilty party," Grosvenor said. "Now, of course, you'll think it should be her. But, if Veronica's the guilty party, the divorce will be far from a rubber-stamp affair. You see, our Canadian divorce laws —"

"For crying out loud, will you stop lecturing?" Coffey said. "Just tell me the quickest way."

"The easiest way is to set up a false adultery scene," Grosvenor said. "I know a lawyer who can arrange it. They provide everything. A girl, a detective, the works. You check in to a hotel with the girl, and half an hour later the detective shows up. Case is heard by the Senate divorce committee in Ottawa. It's a cinch."

"And Vera gets custody of Paulie," Coffey said. "No thanks."

"No, no," Grosvenor said. "Vera and I intend to get married and have children of our own, if possible. I know *I* don't want a fourteen-year-old daughter."

Involuntarily, Coffey fingered the part in his mustache. Was that why she was marrying Grosvenor? To get the kids they'd never had?

"Another thing we talked about," Grosvenor said, "was the expense of a divorce. Veronica thinks that because you're going to have the burden of supporting Paulie, it's only fair that we pay for the divorce thing. I agree. After all, you're pretty hard up at the moment. It wouldn't be fair to saddle you with an additional financial burden at this time."

Coffey, his face hot, stared at the dashboard of the car. The ampere needle flicked, *wig wag,* one side to the other. She went *wig wag* from him to Grosvenor, Grosvenor to him, telling each what she knew. Poor Ginger's too hard up to pay, you see. Now, Gerry, if you pop down and talk to him. Then tell me.

Last night he had not slept until dawn. Last night he had watched her in bed with Grosvenor as she laughed and made a story of Poor Ginger's attempt to rape her. And Grosvenor had laughed too. Grosvenor, sitting here beside him, probably knew every secret thought or action he'd confided to Veronica in fifteen years of marriage. Bitch!

"All right," Coffey said, in a hoarse voice. "I want rid of her. You pay the divorce and I'll be the target. When can we get it over with?"

"What about next Saturday night?" Grosvenor said. "You don't work on Saturday nights, Vera says."

Coffey nodded. "Where?" he said. "And how?"

"There's a hotel called the Clarence which isn't too particular. I'll try to set it up with the lawyer for Saturday night. You go there at ten. I'll have a girl waiting for you in the lobby. The detective will be along later."

"Not much later," Coffey said. "I want to be home at midnight. I have my daughter to think of."

"Of course. Shouldn't take more than an hour. I'll phone you and let you know the details, okay?"

Again, Coffey nodded. They drove the rest of the way in silence. When they arrived at the *Tribune,* Grosvenor reached over and put his hand on Coffey's knee. Coffey stared at that hand. It was very white, backed with very black hairs. He saw the hairy flanks she kissed in those nightly scenarios. Quickly, he moved his knee away.

"I just wanted to say thanks," Grosvenor said, sounding hurt.

For the first time since he had got into the car, Coffey looked Grosvenor full in the face. It was an ordinary face. A year ago he had not even known it existed, yet now it was joined to his in a resemblance stronger than brotherhood, in an intimacy he and his true brother would never share.

What chemistry of desire made Grosvenor willing to face a surly husband to discuss the settlement of Veronica's divorce? What made him willing to pay for that divorce, to marry another man's woman, a woman older than he? Coffey did not know. He knew only that it was the same violent illness which, after fifteen years of marriage, had suddenly revived his own desire, leaving him prepared to commit any equal folly. He could not hate Grosvenor, for Grosvenor in turn would suffer the same feminine ritual of confidence and betrayal. He felt compassion for Grosvenor. He was cured of this sickness: Grosvenor had inherited it.

"Good-by," he said, and held out his hand.

Surprised, Grosvenor shook hands. "Till Saturday then?" Grosvenor said.

"Saturday it is."

His decision made, Coffey went to bed that night, confident that all his fevers had passed. He went to sleep and slept. He did not dream. In the morning Paulie heard him singing in the kitchen.

"Somebody's in good form," she said, coming in, her hair in curlers, her toothbrush in her hand.

Coffey turned an egg in the pan, still singing. "Why not?" he said. "Less than two weeks to go, Pet. I wonder what sort of a journalist I'll make? I wonder now, will they send me off to faraway places? That's a great thing about the journalistic profession, you never know where you'll end up. You see, you're very much your own boss in that field. Ah, it just shows you now, doesn't it?"

"Shows you what?" Paulie said.

"That the old saying is true. The darkest hour is just before the dawn. You have to remember that. Hope, now that's what you need. While there's hope, there's life."

"Somebody's in a philosophical mood this morning."

"And why not? Do you know another thing I was thinking this morning, Pet? The old saying, Man wasn't born to live alone . . . Do you know, that's a lot of malarkey?

166

For Man was, and the sooner he faces up to it, the better."

"Does that mean you want to get rid of me?" Paulie asked.

"Never!" He kissed her on her brow, cold cream and all. "By the way," he said. "That reminds me. I have to go out on Saturday night. I won't be back till nearly midnight."

"But, that's perfect," Paulie said. "I was going to ask some of the kids over, anyway. Maybe you could go out early and leave us the place to ourselves?"

Well, he could go to a film, he supposed. Ah, he wasn't like some people: he knew that children hated grownups around when they were having a party. "Good idea," he said cheerfully. "I'll do that. Go to a film, or something, and leave you a clear field."

On Friday, when he returned from his TINY ONES round, Mr. Mountain handed him a message which had come in during the day. It was to call Mr. Grosvenor before seven. So when Coffey arrived at the *Tribune*, he rang Grosvenor at home.

"Ginger? Good, I've been trying to get you. It's all set for tomorrow night. You're to go to the Clarence Hotel at nine forty-five. Go to the bar and there'll be a girl there wearing a green overcoat and a black fur hat. Her name is Melody Ward. Got that? Melody Ward. Have a drink with her, then take her upstairs. There'll be a visitor at ten forty. Okay? And Ginger — you won't even have to pay the hotel bill. I'll reimburse you later."

"Fair enough," Coffey said. He hung up, feeling like a man in a thriller. It wasn't sordid at all, it was an adventure. Melody Ward. He even found himself wondering would she be pretty? He did not think of Veronica. Because he was finished with all that, you see. He was cured.

Saturday evening, he returned from his delivery round in good spirits. He finished his supper at seven and, determined to be agreeable, put on his coat and hat and went out, leaving the flat free for the children when they came. He told Paulie he would be home about twelve.

It was a clear cold night, electric and anticipant. When Coffey alighted from a bus in the center of the city, he was at once caught up in the hurry of a Saturday-night spree. Neon lights promised, spelled pleasures, performed tricks. A neon Highlander danced a jig over a clothier's, a comic chicken popped its head in and out of the Q in a BAR-B-Q sign, a neon hockey player jiggled his stick over a tavern doorway. In movie house entrances, bathed in the fairground brightness of million-watt ceilings, diminished and humbled by enormous posters proclaiming current attractions, anticipant girls fidgeted, waiting for their dates; solitary boys consulted wrist watches and dragged on cigarettes, nervously checking their brilliantined pompadours in reflections from the glass-walled cashier's shrine. And as Coffey strolled, slow, slower than the crowd, not sure what to do, he was swept up in a change of shows and eddied into one of these entrances. He stood undecided under the myriad lights, watching the anticipant girls smile and wave in sudden recognition, the boys drop their cigarettes and hurry forward; the pairing, the claiming, the world going two by two.

Watching, he absently stroked the part in his mustache: felt a sadness. All these thousands, hurrying to meet; yet he was alone. Saturday night and they came down in their thousands to laugh, to dance, to sit in the dark watching colored screens, holding hands, sharing joys. While he waited to meet some unknown woman in a strange bar, to go upstairs with that stranger to an unknown room, perhaps to lie down on a bed with her, in

168

make-believe of an intimacy he now shared with no one. And when it was over, he would have no one: not even Paulie. For Paulie had put him out tonight so that she, with other youngsters, could laugh and dance, listening to shared music.

He had no one. He was three thousand miles from home, across half a frozen continent and the whole Atlantic Ocean. Only one person in this city, only one person in the world, really knew him now: knew the man he once was, the man he now was. One person in the whole world, who fifteen years ago in Saint Pat's in Dalkey had stood beside him in a white veil for richer for poorer, in sickness and in health until death. One person had known him — or known most of him. Would anyone ever know him again?

Well now, enough of that. Do something.

He went up to the cashier's little glass shrine; put a dollar in the opening. The cashier pressed a button and an aluminum machine spat a ticket at him. The cashier made change by manipulating another machine. A nickel dropped into its little metal change bowl. He picked it up. That was the way of this world. You saw someone in a glass cage, stepped up, exchanged things, but never touched. Oh, come on now! Enough of that, I said.

At the back of the theater, penned two by two behind a velvet rope, a line of people waited. The usherette, a girl not much older than Paulie, came up to him. "Single, sir? We have seats in the first six rows."

There was something about her: her accent was not Canadian. He smiled at her, drawn by that immigrant bond, and followed her from the lighted area into the darkness of the theater. Poor kid. Her scapula bone stuck out at right angles against the maroon stuff of her uniform. New Canadians: thousands like her came here each year; thousands started all over again in humble circs.

You heard such stories: lawyers forced to take work as checkers, doctors as lab assistants, professors driving trucks. And still they came, from every country in Europe, riding in old railroad colonist cars to the remote provinces of this cold, faraway land. Why did they do it? For their children's sake, it was said. Well, and wasn't he driving a truck now for his daughter's sake? Wasn't he one of them? Wasn't he, too, a man who would always be a stranger here, never at home in this land where he had not grown up. Yes: he too.

The girl's flashlight showed him an almost empty row, lowering its beam as she waited for him to enter his seat. He wanted to stop, take her by the arm, lead her back up the aisle into the light again. To say: "I too am an immigrant," to compare impressions, reminisce, to tell the things that immigrants tell. But the flashlight beam snapped off. He could no longer see her. He sat down, purblinded by the colored images on the huge screen above. He looked around. Here were the solitaries. Some slept, some slumped in morose contemplation of the film giantess kicking yard-long legs, while some, like him, ignored her and peered about them in the shadows, hoping for a glance, a promise of company.

How long was it since he'd sat down here? Years, years. But he remembered: mitching away long school afternoons in the picture houses off O'Connell Street, huddled down in his seat for fear someone might see him and tell his parents. And later, as a university student, the lonely Saturday nights in cheap front seats, hoping that some American daydream would banish the private misery of having no girl, no place to go. Well, and was he going back to all that? For if he lost Veronica now, who would have him, a man nearly forty with a grown-up daughter on his hands? Wouldn't he end his days here among the solitaries?

170

Enough of that. He tried watching the film, but somehow the filmed America no longer seemed true. He could not believe in this America, this land that half the world dreams of in dark front seats in cities and villages half a world away. What had it in common with his true America? For Canada was America; the difference a geographer's line. What had these Hollywood revels to do with the facts of life in a cold New World?

At half past eight, unable to watch the film any longer, he went upstairs and sat in the lobby, waiting to go to the Clarence Hotel, waiting to meet a girl in a green coat and a black fur hat. He thought about her, Miss Melody Ward. How many of her customers really went to bed with her? Did she charge you extra for that? That made him smile. By the holy, it would be great gas to charge Grosvenor for that.

At nine fifteen he left the theater and began to walk towards Windsor Street. He thought of Veronica and wondered if she were thinking of him this minute as he started off to end it. And if she were thinking of him now, didn't she feel as he did, some sorrow that tonight, after all those years, it was ending? She must feel some sorrow, he decided. Anybody would.

The Clarence was a small hotel opposite the Canadian Pacific Railway terminus. The neon sign over its side entrance read MONTMORENCY ROOM and a display case showing photographs of glossy nonentities advertised CONTINUOUS ENTERTAINMENT. He went in. The hotel lobby was on the right and consisted of a single desk-cum-cigar stand with three armchairs in a row facing the street window. At the desk was a night reception clerk and in the armchairs three old men stared out at the snow, watching traffic. On the left, in the Montmorency Room, a pallid French-Canadian sang a cowboy lament to an audience of eight drinkers. Coffey entered, sat down at a

171

table and ordered a rye. There was no girl in a green coat and a black fur hat. He was glad. Wasn't this whole thing daft? Why should he go through with it? He would not go through with it. Stranger or not, Veronica was his lawful wedded wife: his, not Grosvenor's. Why should Grosvenor have her? Why should he be the one who was left alone?

But the clock over the bar said nine thirty-seven and it was too late to ring Grosvenor and call this off. The girl would be here any minute, the detective was probably on his way already, the lawyer had arranged things —

And — and all his life, he had hated scenes, hated making a fuss. It was too late now, far too late to change things, because — because at that moment a girl walked in. She wore a green overcoat and a black fur hat. She went up to the bar, spoke to the barman, then turned and looked around the room. She looked at him. And, by J, she was not the sort of girl who'd stand any nonsense. She was tall and pretty and tough. And, by J, she was coming right at him!

"You're Mr. Coffey, right?" she said.

"Yes." He stood up.

"The mustache," she said. "I was told to look out for it."

Yes, he said, and would she please sit down. And what would she have to drink? A brandy? He called the waiter. He joined his hands under the table. *Here's the church* . . . How could he get out of it now? *And here's the steeple* . . . Because she wasn't the sort who would let him off lightly. *Open the gates* . . . good-looking too, in other circumstances he wouldn't half-mind . . .

The waiter brought a brandy and Coffey paid. The French-Canadian singer sang a song about Paree, Paree. The girl sipped her brandy, listening to the song. *And here's the minister coming upstairs* . . . Too late, wasn't it? Of course it was. Besides, it wasn't his idea, it was Grosvenor's, all Grosvenor's fault . . .

And here's the minister . . . Grosvenor's fault. He remembered sitting in the Ritz, his hands joined as now in the steeple game. And remembered what Veronica said in the Ritz: Gerry's fault? Not your fault, of course. Never your fault, is it, Ginger?

He unclasped his hands and looked nervously at the girl. What sort of man would worry more about offending a strange whore than about losing his wife? Ah, dear God. The sort of man who had been ready to walk away from Grosvenor's apartment door one night for fear of a scene, who had only rung the bell that night because some total stranger gave him a suspicious look. The sort of sad impostor who now, seeing Miss Melody Ward applaud the singer, raised his hands and applauded too.

The singer bowed and went behind a curtain. The lights went on. "Well," said the girl, putting down her glass, "I guess we'd better go up, huh?"

Who was he to talk about in sickness and in health until death? He, who half an hour ago had thought of taking this strange whore to bed, not of fifteen years of marriage. Who was he to condemn Veronica?

Miss Melody Ward stood up. She preceded him across the room and waited for him in the lobby. Through the reflection from the street window, the three armchair ancients watched him join her.

"Okay," she said. "Now sign us in as Mr. and Mrs. Your right name, mind. But give an out-of-town address, like Toronto, huh? And act sort of loaded so's the clerk remembers you."

He began, his large trembling dignity compromised by a sudden mulish stammer. "Nu-no," he said. "No, I can't."

"Oh, come on," she said. "Don't worry."

He avoided her eye, looked at the linoleum squares of the lobby floor.

"Oh, listen," she said. "This happens all the time. A lot of guys are nervous, so what? I mean, you don't have to do anything, see? I mean, we just go up and have a drink in the room and then I take a shower. I'm in the shower when the lawyer's man comes."

The three old men sat silent in their chairs, their faces fixedly vacant in the manner of surreptitious listeners.

"So come on," she said. "I won't eat you."

If only she knew: to go up would be so easy. They were all waiting: the girl, the lawyer's man, the desk clerk, Veronica. All trying to shame him into compliance.

"No," he said. "I'm going home."

"Well, for Christsake," Miss Melody Ward began, her voice rising to a terrifying decibel count. "What are you playing at, huh? I mean to say, I came all the way down here, I gave up another appointment —"

"You'll be paid," he said. "Good night."

And turned away, his military manner failed completely in the desk clerk's curious stare, in the peering and whispering of the old men as he fled towards the sanctuary of the hotel door. Outside, he stood for a moment in the slush of the gutter and raised his face to the sky. Snow fell, wetting his cheeks. He felt his body tremble. Yes, it *was* a victory.

He went home. He had promised Paulie that he would stay out until her party was over, but in his victorious mood, he forgot all that. Somehow or other he must try to get Veronica back; that was all he thought of now. And so, at ten-fifteen, he paused outside the door of his flat, hearing from within that loud rockabilly nonsense that Paulie loved so well. He hesitated, but suffering J, wasn't this *his* home as well as hers? Why shouldn't he take the bull by the horns twice in one night? He let himself in.

In the tiny living room, furniture had been cleared against the walls and two boys danced cheek to cheek with two of Paulie's schoolmates. The girls he knew; like Paulie they were children playing at being women, their childish bodies tricked out in low-necked blouses and ballerina skirts; their faces unnaturally aged by lipstick and eye shadow.

The boys were older; they wore leather windbreakers, Western-style shirts, bootlace ties. Peculiar, brilliantined haircuts gave them the appearance of wet sea birds. Where was Paulie?

He turned. In the narrow trough of kitchen, a third sea bird faced him, eyes shut, spread hands distributed, one over Paulie's small rump, one on her back, pressing her breasts tight against him. Paulie's body moved in time to the music but her feet did not. Eyes shut, her pale face flowered upwards to the electric light bulb, she undulated in a fixed position, rubbing against the boy.

Coffey took three steps into the living room and knocked the player arm off its thundering course. Eyes opened. The dancers stopped. The arm scratched in the silence, its needle frustrated: slipping, circling, slipping again.

"Daddy?" Paulie said, coming out of the kitchen. "What time is it?"

But Coffey did not look at her. He pointed to the boy behind her. "What's *your* name?" he said.

"Bruno," the boy said. He had a slight inward cast to his eyes which gave him an aggrieved look. "Why? You Paulie's Dad?"

"Do you go to school?" Coffey asked.

"Me?" the boy seemed puzzled by the question. He turned to Paulie. "What'd *I* do?" he said.

"No, Daddy, Bruno doesn't go to school. He works."

"I thought you said these were all school friends, Apple?"

One of the girls giggled. The boys exchanged glances and winks. "Apple?" one of them said to Paulie. "That what they call you at home?"

All laughed, except Paulie.

"Is there something funny about that?" Coffey said to the boy.

The boy, caught in Coffey's stare, was silent. The girls, saving him, said it was late, they really must go. The boys said they would drive them in their car. They ignored Coffey, as did Paulie, who rushed around, helping them find their coats, talking pointedly about how sorry she was; it was early; it was a pity they couldn't stay.

" 'Night, kid," said the boy who had been dancing with her.

"Be seeing you — *Apple*," another boy said.

"Good night Mister — ah — Coffey."

"Good night."

"Good night." Paulie shut the door and went into the kitchen to clear away the litter of Coke bottles and plates, while her father started to restore the furniture to its former scheme.

"Why did you call me Apple in front of them?" an angry voice said from the kitchen.

"I'm sorry."

"And why did you come home when you said you'd be late? You've ruined my party."

He pulled the sofa back into place and paused, his lips shut tight under his mustache. After all he'd been through tonight! "Come here a minute," he called.

She came from the kitchen and stood in the doorway. Her face was pale. Her eyes were bright. Anger? She was his girl; she looked like him. But he saw Veronica there. Not anger, no. Hate.

176

"These boys," he said. "They weren't school friends. They're older boys, aren't they?"

"Yes."

"Little thugs," he said. "If you ask me."

"Nobody asked you, Daddy."

Was it for this that he was working day and night? Was this all he had left now, this — this cheekiness?

He slapped his daughter's face. It was the first time in his life he had done such a thing.

Tears formed in Paulie's wide eyes. She stared at him as though she had lost her sight, then, with a wail of rage, began to weep. "Leave me alone! You don't touch me. You — You — Everybody'll be making fun of me. I'm not your Apple, do you hear? You and your Apple! I'm nearly fifteen."

"Exactly," he said. "So what are you doing painted and powdered like an old woman? Go and wash that muck off this instant."

"No, I won't!" she screamed.

He took her arm. "Do what you're told, miss, or I'll put you over my knee and teach you some manners."

"Don't you dare." She wrenched free, ran into the kitchen and reappeared, an aluminum saucepan in her hand. "Just you come near me."

"Put that down, Paulie. Paulie, put that down."

She threw it down. It clattered on the linoleum of the hall. She turned, ran into the bathroom and locked the door. Ah, Dear God. Contrite, he went to the door and knocked on it. "Paulie? Now, listen Pet, listen to me —"

"I'm not your Pet. You're not going to bully me the way you bullied Mummy. I'll run off with somebody too. I can run off with Bruno. Just remember that."

Run off with Bruno? He felt dizzy. He backed away from the door and sat down on the first chair his hand touched. In his mind, a child's voice spoke: *Do you like*

big elephants best of all, or do you like horses best of all?
He remembered her asking that. Or: *Why do my dolly's
eyes stay open when she sleeps?* Conversations which
ended with him telling her something she did not know.
Now, she had told him something he did not know.

Paulie came out of the bathroom. She crossed the living
room. "I'm going to bed," she said. "Will you put the
lights out?"

He heard her shut and bolt her bedroom door. She too
could run off with some male. Once, if Daddy liked big
elephants best of all, then Paulie liked big elephants too.
But now . . .

He covered his eyes, his fingers pressing against his eyeballs until it hurt. Now, she was not his little Apple any
more. Big elephants were no longer relevant.

Eleven   Bells, calling to the noon mass in the Basilica, tolled out across the city in a clear and freezing tone,
waking him from an exhausted sleep into a world without
end, amen. Slowly they focused, the facts of his life. Someone lost, someone stolen, someone strayed. But the morning habit of a lifetime, kicking now with its head cut off,
must begin to balance the good with the bad. The habits
of an habitual ratiocinator must be fixed in hope. And so,
let's see. At least he had gained a little victory by running
away last night. At least, last night, he had had his eyes
opened to Paulie's true intentions. There was still time to
stop her running wild. And so . . .

And so, when the bells stopped tolling and the wor-
shipers went up the steps to pray, Ginger Coffey, with no
God in whom he could place his trust, placed it as he
must, in men. By ratiocination, MacGregor became his
hope. If he could last one more week, MacGregor had
promised to promote him. And once MacGregor promoted
him, as J. F. Coffey, Journalist, he would have time to
oversee and correct his daughter's upbringing. As J. F.
Coffey, Journalist, he would have a job he was proud of
at last. No glorified secretary, no galley slave, no joeboy;
but a Gentleman of the Press.

179

And so, he had been right to come to Canada, after all. He had picked a winner. In the winner's circle, by his habitual processes of ratiocination, he thought it natural that Veronica would salute his silks.

So, one-two-three, lift up your big carcass, you winner you. Up! And up he got, feeling a twinge in his left leg, going heavy and slow to the kitchen where Paulie was. He started right in.

"Hello, Pet. About last night. I mean, I'm sorry. Now, listen to me —"

The phone rang, postponing his armistice plans. He answered. It was Veronica. "Ginger? I want to know if I can come and see Paulie this afternoon."

"Of course you can," he said.

"But if I come I don't want any repetition of the last time. I want you to be out."

"Look," he said. "I have to have a chat with you."

"Why?"

"Well — Well, last night — I mean, last night I didn't go through with that business."

"You didn't? Why?"

"Well, I'll explain it to you when I see you. And I want to talk to you about Paulie."

"What about Paulie?"

"Little pitchers."

"Oh, don't be ridiculous," she said. "Have you had a row with her? Let me speak to her."

"No, wait, dear, I want to explain —"

"Let me speak to Paulie!"

He sighed, put the phone down and beckoned to Paulie who was listening at the kitchen door. He went into the kitchen and listened himself, trying to make sense of what was being said.

"No, Mother. . . . No. . . . We had a row last night.

. . . He hit me. . . . Yes, he did. Because, well, I'll tell you when I see you. . . . Yes, I'll come now."

Paulie came back into the kitchen. "Isn't your mother coming here?" Coffey said.

"No. I'm meeting her downtown for coffee. Now, if you'll excuse me, Daddy, I've got to get dressed."

She went out. He looked at the stove. For the first time since they'd been together, she hadn't made his Sunday breakfast. He got up, spooned a dollop of instant coffee into a cup and sat down again, waiting for the water to boil. A few minutes later he heard Paulie go out. He sat alone, thinking of her meeting Vera in some restaurant, knowing that, in their womany way, he would be blamed for all that happened last night.

Somewhere in the bowels of the apartment the furnace coughed and whirred into life. He drank his instant coffee. Upstairs, someone knocked on a radiator and the noise echoed down through the pipes to the basement. The whirring ceased. The furnace went off. Yes, it was hard to hope.

At ten minutes to two, the telephone rang. He expected it would be Grosvenor, asking why last night's plans had gone agley. But it was Veronica.

"Ginger," she said. "Paulie's just left and she's on her way home. I want to see you at once, it's very important. After what she's told me, you and I have to come to some decision."

"All right," he said.

"Can you come up to my room?" she asked.

"When?"

"Now. Paulie has a key, hasn't she? You don't have to wait for her?"

"No."

"All right then, hurry. Here's the address."

In his dreams which were not dreams, he had sometimes seen her room. She did not spend much time in it
but it was large and elegant, furnished with spindly Swed-
ish things and a large, un-slept-in bed. It was close to
Grosvenor's flat.

The reality was an Edwardian gingerbread house on
the dividing line between the English and French sections of the city, a slum whose sagging porches and bal-
conies were weighted with a winter's accumulation of
crusted, filth-spattered snow. The hallway was bare and
uncarpeted; the staircase supports were loose. Communal
cooking devices were placed on the landings and large
garbage pails stood sentinel at each turning of the stairs.

She lived on the third floor. She was waiting for him on
the landing as he came up, his face slapped red by the
cold, his car coat unbuttoned, his unhusbandly status
plain by the polite way he took off his little green hat as
he went to greet her. And she, still the stranger, wearing a
navy-blue dress and a white bead necklace, her stocking
seams straight. He thought how a certain kind of drunk-
ard hides signs of his failing in a meticulous attention to
dress. A certain type of lady hides her nights of orgy . . .

"Come on in," said the lady, without preamble. "I just
got back myself a minute ago. Mind that step."

Large? Modern? The room alarmed him. It was smaller
than the cell he had briefly occupied at the Y.M.C.A.
There was no closet, so her clothes were hung on hooks
all around the walls. The bed was an unwieldy double,
occupying two thirds of the floor space. There was a
small washbasin, its enamel browned with age. There was
a small window, its panes covered with diamonded paper.

Of course she was never here; of course she just used it as a place to keep her things. Why, then, were there tins of food under the basin? Why was there milk on the window sill, why those dishes stacked in a corner? He sat on the only chair; watched as she went to the mirror over the sink and unfastened her necklace. "Filthy place, isn't it?" she said. "They never clean it. I'm going to take my good dress off, if you don't mind. Oh, I'm in such a state about Paulie. I knew she was running around with boys. I just felt it."

Desirable stranger pulled the dress over her head. Her white slip rose also, revealing her stocking tops and garter straps. It was the beginning of one of his nightly scenarios. He put his little green hat between his feet. The floor was not clean. How could she stay so clean here?

"I gather his name is Bruno," she said, "and that he's a mechanic."

"He's a little thug," Coffey said. "And she's only a child."

"Well, that's got to stop," she said. "No two ways about it: that's stopping right now."

She went past him in her slip and reached behind the door for her dressing gown. It, at least, was familiar. He had bought it for her as a Christmas present one hundred years ago in a shop in Grafton Street. She sat on the bed, reaching across the bed for her cigarettes while he stood, enormous and clumsy, in the tiny, ill-lit room, his hand trembling as he held out a match flame.

"Thank you." She sucked in her cheeks, expelled smoke and leaned back on the pillows. She drew one knee up, lacing it with her joined hands. He looked at, then looked away from her bare white thigh, her tan stocking top. Whorish beauty, cover yourself! But oh! Wasn't that gesture of drawing one knee up, holding it in her hands, wasn't that familiar from the years he had known her? Of course it was. Then, why had he never really looked at her in all those years? Why was it so distracting now? He did not hear a word she was saying. He shifted in his chair, shamed and troubled by his desire.

". . . And supervision," she said. "No more leaving her alone every evening. So, what are we going to do about it?"

We. We is you and me. He looked again at the cans of food under the sink. Maybe his imaginings about her and Grosvenor had been only that? Maybe —

"Listen," he said. "If only you'd come back. I mean, even as a temporary arrangement until I get this new job. Listen, Vera —"

Listen? As he said the word, he saw her face. Of course she would not listen. As of old, she merely waited her turn to speak.

"For instance," he said. "Paulie's wearing lipstick and powder and her nails are orange. Now, I don't know about these things. She says the other girls in her class use them. How do I know?"

Veronica stubbed out her cigarette and turned her face against the pillows. "Oh God! It never changes, does it? Am I never to have any life of my own? The pair of you," she said, "you'd think you planned it. You can't look after Paulie, and of course she refuses to come and live with me. And of course, you won't go through with the divorce — oh, that would be too easy, that would be helping me, wouldn't it? And of course, Gerry can't wait forever."

She stubbed out her cigarette and sighed, a woman beyond all hope. "All right," she said. "I'll go back until you get this other job. All right. Oh, it would have been too much to expect that I'd have some life of my own after all these years wet-nursing the pair of you."

He avoided her angry eyes. He looked away and was

184

caught in another stare, that of his own image in the mirror above the sink. The mirror man was flushed and guilty. Well now, fellow, and do you hear that? She's coming back for a while. Not because she wants to come, mind you, but because she has to stop you messing up Paulie's life. Do you follow me there, my alter ego? Do you want her?

He looked at her. Yes, he wanted her, no matter what the terms.

"And if I *do* come back," she said, "it's temporary. I'm keeping my job on. And I'm to be in charge of Paulie. Do you understand?"

He nodded, all right.

"And another thing," she said. "I'd like to have my own room."

The mirror man watched his embarrassment. "There's ah — there's only two bedrooms," he said. "There are twin beds in my room."

She sighed in swift exasperation. "Oh well, I suppose we may as well get started. Get my suitcases, will you? They're under the bed."

The mirror man watched as he went down on his knees.

So, she came home. That night when he returned from his proofreading duties, he found her asleep in the twin bed next to his. Quickly he began to undress, remembering all the waking dreams of her absence, and in a few minutes, large, naked and vulnerable, he shyly approached her bed. He hesitated, then bent over and placed a bristly mustache kiss on the nape of her neck. Immediately — she could not have been asleep — she sat up and switched on the light. She stared at him. Naked, it was plain what ailed him.

"Go back to your own bed," she said.

"Ah now, Vera —"

"Either you go back to your own bed or I'll dress and leave tonight."

"Suffering J!" he said. But he went back to his own bed. He slept. He dreamed about her. And next morning awoke to a new torture. Covertly he watched as she got out of bed. She was wearing flannel pajamas which were not exactly Gay Paree but which nevertheless brought him to sudden desire. He turned towards her, the ends of his mustache lifting in a hopeful smile . . .

She stared him down. Without a word, she picked her clothes off the chair and went into the bathroom, leaving him alone, his desire drooping to a sadness. Unshaven and unfed (for she stayed in the bathroom) he fled to another day of diapers.

Still, wasn't it better to have her in the house, no matter how cold she was, than to torture himself with imaginings? Soon she'd thaw; the KEEP OFF THE GRASS signs would come down; Grosvenor would be forgotten. Soon they'd be friends again. Paulie would be friends with him too. Soon MacGregor would promote him. Soon everything would be all right. Soon . . .

Yes, he put all his hopes in one basket, an ancient basket by the name of MacGregor. That night, when he went to work at the *Tribune,* he attacked his galleys like a driven man. That night when MacGregor passed through on his usual sortie, Coffey looked up from the dirty steel desk, not in fear but in hope, proud of the great mass of corrected proofs on his spike, hoping MacGregor would see in him a man worthy of advancement.

But MacGregor did not single him out. MacGregor passed him by.

Ah well. Maybe tomorrow night?

Tomorrow was Tuesday. When he came back for his supper on Tuesday night, Veronica was not there. Nei-

186

ther was Paulie. Not that that made much difference, as Paulie hadn't spoken two words to him since her mother's return. Still, it couldn't last much longer, could it?

He went to work. Again he drove himself to produce the greatest number of corrected galleys. Again he lived in hopes. And Hooray! At a quarter to ten, just before the supper break, a copy boy came into the composing room and said Coffey was wanted at the city desk.

"Did you hear that?" Coffey said to Old Billy Davis. "The *city desk.* Ah, now, MacGregor isn't such a bad old basket after all. He's given the order and the city editor's going to find a spot for me."

Old Billy fingered his feathery goatee. "Just so long as it isn't trouble," he said. "Best you can hope for is keep out of trouble. Watch your step."

Poor old sausage, what would *he* know? In joyful disparagement, J. F. Coffey, Journalist, donned his jacket and hurried out into the great cavern of the city room, sure that now, his ship rounding the harbor bar . . .

False alarm. Leaning against a pillar a few steps from the city desk a visitor awaited Coffey. Waited, slightly disarranged as though the window dresser had gone to lunch and left him unfinished.

"Hi," he said. He turned towards the City Editor and said in a slurred, half-drunken voice: "Okay if I borrow this guy?"

"Go ahead, Gerry boy," the City Editor said.

Gerald Grosvenor waved his thanks, then, detaching himself from the pillar, came towards Coffey. "Come on in the cafeteria," he said. "I want to have a talk with you, Buster."

He was drunk, that was plain. Uneasily, Coffey accompanied him along the corridor to the cafeteria, praying that MacGregor would not spot them. Uneasily he waited as Grosvenor, after a noisy exchange of greetings with two reporters and the counterman, brought steaming mugs of coffee to the table. MacGregor had not yet paid his nightly visit; Coffey was supposed to be at his desk, not here. "Look," he said to Grosvenor. "I'm busy and it's not my supper time yet. Now, what is it?"

"Want to talk to you," Grosvenor said. "Just left Veronica half an hour ago. You bastard. You're crucifying that girl."

Uneasily Coffey looked around the cafeteria. The counterman was listening.

"Left her in tears," Grosvenor said in a loud voice. "At the end of her rope, see? Goddammit, I love that girl. And she loves me too. Yes, she does."

To Coffey's intense embarrassment, Grosvenor began to weep. Worse, Grosvenor did not seem to care who saw him. "What *are* you?" Grosvenor said tearfully. "A dog in the manger, or something? You're ruining Vera's life."

"Will you shut up?" Coffey whispered urgently. "Lower your voice and stop sniffling."

"Forcing her to come back," Grosvenor said. "Using your daughter as bait. Don't you see what you're doing to both of them? It's criminal."

"Shut up! Shut up, or I'll shut you up."

"No, I won't shut up. You're a menace, Ging'r, that's what you are. You're one of those guys, you don't care about anybody except yourself. Veronica hates your guts, you know."

"She does nothing of the sort," Coffey said, unwisely.

"No? Only went back because you were messing up Paulie's life, didn't she? That's what she said tonight. I mean —" and Grosvenor reached across the table, his hairy black hand gripping Coffey's wrist. "I mean, I'm not going to let you get away with this. I'm going to kill you, you sonofabitch."

188

Quickly, Coffey disengaged his wrist. Until now Grosvenor had been merely a lay figure in his imaginings, a self-important dummy which Veronica had picked to affront him with. But now, look at him. Weeping, revengeful, not ashamed to make a fool of himself for love's sake. Is this why Veronica loves him? Because he cares more about her than about himself, because, unlike me, he's prepared to weep in public? Suddenly — and for the first time — Coffey feared Grosvenor; feared the recklessness of Grosvenor's love.

"Now listen to me," he said, staring at Grosvenor. "Listen, now. Veronica's my wife and I intend to hold on to her. Get that straight. I'm a newcomer in a new country and I've had my troubles finding a spot, as who wouldn't? But things have changed. I'm on the right track now. I'm getting a better job soon and we're going to be all right, all of us. So bugger off, Grosvenor. I'm warning you, if I catch you hanging around Vera any more it's you that will be killed!"

"You don't scare me," Grosvenor said drunkenly. "You big Irish ape. You and Veronica are finished, do you hear? She loves *me*. She's coming back to *me*. Know what I'm going to do? I'm going to beat the piss out of you, Buster."

With that, Grosvenor stood up, wiped his wet eyes with the back of his hand and moved out from the table, spilling coffee from the untouched mugs. He stood in the aisle, raising his arms in the exaggerated stance of an old-style barearm boxer. Drunkenly he began to circle Coffey, who hesitated, embarrassed by the rapidly forming audience of reporters and copy boys, uneasily aware that MacGregor might walk in at any moment, yet itching to lay Grosvenor in his tracks.

"Come on," Grosvenor jeered. "Fight! I'm going to kill

you, you sonofabitch. Somebody should have done it long ago."

His face ruddy with anger, Coffey ducked the long loping clout which Grosvenor aimed at him. Then he moved in. He knocked Grosvenor's right arm aside and stiffened Grosvenor with a vicious punch in the mouth. Grosvenor stumbled, hit a chair and sat down in it, his hands going to his mouth. After a moment a trickle of blood ran down his wrists. He took his cupped hands away and stared into the bloody spittle in his palms. There were bits of teeth there. The spectators looked at Coffey with new respect and one of the older reporters came forward, blocking his path. "Hold on," he said. "Guy's hurt."

Coffey did not need the restraint. His anger bled to shame at sight of Grosvenor, pathetic and beaten, the underdog beloved by the crowd. Whereas he, the man with right on his side, stood convicted as a bully. He dropped his arms and, at that moment, as though announcing the end of the contest, the composing room bell rang in the corridor. Supper break. Now, it did not matter if MacGregor walked in. A victor, wanting the crowd to think him a good sport, he went over to Grosvenor and tried to help him up. "Come on," he said. "You're in no condition to fight. Better cut off home."

Grosvenor pushed him away. He stood up, watched by all the cafeteria customers and, staggering slightly, put his hand to his mouth as though he were about to vomit. He rushed into the corridor, Coffey following.

"Do you want to go to the Men's Room?" Coffey called after him. "It's the other way."

"Go to hell," Grosvenor mumbled. He lurched along the corridor, one hand over his mouth, the other fending the corridor wall away. At the end of the corridor a service elevator waited, its gate open, its operator squat on his little stool. Grosvenor lurched inside, then turned, looking curiously like a performer on a tiny, bright-lit stage. He pointed an accusing finger at Coffey. "You won't get her," he shouted. "She's coming to me. Irish Ape, you'll fail! She's mine, do you hear me? Mine!"

That crying voice, that bloodied mouth, that accusing finger, the sight of Grosvenor in the bright-lit elevator cage — all filled Coffey with an unreasoning dread. It was as though Grosvenor had formally pronounced a curse on him. And at that moment, MacGregor appeared, Jehovah at the far end of the corridor, attended by Clarence, his fat ministering angel. In sudden panic Coffey ran forward, tried to close the elevator gate.

"Take him down," he whispered to the operator. "Hurry, hurry —"

Startled, the elevator operator closed the gate. The elevator cage fell shuddering into the black shaft. Coffey turned and walked back up the corridor towards MacGregor, a man approaching the altar of his hope. Surely in this minute his luck must change? Surely in this very minute MacGregor would dispel the curse of Grosvenor's hate?

Clarence, riffling through his notebook, said: "Eleven hundred lines, sir."

"That's it," MacGregor said. "Shoe Week Convention. Tell the city desk to send a man to cover it. Good advertising tie-in."

"Yes, Chief," Clarence said.

Coffey was level with them now. He turned towards MacGregor, his face like a child's in its longing.

"A few wee features on the local page," MacGregor said. "To keep the advertisers happy."

"Right, Chief."

They passed him by. They had not seen him. He did not exist. *Irish Ape, you'll fail!*

191

That night when he got home, Veronica was sitting up in bed reading a book. "What did you do to Gerry?" she said.

"He started it. He came in drunk and acting like a blithering idiot."

"So you broke two front teeth for him?"

"That was an accident, dear. Besides, he asked for it."

"An accident?" she said. "Well, let me tell you, you're wasting your time."

"What do you mean?"

"I mean, hitting Gerry, what good's that going to do you? Gerry's more of a man than you'll ever be. Gerry loves me. That's why he was so upset tonight when I told him I'd have to stay here. That's why he got drunk."

Coffey began to undress.

"And another thing," she said. "I've no intention of staying here one minute longer than I have to. Today, I spoke to the mothers of those girls Paulie goes around with, and we're all going to make sure that gang of hoodlums are chased out. We're going to arrange more evenings at home for Paulie and the others. I can come over here two or three evenings a week and supervise. I don't have to live here all the time, just for that."

"Ah now, wait, Kitten — why, at the end of this week, I'll have that new job and maybe then we could —"

"New job," she said. "Oh, for God's sake!"

"No, I'm getting it, dear. Honestly."

"Want to bet?" She reached up and put the light off. "Good night," she said. "I have to work tomorrow."

Slowly, he finished undressing. He put on his pajamas. If she left now . . . He went over to her bed, sat on the edge, and put out his hand. It hovered over her, then settled on her shoulder. "Vera?" he said.

"What?"

192

"Vera, I know Grosvenor loves you. But I do too."

"Ha, ha!"

"Don't laugh, Vera. I do love you. Honestly I do."

"Listen to me," she said. "You don't know what love is. Just remember this, Ginger. Love is unselfish, it's doing things for other people and not asking them to do things for you. If you really loved me, you'd let me go. You'd give me a divorce. You'd think of my happiness and not your own. Gerry does. Now, go back to your own bed. Good night."

He stood up. Heavily he recrossed the room. He got into his bed and lay down on his side, looking at the darkness where she was. *Unselfish.* So that was what she wanted. Some proof of devotion greater than self. Was that the thing that would win her back? Was it? He rolled over and stared at the invisible ceiling. Love is unselfish. Was that what she had found lacking in his love for her? Was that why Grosvenor, weeping but prepared to wait, had won her instead? If only he could think this out. If only his brain could puzzle out what she had said and find the answer, that absolute answer he felt he had almost grasped.

It was tiring to think. He was not used to thinking in abstractions. But still — was selflessness what he lacked? Was *that* true love? Would the greatest proof of his love for her be his willingness to sacrifice himself, the way Jesus had sacrificed himself for mankind? Jesus considered that the highest form of love, didn't he? Well, there you are, then.

"Vera?" he said.

"Go to sleep."

"Listen, Vera," he said. "I've made up my mind. If I don't get that reporter's job at the end of this week, I'll bow out. If I don't get it, you can go back to Grosvenor and you can take Paulie. And I'll give you your divorce into the bargain. Now, isn't that unselfish of me? Isn't it?"

He waited for her answer. There was no answer. "I mean it," he said. He did mean it.

Twelve   Next morning he awoke on the cross of his
new obsession. He woke and went to work, a man who
had decided to gamble his all on one event. He started
fresh on that Wednesday morning, convinced that if he
got the job, all his worries would end. Veronica would
stay, Grosvenor would disappear, Paulie would be his
Apple again, his future would be assured.

And if he did not get the job? If he did not get the job
he would go down like a man. Lonely and proud, he
would cast himself adrift from all who knew him, his
boats burned forever. He would prove to her that he was
a man of his word, the most unselfish lover in all the
world, a man who could do a far, far better thing than
Grosvenor ever would.

Not that he thought he'd have to, mind you. No, he
was going to get the job, for sure. J. F. Coffey, Journalist,
Coffey of the *Tribune,* why that was only a matter of
days and hours now. And so, that Wednesday morning,
fixed on the cross of his obsession, he began to measure
off those hours. As he drove through the city delivering
diapers, his mind moved from hopes to *faits accomplis.* By
mid-afternoon he had convinced himself that he had no
time to lose. For, since he was getting this new job on

Friday next, he should be starting his preparations now, shouldn't he? Right, then. He had no time to lose.

At four-thirty that afternoon, his delivery route completed, he walked into the Tiny Ones depot and gave notice.

"What?" Mr. Mountain rose up in alarm, his great stomach overlapping the military array of folders on the desk. "What's the matter, Coffey, we not treating you right?"

"It's not that, sir. It's just that this other job is more in my line. The job with you was more or less a stopgap."

"Well, eff me," Mr. Mountain said. "Reporter, eh? What paper?"

"The *Tribune,* sir."

"The *Tribune,* eh?" Distractedly, Mr. Mountain ran four plump fingers through the soft thickness of his detergent-colored hair. "This puts me on a spot," he said. "What am I going to tell the boss?"

"What do you mean?"

"Well, this is strictly classified info, Coffey, but the fact is you're up for promotion."

"Oh?"

"Mr. Brott himself is interested. Told me to keep you happy. Said he was finding an office spot for you soon. It's going to reflect on my department, you walking out like this."

Now that was nice to hear, wasn't it? Damn right it was. He wished to goodness Veronica were in the room. They want to keep me on and promote me. Well Vera, what do you think of that?

"Look, I'm not unhappy with the job or with the way I've been treated," Coffey told Mr. Mountain. "I'll be glad to explain that to Mr. Brott, if you like."

"Tell you what," Mr. Mountain said. "I think this is a

case for top brass. Tell you what —" He paused, staring with great solemnity at Coffey. "I'm going to the boss himself!"

He picked up the phone, a man assuming command. "Wait outside," he said.

So Coffey stepped outside. In a moment or two, Mr. Mountain dashed to the door, beckoning him. "Wants to speak to you *himself*," he whispered. "Mr. Brott."

He handed Coffey the telephone. At the other end of the line a crackly, testy voice said: "That you, Coffey? A. K. Brott here."

"Yes, sir."

"What's this about quitting? Now, you listen to me. You come right over here. I want to talk to you."

"But I have to start my night job, sir, I wouldn't be able to manage —"

"What time do you start?"

"Six, sir."

"Give me Stan."

Coffey gave him Mr. Mountain. "Yessir," Mr. Mountain said briskly. "Right, sir. Roger, sir. Thank you, sir." He put the phone down. He picked up his hat, stared at Coffey with some distaste. "Get in my car," he said. "I've got to deliver you."

So they got in Mr. Mountain's car and drove up to the TINY ONES head office. There was no conversation en route: Mr. Mountain clearly believed this disruption in the chain of command to be above and beyond the call of duty. Coffey felt embarrassed. It was not Mr. Mountain's job to chauffeur him. Especially when it was all a waste of time.

Among the display of ex-voto scenes in A. K. Brott's office several advertising roughs were pasted on a board. They bore a vaguely familiar slogan:

RENT-A-CRIB SERVICE
Why Buy? We Supply
TINY ONES INC.

"That's right," Mr. Brott said, pointing to the board. "I checked into that idea, had a survey done and now I'm ready to go. That's what I want to talk to you about. What's this about you quitting?"

"I'm going to become a journalist, sir."

"Reporter?"

"Yes, sir."

"Never saw a reporter in this province you couldn't buy off for twenty bucks in a plain envelope. So, forget that. You're a smart fella, Coffey, and I'm going to make you a good offer. A once-in-a-lifetime offer — take it or leave it."

Coffey fiddled with his little green hat. Nice to know that old Brott thought well of him, but to tell the truth, if he never saw a nappy again, it would be far too soon. Still, it was a good omen, wasn't it? The tide was turning, his luck had changed and surely, surely, in less than forty-eight hours, MacGregor would come through and J. F. Coffey, Journalist, Coffey of the *Tribune* —

"Matter of fact, I should have acted sooner," Mr. Brott said. "Just goes to show, in things like this you've got to pee or get off the pot. So, okay. Here's what I'm going to do. I'll make you my personal assistant at ninety bucks a week."

Personal Assistant to the Managing Director of Kylemore Distilleries . . . Personal bumboy to old Cleery in the advertising . . . glorified secretary at Coomb-Na-Baun. Coffey stared at A. K. Brott's small gray face.

"No," he said in a strangled whisper.

"No? Look, what's the matter with you? *Personal Assistant*, do you realize the chance I'm giving you?"

198

"Do I?" Coffey echoed. "Fetch me this and fetch me that. Run down for cigarettes. Book me a table. I'm no glorified secretary, I'll have you know. I'm going to be a reporter by the end of this week."

"You're crazy."

"Ah no," Coffey said. "What do you think I came to this country for? Sure, didn't I leave a job as Personal Assistant in a far bigger company than this — this laundry will ever be? No thank you."

"Well, that's your mistake," Mr. Brott said, shaking his little gray head. "Rent-A-Crib — now there you were using your head, Coffey. When a guy gives me a worthwhile idea, I like to pay for it. As my assistant, you could have had yourself a nice steady job. Reporter? You're nuts. Come on now?"

"No," Coffey said. "I want to be a reporter."

"Well, it's your funeral," A. K. Brott said. "Sorry you feel this way. Stan?"

Mr. Mountain appeared in the doorway. "Yessir?"

"Stan, drive Coffey down to his newspaper. And get a replacement. He's quit us. Take him off the payroll."

"Roger Dodger," said Mr. Mountain.

Personal Assistant! It just showed you, unless you had the guts to believe in yourself, what you started off as you would wind up as, even over here. Thanks be to God he would never go back to that, thanks be to God he had the strength to refuse once and for all. Glorified secretary, indeed! Running errands now and forever more, amen. Ah, shove your bloody Personal Assistant once and for bloody all! Shove it!

"What's the matter with you? You look mad," Fox said.

"Nothing," Coffey said. "I was just thinking about something. I turned down a job today."

But Fox did not seem to hear. He fed two new galleys in Coffey's direction. "Let's get rolling," he said. "Old Billy Davis has reported sick tonight. We're a man short."

"What's the matter with Old Bill?" Kenny asked.

"A cold, he says."

Blast Old Billy, Coffey thought. What's he getting sick for when I need him here? But a cold was nothing. No need to panic, was there? Right, then. He picked up a fresh galley.

Next morning, Coffey broke the breakfast silence with an announcement. "This is my last day on the delivery job," he said.

"What happened?" Veronica wanted to know. "Did they lay you off?"

Now, wasn't that typical?

"They did not," he said. "I resigned. Matter of fact they offered to promote me and take me into the office. That's how well they think of me, if you want to know."

"And you *resigned?*"

"Too right, I did. I told you, I'm going on the editorial staff of the *Tribune* as of next week. Friday will be my last night in the proofroom."

"Honestly, Daddy?" Paulie said. It was the first direct word she had spoken to him in days.

"Yes, Pet. Word of honor."

"Oh, that's super," Paulie said, looking pleased. "Then you and I can go skiing. Remember, you promised?"

"Don't count your chickens," Veronica said to Paulie. "And hurry now, you'll be late for school."

Don't count your chickens . . . Wasn't that the height of her, putting the child against him every chance she got? But he would not let her annoy him. He went off to his last day of TINY ONES deliveries and spent it happily, settling up his accounts with the housewives on his route. Naturally, he told all his customers the good news. And the ladies were impressed. A reporter, now that was a glamorous job, one woman said. And another said he was a credit to his family. Yes, they congratulated him, wished him the best of luck and one or two of them even offered him a tip. Which was well meant, not mortifying at all; there was no harm in it. He took the money so as not to hurt their feelings and bought candies for all the little boys on his route.

At four sharp, he turned over his uniform, his accounts and his truck to Mr. Mountain. At four-thirty, after saying good-by to Corp and the other lads, he walked out of the depot, a free man. By six he was at the *Tribune*, ready for a good night's work, his hopes high, his obsession well stoked. And at five past six — hooray! Fox came in with a brand-new proofreader.

A new man. Coffey studied him. He was elderly, the new man. He wore long combinations under his rolled-up shirt sleeves and he read the first galley as carefully as if it were his own insurance policy. Ah, good man yourself, New Man. You'll do. A night to learn the ropes and Ginger Coffey will give you all the hand you want. And lend a hand he did, hitching his steel chair close to the new man's, keeping a brotherly eye on the new man's performance.

MacGregor came at ten, did not look at Coffey, examined the new man's work with his customary displeasure, said that Old Billy Davis was still sick, and passed on out of the composing room. Later, Fox told them that Old Billy had flu.

"Flu," Coffey said. "Sure, that's nothing."

"Old Billy's seventy-two, you know," Fox said.

Coffey put that worry out of his mind. Next morning, when he woke, he believed his only remaining trial was how to wait out the day. For it was Friday. *Mafeking Relieved. Irish Guards Pull Out.* He lay late, listening to the indistinct mumble of his womenfolk in the kitchen, half wishing that he had a day of diaper deliveries to occupy him until the news came through this afternoon.

At half past eight, just before she left for work, Veronica put her head in the bedroom door. "Isn't today the day you expect to be promoted?" she said.

"Didn't I tell you it was!"

"You did, Ginger. You also made a promise to me the other night in bed. Do you still feel that way?"

"You never even answered me the other night," he said, reproachfully.

"What was the use answering you, when you'll renege on it for certain."

"Did I say I'd renege on it?" he asked her.

"Well — are you going to?"

"I am not," he said. "As I told you the other night, if I don't get that job today you can have your divorce and Paulie and all the rest of it. I'll show you who's selfish!"

"Do you mean that, Ginger? Honestly and truly?"

"I do," he said. "But I *am* getting the job, don't forget. It's promised."

"All right. I was only asking. I wanted to see if you were serious."

She went out. He lay for a while, thinking of their exchange. Wasn't that women for you, never letting on they heard a word and then, two days later, coming out with the whole thing. So she thought he'd renege, did she? Well, he'd show her. Not that he'd have to, of course. Of course not.

He lay abed, listening as Paulie left for school in her usual, late-flying rush. Then he got up, shaved and dressed with the care of a man preparing for some court function. His only worry, as he saw it, was how to wait until four. At four, the night staff were entitled to go and pick up their pay checks. And as all staff changes were reported on payday in the pay office, Hennen would know. But, flute! It was a long, long morning.

At a quarter to four, having already waited fifteen minutes in the corridor, Coffey went into the *Tribune* business office and idled by the cashier's wicket, trying to catch Mr. Hennen's eye. Mr. Hennen, an old bird in his cage, busied himself with his ledgers, aware of Coffey, but determined to make him wait each agonizing second until the hour. The office clock's second hand circled, the minute hand jerked up one black notch, the hour hand moved imperceptibly closer. At the precise moment that all three reached the hour, Coffey stepped up to the wicket. Mr. Hennen laid down his pen, fussed with his black sleeve protectors and looked in Coffey's direction. "Name?" he shouted.

"J. F. Coffey."

Mr. Hennen riffled through a sheaf of pay checks and slipped one through the wicket. "Don't spend it all at once," he said.

"By the way — I — ah — I wonder if you'd have a note about a staff change?" Coffey said. "A transfer for me?"

Mr. Hennen cocked his old parrot head to one side. "Transfer?" He opened another ledger and took out four little yellow slips. He riffled through them. "These here are all the new staff changes. Your name's not in."

"Perhaps it hasn't come down yet?"

"All changes came in at noon. So it won't be for next week, fella."

"But Mr. MacGregor promised me . . ."

"Did he now?" Mr. Hennen said, and winked.

Coffey turned from that wicked parrot eye, afraid. What did that wink mean? Surely . . .

"Hey, wait a minute," Mr. Hennen said. "One of your fellas is sick. Phoned up, wants someone to take his check over to him. Let's see. Davis is the name. Want to take it to him?"

Old Billy. *There* was the reason he had not been promoted. That was what Mr. Hennen knew and had not said. Coffey went back to the wicket, heartsick with anger against old doddering Bill. Why did he have to get sick this week, of all weeks? It was not fair. Bloody Old Bill! "All right," he said. "I'll take it to him."

Mr. Hennen passed over an addressed envelope and Coffey went out into the streets again. Bill's place was a room over a small clothing store, in a street three blocks from the *Tribune* offices. The landlord, an aged French-Canadian who spoke no English, looked at W. DAVIS on the pay envelope, then nodded and led Coffey up the back stairs to a door at the end of a dark corridor. Coffey knocked.

"Come in," an old voice called.

The room reminded Coffey of Veronica's, but there was a difference. Old Billy had lived here a long time. There was a small electric hotplate, an old icebox, a green card table on which a large orange cat licked its paws. The walls were shelved with many books in fruit-crate containers. There were several snapshots on the walls, and an ingenious device of extension cords and three-way plugs so that Old Billy could turn on and off the lights from any chair or corner. On the bed lay the master of the room, his frail body invisible beneath a heap of quilts, his plumy goatee jutting upwards in the direction of the water-stained ceiling. "It's Paddy, isn't it?" he said. "Did you bring my check, Paddy?"

Coffey removed a fold-up chair from the stack beside the card table. The cat made a hissing noise of dislike. The chair had not been opened for many a year; dust lay thick in its crevices; its hinged joints were stiff. He put it at the head of the bed and sat down. He handed over the envelope.

Frail old fingers fumbled with the flap. "Full check," Old Billy said. "Didn't dock me sick pay, I see. Good. And how are you, lad? What's new?"

Coffey did not answer. He looked at the old man's arm, protruding from a worn pajama sleeve. On the skeletal wrist was a faded tattoo. A harp, a shamrock and a faint script: ERIN GO BRAGH. Above this tattoo was another, a heart pierced by an arrow, and entwined with a motto: BILL LOVES MIN.

"Are you Irish, Billy?" Coffey said. "That harp?"

"Course I'm Irish," Old Billy said. "William O'Brien Davis. Fine Irish name."

"But you were born over here?"

"No, sir. I'm an immigrant, same as you. Donegal man, born and bred. Came out here when I was twenty years old, looking for the streets that were paved with gold." Billy's mouth opened in a chuckle, showing his hard old gums. "Yes," he said. "I've been all over, Atlantic to Pacific and back again. Been north of the Circle too, and down south as far as the Gulf of Mexico. Yes, I been all over the States; seen them all, all forty-eight. Never found any gold streets, though. No sir."

But Coffey did not join in the old man's laugh. He stared at that skeletal forearm. BILL LOVES MIN. Where and in what long ago had Bill loved Min? Where was Min now? How many years had Old Bill lain here in this room, watched over only by the inhuman, unblinking eyes of his orange cat?

"Yes, all I got to show now is forty dollars a month on the Old Age pension," Bill said. "A man can't live on that nowadays. Even me, and I don't hardly eat but a bowl of Campbell's Soup once a day. And beer. Beer's what keeps me going. That's why this proofreading job was such a blessing. Lots of beer."

"But you still have the proofreading job," Coffey said. "We've been expecting you back tonight."

"Not tonight," Old Billy said. He touched his chest. "Got something in here, the doctor says. I've got to rest."

"But you'll be back," Coffey said. "In a day or two—"

"It was the *Tribune* doctor who saw me," Old Bill said. "They have my number. Hear they hired a new man already."

"The new man's not a replacement for you," Coffey said. "He's my replacement. They're making me a reporter next week. Now, listen, Bill. Tonight, I'm going to see MacGregor. I'll tell him you'll be back in a day or two. You'll be up and about in no time."

The old man's eyes had closed. He appeared to be sleeping.

"Bill, listen?" Coffey said. "Bill, are you asleep?"

"Plenty of time to sleep," the old voice said. "Not much else to do but sleep when you're living on the Old Age. Be all right, though. I've got all my things here. Bowl of soup, that's good enough. And a beer. The odd beer . . ."

His toothless mouth remained open on that sentence. His hand, holding the pay check, slid over the quilt and bumped against Coffey's knee. The envelope fell on the floor. Carefully, Coffey picked it up and put it on the card table. Carefully, he leaned over the old face. Yes, Bill was asleep.

"I'll be back, Bill," Coffey said in a whisper. He lifted up the skeletal arm, covered it with the quilt. Yes, J. F. Coffey, Journalist, would come back; oh yes, Billy, I promise you, I'll come back every week, I won't forget you. I'll bring beer. Every time, a case of beer.

But would he? Another promise. Would he Judas Old Billy along with the rest of them? For Old Billy might not come back to work. Old Billy might never be back. Coffey tiptoed to the door, opened it with infinite precaution, and went out into the dark corridor.

Irish. *An immigrant, same as you.* A young wanderer, once, traveling through this land of ice and snow, looking for the bluebird. ERIN GO BRAGH. But was it really ERIN FOREVER? What trace of Erin was left on William O'Brien Davis save that harp and shamrock, that motto, faded as the old reminder that BILL LOVES MIN? Would Ginger Coffey also end his days in some room, old and used, his voice nasal and reedy, all accent gone? "Yes, I'm Irish. James Francis Coffey. Fine Irish name."

No, no, that wasn't going to happen to him. Not to J. F. Coffey, Journalist. Never mind Old Billy, he was going to get that reporting job. Tonight he was. It was all arranged. He wasn't going to wait for MacGregor to speak to him, he must speak to MacGregor himself, remind him — yes, MacGregor was a busy man, it might have slipped his mind. And a promise is a promise. So, all right then. See MacGregor.

Because it was pay night, Fox and the others had spent their usual two hours in the tavern before coming to work. This meant that only Coffey and the New Man were not under the weather. So Coffey read the major number of galleys before the first edition. He and the New Man were working at the same desk, sober men and true. Ah,

New Man! Good man yourself. You front-line troop relief!

At ten, when supper bell sounded, MacGregor had not put in an appearance. Coffey could wait no longer. He went to the office. But MacGregor was in conference with the telegraph editor, which meant that Coffey had to wait in the corridor until ten past ten. At last, when the telegraph editor went out, in went Coffey.

"What do you want?" MacGregor said.

"It's the two weeks, sir. It's up, as of tonight."

"What two weeks?"

You see! It *had* slipped MacGregor's mind; so it was a lucky thing Coffey had decided to take the bull by the horns, wasn't it? Glad that he had come, he spoke up. "You remember, sir, about making me a reporter? You promised two weeks ago."

"Aye," MacGregor said. "Well, we're still short-staffed in the proofroom, as you know. Man sick."

"Yes, sir. But I went to see Old Billy Davis today and he's feeling much better. He'll be back to work in a day or two at the latest. Now I wondered, in view of that, perhaps you'd make the change now and start me off as a reporter next week?"

"No."

"But I've been expecting it," Coffey said, feeling his face grow hot. "I've been counting on it, sir. I hardly think it's fair."

"Fair? What? What the hell are you talking about? Now go on — take your arse out of here before I kick it out."

"No!" Coffey said, in a sudden shocked rage. "You made me a promise. I've been working like a bloody slave for the past three weeks in hopes of this. I gave up another job because of it. I promised my wife and daughter. You don't know how much this means to me, sir. It's very important."

"Clarence?" MacGregor shouted. The fat man rushed in, notebook at the ready. "Now, Coffey," MacGregor said. "Tell it to us again."

"You promised me," Coffey said, feeling his tongue thick and confused. "You promised that you'd promote me as soon as you had a replacement in the proofroom. Well, that new proofreader's been here three days now. He's a good man too."

"What new reader?"

"Rhodes, sir," Clarence said. "Replacement for old Davis."

"But Billy's coming back," Coffey began. "He needs the job. You're not going to throw him —"

"Doctor said bronchial trouble, sir," Clarence told his chief.

"Aye." MacGregor nodded his head. "Bronchial trouble. He won't be back."

"But you promised me." Coffey turned to Clarence. "You were here. You heard him."

"I don't recall any promise," Clarence said.

"Aye," MacGregor said. "Go on back to your desk, Coffey."

"No, it's not fair! Dammit, is that the way you keep your word?" Coffey shouted.

"Perhaps I'd better phone the lobby, sir," Clarence said. "And ask them to send Ritchie up."

Ritchie? Ritchie was the doorman. A blackness sealed Coffey's eyes. For a moment he stood, dizzy, their voices fading in his ears. Doorman? To throw him out?

". . . had quite enough of this," MacGregor's voice said. "Now go on back to your wurrk or you'll not be paid."

"That's it, fella," Clarence said. A hand took Coffey's arm. "Come on, now."

"No," Coffey said. "Dammit, no!"

"Listen to me, you." The blackness cleared from in front of Coffey's eyes and he saw MacGregor leaning across the desk. A large blue vein pumped in MacGregor's pale, bony skull. "If you think I have any notion of making you a reporter after the way you carried on tonight, you're sadly mistaken. Now, get back to that proof desk and thank your stars I don't kick your arse right out of this building. Is that clear?"

Clear? He shook himself free of Clarence's arm. He turned back into the corridor. The composing room bell shrilled, calling the readers back to work. Dazed, he walked towards the sound of the bell.

The new proofreader, Mr. Rhodes, was surprised at the difference in the Irishman's behavior when the Irishman came back from his supper break. Until now he had thought of the Irishman as the hardest-working, most respectable man on the shift, the only one you would not be ashamed to introduce to your friends. Obliging, sober, well-spoken, not cursing and half drunk like the rest of these bums.

Mr. Rhodes was on pension from the railroad and had only taken this job to help his wife make payments on a little place they were buying up North. He had been unpleasantly surprised by the class of man he found himself working with, and, in fact, would have resigned the second night had it not been for the Irishman's helping hand and courtesy. But now, when the big fellow came back and sat down at the desk beside Rhodes, he began to show signs that he might be every bit as unstable as the others. For one thing, he hardly did a tap of work for the rest of the shift. He sat there, his face like a wooden idol, muttering filthy language under his breath. Had he too been drinking, Rhodes wondered? Indeed, it would be no surprise, for in all Rhodes's years in the railroad's ac-

210

counting department, he had never met such a low class of man as Fox or Harry or that young lad with the eczema. So at the end of the night's work, when he heard the big fellow say that he would go out for drinks with the rest of them — well, thought Rhodes, I was mistaken, he's a bum like the others. No money was worth it, to be forced to spend your retirement years in the company of men like these. No. Next Friday, Rhodes decided, I'll give notice.

"Come on, Paddy," Harry said. "We have a jug at Rose's place."

They stood on the steps of the *Tribune* building. Down the street, brightlit in the night silence, a sign winked on and off. FIVE-MINUTE LUNCH. "Rose?" Coffey said.

"Rose of the rosy teats," Fox shouted. "Come on, lads."

The Five-Minute Lunch was open all night. There, under the rumble of transcontinental trains leaving on track, arriving on track, gathered a nightly cross-section of city owls. Bus drivers on the late trick, their change machines extracted and placed carefully beside their coffee and eggs; colored sleeping car porters from the railroad terminus across the street, magpie collections of abandoned newspapers and magazines stuffed in the handles of their overnight bags; consumptive-looking French-Canadian waiters stealing a break from the boredom of fifth-rate nightclubs; middle-aged whores, muffled in babushkas, snow boots and sensible wool scarves, condemned by the winter to come in often out of the cold; night postal clerks; ticket collectors; cleaning men. And behind the long mica-and-chrome serving-counter, under framed, hand-lettered cards — WESTERN SANDWICH, KNACKWURST & BEANS, SPAGHETTI & MEATBALLS — the queen of this night hive moved, never off her paining feet, never hurried, never done. Rose Alma Briggs.

211

"Rosy, dear," Fox said, rapping his cane on the counter.

Rose sent two eggs, sunny side up, flipping onto a plate. She turned, acknowledged the greeting with a nod. She was powdered and clean; she wore a white nylon coat, white rubber shoes and white lisle stockings. Under the transparent coat, a white slip. And biting tight into the soft pink flesh of her fat soft shoulders, white straps like tiny tent ropes converged to a double support of the mammary mountains trembling in bondage underneath.

"Evening, Mr. Fox. What'll it be?"

"Ever practical," Fox said. "We will have the usual. Three times. This is our co-worker, Mr. Coffey."

"Pleased to meet you," Rose said. She opened a glass jar, removed three pickled eggs, put three slices of rye bread on three plates; then, turning again, looked at Coffey. "What's the matter with him?" she asked Fox.

"He needs cheering, that's all," Fox said. "Go, lovely Rose, bring us that which cheers and doth inebriate."

"Now watch yourself," Rose said. "The Provincials was in here last night. They'll be back."

"We'll wu-watch it," Harry assured her. "Give us tu-two cu-Cokes to color it."

From beneath the counter, Rose took a large paper bag, added two Coke bottles to its contents, and handed the bag to Harry. Fox led the way into a small back room near the toilet. The bag was opened and a large bottle was placed on the table. The label read: *Vin Canadien-Type-Sherry*. Fox uncorked it and drank several swallows. "Now, Harry," he said. "Pour the Cokes in. And if any policeman pays a call we are enjoying the pause that refreshes. Right?"

"Right," Harry said. The Cokes were added and full glassfuls distributed. "Du-drink up," Harry said.

Coffey picked up his drink. It tasted sweetish but not

212

strong. He drank it down and poured another. Yes, what matter if he got drunk? Drink and these companions would be his future life. Down, down, down, all his boats burned. He had failed. Now he must do a far, far better thing . . .

"Count your blessings," Fox told him. "Think of Old Billy. You have your health and strength."

He drank a third glass, not listening. Alone he would be, an ancient mariner who had looked for the bluebird. He would grow a feathery goatee, his voice would change, nasal and reedy. Old Ginger Coffey, fifty years a reader, a man in humble circs. He stared through the open doorway at the customers in the outer room. Humble circs, all of them. How many of them had dreamed, as he had once, of adventures, of circs not humble in the least? And what had happened to those dreams of theirs? Ah Dear God, what did you do when you could no longer dream? How did you reconcile yourself to those humble circs? "Suffering J," he said. "So this is what it's like."

"What *what's* like?" Fox said, pouring.

"The bottom. The dustbin. The end of the road."

"Bottom?" Fox shouted. "Why, you don't know what bottom is, Paddy. Now, take me. Three years ago you could find me up the street outside Windsor Station, panhandling dimes at two in the morning. Without an overcoat, mind you, and the weather at zero. That's bottom, Paddy. Bottom is a dime. A dime and a dime and a dime until you can buy your peace of mind in the large jug of Bright's Hermitage Port. Bottom is when your clothes are too far gone for anyone not to notice, and there's no chance of a job because they do notice. Bottom is that, Paddy. Not this. Why, this is regular employment."

"Bottom's when you lose your wife," Coffey said thickly. "That's bottom. Bottom's when bloody liars make promises and bloody wife-stealers run off with your wife. Bottom's this bloody country, snow and ice, bloody hell on earth —"

"Yu-you leave Cu-Canada out of this," Harry said menacingly. "Gu-goddamn immigrants. Go on back where you came from."

"No, we have room for all sorts," Fox said. "We're the third largest country in the world, remember. We need our quota of malcontents."

"I'm sorry," Coffey said thickly. "Didn't mean to insult you fellows. Thinking about my wife. Not Canada. Leave Canada out of this."

"He doesn't want to talk about Canada," Fox said. "Leave Canada out. There you have the Canadian dilemma in a sentence. Nobody wants to talk about Canada, not even us Canadians. You're right, Paddy. Canada is a bore."

"No, I didn't mean that," Coffey said. "I'm just — listen, I've just lost my wife. And my little girl. Lost them."

But Fox was not listening. "Poor old Canada," he wailed. "Not even a flag to call its own. Land of Eskimo and Mountie, land of beaver and moose —"

Coffey poured another glass and tried to stand up. Suffering J, what was in this wine, what's the matter? His legs felt like melting wax. How could he go home tonight to tell her that he would keep his word? How could he make his lonely exit in dignity, and him half drunk? Ah, dear God —

"Sit down," Fox shouted.

He turned towards the shouting voice, confused. "Must go," he said.

"Sit down!" Fox's cane caught him a smart blow behind his woozy knees and Coffey sat down. "I'm speaking to you, you bogman, you!" Fox shouted.

In trembling pain Coffey leaned across the table, inches

from his tormentor's stubbled face. Cruel cripple doomsayer! He bunched his fist, raising it to strike that yelling mouth —

"Now don't hit me. Don't!" Fox shouted.

Dully, Coffey lowered his fist. At once Fox picked up the wine jug, swinging it in a menacing sweep. "Don't you dare walk out on me," he yelled. "I can't stand people walking out on me!"

White shoes, soundless on their rubber soles, moved up behind Fox. Rose Alma Briggs deftly caught the swinging jug. "That's enough of that," she said.

"Oh, Rose of all the world," Fox shouted. "Go, lovely Rose."

Rose moved behind him, reached under his armpits, set him tottering on his feet. "Out," she said. "That's an order. And this is the last time you use my place as a wine drop, any of you. Come on, Harry. Help him."

For an instant Fox's glazed eyes grew bright with rage. He gripped his cane, raising it like a club; held it suspended over the table for a moment, then lowered it. "No," he said. "No violence. No police. No doctors. Give me liberty or give me death, right, Rose? Yes, Rose. Yes, all. Good night, all."

Harry took his arm. Together they threaded their way among the tables of the outer room. The street door opened with a huff of wind, then banged shut as the drunkards met the winter snow, circling like lost birds on the pavement. Rose Alma turned to Coffey. "Poor man," she said. "He was in the asylum, you know. Dee-Tees." She bent and began to stack the dishes on the table. "You don't want to get mixed up with the likes of them. They're winos."

Coffey felt for a chair and sat down. His legs were trembling, the sweat on his brow was cold, his head felt swollen and heavy. "Not mixed up," he said drunkenly. "This job — just a stopgap, you see. I'm a New Canadian, you see."

Rose looked at him. "You married?"

"Yes."

"Well, why don't you go home to your wife then? It's late."

He put his hands up; felt his face fall into them. He rested his face in his hands. "My wife's leaving me," he said.

"No wonder," Rose said, "if you carry on like this."

"I didn't carry on. She did."

"Maybe she had a reason; did you ever think of that? Now, go on home."

He raised his face from his hands. Two Rose Almas stacked dishes, side by side. "A reason?" he said.

"Carrying on like this," said the double images of Rose. "You men. Do you know what women have to put up with? Now, go on home."

"Home?" he said. "I have no home," he told them.

"Where do you sleep then?"

"In my own bed. Not allowed in hers, you see."

"Come on now." The two Roses came close to him. "This way."

They raised him up. He tried to focus on the outer room. There were twins of all the customers. He rubbed his eyes, trying to make them come together, but they, like Rose, remained bifocal. "Come with me," Rose said. "Watch out for those girls over there. You don't want to get in trouble, now do you?"

"What girls?" he said. "Where girls?"

Rose took his arm, led him across the room, past the whores' table. "Have a girl," he said. "My own little girl. Going to lose her now."

"No, you won't," Rose said. "Now, come on. Bus stop's right across the street. You got a ticket?"

He nodded, not hearing, hearing only words.

"You'll feel better tomorrow," her voice said. "Things will look better then."

"No." He stopped, turned to her, his face pale and confused. Behind that large trembly dignity, behind that military façade of mustache and middle age, Rose Alma saw his true face. Like a boy, she thought. Lost.

"Never better now," he mumbled. "Got to give them up . . . promised . . . word of honor . . . word — of — honor. My Paulie too. Growing up. Trouble with boys. I — made mess that too."

"Never mind," Rose Alma said. "They need you. Go home."

She opened the café door and suddenly he faced the street. A gust of wind struck a nearby rooftop, whirling a powdery gust down to blind him, covering his mustache and eyebrows with a fine white granulation. Aged white in one moment, old Coffey crossed the street, stumbling over a snowbank, headed for two street lamps, each labeled with a tin sign: BUS. BUS. He was going home, wake Veronica, renounce her and then, lonely, his barque cast adrift, he would leave again, going into the Arctic night, condemned forever to this land of ice and snow, this hell on earth, alone forever in his Y.M.C.A. room . . .

He tried to focus down the street, looking for a bus. No bus. Instead, a huge trailer truck came uphill, red warning lights aflicker, a groaning giant condemned to move at night. It drew near and, bifocally, two tiny drivers looked down on Coffey from their high-riding cabs.

The driver looked out, saw the man standing under the lamp, tiny green hat snow-matted, his mustache and eyebrows white, peering up, a lost drunk night-face. The great truck rode on.

A night wind crossed the frozen river, whirled along the empty ice-locked docks, rushed into the street. Coffey bent his head to the wind and, cold, confused, began to feel a natural urge which would not wait. The street was quiet. Only in the Five-Minute Lunch was there light. Still trying to focus, he peered at the buildings on his side, looking for a lane. There was no lane. But there was a large darkened doorway, some office building entrance, he thought, and there, unable to wait any longer, he stepped into the shadows.

A police prowl car turned the corner from the railroad goods depot behind the station, its tires noiseless in the thick night snow. In the front seat, two uniformed constables looked over at Rose's place, then swept their searchlight beam along the front of the hotel opposite. The constable who was not driving rolled down the window and stopped the searchlight glare on what he saw. In the main doorway, legs apart, head bent in humble concentration, a man.

"*Tu vois ça?*" the constable said to his colleague.

"*Calvaire!*" the driver said, revving his engine.

Coffey, fumbling to adjust his dress, heard the engine sound. Still blinded by the harsh eye which had picked him out, he did not see the constable but felt a hand touch his elbow.

"*Viens ici, toi,*" the constable said.

"I — what?"

The constable did not reply, but led him towards the waiting prowl car. The other constable sat quiet at the wheel.

"What do you think you're doing?" the first constable asked.

Coffey told him. "Just waiting for the bus, waiting a long time, you see, so I had a call of nature. I mean, there was nobody —"

218

"You hadmit the oohfense?" the second constable said in a strong French-Canadian accent.

"Well now, look here —"

"Where do you work?"

"The *Tribune*."

Constable One looked at Constable Two. This was a matter for caution. Police and press relations. "What do you do there, sir?" said Constable One.

"Proofreader. Galley slave."

"*C'qu'il dit?*" the second constable asked the first.

"*Zéro,*" said the first.

"He's been drinkin' the wine," the second constable said, sniffing Coffey.

"Well, I was with some friends — Look here, officer — Ah now, for the love of God, man, be fair. I'm not drunk."

"Get in the car."

"Ah now, we don't have to do that, we can settle this, can't we?"

The first constable seized Coffey's left wrist and jerked it up against his back, bending Coffey double. In that way he was led towards the car. "Get in!"

So he got in and the first policeman got in the back beside him. The car started its engine, the police radio crackled and the driver made a report to radio control as they drove through the deserted streets. The report was in French, so Coffey did not understand it.

At the police station they made him wait. He sat on a bench, staring at a room full of two-headed policemen. Veronica must not know. Paulie must not know. Must get out of this. Just a fine or a warning, probably. Now see here, Sergeant . . . Reason with them. Och, now, listen to me sergeant, married man, little girl and wife, one over the eight, no harm meant, *hmm?*

But still . . . there were so many tabloid weeklies in this cursed city. Suppose it were reported in one of them. All full of rape they were, and other sexual misdemeanors . . .

He exhaled, feathering up the ends of his large mustache. *IMMIGRANT CHARGED WITH DISORDERLY CONDUCT*. A nice thing for Paulie to see. Nice thing indeed. Flute! You're not going to let that happen, are you? Not likely. He'd give a false name, that's what he would do. False name, that was the ticket. With any luck he'd get a fine and be home by morning. Right, then!

The double images had diminished to single ones by the time he was called up to the sergeant's desk. "Name and address?" said the sergeant.

"Gerald MacGregor," Coffey said, and gave the address of Madame Beaulieu's duplex.

The desk sergeant started a long conversation in French with the radio car officers. They reached an agreement. "Okay," the sergeant said to them. He turned to Coffey. "We're not booking you on a vag," he said. "We're going to book you for indecent exposure. That's the charge."

"Wait a minute, sergeant," Coffey said. "Couldn't we settle this here — it was all an accident. A mistake."

"Now, put all what's in your pockets in this bag," the sergeant interrupted.

"Ah now, wait sergeant —"

"And take your tie off."

"Ah, sergeant, ah now, listen, I'm an immigrant here, I didn't know it was any crime —"

"And give me your belt."

"Sergeant, did you hear me? Listen — I'm a married man with a little girl. Ah God, you've no right to enter a thing like that in the record."

220

"Prends-lui," the sergeant said to the jailer. *"Numéro Six."*

The jailer took him in the back and led him down a flight of stairs. A detective was coming up. They stopped to let him pass. The detective, a fat young man with a crew cut and a mustache almost as large as Coffey's, stopped and said: *"Le gars, c'qu'il a fait, lui?"*

The jailer laughed. *"A fait pisser juste dans la grande porte du Royal Family Hotel."*

"Oh-hoh!" the detective said, grinning at Coffey. "What's de matter? You don' like the English, eh? Or the Royal Family? Or maybe you just don' like the hotel?"

"What — what do you mean?" Coffey said. "What does he mean?" he asked the jailer.

"Move your ass," the jailer said. He pushed Coffey towards the last flight of steps, led him along a corridor and unlocked the door of a cell. There were two men sleeping inside. Coffey, undignified, holding up his trousers with both hands, made one last appeal to justice. "Listen to me," he said. "Please, will you let me speak to the sergeant again?"

"Don' piss on de other boys in here," the jailer said, shoving him in. "Dey won' like it."

The cell door shut. The lock turned. The jailer went back upstairs. Sick, Coffey let his trousers sag as he groped for and found a bench. He sat down, hearing the harsh cough of his cellmate. The cell was clean but stank of beer or wine or something. Or, was it he who . . . ? He did not know. One floor above him he heard the policemen walking about, talking, laughing at an occasional sally or bit of horseplay. Up there, just one flight of stairs, men were free. While down here — Oh God! Childish memories of being shut in a closet, of calling out to playmates who had run away, of beating on the door, unanswered: these swam in on him now, making it impossible to say Chin up, Steady as she goes, or any of the rest of it. Ever since he could remember he had read of prison sentences in secret dread. *Jail.* Yes, they could send him to jail. O God, he prayed. . . .

O Who? What did God care, if there were a God? Or was it God who had pulled the rug out, once and for all, who had now decided to show him once and for all that he had been a lunatic to have hopes, that his ship would never come in, that he had lost his wife and child forever?

Steady. Steady as she goes, he told himself. Don't panic. Steady on there.

But it was no good. Upstairs, the policemen broke out another round of laughter. He put his face in his hands, his lower teeth biting into the hair on his upper lip. Ah no, no, there was no sense blaming a God he could not believe in, there was no sense blaming anyone. Vera was right. *He was to blame.* If he had been content with his lot at home, he would never have come out to this cursed country. If he had never come out here, he would not have lost Veronica to Grosvenor; Paulie would not be running around with young hoodlums older than she. If he had not come out here, he would not be a proofreader with no hope of advancement, he would not be in jail tonight. Why hadn't he gone straight home? Whose fault was it he was drunk? His fault.

Yes, his fault. What a bloody fool he had been giving that wrong name and address. They had put his belongings in a bag but if they looked in his wallet they would crucify him. He should call out now, go upstairs, apologize, get a lawyer, tell them his real name . . .

He went quickly to the cell door and peered out of the small Judas window at the corridor. The window was thick-glassed, with a wire netting grille. He could see no one. He stepped back, trying to peer sideways down the corridor and, as he did, he saw his own face, angled in the reflection from the glass pane. He stared at that sad impostor, at that hateful, stupid man. Yes, look at you, would you? You that promised you would drop out of sight. You that would do a far, far better thing, look at you! What sort of man would call out now, what sort of man would disgrace Veronica and Paulie because he was afraid of being locked up?

He stepped back into the darkness of the cell again. He could not bear to look at that hateful, stupid man. He was not that man. He was Ginger Coffey who had given a false name to protect the innocent and now must take his punishment.

He sat down, his trousers loose around his hips. It was dark. He was afraid.

But oh! He knew something now, something he had not known before. A man's life was nobody's fault but his own. Not God's, not Vera's, not even Canada's. His own fault. *Mea culpa.*

Thirteen   Shortly after dawn someone in a nearby cell began to beat on the door and call out in French. This woke everyone up. The jailer came downstairs, unlocked the cell and led the prisoner out. One of Coffey's cellmates wiped his nose on his sleeve and said: "They never learn."

"What d'you mean?"

"They'll take him up in the back room now and tire him a bit."

"Oh?" Coffey went to the cell door and listened. He could hear no sound upstairs. He heard his third cellmate say: "You bother them, they tire you, that's right. Just keep quiet is the best."

Several minutes later the jailer brought back the man who had been shouting. The man held both hands over his stomach and his face was pale. After he had been locked in again, he could be heard retching. Coffey's cellmates exchanged nods. One said: "In Bordeaux they beat the shit out of you whether you bother them or not. Minute you get in, they fix you."

"Where's Bordeaux?" Coffey asked.

"Provincial jail. What are you up for, Jack?"

"Ah — I was taking a leak in the open last night and the police found me."

224

"A vag, eh?"

"A vag?" The word was familiar. "No, it wasn't that they called it. Indecent exposure, it was."

His cellmates exchanged glances. One of them coughed. "Well," he said. "I'd rather it was you, not me."

At eight o'clock a bell rang. A jailer came down to the cells, called a roll from a typewritten list and ordered the prisoners to line up at their cell doors. Several other policemen appeared. The prisoners were marched upstairs and Coffey, with three other men, was put in a waiting room. There was a policeman in the room. One of the prisoners begged a light.

"NO TALKING!" shouted the policeman.

At eight thirty-one, Coffey and three others were taken to the back door of the police station. A van was backed into the alley, its engine running. A policeman helped them up, a second policeman handed the driver a list and the doors of the Black Maria were locked. There were already two prisoners in the van and it stopped at three police stations in the next half hour. By the time it reached a courthouse somewhere in the harbor area, the van was crowded with men and smelled of alcohol and sweat. They were disembarked in a yard and, as they waited to be marched away, Coffey saw a newspaper kiosk in the street outside, its walls plastered with tabloid headlines. One of them read:

CADI SENTENCES "FOUL EXPOSER" MERCY PLEA REJECTED

Suffering J! Better they sentence him to jail than Paulie ever read the like of that. This was his fault. Everything was his fault. He must pay for it himself.

"Right," said a warder. "MARCH!"

One of the prisoners, an old man, said: "Is there a toilet inside? I need to go to the toilet."

The warder turned and bellowed as though struck: "NO TALKING IN THE CORRIDORS."

They were marched downstairs and locked up.

Above the judge there was a large crucifix. The Christ figure seemed to recline, head to one side, as though trying to catch the half-audible mumble of the clerk of the court.

"Criminal Code . . . Statute . . . Section . . . Said Gerald MacGregor . . . night of . . . premises . . . did indecently expose himself — as witness . . ."

A lawyer, arriving late, entered the courtroom and hurried up the aisle, shaking hands with his colleagues. The reporters on the press bench were reading a newspaper called *Le Devoir:* they did not appear to have paid attention to the charge. The judge, a florid man who might have been mistaken for a bookmaker, was having trouble with his Parker pen. He signaled a court functionary, who went through the door leading to the judge's chambers. A detective-sergeant came in and stood beneath the judge, waiting. The clerk of the court finished his mumble and sat down. The judge unscrewed his Parker pen, and noticed the waiting detective-sergeant. The sergeant stepped forward and whispered. The judge looked at Coffey.

"Swear the accused," he said.

Coffey was sworn in. The judge said: "Now — is your name Gerald MacGregor?"

Coffey looked desperately at the crucifix over the judge's bench. The Christ figure lent an ear: waiting.

"I warn you," the judge said. "No one by the name of MacGregor lives at the address you have given. Do you still say that is your name?"

226

In terror, Coffey looked at the detective-sergeant. Vera and Paulie? — must protect . . . "Yes, Your Honor," he said.

"All right." The judge nodded to the sergeant. "Bring your witness in."

The sergeant signaled to a court attendant and the court attendant went outside. In her best blue coat, her eyes downcast, Veronica was escorted to the bench. She was sworn in. Her eyes met Coffey's, then flittered towards the press bench. The reporters were taking notes now. She gave her name and address.

"Is this man your husband?"

"Yes."

"What is his given name?"

"James Francis Coffey."

"You may stand down. Clerk, read the charge again in the name of James Francis Coffey."

She went to a front seat and sat down. She looked up at him and her fingers fluttered in a tiny, surreptitious greeting. She was afraid.

"Now, Coffey," the judge said. "Why did you give a false name?"

"I — ah — I didn't want my wife and daughter mixed up in this, you see."

"I do not see," the judge said. "You have heard the charge. Have you any idea of the gravity of this charge?"

"Well, no, Your Honor. You see — I mean, I wanted to avoid — I mean, it wasn't their fault. I didn't want them to be worried."

"This charge," the judge said, "carries a maximum penalty of seven years in prison."

Coffey looked at Veronica. She seemed about to keel over. *Seven years.*

"Well, Coffey? What do you have to say for yourself?"

"I — I'm an immigrant here, Your Honor, and I've not

227

done very well getting settled. My wife . . ." He stopped and looked at Veronica, who lowered her head, not answering his look. "My wife and I had agreed to separate unless I did better. I'd promised her that unless I got a certain promotion, I'd let her go back to — I mean, leave me. And I promised she could take my daughter as well. So last night, I didn't get the promotion, and so . . ."

He could not go on. He stood, looking down at her, looking at the white nape of her neck beneath the hairline of her new short haircut. The judge said: "What's all this got to do with perjuring yourself?"

"Well, I'd lost them anyway, Your Honor. I didn't want them to suffer any more for what I'd done. So I thought of a false name . . ."

The judge looked at the sergeant. "Is the prisoner represented by counsel?"

"*A pas demandé*," the sergeant said.

"This case is being tried in English," the judge said, testily.

"Sorry, sir. He didn't ask for a lawyer."

The judge sighed. He put both halves of his Parker pen together, screwed them tight, then laid the pen down. "How do you plead?" he said to Coffey. "Guilty or not guilty?"

"Not guilty, Your Honor."

"Very well. Call the first witness."

Constable Armand Bissonette, Radio Mobile Unit, Station Number 10, took the stand. Following the witness's testimony, he was cross-examined by Judge Amédée Monceau.

His Honor: "Was there anyone else in the street at the time?"

Witness: "Not so far as we could see, sir."

228

His Honor: "Then no one witnessed the act except the police?"

Witness: "Maybe there were people inside the hotel lobby who saw it."

His Honor: "Did you actually see any people?"

Witness: "No, sir."

His Honor: "And the doorway was dark?"

Witness: "Yes, but there were lights in the lobby, inside the door."

His Honor: "Were those lights visible from the doorway?"

Witness: "Yes, if he had looked in, he would have seen that it was a hotel lobby. But he was on the wine, sir. He could hardly see straight."

His Honor: "He was intoxicated?"

Witness: "He's a wino, sir. I smelled the wine off him."

His Honor: (*To accused*) "What did you have to drink?"

Accused: "Your Honor, I had some glasses of wine. It was a sort of a mixture of sherry and Coca-Cola. I didn't intend to get drunk."

His Honor: "You're Irish, by the sound of you. Is that an Irish recipe?"

[LAUGHTER]

His Honor: "If that didn't make you drunk, it should have made you ill. Were you ill?"

Accused: "Yes, Your Honor. I felt a bit dizzy. And I had been waiting a long time for the bus."

His Honor: "How long?"

Accused: "More than twenty minutes, sir. Maybe half an hour."

His Honor: "Half an hour? Well, I can see you're not a native of this city. Half an hour is not a long time here."

[LAUGHTER]

Coffey looked at them: the judge grinning at his witticism, the lawyers looking up to laugh with the bench, the

229

spectators lolling back in their seats like people enjoying a joke in church. Seven years in prison and yet they laughed. But why not? What was he to all these people except a funny man with a brogue? Not a person; an occasion of laughter. His whole life, back to those days when he ran past the iron railings of Stephen's Green, late for school, back through the university years, the Army years, the years at Kylemore and Coomb-Na-Baun, through courtship, marriage, fatherhood, his parents' death, his hopes, his humiliations — it was just a joke. All he was this morning, facing prison and ruin, was an excuse for courtroom sallies. So what did it matter, his life in this world, when this was what the world was like? Unsurely but surely he came to that. His hopes, his ambitions, his dreams: what were they but shams? Only one face in that courtroom suffered with him, knew him as more than a joke, was one with him on this awful morning. One face, which fifteen years ago in Saint Pat's in Dalkey had turned from the priest to look at him and say "I do."

The judge rapped on his desk. The laughter stopped.

His Honor, Judge Amédée Monceau, addressed the prosecution. His Honor stated that under the circumstances, the lateness of the hour, the absence of proven intoxication, the lack of witnesses to the action, the fact that there was no known previous criminal record, there was some question in His Honor's mind as to why the police had preferred the more serious charge. A charge of vagrancy might, His Honor suggested, have been more appropriate in this instance.

DETECTIVE-SERGEANT TAILLEFER: "Your Honor, this act was committed in the doorway of one of the biggest hotels in the city."

His Honor: "Yes, but you have not proved that there were any witnesses."

Detective-Sergeant Taillefer: "Well, the police took such speedy action, sir, that nobody was disturbed."

His Honor: "Sergeant, if the police department is ever in need of a public relations officer, I'll be very happy to recommend you. But if there are to be any further compliments to the police department this morning, will you please allow them to come from me?"

[LAUGHTER]

Down there in the courtroom the spectators looked up, enjoying the discomfiture of the police sergeant. No one looked at him, the central figure in this drama. No one, not even she. For she sat, her head bent; humiliated. Was she humiliated because this laughter was a criticism of her, a mockery of her taste in marrying a man who had indecently exposed himself to the world's ridicule, whose sufferings merited the world's attention only as a subject for farce? Likely that was it, he thought. For didn't she want shut of him too, wasn't she here only because the police had found his true address and ordered her presence in this court? Oh, Vera, Vera, look at me, would you . . . ?

But she did not look at him. She did not care for him any more than the rest of them. Nobody cared for him.

His Honor: "Accused, stand up. Have you anything to say in your defense?"

Accused: "I didn't know it was a hotel, Your Honor. I thought it was an office building. It was an accident."

His Honor: "I see. And in your country is it common practice to relieve oneself in office doorways? Are you asking me to believe the Irish are uncivilized?"

Accused: "No, Your Honor."

His Honor: "I see. Well, let me inform you, Coffey, your actions last night constitute a serious crime in this Province. Now, as I understand it, there were certain extenuating circumstances. It was late at night and you were at the mercy of the Montreal Transportation Commission —"

[LAUGHTER]

His Honor: "And certainly, having imbibed the concoction which you described to this court there is every reason that your system should seek to expel it as soon as possible, in one way or another."

[LAUGHTER]

His Honor: "However, the fact remains that your action in a public — a very public — place might have caused considerable shock and outrage to innocent bystanders. In the event of your action being committed deliberately to shock and outrage such bystanders, the charge laid against you by the police would seem justified. And, as I have already told you, the maximum sentence for that offense is seven years in prison."

Veronica raised her head. There were tears in her eyes and her face was terribly pale. She stared at him as though only she and he were in the room. He looked at her; his legs no longer trembled. He saw it in her eyes: it was not shame of him, it was fear for him. He looked up at the judge, no longer afraid.

His Honor: "Now, Coffey, in the absence of defending counsel, this Court considers you to have thrown yourself upon its mercy. And despite the charge laid against you by these officers, I am inclined to believe that in view of the mitigating circumstances there was no criminal intent on your part. So I am giving you the benefit of the doubt. I hereby sentence you to six months in prison . . ."

His eyes left the judge's face; went to her below him. Something had happened. A court usher and a spectator were bending over her. Fainted? The court usher was helping her from her seat. Watching, Coffey barely heard the judge's next phrase.

". . . However, in this case, sentence will be suspended, in view of the fact that you have no previous conviction and are an immigrant with a wife and child to support. I am dealing with you leniently, Coffey, because I am sorry for your family. To be alone in a new country, with their breadwinner in jail, seems to me a fate which your wife and child do not deserve. But let me warn you that if for any reason you again find yourself before this court, you will, I assure you, have every cause to regret it."

They had taken her outside. He was all alone now. He stared at the judge.

HIS HONOR: "In conclusion, let me remind the police officers concerned that in cases of this kind all available evidence should be weighed before a charge is preferred. It is because of carelessness in determining the charges against defendants that this court has been obliged, time after time, to render verdicts against the prosecution. That is all, gentlemen."

A warder tapped him on the shoulder. He was led back to the detention room.
"My wife . . . ?"

One of the warders stepped on Coffey's toes. It hurt. "Sorry," the warder said. "What's that you said?"

"My wife, is she . . . ?"

The detective-sergeant, smiling, stepped on Coffey's toes. "Twenty years on the Force," he said. "And I never saw a judge give a guy a break like you got. Luck of the Irish, it must be, eh, Irishman?"

The sergeant poked him in the ribs. It was not a friendly poke. The warder made him sign for his belongings. Then, they let him go.

The corridor outside was crowded with people. Witnesses, waiting their turn in court, lawyers in corner conference with clients and colleagues, policemen walking up and down with the proprietary air of museum guides. He ran past them all, ranging this way and that, finally emerging into a large hall where two court ushers sat on a stone bench near the main door. He went to them.

"Excuse me," he said, newly afraid, for they were policemen. He expected them to shout "NO TALKING." But instead, they were the police he had always known.

"Yes, sir?"

"Did you see a woman? I mean a woman fainted in the court there, did she go out this way?"

"In a blue coat, right?" the usher said. "Yes, we put her in a taxi a minute ago."

"I'm her husband," he said. "Do you know the address she went to?"

They thought this over. One said: "A number on Notre Dame Street, I think."

He thanked them and turned towards the doorway. He felt weak, as though he had risen from a month in bed. Notre Dame Street was Grosvenor's office. Ah, God, it was plain as the nose on your face. She had fainted: she had

234

not even waited to hear the whole thing. She had not waited for him but had gone off to her lover. Ginger's in jail. Gerry, we're free.

Yes, he had been wrong to hope. He was right the first time. She did not care about him. Nobody cared.

Through the main doorway, under the Latinate scrolls to justice and truth, he moved, his step that of an old, old man. He was a wanderer who had sought the bluebird, who had seen all, who knew now that this was what the world was like. He stood at the top of the wide fall of steps which went down to the streets of the city, that city of which he had hoped so much, which had laughed at his hopes, which had turned him out. He looked up at the sky. Gray clouds ballooned down like the dirty underside of a great circus tent. Yet, oh! Never since he had lain in a field as a small boy had the heavens seemed so soaring, so illimitable. And in that moment his heart filled with an unpredictable joy. He was free. The night that had passed, the cells below stairs, the shouting warders, the terrifying laughter of the spectators in court; it had happened and yet it had not. It was a nightmare washed into nothingness by the simple and glorious fact of freedom. The city, its roofs and cornices crusted with snow, its rushing inhabitants muffled in furs, seemed a busy, magical place, a joy to be abroad in. For one liberating moment he became a child again; lost himself as a child can, letting himself go into the morning, a drop of water joining an ocean, mystically becoming one.

He forgot Ginger Coffey and Ginger's life. No longer was he a man running uphill against hope, his shins kicked, his luck running out. He was no one: he was eyes staring at the sky. He was the sky.

A passer-by bumped against him; went down the wide steps. The moment detached itself, leaving him weak and wondering. That was happiness. Would it ever come

235

again? Wishing would not bring it back, nor ambitions, nor sacrifice, nor love. Why was it that true joy, this momentary release, could come even in his hour of loss and failure? It could not be wished for: it came unawares. It came more often in childhood, but it might come again and again, even at the end of a life.

Slowly, he descended the courthouse steps. Yes, a momentary happiness might come to him again. But was that all he could hope for now — a few mystical moments spaced out over a lifetime? Yes, it might be all.

Wish — if I could wish, what would I wish for now?

But he thought of her. He thought of his promise to go away. He must not wish. He must go. Yes, he must go.

Fourteen   He let himself in, cautiously. There was always the chance that Veronica might have come back. But when he opened the hall closet, her coat was not there. As Paulie was at school, there was no further need for him to be quiet. He went into the bedroom and began to pack a suitcase. He took shirts from the dresser drawer, avoiding the man in the mirror. He no longer felt any interest in that man. He no longer felt any interest in Ginger Coffey. He felt like someone else.

Suddenly, down the hall, the shower went on. Saturday! Of course. Paulie was at home. He wanted to hide. He did not want questions; did not want to be forced to explain why he must go. Hurriedly, he tried to finish the clumsy job of stuffing his clothes into the suitcase. But the suitcase slid off the bed with a thump. The shower stopped. He heard Paulie's footsteps in the corridor.

"Mummy, is that you? . . . Mummy? . . . Who's that?" Her voice changed from inquiry to doubt, to fear, and of course it was not fair to frighten her by letting her think he was a thief or something. He opened the door and there was Paulie in her bathrobe, her face and neck still dewed with shower steam. "Oh, it's you, Daddy," she said. "Where were you?"

"In here."

"No, I mean where *were* you? We were nearly demented. And then, this morning, when that policeman came in the car for Mummy, I was sure you were in a hospital or even killed. Now what *happened?*"

"I was in jail," he said.

"Oh, you're joking!" But as she said it, she ran to him and hugged him. "I was worried, Daddy."

"Were you, Pet?" He was surprised. He took her face in his hands and raised it up. Yes, she took after him: there was something of him in her reddish hair, her worried eyes. She was his child and she had worried for him. If he asked her to come away with him now, she might come. . . .

But where? And why? His hand stroked the back of her head. She loved him: it was more than he had a right to expect. Let her be.

"My hair's just set," she said. "Please don't mess it, Daddy."

He released her. He must finish his packing, without her knowing. "What about getting me some coffee?" he said.

"Okay, Daddy. But what *is* all this about jail?"

"It's a long story, Apple. I'll tell you some other time."

"Tell me now."

"Some other time," he said.

She went to the kitchen. He shut the bedroom door and picked the bag off the floor, repacking it. She had worried for him: she loved him. That moved him more than he thought he could be moved again. Still, he had made a promise. He must go. He shut the suitcase and, so that she would not see it, he went to the hall closet and hid it. After the coffee, he would slip away . . .

But the hall door opened as he closed the closet. Veronica. Slowly, he turned to face her. It was like those long

238

ago days when, having failed the examination, you must face the anger, the reproach.

"Is it you?" she said.

"Yes."

"But you're supposed to be in jail?"

"It was a suspended sentence."

"Oh."

He looked at her. She looked at him. Caught, like strangers who eye each other on a train, they pretended the glance was accidental.

"Well . . ." he said. He opened the closet and took out his car coat.

"Are you going out?"

He put on his coat and reached in again for his little green hat. "I'm going away. They're not going to make me a reporter, now or ever. So you can get the divorce. I'll be in touch with you."

He stood for a moment, facing the closet; feeling watched; not wanting to meet the eyes that watched him.

"What about Paulie? Does Paulie know?"

"No," he said.

"Well, don't you think you should tell her?"

"You tell her." He turned, little green hat in one hand, suitcase in the other. "Would you open the door for me, Vera?"

Their eyes met. One person in the whole world who had known him; one person who knew him as more than a joke. A person who, fifteen years ago in Saint Pat's in Dalkey, had knelt beside him at the altar and promised . . .

"Before you go," she said. "There's one thing I want to explain. I didn't run away this morning."

He put down his suitcase. He would have to open the door himself. She wasn't going to help him.

"Listen, Ginger. When I heard the judge say 'Six

months,' I keeled over. Then, when they took me out, I thought the best thing to do would be to go to Gerry's office and try to get a lawyer so that you could appeal."

He opened the door and picked up his suitcase.

"You don't believe me, is that it?"

"It doesn't matter," he said. It did not matter.

"Gerry refused to help you," she said. "That's why I came back here."

"Look, Vera, I have to go now."

"But, just a *second*, will you?" Her voice was urgent and strained. "I want to tell you what Gerry said to me. He said it was the best thing that could have happened. He said it would make the divorce easier. That's all he cared about."

"Well, it doesn't matter, does it?" he said. "It's former history."

She bent her head, and suddenly rubbed at her eyes with her knuckles, leaving a smudge of mascara on the bridge of her nose. "Dammit," she said. "I'm sorry. Don't you see, I'm sorry?"

Sorry? What was she sorry about? What did "sorry" cure? She'd told him that once. Now, he knew what she meant. He stood, suitcase in hand, at the open doorway. He must go.

"Wait," she said. "There's something else too. Only I can't tell it, with you standing there like some door-to-door salesman. Come into our room a minute. I don't want Paulie to hear."

Unwillingly, he put down his suitcase and followed her back to the bedroom. What use was there in all this? Why must she make it so hard?

She shut the bedroom door. "Now, listen," she said. "I never slept with Gerry. On my word of honor. I wouldn't do it until you and I were legally separated."

He nodded. Get it over with.

"You should have seen Gerry just now," she said. "He behaved like a total stranger. How could anyone love a person who'd let someone go to jail and be glad of it? He doesn't love me, either, he just wants me. Whereas you — you stood up in the courtroom this morning and gave a false name for my sake and for Paulie's —"

She stopped. She seemed to be waiting for him to tell her something.

"All right then," she said. "If that's the way of it, won't you even kiss me good-by?"

Kiss this stranger? Unwillingly, he put his arms around her. She was shaking. He looked down at the nape of her neck, bared by her new hairdo. It was unfamiliar, yet familiar. Ah God! Had he been wrong in that, as well? For, now that he held her, she was no stranger at all, but Veronica, the woman he had slept with how many thousand nights. Veronica: older and heavier than the girl he had married, her breasts a little too big, her eyes edged with small white lines, her hand, now touching his cheek, roughened by years over sinks and washtubs. Veronica. No stranger: not desirable.

"Ginger," she said. "You still love me, don't you? You said you did."

Love her? This body familiar as his own . . . Desire her? This woman growing old . . .

"Even if you don't love me," she said. "There's Paulie. That child wept half the night, worrying about you. You can't walk out on her now."

Didn't you walk out on Paulie? he thought. But what was the use in blaming her? Blame was his. "Look," he said. "You'd be better off, you and Paulie . . ."

He did not go on. Someone else was saying all this. Not Ginger Coffey. Someone who had stopped looking for the good in the bad; who had stopped running uphill in hopes; someone who knew the truth. He did not love her:

241

he could no longer love. He did not want to watch her cry. She was getting old: she was just another illusion he no longer had.

He began to button his overcoat.

"No, we wouldn't," she was saying. "Because it wasn't only your fault, it was mine. When I saw Gerry just now — I mean, saw the real Gerry — I knew it was my fault. What I mean is, I'd like to start again. Listen, we *could* start again if you wanted to? You could get that job as Mr. Brott's Personal Assistant, if you went and asked for it."

He looked down at her. Yes, that was true. He might get that job. He could become, now and forevermore, amen, the glorified secretary she had always thought he was. What did it matter? What was so terrible about that? Didn't most men try and fail, weren't most men losers? Didn't damn nearly everyone have to face up someday to the fact that their ship would never come in?

He had tried. He had not won. He would die in humble circs.

"I'm sure he'd give you the job," she said. "Honestly, Ginger, I'm sure of it."

He smiled. Wasn't that familiar, somehow?

"Don't laugh," she said. "You'll see!"

"I'm not laughing," he told her.

"Why, listen," she said. "In a year or two we'll have forgotten this ever happened."

He did not feel like someone else now. She did.

"And if you do stay," she said. "I'd never ask you to go home again. You were right. Home is here, we're far better off here. Why, in a month or two, with my job and your job, we'd be sitting pretty. You were right. This was only a crush, I had. Why, I'll bet you —"

"A brand-new frock, Vera?"

She stopped. She looked at him, her eyes blinding with tears. "Oh, Ginger," she said. "I sound like you."

242

"I know you do." He went to her, put his arm around her and opened the bedroom door.

"Your coffee's ready," Paulie called from the kitchen. "And do you want an egg, Daddy?"

Beside him, Vera waited his answer.

"I'll have two eggs," he said.

"Good. I'll put them on," Paulie said.

"No, *I'll* do it," Vera said. Quickly, she went out of the room and down the hall.

He pushed the bedroom door, let it drift shut. He unbuttoned his overcoat. In the dresser mirror, the man began to cry. Detached, he watched the tears run down that sad impostor's face, gather on the edges of that large mustache. Why was that man boohooing? Because he no longer lusted for his wife? Because he wasn't able to leave her? Ah, you idjit, you. Don't you know that love isn't just going to bed? Love isn't an act, it's a whole life. It's staying with her now because she needs you; it's knowing you and she will still care about each other when sex and daydreams, fights and futures — when all that's on the shelf and done with. Love — why, I'll tell you what love is: it's you at seventy-five and her at seventy-one, each of you listening for the other's step in the next room, each afraid that a sudden silence, a sudden cry, could mean a lifetime's talk is over.

He had tried: he had not won. But oh! what did it matter? He would die in humble circs: it did not matter. There would be no victory for Ginger Coffey, no victory big or little, for there, on the courthouse steps, he had learned the truth. Life was the victory, wasn't it? Going on was the victory. For better for worse, for richer for poorer, in sickness and in health . . . till . . .

He heard her step outside. He went to join her.

The
GREAT
VICTORIAN
COLLECTION

BRIAN MOORE

FARRAR · STRAUS · GIROUX

NEW YORK

For Jean

Copyright © 1975 by Brian Moore

All rights reserved

First printing, 1975

Printed in the United States of America

Designed by Cynthia Krupat

Library of Congress Cataloging in Publication Data

Moore, Brian.

The Great Victorian Collection.

I. Title.

PZ4.M819Gr3   [PR6063.06]   813'.5'4   75-5553

1

There is still some confusion as to when Anthony Maloney first saw the Great Victorian Collection. Can it be said that he first envisaged the Collection in his dream? Or did he create it in its entirety only when he woke up and climbed out of his bedroom window?

Maloney himself proved an unsatisfactory witness on this point. He was, of course, confused after the event. Indeed, he seemed a different person from the ordinary, rational young man who had checked into the Sea Winds Motel in Carmel-by-the-Sea, California, on that extraordinary night.

That ordinary young man was twenty-nine years old and an assistant professor of history at McGill University in Montreal. It was his first trip to the West Coast. He had flown out to San Francisco to attend a seminar at Berkeley. On the last day of the seminar, he rented a car and drove south, intending to spend the weekend exploring the Big Sur region. He arrived in Carmel on a

Saturday afternoon. On Monday he was to fly home to Montreal.

But Maloney did not make his flight. A year later, he was still living in Carmel in the same motel room he had checked into on the night of his arrival. A wall had been removed so that the adjoining room could be used as a study. But, in essence, his motel bedroom remained unchanged.

A word about Carmel. It is a small California coastal resort which is sometimes described as an "artists' paradise." But even on that first evening, walking past galleries filled with local paintings, arcade shops selling homemade candles, and bookstores displaying the complete works of Kahlil Gibran, it occurred to Maloney that a true artist could hardly fail to be appalled by the values evidenced in this place. Indeed, later, he became irritated when the Vanderbilt University researchers purported to find significance in his choice of Carmel and the Sea Winds Motel. The truth is, he stopped in Carmel because he had been told it was a convenient jumping-off ground from which to explore the Big Sur region. As for his selection of this motel, when he arrived in Carmel he had gone into a Chamber of Commerce tourist bureau and inquired about accommodations. A clerk in the bureau recommended the Sea Winds.

Maloney arrived there shortly after 5 P.M. Henry Bourget, the motel owner, greeted him in the lobby and showed him to a second-floor room. Maloney looked out of the window and saw a very large, empty parking lot, which fronted on Bluff Road. He asked if he should

4

park his car there, but Bourget said the lot was not in use, as it was about to be built on. He advised Maloney to leave his car in the street.

Maloney then brought his bag in. He inquired about restaurants and Bourget recommended the restaurant at which Maloney subsequently ate dinner. After dinner he returned to the motel, intending to retire early and be on the road to Big Sur at seven in the morning. He later said that when he entered the motel bedroom the blind was drawn and the bed was turned down. This has since been confirmed by Mrs. Elaine Bourget, wife of the proprietor, who customarily performs this service for guests.

Maloney was a normal sleeper. He had not had extraordinary dreams in the past. And, finally, his dream, as a dream, did not seem extraordinary to him at the time. To dream of Victoriana was not, given his background, an improbable conjunction. His Ph.D. dissertation had been "A Study of the Effects of Gaining a Colonial Empire on the Mores of Victorian England as Exemplified by the Art and Architecture of the Period." In connection with his thesis he had journeyed to England to visit museums and libraries and to look at various public buildings. Thus, while not a recognized expert on Victoriana, he could at least claim a degree of familiarity with the subject.

But, to return to the Sea Winds Motel. Maloney went to sleep in a normal manner and passed an uneventful night. Sometime in the early morning he awoke for a few minutes, then, falling asleep again, began to dream. The dream is given here as he recounted it in a television interview on the following day.

5

"I dreamed that I was in London having lunch at an old public house called The Cheshire Cheese, which is located just off Fleet Street. When I looked around I saw that the other people having lunch there were, unmistakably, transatlantic tourists like myself. I remember being irritated at finding myself lunching in such an obvious 'tourist attraction.' There was only one other customer who did not seem North American. He was a tall man who wore dark, old-fashioned clothing. I didn't see his face, but when he rose and left the room I felt compelled to get up and follow him. The waiter shouted out that I hadn't paid my bill, but I ignored this, went outside, and found myself in an ill-lit alleyway behind the pub. The man in dark clothes stood, waiting, with his back to me. I knew then that he had been sent to guide me. The man walked up the alleyway and, pointing to an oak door at the end of it, beckoned me to go ahead of him. I went to the door and pushed it open, believing it would give onto the street. Instead, I found myself in the darkened bedroom of the Sea Winds Motel, the same room in which I had gone to sleep. The bed was empty and the bedclothes were disarranged. I went to the window, raised the blind, and looked out at a pale pink sunrise. Below me was the motel parking lot, large as a city block. But now the lot resembled a crowded open-air market, a maze of narrow lanes lined with stalls, some permanently roofed, some draped in green tarpaulin awnings. I unfastened the catch of the window, opened it, climbed out on the sill, and eased myself onto a wooden outdoor staircase, which led down to the lot some twenty feet below. I began to walk along what seemed to be the central aisle of the market, an aisle dominated by a glittering crystal fountain, its columns of polished glass soaring to the height of

6

a telegraph pole. Laid out on the stalls and in partially enclosed exhibits resembling furniture showrooms was the most astonishing collection of Victorian artifacts, *objets d'art,* furniture, household appliances, paintings, jewelry, scientific instruments, toys, tapestries, sculpture, handicrafts, woolen and linen samples, industrial machinery, ceramics, silverware, books, furs, men's and women's clothing, musical instruments, a huge telescope mounted on a pedestal, a railway locomotive, marine equipment, small arms, looms, bric-a-brac, and curiosa. As I moved on, staring about me, I became aware that the stalls were unattended and that my guide had not followed me into this place. I knew then that all of this had, somehow, been given into my charge. And, as soon as I knew it, I woke up.

"It was morning. I was in the motel room I had dreamed about, that same room in which I had gone to sleep. I got out of the bed and, barefoot, wearing only my pajama trousers, went to the window, raised the blind, and saw that same pale pink sunrise. There, below me, just as in the dream, was the large open-air market and the maze of stalls occupying the entire area of the parking lot which had been empty last evening. I opened the window, climbed down onto the main aisle, and began to walk along that aisle, exactly as I had done in my dream, coming to the selfsame crystal fountain which I recognized now as the work of F. & C. Osler, a marvel of casting, cutting, and polishing of faultless blocks of glass, erected originally in the transept as the centerpiece of the Great Exhibition of 1851.

"I walked on. Everything in the stalls, booths, and showrooms was vivid and real. But I knew, of course, that I must be dreaming. There was no possible way that this lot, empty last evening, could have been filled

7

with so many large and varied exhibits in a single night. I remember that as I continued to walk I became aware that everything I laid eyes on was, in some sense, familiar. I stopped at a stall and picked up a small object, a child's wooden fire engine, circa 1840. I remembered I had seen it before in the Marvell Collection of Toys at Kensington Palace. I fingered the engine's painted surface, sniffed its faint odor, reminiscent of snuff, and put it back on the stand. I then noticed a mechanical cat sitting next to it, a tin toy which does not exist in any known collection of Victoriana. I recognized it from a description of its workings which I had read in a book on rare Victorian toys.

"But now I held in my hand a real toy, seven inches long, made of tin, painted with black and orange stripes, and containing a winding mechanism which enabled it to run along the ground on concealed wheels and, by a twist of its tin tail, roll over. When I wound it up and set it in motion I remember that, for one moment, I thought: What if it *is* real? What if I am not dreaming?

"I grew excited. I went quickly down the main aisle, discovering that each of the narrow, crowded side aisles contained stalls and sheds which displayed groupings of objects which themselves comprised collections within the Collection. A first, I stopped only at the very large pieces, such as the giant telescope which I recognized as the famous instrument designed by A. Ross; one of the more popular sights in the Great Exhibition of 1851. The locomotive I had noticed earlier was, of course, the South Eastern Railway Company's 'Folkstone,' designed by T. R. Crampton.

"In fact, it was as though I had memorized a huge catalogue. I recognized the 'Thebes' stool made for Liberty & Co. Beside it was a grand piano of walnut with inlaid ornament of boxwood and mother-of-pearl made by John Broadwood and Sons, which, in turn, sat on a Hammersmith rug, designed by William Morris. All were from the 1880's. Near them was a clawfoot sofa of carved mahogany upholstered in red silk, about fifty years older, I believe.

"I had never seen such a collection. On the opposite aisle to these furnishings I noticed the 'Day Dreamer' easy chair in papier-mâché, decorated at the top with two 'winged thoughts,' and made by Jennings & Betteridge; an ivory throne and footstool presented to Queen Victoria by the Rajah of Travancore; a marquetry dressing table with botanical woodcarvings by Messrs. Trollope. I turned away and, in the maze of aisles, no longer pausing to examine individual pieces but simply roving among this glut of objects, came on collections of Victorian silver tea sets, bridal breakfast services, ornamental urns, statuary, cheval glasses, tallboys, ottomans, poufs, corner cupboards, gaming tables, stoves, kitchen utensils, fireguards and firedogs. Among the larger rooms I recognized the parlor of a famous Victorian brothel and a room containing the furnishings of a Victorian music hall.

"I moved on. I was walking down an aisle which reflected life in the Victorian streets, with a display of costermongers' barrows, carriages, penny-farthing bicycles, and so on, when, up ahead, I saw something move.

"It was a man. He was in his sixties, heavily tanned, with longish gray hair. He was outside, on Bluff Road, moving past the entrance to the parking lot, pulling behind him a metal trolley containing two green plastic garbage cans.

"The newcomer (I later discovered that his name is

9

John Rockne and that he lives down the road) stopped and called out in greeting: 'Hi there. What the heck is this, some kind of exhibition? How in God's name did they get it up so fast?'

"I remember that I did not answer him. There was something about him, some living reality, I suppose, which left me tongue-tied and alarmed. Again, the thought came into my mind: What if I am *not* dreaming?

" 'I just can't believe it,' Mr. Rockne said, peering in. 'Look at that fountain! And look—is that a locomotive, sticking up over there? Are you in charge of this?'

" 'Yes,' I said. I don't know why I said it. I simply said it.

" 'But there was nothing here yesterday. I came by yesterday evening. I just can't believe it.'

"I didn't answer him. I didn't know what to say to him. Besides, in a dream you don't have to behave politely. I smiled, then turned and walked back up the central aisle, passing by the fountain, which, I noticed, had water in its pool and a mechanism to turn on the jets. But I did not stop to see if it worked. I felt chilly. I was wearing only my pajama trousers, after all. I returned to my window, climbed up, and re-entered the motel room. At once, I began to dress in a great hurry, all the while staring out of the window. I saw Rockne move on, looking back at the Collection as he dragged his trashcans toward the garbage pickup point. Then, just as I finished dressing, two cars passed by on Bluff Road. Both slowed down and their occupants peered in at the Collection. And, again, the thought came to me: If those are real people and they see what I see, then I am not dreaming. I have made this Collection come to life. No one has ever done anything remotely like it before."

In the television interview, Maloney then described how, at that point, one of the cars pulled over and parked and its occupants, two women and a small girl, got out and walked boldly into the parking lot, staring at the contents of the stalls. At once, Maloney grew agitated. If this was not a dream, the exhibits were completely unprotected from thieves and souvenir hunters. The lot must be fenced in and guarded at once. And so, in a hurry, not thinking of what he was going to say, he went out to the lobby.

Mr. Bourget had obviously not yet stepped outside that morning. "Hi there. Sleep well?"

"Yes. There's something I want to mention to you. There's a lot of stuff out there in your parking lot. It's quite valuable. I wonder if we could hire somebody, some private guards, to look after it."

"What stuff? What's it doing in my lot? I told you not to use the lot."

"I'm very sorry. I just had nowhere else to put it."

Mr. Bourget is a white-haired man who walks with a pronounced limp, the result of an injury to his heel while serving with the Seabees in World War II. He got up from behind the counter, took his cane, and went with Maloney to the parking lot. Later, describing his impressions in a newspaper interview, he stated that he was "bowled over by the beautiful stuff I saw out there." But, in truth, Bourget did not seem "bowled over" by his first sight of the Collection. He entered the parking lot and walked up the center aisle, gesticulating with his cane. "What's all this junk? How in hell did this stuff get in here? I don't believe it. A fountain! I've got to be dreaming."

11

"Well, maybe one of us is dreaming," Maloney said. "I think it's me."

"Who the hell gave you permission to stick this stuff in here?"

"I'm very sorry. It was an emergency."

"What emergency? How did you get all those structures up? You must have used fifty trucks."

"Well, I wanted to explain to you. These things are very valuable."

"Listen to me!" Bourget said, interrupting. "I don't know how you got it set up like this. And, come to think of it, I don't want to know. But if you got it in in one night, you can get it right out again, do you hear? I want this lot empty by noon."

"I know. I should have spoken to you. But I was wondering. Would you consider renting me the lot on a day-to-day basis?"

"No, sir. No way."

"I'd pay well. Just tell me what you'd consider a fair price."

There was a silence. Then: "A fair price? You mean a cheap price? Well, let's say a hundred a day, that's a dirt-cheap price. Because that's a big area you got there."

As he spoke, Bourget waved his cane in illustration, seriously endangering the delicate funnels of some rare "student" lampshades.

"All right," Maloney said. "I'll take it at a hundred a day."

"Just a minute. You can't put this on your Diners card. It's got to be cash. And in advance."

"Would traveler's checks be acceptable?"

"Come in the office," Bourget said.

There Maloney paid Bourget a two days' rental of two hundred dollars and, with his permission, phoned a

12

guard service, Securiguard Inc., and arranged for two uniformed men to be sent over at once at a daily rate of thirty-two dollars apiece. As the men worked eight-hour shifts and as at least one night guard must also be arranged for, Maloney estimated that even if he were to wire Montreal for his entire savings, he would be unable to maintain the Collection for more than two weeks.

The security guards arrived within the hour. Until they did, Maloney stood in anxious vigil at the entrance to the parking lot, turning away passers-by who wanted to come in and look at the exhibits. He no longer asked himself if he were awake or dreaming: indeed, he had no time for self-examination, being kept constantly on the move discouraging people from picking up objects, and providing evasive answers to such questions as: "What's it for? What sort of fair is it going to be? Where did it all come from? Who owns it?" and so on.

But as soon as the uniformed guards took up their stations at the lot entrance he became victim of a new anxiety. What if the Collection, which had appeared in a dream, were now to disappear again before he had time to prove to the world that it had actually materialized? With this in mind, he hurried into his motel room and telephoned Professor William Henning, his host at Berkeley. It was the first of many strange conversations he was to have with friends and colleagues.

"Bill, this is Tony Maloney."

"Hey, Tony, how's it going? Let's see. Where are you? Big Sur?"

"No, I'm still in Carmel. Listen, Bill, something has come up. I need your advice."

"What's your problem?" Henning asked and waited, silent in San Francisco while Maloney, stricken with aphasia, was for some moments unable to formulate any reply to his friend's query. What could he say? Who would believe this unbelievable story? To mention it at all was like saying that you'd lost your mind. Thus, when speech returned to him, Maloney found himself mumbling, "Listen, I've come upon something, a collection of Victoriana—"

"That's kind of a hobby of yours, isn't it?"

"Well, yes. This collection is very interesting, very valuable. I'd like to get some pictures taken of it at once."

"Who owns it?"

"Well, in a way, I do."

"You mean you just got hold of it?"

"It's hard to explain over the phone."

"Got you," said Henning, in the voice of a man who appreciates sharp trading. "Still negotiating, are you?"

"No, not really. But it's such an important discovery, I mean—collection. I think perhaps I need some institution to sponsor it. You know, to fund it so that it will be properly looked after and displayed and so on."

"How about a commercial sponsor?"

"Well, no, I wasn't thinking of that."

"Shell Oil is doing a lot culturally. And so is Xerox. You'd be surprised."

"Well, I'm not sure what to do at this stage."

"Tony," Henning said, patiently. "If you've discovered some great Victorian collection, what you need now is publicity. If you get the right kind of publicity, things will begin to happen."

"Publicity?" Maloney said, his voice shaky with new excitement. "You're quite right. This is a fantastic news story. Hey, Bill—didn't you tell me your brother-in-law works in the San Francisco bureau of *The New York Times?*"

Henning said, dubiously, "He does. But you know the *Times* is pretty picky about what stories it runs. They have to be—you know—of national interest."

"This is of national interest," Maloney said. "It's of *international* interest. Wait till they find out in London that this stuff has turned up here. Out of the blue! Believe me, Bill, your brother-in-law is going to thank you."

"So, you're really sure this is something big?"

"I'm certain."

"Well, I suppose I *could* call Jerry. But, listen, how should I explain it? I mean, the collection?"

"Just say that it's, ah, that it's *the* Great Victorian Collection, the greatest in the world. And that I've just discovered it in Carmel."

"And that you're a leading authority in the field."

"Well, I wouldn't say that."

"Tony, if you want to promote this you've got to go all the way."

"Yes, I suppose so. Yes, you're right."

"Okay, give me your number and I'll call you back."

Maloney read off his number, put the phone down, and went to the window. On the side of the parking lot fronting the street, one of the guards, armed with revolver and nightstick, stood with his back to the stalls and booths, watching the cars slow down as they passed by on Bluff Road. The second security guard sat on a chair in the middle of the main aisle of the Collection, shoulders slumped, hands hanging between his thighs in the abject posture of bored museum guards everywhere: jailers, themselves jailed, such guards had always seemed to Maloney the personification of that public which, left to its own devices, could not be induced to walk ten steps to view any museum exhibit in the world. Indeed, there was something about a museum guard sitting in the midst of the Collection, a real toad, so to speak, in this imaginary garden, which reinforced his feeling that he was not dreaming: he had really created these things and had made them visible for others to see and admire. It had never been done before. It was unique.

At that moment, as he stood at the window, an idea came to him. If he was not dreaming, if he had been able to will these items to appear, could he now will them to disappear? Or—an interesting possibility—could he will them to appear somewhere else? What if, as an experiment, he willed one piece to move now, from the parking lot into his motel room? He shut his eyes. The first object which came to mind was the first item he had examined, the child's wooden fire engine from the Marvell Collection of Victorian Toys. He concentrated. *Make it move from its stall and reappear here on my bed.*

He opened his eyes. He looked at the bed. There was no toy engine there. A feeling of dread assailed him. Turning, he ran out of the motel, going straight to the parking lot and the booth where the Marvell Collection was on display. At first, as he ran up, his sensation was one of relief. The grouping was as before. The toy engine sat exactly where he remembered it to have been. But, on picking it up, he knew at once that something was wrong. It looked the same, but when he turned it over he saw, stamped on the forward axle, the words "Made in Japan."

He was absolutely sure that the words had not been

there when he first examined the engine. He scrutinized each of the remaining toys. The engine was the only imitation. He stood for a moment, looking at it in dismay, then covertly put it under his suit jacket and, retracing his steps, went back into the motel with some vague idea of destroying it. But although he could feel the bulge of the wooden toy under his coat, when he reached his room and sought to uncover it, the toy had disappeared.

His first reaction was joyful. Nothing could be more damaging to the status of the Collection than for a cheap Oriental imitation to be discovered among its pure period pieces. The fake seemed, simply, to have vanished into thin air. Of course, there was the possibility that, unwittingly, he had dropped it in transit from the parking lot to his room. So he retraced his route, coming once more to the Marvell Collection, where he saw, restored as if by magic to its original position, the selfsame wooden engine. And, on picking it up, read the same incriminating legend: "Made in Japan."

Then, and only then, Maloney realized the laws of this creation. Already the toy engine reproached him, a small cancerous blemish on the perfect bloom of the whole. It had been given to him to envisage the Collection here, in a parking lot in California. Any further attempts to remove these items to some other location would result, not in the greatest collection of Victoriana the world had ever seen, but in an astonishing conglomeration of Japanese fakes.

A few minutes after this experience, the telephone rang.

"Tony? This is Bill Henning again. I just talked to my brother-in-law."

"And?"

17

"Well, I think I was pretty convincing. Anyway, I got him to promise that they'll look into it. He said they're sending their Monterey stringer over to check it out. You going to be there for a while?"

"Yes. Did he say when they'd be likely to arrive?"

"No, and I didn't ask. You can't push these press people, you know."

"Yes, of course. Well, thanks, Bill."

"Not at all. And, listen, if you need any more help, call me at my office. Call me anyway, and let me know how you make out. Oh, and by the way, Peg says let's all get together for a drink, as soon as you get back to San Francisco. You're coming back through San Francisco, aren't you?"

"Yes. I think so. And thanks again, Bill. I really appreciate this."

"Okay. Take care."

Maloney put the receiver down and went to the window, staring once again at those roofs, sheds, and awnings. For a long time he stood as though in trance, remembering with a shiver of recognition that he had once thought of creating a collection such as this. It was in his graduate student days, after his return from England. He had asked his adviser about the possibility of the Canada Council's funding a research study to investigate the possibility of assembling a National Collection of Victoriana. "Impractical," his adviser said. "You would have to start by finding some collection and a donor willing to present it. You'd have to have promises of further funding from private sources. And nobody has that kind of loot any more."

And so he had done nothing about it. Or had he? Now, staring at this strange reality of an old dream come true, he realized that it was, indeed, his responsibility. He could not abandon these objects. He must stay here and watch over them.

But at once, in counterpoint, new glooms of guilt arose. The face of his wife, Barbara, loomed like an angry icon, reminding him that on Wednesday he had promised to meet her in Montreal. They were to have coffee in the Café des Arts, and a talk—the long-awaited talk. It had been more than a year since Barbara had walked out on him. They had not met or spoken to each other since.

No, he would have to go back. He had made a solemn promise to Barbara's sister, who had been the intermediary. He *must* show up on Wednesday. That was the all-important meeting. If he stayed on here over Wednesday, any possibility of fixing things up with Barbara would vanish like a dream.

So that was that. Real life. The Collection was wonderful, it was beautiful, it was absolutely astonishing. But, once he had it photographed and authenticated, he would have to head home. No question about it.

The telephone rang. "Professor Maloney? This is the desk. I've got a gentleman, says he's from the press. Will I send him in?"

"Yes, please."

He had expected someone older than himself. But the reporter, dressed like a student, in khaki bush jacket, jeans and red tennis shoes, was probably five years younger than he. Plump, with whitish blond hair worn fashionably long about his shoulders, the visitor stepped into the room, did not speak, but at once handed Maloney a small visiting card, much as though he were a deaf-and-dumb beggar soliciting alms. He watched with a cold blue stare as Maloney read the card.

19

"I am also the local correspondent for *The New York Times*."

Maloney asked him to sit down.

Vaterman sat on the bed. He produced a notebook and a ball-point pen. "This morning I received a call from the San Francisco office of the *Times*. They tell me you claim to have discovered here in Carmel a fantastically valuable hoard of Victorian treasures. May I ask where these—treasures—are hidden?"

"They're not hidden," Maloney said, beckoning his visitor to the window. "There they are in the parking lot."

Vaterman stood, looking out. Sunlight rinsed his ash-blond locks, revealing a downy fuzz on his porcine cheeks. "My God! All of those stalls?"

"Yes."

"How many items would you say, roughly?"

"I don't know yet."

"Why not?"

"I haven't had time to count them."

"So. May I ask, where did you find these things?"

Maloney looked into those cold blue eyes. Of course, he would have to tell about the dream. That was the story. But how? He hesitated, then said: "Perhaps you'd like to go out and have a look at the stuff?"

"Later. First we will get the details, if you don't mind."

"All right," Maloney said. He felt himself grow tense.

"So, if you will begin at the beginning?"

"Well, I know this is going to be hard to believe." His

voice seemed to him disembodied, floating in the room as though spinning from a tape recorder. "But last night I had a dream. I dreamed I was having lunch in London—"

"London, England?"

"Yes. I was in a restaurant. A man who was lunching there, a man who wore old-fashioned clothes, got up to leave and, in my dream, I followed him out into an alleyway. He led me to a door in the alley and beckoned me to go through. I opened the door and found myself in a room. It was this room."

"Which room?"

"This room."

"This particular room," Vaterman said. He began to write in his notebook. "So?"

"So, in my dream I went to the window and looked out. There was the parking lot and it was just as you see it, all those stalls, all those objects. Then—and this is the astonishing part—then I woke up and got out of bed. It was morning."

"What time?"

"I don't know."

"You couldn't make a guess?"

"Oh, just after dawn. Anyway, I opened the window, climbed out and began to explore—"

"Why did you climb out of the window?"

"What do you mean?"

"Why didn't you use the door? You could go through the lobby into the parking lot."

"Well, I didn't think of it. I was excited. I mean, I couldn't believe my eyes."

"Could not believe his eyes," Vaterman said, writing it down. "And why could you not believe?"

"Why? Good God, man, this is the most fantastic collection of Victoriana in the world. There's nothing like it anywhere. What's it doing here?"

Vaterman smiled, warily. "Wait a moment. Let me, please, ask the questions. First, you are an established expert on this Victoriana stuff?"

"Well, it's a hobby of mine. I do know something about it."

"But your opinion of its value could be challenged by other experts?"

"Well, yes, I suppose so."

"So, it's possible, then, that this stuff could be ersatz? Imitation?"

The Japanese wooden engine jumped into Maloney's mind, causing his shoulders to contract as though in anticipation of a blow: this guilty movement, he felt, was not missed by Vaterman. "Well, hardly," Maloney said. "I mean, I recognize a great many, if not all, of these objects."

"How do you recognize them?"

"Because I've seen them in other collections."

"So they are stolen?"

"No."

"Then they are, or could be, copies?"

"Whether they're copies or not isn't the point. The point is, I dreamed them up and now they're here."

"Ah!" Vaterman said. He stopped writing. "Then, if they are here, they cannot be there?"

"In England? Yes, I suppose that's the logical assumption. But then, it would be an equally extraordinary thing, a telepathic theft, so to speak. Still, I don't think that's the case. I suspect these things exist *both* here and in England."

"Then one set is original, and one set is fake. You claimed these things to be 'fantastically valuable.' Yet, now you admit they might be fakes."

"Mr. Waterman, why do you keep missing the point? The point is, I dreamed them up and they've appeared here. Out there in that parking lot."

"Vaterman," Vaterman said. "With a V. Not like the pen."

"I'm sorry."

"That's all right. People often make this mistake. Now, to go back to what you just said. That is, don't you see, my problem. I mean, how do I explain this to my editors?"

"I realize that," Maloney said. "And let me say that if I were you and some stranger told me he'd dreamed this Collection into existence, I'd think there was a trick. I'd think he was some sort of crook or publicity seeker. I'd be just as suspicious as you are, but"—and here Maloney held up his hand, fearing that Vaterman would interrupt—"I want to say that this whole event baffles me as much as it does you. I mean, I don't know if this stuff is going to vanish again five minutes from now. That's why I got in touch with you."

"I don't quite understand."

"I need photographs and witnesses. I need someone to tell me I'm not mad or dreaming, don't I? Supposing it disappears again in the next hour or so? Then what? Nobody will ever believe it happened."

Vaterman nodded and stood up, putting his notebook and pen in his pocket. He smiled placatingly, then made for the door. "Will you excuse me a moment, Professor? I'll be right back."

The door shut. Maloney sat for a moment and then,

as though hypnotized, went once more to the window to stare out at the roofs and awnings. Where had the reporter gone? To telephone? To check something?

Quickly, Maloney went to his room door, opened it and peered out. At the end of the corridor, in the lobby, he saw Vaterman in earnest conversation with Bourget. There was a great deal of head-nodding and agreeing. Maloney shut the door. For a moment, he thought of locking it, climbing out the window, getting into his rental car, and putting as many miles between himself and Carmel as possible before the police or the asylum men arrived.

But, with a perfunctory knock, Vaterman re-entered the room.

"So," he said. "It checks out, so far. Fantastic! Yes, it has to be something like you said. It couldn't get set up in one night. But tell me. Why did you not say anything to the motel man about having a dream?"

"I don't know. I just thought he wouldn't believe me. He was pretty angry at me for using his lot."

Vaterman went again to the window and looked out. "*Who* will believe it?" he said. "Professor, may I tell you something?"

"Yes, of course."

"It is something about myself. First of all, the name Vaterman is well known in Bavaria. I come from a family which has a great tradition. You have heard, perhaps, of Oberammergau?"

"Where they have the Passion Play?"

"Exactly. My grandfather and my great-grandfather both played leading roles in the pageant. My father played John the Baptist. So, we are a family with achievements. And I, who am the first member of this family to become a citizen of the United States, have my own dream of achievement. I want to become a great newspaperman in the American tradition. Like Jack London. Or Reston of the *Times*. Do you follow me?"

Maloney nodded. Vaterman reminded him of a graduate student. They never could come to the point.

"Anyway," Vaterman said. "Today, at long last, I have my chance. My editor, Mr. Yorkin, is the local correspondent for the *Times*. He is sick with flu and so I am covering for him. Sheer luck. But here is my problem. What are you, are you a nut or a crook, or am I sitting on a story so big that if it checks out all the way—my God! Do you follow me?"

"Of course I do," Maloney said. "Look, I'm in exactly the same boat. I can only tell you that this *happened*. It happened just the way I told it to you."

Distractedly, Vaterman ran his fingers through his ash-blond locks. "Okay, let's assume for a minute that it *is* true. How am I going to keep it for myself? Exclusive. Excuse me, confiding in you like this. But you have a dream and I have a dream. How can we make both these dreams come true?"

"My dream *has* come true," Maloney said. "That's my problem. Now, I need to prove it. I need pictures to be taken at once."

"Pictures? Oh, my God!" Vaterman seemed transfixed. "May I use your phone to call the *Times*? All charges will, of course, be reversed."

"Go ahead," Maloney said. Suddenly, alarmingly, he felt drowsy. "I've got to step outside for a moment."

"No, better wait here. The *Times* office may have questions for you."

"I'm sorry. I *must* step out."

"You mean you want to go to the bathroom?"

"No. I need fresh air. I feel sleepy. Look. Normal

dreams disappear when a person wakes up. Maybe this Collection will disappear if I fall asleep again."

"Yes, that is possible, isn't it?" Vaterman said. "All right, you go ahead. I'll phone on my own."

Maloney went out of the room. As he crossed the lobby, Bourget looked up from his desk and called: "How's it going? Getting a nice write-up?"

He pretended not to hear. Hurrying, he reached the parking lot, and, pausing for a moment, took a deep breath, then began to jog along the aisles of the Collection, moving deeper and deeper into the maze. After a few minutes his drowsiness abated and, out of breath, he paused by a shed which contained an exhibition of oils and watercolors by Victorian Royal Academicians: landscapes, stormy seascapes, portraits, illustrations from novels of the day. Sentimental and literary, these paintings reminded him that in the time of the old Queen, something like this Collection would first have been announced to the world in a series of artist's drawings in *The Illustrated London News* as a marvel, a far-off miracle, to be accepted by most of the populace as yet another wonder. But, today, in this age of instant distrust, who would believe it? He knew then that he would be challenged, cross-examined, probed. His brainwaves would be monitored, his childhood investigated, his body fluids tested, his privacy destroyed. And for what?

At that moment, looking up from the paintings, he saw Vaterman, framed in the motel window above, talking excitedly on the telephone. Vaterman was talking to the *Times* about the dream. It would soon be public knowledge. Oh, God! The sensible thing to do would be to duck across to the entrance to Bluff Road, find the rental car, drive back to San Francisco, and take the first plane home to Montreal. And if they tracked

26

him down, he would simply deny he ever gave this interview. He would deny that he knew anything about the Collection or where it came from. It was the only sane thing to do.

But at that moment Vaterman threw open the window and shouted down, "Professor? They're sending a reporter and a photographer up by plane from Los Angeles. And they want to interview you."

He stared at Vaterman. Would *The New York Times* believe this story? What if they did not believe it? What would convince them?

He looked back at the Victorian paintings, alien and vulnerable under this metal American sun. This sun is a danger; it could fade those colors and diminish the paintings' claim to authenticity. There should be a larger tarpaulin on that stall. At once.

2

On that same afternoon Lieutenant Henry Polita of the Salinas County Sheriff's office arrived with his partner to investigate an anonymous complaint that a fairgrounds was being set up illegally in the motel's parking lot. Both were uniformed officers. They were shown at once to Maloney's motel room. Polita, a heavy young man with a sarcastic manner, chewed gum disconcertingly all through Maloney's explanations as though he, Polita, were silently mouthing obscene words of disbelief. From the outset he acted on the assumption that the Collection had been stolen. His first question was to inquire if Maloney was the owner of the objects in the parking lot. Maloney said he was, but there were special circumstances which he had better explain. Polita then asked if it was not true that Maloney had informed Mr. Bourget, owner of the motel, that the Collection was his, and also if he had made a deposition to that effect to an official of the Securiguard service. Maloney said this was the case, whereupon Polita asked if he, Maloney, had a city permit to exhibit merchandise in a public place. Maloney explained that he was not exhibiting the Collection but merely guarding it pending its ultimate disposition, which had not yet been determined. Polita then said the way the Collection was set up in aisles, it certainly looked as though somebody was planning to exhibit it. He inquired as to the country of origin of the goods and asked by what right they had been imported into the United States. It was then that Maloney, knowing the extreme danger of telling his story to a policeman, nevertheless began, haltingly, to recount exactly what did happen, namely that he was a Canadian passing through Carmel, and that he had had a dream. And so on.

On completion of Maloney's account, Lieutenant Polita, masticating gum, stared out of the window for what seemed an unconscionably long time. Then said: "You say you woke up, went to this window here, looked out, and that this stuff you dreamed about is what's sitting in the parking lot there? Is that what you just said?"

Maloney agreed it was. Lieutenant Polita then asked: "Are you Catholic?"

"No."

"That's funny."

"What do you mean?"

"I mean this is a miracle, isn't it?"

At this juncture the second police officer looked up and uttered a loud laugh. Lieutenant Polita joined in. Still laughing, both men went toward the bedroom door, but as they were about to leave the room, Lieutenant Polita turned, unsmiling, to announce that Maloney's story was in no way to be believed, that his possession of the Collection laid him open to several possible charges, that the police proposed to look into his record and the circumstances of his arrival in the United States, and that further proceedings could be taken in the matter. After the departure of the police officers, it became evident that they had also sown seeds of mistrust in those who harbored Maloney and the Collection. This became apparent almost at once when Bourget knocked on the bedroom door.

"When the photographer is through, I want that stuff removed from my lot. I want the place clear by morning, you understand?"

"But you accepted two days' rent."

"I'll give you a refund. I don't know what your business is, but I don't want any part of it. I've never had any trouble here."

"Mr. Bourget, I've done nothing wrong. On the contrary."

"You've got no per*mit*. That's what the officer said."

"What sort of permit?"

"How do I know what sort of per*mit*? You're in the antiques business, not me. You say you own this stuff, then you should know what sort of per*mit* you need."

Maloney told Bourget he would see what he could do. Bourget left. A few minutes later a man named John Lilley phoned from the motel lobby, saying he was from the Monterey television station and asking for an interview. He had, it seemed, heard from the local police of the Collection's existence. Maloney agreed to see Lilley, and as he stood in the motel bedroom, telling his story to the reporter, the following incident occurred. This description of it was later tape-recorded by the Vanderbilt University researchers:

"I remember when I talked to Lilley, it was about five

o'clock and still quite light. But I had a feeling that the sky was getting dark. At the same time I felt myself becoming sleepy, as I had earlier in the day. I went to the window and opened it, hoping the fresh air would revive me. Below me, moving in an aisle of the Collection, was a man with cameras and lighting equipment, the photographer, I supposed, from *The New York Times*. I saw him turn some floodlights on a stall containing a pianoforte, an equitone saxophone, and other musical instruments. The photographer approached the stall and, raising his camera, clicked the shutter. The objects he had photographed seemed to shimmer, fade for a moment, then reappear, not as they had been before but with a slight—I can't quite explain it—well, a slight difference in their texture. I remember that I called out: 'Wait! Stop!' and that Lilley, coming to my side, asked me what was wrong and I said: 'They're being spoiled.' I had no idea why, but I saw that the original bloom was no longer present on these particular instruments. It was as though, by being photographed, they had lost some of their natural freshness.

"At that moment a second man appeared behind the photographer, a large bald man who shouted to me: 'I'm Brewster from the *Times*. Are you Professor Maloney? What's wrong? Is something wrong?'

"I was unable to answer. I had invited these people to come here. I sensed that, while they were performing their job, their attitude was wholly skeptical toward my claims. If I now forbade them to photograph the Collection, how could I secure the record I needed in case it disappeared before the day was over? The slight fading, the difference in the objects before and after photography, was visible to me, but might not be to other people. The truth is, I had got myself into an awkward situation and didn't know how to get out of it. The bald man, Brewster, was at least ten years older than I and was obviously accustomed to giving orders. He intimidated me. And, at that very moment, Lilley, standing by my side, asked permission to do a filmed television interview with me. I told myself I must not be overprotective of the Collection. Other people were now involved. In a way, the Collection seemed to be passing out of my hands."

It was true. From that point on, not only the Collection but he himself seemed to be passing into the control of others. Brewster and his photographer bustled in and out of the motel bedroom, as did lighting and sound men and other members of the local television crew. A makeup girl arrived to put tan coloring on his face. Lilley began to prepare a list of questions. In the midst of all this, Maloney began to feel hungry. "I think I'll run out and get a sandwich," he told Brewster. "I haven't eaten all day."

"No, better stay here. We might need you. We'll get some food sent in. Hey, Vaterman! Go get some food— pizza, chicken, beer, and whatever. Professor Maloney is hungry."

"Brewster, I am a reporter. I am not your servant."

"Are you working for us, or aren't you? Go get some food."

"Are you trying to insult me? Who the hell do you think you are?"

"Wait," Maloney said. "Why can't we just phone for some food?"

Brewster at once backed off. "Fine by me. Whatever you say, Professor."

Vaterman, his pale anger subsiding, came confidentially to whisper in Maloney's ear. "Thank you, Professor. I'll be delighted to phone. Just tell me what sort of food you wish. As for beer, perhaps I can ask my girlfriend to pick up a case. I would like very much for you to meet her. Will that be all right?"

"Of course."

Half an hour later, Bourget telephoned from the lobby. "Professor Maloney? Listen, I'm not running a restaurant here. What is this?"

"What is what?"

"Some girl looking for you. Beer delivery. And two delivery boys with a whole heap of food blocking up my front entrance. That entrance has got to be kept clear. That's the law."

"That will be my girlfriend," Vaterman told Maloney. "Let's go and get her, okay?"

Together they went out into the lobby.

Vaterman's girl was about twenty years old, tall and slender, with glossy auburn hair which fell to her shoulders. She wore a simple, long, white cotton dress and a red velvet cape. Her feet were shod in thong sandals.

"This is Professor Maloney, Mary Ann. Professor, this is my girlfriend, Mary Ann McKelvey."

Her eyes met Maloney's and at once she blushed. "Pleased to meet you," she murmured in a voice so low he barely heard it.

"Where do you want the stuff?" one of the delivery boys asked. "It's forty-one fifty with the side orders."

Vaterman took charge. "This way, please"—ushering the delivery boys toward Maloney's motel room. And, as she did not move to follow, Maloney found himself alone with the girl. "You go ahead," she said in her half whisper. "I'll just wait here."

"Maybe you'd like to join us for supper? There seems to be plenty of food."

Again she colored and, avoiding his eye, seemed to search the ceiling for an answer. "Well, I guess not. I mean, I'd have to ask Fred."

"Let's go and see him then. He's in my room."

The shy have a power to transmit, like disease, their awkwardness of movement. Maloney at once became clumsy, maneuvering her across the lobby toward his motel room, where Lilley, the television reporter, ignoring her, pushed past her, his smile fixed on his subject. "If you're ready now, Professor? Perhaps we can do the interview before you eat?"

The television interview. Cameras pointing at him. The lights. The deferential yet inquisitorial tones of the interviewer. This moment, more than his dream, had the unreal, minatory quality of a dream. And, later, when the television crew had departed and supper had been eaten, companionably, with Brewster and his photographer and Vaterman and his girl, Maloney turned on the television set and, within minutes, was presented with his first sight of himself on a television screen. Not that self he thought he knew, but a shabbily dressed stranger, a person whose hands clenched and unclenched as he spoke, that same stranger he sometimes caught sight of when trying on a jacket in a triptych mirror in a clothing store, a person not to be trusted, now telling an absurd-sounding story until, mercifully, the camera cut away from him, leaving the disembodied voice to stammer on as it panned down from a nearby rooftop, roving among aisles and stalls,

34

inspecting a tiny part of that plethora which was the Collection.

"Hey, they shouldn't have done that," Vaterman said. "You never gave them permission to take any shots."

"Quiet!" Vaterman's girl's voice was suddenly loud. Everyone stared at her as, squirming, she seemed to fold herself inward in instant embarrassment. "I'm sorry—it's just—what Professor Maloney's saying is so interesting."

Maloney looked at her. She sat, hunched before the television set, her dress rucked up to reveal her elegant, coltish legs, as, mesmerized, she stared at the television screen. And suddenly it came to him. This girl believes in the Collection. As other people will believe in it. Unlike those ghost things you read about, this can be photographed. People will know it really happened.

Roughly half an hour after the local television news ended, cars began to appear on Bluff Road, moving in a clogged procession toward the Sea Winds Motel. A red chain of taillights winked on and off all the way down to the ocean and back up through a maze of connecting streets into the center of Carmel. Some drivers, abandoning their cars, moved on foot toward the parking lot, to stand, a frieze of faces, facing the security guards at the entrance, watching the photographer at work. In time, as the press of the crowd grew, a few adventurous teenagers managed to duck past the two security guards. The guards, running to pursue them, left the main entrance unattended. Within minutes the aisles, stalls, booths of the Collection were filled with a throng of curious sightseers.

Brewster phoned the police. The Salinas County Sheriff's office, on learning that the request for assistance came from *The New York Times,* at once promised full cooperation. Two patrol cars, followed by a crowd-dispersal unit, arrived at full siren. Sheriff's deputies, equipped with bullhorns, entered the parking lot and evacuated the mobs of sightseers. Warnings were broadcast that souvenir hunters would be prosecuted. Within minutes, the lot had been emptied, apparently with no damage or loss to the many groupings of the Collection. Police barriers were then set up, sealing off the block containing the motel, and through traffic was rerouted by a detour. Shortly after eleven, the flow of sightseers having been diverted and the crowds dispersed, the sheriff's deputies left the scene. The photographer's floodlights were switched off. Coffee was served and Brewster announced that the job of photographing the Collection was complete.

"No, it's not. Not yet," Maloney heard himself say.

"What?"

"There are a number of concealed drawers, cupboards, and compartments which have things hidden in them. The Victorians had many secrets. For one thing, there is the Carrington Collection of Flagellatory Instruments and Literature, which is concealed behind a false wall in the Zollverein Indian Room. There is the Dodson-Hutter Collection of Pedophilic Photographs, concealed behind false panels in a sideboard carved in oak in the Renaissance style by Graham and Sidgwood of London. There are some holograph wills concealed in double-bottomed drawers. The Victorians were secret hoarders. There are at least two golden-sovereign collections which you have not yet uncovered. There is a silver-coin hoard. There is an artificial phallus concealed in a false compartment in the statue 'The Turkish Slave' by Henry Powers. There are a number of wonderful things like this, which you've missed."

Brewster, who hitherto had conducted his inquiries in

a polite, if skeptical, tone, now showed his first sign of irritation. "Why didn't you mention this before?"

"I didn't know about it before," Maloney said. "I just sensed it now, when you said the photography was finished."

Brewster sighed. "All right, Harry," he told the photographer. "You can wrap up now. We'll get those other shots in the morning."

"But that may be too late," Maloney said.

"What do you mean?"

"I mean, if I fall asleep tonight, maybe the Collection will go out of my mind and vanish."

For a long moment Brewster was silent. Then he signaled his photographer. "Okay, we'll do it tonight."

"But how will I find the hidden stuff?" the photographer asked.

"Professor Maloney will have to show us. Right, Professor?"

"Yes, fine."

At that moment Vaterman's girl whispered, "Fred, I'd better be going."

"I'll see you home," Vaterman said.

The girl, Mary Ann, stood, then, awkward, turned to Maloney. "It certainly was a great pleasure meeting you, sir."

"Please. My name is Tony."

She blushed and shook her head, as though this familiarity would be impossible, then said in her whisper, "I'd really like to, you know, to really see some of those wonderful things, sometime."

"Well, come back tomorrow. I haven't seen most of it myself."

"Oh, no, I couldn't disturb you."

"No bother."

The photographer, girding himself with cameras, interrupted. "Ready, Professor?"

"Right. Good night, ah—Mary Ann."

"Good night."

And so Maloney went with Brewster and the photographer down to the darkened aisles of the parking lot, going unerringly toward the secrets of the Collection, opening first a hidden back panel in an oaken cabinet by Grace of London to reveal the rare holograph will of a poor clergyman, bequeathing his four young daughters as an aid and comfort to the knight who paid for his living. From there he went to the hidden Papist codicil signed by Lord Craigbroke, which was concealed in a statue entitled H.R.H. the Prince of Wales as a Young Shepherd, a work by T. and A. Thornycroft. From this discovery he led the photographer to the grand center portion of a service of plate presented to the Earl of Ellenborough in India. Within the largest urn, he uncovered a hoard of one hundred golden sovereigns. From a massive tea service made of California gold by Ball Tompkins & Black, he took a treasure of five hundred silver crowns. Then, from a variety of false drawers, hidden panels, and double-door bookcases, he withdrew a dozen or more smaller hoards, purse after purse of sovereigns and half sovereigns, so well hidden by thrifty Victorians as insurance for a rainy day that they remained undiscovered after their owners' untimely deaths. But the first great shout of surprise came from the photographer when Maloney pressed a concealed button in the wooden nipple of a carved rosewood nymph which stood at the entrance to the Indian Room, a room in the manner of the Raj, designed by Sir Arthur Zollverein for a former viceroy. Slowly, a false wall rolled aside at the rear of the room, to reveal a secret chamber within, an inner room some fifty feet long by eighteen feet wide. This was the Correction Chamber, designed by Charles Carrington, master of that Paris publishing house which dominated the field of English erotica at the turn of the century. There, in addition to a wall displaying various instruments of flagellation, were two stout wardrobes filled with choice items of bondage, a selection of whipping horses and torture racks, and some punishment costumes for females, featuring removable posterior panels. Further cries of surprise went up when Maloney pressed a concealed button in the nymph's left nipple. At that moment a second false wall fell away inside the inner, secret Correction Chamber, to reveal the entire collection from Carrington's Flagellation Desk, volume after volume lavishly illustrated, showing both youths and maidens engaged in scenes of Sadean torture and fornication. The photographer, loitering lasciviously over these drawings, at first showed interest in photographing a selection of plates, but Brewster, worried about the hour, vetoed this, ordering instead an overall shot simply showing a wall of books.

At one o'clock in the morning, while work was still in progress, Mr. Bourget came down into the lot and told Maloney that there was an urgent long-distance call for him from a Dr. Someone in Amsterdam, Holland. Maloney, on taking the call, found himself speaking to Dr. Johannes Fetema, the renowned Dutch clairvoyant and president of the International Society for Parakinesic Research. Dr. Fetema, who had heard a radio account announcing that Maloney had dreamed these objects into life, was, understandably, excited. After introducing himself and giving his credentials, Dr. Fetema engaged Maloney in the following exchange.

"Professor Maloney, first may I ask you a personal question? Do you have a spirit, an animus? Are you a medium?"

"No, I'm not a medium. I don't believe in spiritualism."

"That doesn't matter. Has someone tried to get in touch with you? Some man or woman? A voice, perhaps?"

"No, nothing like that, sir. It was a dream."

"My animus indicates to me that you have met someone today who may be very important to you. The presence of this person may be connected with what has happened."

"No, sir, I don't think so."

"Yet, you had someone in mind just now? Someone you just met?"

"Yes, a girl. But I don't see the connection."

"Is she physically close? Say, in your building?"

"Well, she was here earlier."

"This is good. My animus indicates she may be of importance. Will you be seeing her again?"

"I don't know, sir. I think so."

"Excellent. Now, I have another question. Is it true that the objects you have materialized have disappeared from their former locations?"

"I don't know, for sure. Some of these things don't exist in other places. They are descriptions I read in books."

"Excellent! Congratulations."

"Sir, could I ask you a question?"

"Of course."

"What do you think will happen when I go back to sleep tonight? Will the Collection disappear?"

"No, you can sleep. Take my word for it."

"There's no danger, then, that the stuff will disappear?"

"There is always a danger. But my animus indicates to me in this instance that your achievement will not dematerialize overnight."

"Thank you, sir."

"Not at all. Get a good night's sleep. And again, my sincere congratulations."

When Maloney hung up, his former drowsiness had vanished. He felt elated. He at once went to Brewster to ask if the London office of *The New York Times* could find out if any items were missing from English collections.

"Why do you want to know?"

"Because, if nothing is missing, then I haven't merely moved the things from one place to another by some sort of telepathy. It will mean I've created a second set of originals."

"Okay, give me a list," Brewster said.

Maloney at once wrote out a short list, noting only large items which he had seen in the Victoria and Albert Museum. Brewster promised to cable an inquiry at once. Maloney then returned to the parking lot and helped uncover the last hidden items in the Collection. At 2 A.M., the photography having been completed, he left the parking lot and returned to his room. Alone for the first time since morning, he locked his door, went to the window, and raised the blind. Below him, graveyard

41

still in the harsh Pacific moonlight stood the stalls, aisles, and awnings of the Collection. A guard, walking down the central aisle, sent his flashlight circling, will-o'-the-wisp over the booths. Why had this happened? Was this the beginning of some new stage in human history, a time when objects from former eras would begin to materialize, piling up on people's front doorsteps?

Maloney did not believe in God. God was, like Santa Claus, a word his mother used. Nor did he believe in evil spirits, extrasensory perception, or creatures from another planet. Even now, looking out at the Collection, he did not for a moment entertain the notion that some mystical Presence had willed this to come to pass. Nor could he believe it was a hoax: the Collection was too astonishing, too valuable to be anyone's prank. In a way, as its possessor, he was already, potentially, a very rich man.

He pulled down the blind, went into the bathroom, and began to undress. Mirrored in the cold hygienic lights, his naked body seemed angular and ungainly, his face a Judas face, already trapped in damaging admissions. Looking at himself, recognizing that undependable other he had known all his life, he felt he would convince no one: historians, police, press, scientists—imagine the inquiries this face must now face: think of the hundreds of times it will look baffled, deceitful, stupid, when asked these unanswerable questions.

No. One dream was simply not enough. People would dismiss it as a freak accident, a flash in the pan. To make it stick, he would have to dream a second dream and deliver it into the world, real as the Collection. *Then* they would believe him.

He shivered suddenly in an unexpected, almost orgiastic spasm of excitement. *A new dream.* Naked, he went back into the motel bedroom and lay on the bed. What if I've developed a talent for making my dreams come to life? Do I want to be rich? All right, supposing I dream of banknotes filling this room, stacks of hundred-dollar bills, all along that wall in groups of ten thousand. And thousand-dollar bills in groups of hundred thousands, stacked like ice cream bricks along that other wall. And cashier's checks for ten thousand dollars each, lying in a thick carpet across the floor.

He closed his eyes. Within moments, he felt himself nod toward sleep. On the screen of his dozing mind appeared the image of a small copper coin. On the back of the coin was imprinted a tiny bird. He recognized the coin as the British farthing. It was replaced by a half-penny, a penny, a threepenny bit, a sixpence, a shilling, a florin, a half crown, a half sovereign, and a golden guinea, all bearing the likeness of the old Queen. I am dreaming of a collection of Victorian coins—a part of the Great Victorian Collection.

He opened his eyes and sat up, disconsolate. It's just part of the old dream: it's not original. Think of something else. Lie down. Concentrate.

Women. If, in a dream, I could make a beautiful girl walk into this room and lie down here beside me? And then waken to find my dream come true? Eyes shut, he ran his hands over his stomach, caressing the insides of his thighs. I am naked. I will dream of her coming in, closing the door, taking off her dress and, naked, lovely, coming to me, lying on me, caressing me.

Again, he felt drowsy. The key turned in the lock of the motel-room door. A woman entered the room, a tall, long-necked, white-skinned woman, wearing elbow-length black evening gloves and a low-cut black evening gown. She advanced, gliding to the center of the room as

43

though she were being transported on a moving staircase, and now, standing before him, modestly averted her eyes from his frontal nudity. As she stood, immobile, he knew she was not flesh and blood. Familiar, yet false in her proportions, she was not a woman at all: she was a stylized portrait, a Victorian oil, "Portrait of Madame X" by John Singer Sargent.

As soon as he knew this, he awoke with a harsh cry, sitting up as though surprised in nightmare. *Maybe I can't dream any other dream?*

He shivered, but this time it was with tension. Although the night was warm, he reached down and drew the coverlet up over his naked limbs, even covering his face. He lay in this dark tent of his making, and after a moment, his fear subsiding, a drowsiness again touched his limbs and, slave to some Morphean command, he abandoned himself to sleep. And to the dream. And in the dream he rose from the bed, climbed out of the window, and walked again among the aisles of the Collection, examining with pleasure the contents of these stalls and stands—the paintings, the furniture, the manufactories, all those tangible, visible proofs of Victorian life on earth. In his dream, he patrolled his creation, awed at what he had wrought, watching over it, admiring it, guarding it. If it was not wholly original in concept, it was, nonetheless, his own. He had dreamed it into existence and now he dreamed that he guarded it. He was its owner and its custodian. He dreamed all night. And, in the morning, woke.

3

The sun shone. He got out of bed and ran to the window. The stalls, the awnings, the booths all stood. He heard a rush of murmurs, a stirring of feet as in the street beyond the police barrier the crowd sighted him. He looked on them in astonishment, and they on him with a mixture of excitement, curiosity, and disappointment. Saluting, a security guard in the aisle directly below his window called up, "Good morning, sir." Behind him, in the motel corridor, he heard a hurrying of feet, as though his awakening had just been announced. A moment later there was a knock. He unlocked his bedroom door.

It was Brewster. "How're you feeling?"

"Fine."

"I've got bad news for you. We've got an answer from London. Our office there has checked the Victoria and Albert Museum. None of the pieces you list are missing. Therefore, this stuff is fake."

"It's not."

"How can you still say that, Professor?"

"I don't know. I just know that there are now two sets of originals."

"The British don't agree with you. The London *Sunday Times* calls this a great American hoax. They've already commissioned a top Victorian expert and put him on a plane. He should be here later today."

"Good."

"You're not worried, then, Professor?"

"Why should I be? I've nothing to hide."

There was a second knock on the door. Maloney opened to the sight of Vaterman, hovering on the threshold, holding up, like a banner, the front page of *The Monterey Courier*. The entire page was given over to the story, with a photograph of Maloney and an overall view of the Collection. Maloney took the paper and began to read:

PROFESSOR CLAIMS HE "DREAMED UP" MYSTERIOUS
VICTORIANA COLLECTION FOUND IN CARMEL

By Fred X. Vaterman

A collection of Victorian objects worth, possibly, hundreds of thousands of dollars, including a scandalous collection of books and photographs of Victorian pornography and a sex torture chamber concealed behind hidden walls, has mysteriously appeared in a parking lot behind the Sea Winds Motel, Bluff Road, in Carmel-by-the-Sea. An avalanche of inquiries and world-wide interest yesterday followed announcement by Professor Anthony Maloney of McGill University, Montreal, Canada, on local Monterey station KCBC, that he . . .

46

Vaterman, interrupting, announced self-importantly, "It's just the story I wrote for my own paper, but already it has been picked up by all the wire services. It's gone out to newspapers all over the country."

"I only made page 6 in the *Times*," Brewster said. "Our editors are tough on miracles."

At the doorway, Bourget, the motel proprietor. "We held all calls until you woke, Professor. But I have one on the line now from a lady, says she's your mother. Says it's very urgent."

"I'll take it."

He sat on the bed, receiver in hand, watched by his new retinue.

"Tony, is that you?"

"Yes, Mother. How are you?"

"Oh, Tony, are you alone, can you talk?"

"Yes, go ahead."

"Well, look, what happened? What's going on out there?"

"You've seen the newspapers, haven't you? It's true. I had a dream and woke up and here it is."

"A dream? Oh, Tony! I'm your mother."

"But what can I tell you? The stuff is really out there."

"Tony, have you any idea the harm this has done you already? Which is the very reason I'm calling."

"What do you mean?"

"Well, one of the first people who was in touch with me this morning was Susan Morse. It seems Reggie hit the roof when he read the story in *The Gazette*. It identified you as a member of his department. And you know how strait-laced Reggie is."

"Don't worry about Reggie Morse. I have to call the

47

Dean, anyway. I'll need a short leave of absence to arrange things here."

"Dear, do you think that's wise? A leave of absence? I'd come home now, if I were you. Listen, on second thought, why don't I fly out today and we can travel back together. I could call Susan and say you've been sick and that I'm going out there to bring you home."

"Mother, do you hear me, you're *not* to do anything of the kind. I'll phone the Dean. Everything's going to be all right."

"Oh, Tony!" His mother seemed close to tears.

"Mother, please. Calm down."

"All right, I'm calm. But you be very careful what you say to the Dean, won't you? Promise me?"

"I promise."

Maloney hung up and at once put in a call to Dean A. D. MacDonald at the McGill University Department of History. The important thing was to get his word in ahead of Reggie Morse. The Dean's secretary said the Dean was at his Monday Luncheon Club and would return all calls later in the day. As things turned out, he did not call back for two days.

Thus, the morning began ominously. A little later, Brewster came back from a telephone conference with his New York superiors. "Well," he said. "The story seems to be picking up interest. We've decided to send out our own expert to check on your collection. He should be here this afternoon."

"Who is he?"

Brewster consulted his notebook. "A Professor Clews."

"H. F. Clews of Yale. Who's the British expert, do you know?"

Brewster turned a page. "Sir Alfred Mannings. That ring a bell?"

"It certainly does."

"That's the line-up then. Good luck."

At noon, Lieutenant Polita of the Salinas County Sheriff's office arrived at the motel in company with a Mr. Rank, who produced his badge and introduced himself as an agent of the Federal Bureau of Investigation. Maloney was then asked to make and sign two depositions, which were witnessed by Bourget. Mr. Rank asked several questions as to Maloney's family background, marital status, trips abroad, former positions, and earlier visits to the United States. Lieutenant Polita, after telling Maloney he, Polita, would, from now on, be working full time on this investigation, informed him that the bona fides of the Collection would be looked into by both state and federal agencies. He advised Maloney not to leave town and scheduled a further session for the following morning at 11 A.M.

As soon as the police officers had left, Maloney went out into the motel lounge, where he found Vaterman and Vaterman's girl sitting, sipping Cokes in the front parlor. At once he remembered the clairvoyant's remark. Could this girl really have something to do with his dream?

"Hello, Tony," Vaterman said, familiarly. The girl blushed. Maloney went to her and stood, staring at her. "Did you come to see the Collection?" he asked.

"Well, yes, but please, I don't want to disturb you. If I can just sort of look around on my own?"

"No, no. I mean, I enjoy exploring it myself. It's still

49

pretty new to me, you know. Let's go and look at it together."

"What I want to see," Vaterman said, "is that hot stuff you turned up last night after I'd gone home."

Maloney looked at the girl, who at once avoided his gaze. "Well," he said. "Actually it's pretty disgusting."

"Don't kid yourself," Vaterman said. "It will be the most popular part of the Collection."

They went out. Maloney noticed that the girl's shyness seemed to disappear completely while she was viewing the exhibits. Excited, almost childlike, attendant on every word he spoke, she followed him, entranced, as he started a tour of the main aisle. But Vaterman quickly became bored with such treasures as the Ross telescope and the Osler fountain. "What about the hot parts?" he began. "Mary Ann doesn't mind, do you?"

"No, Fred, no. But it's *all* interesting."

"Okay, but let's see the part I want to see. Okay?"

She nodded, her rich auburn hair falling forward, masking her features. "Sure," she said. "But it's up to Tony."

"Okay then," Maloney said. Suddenly he felt excited. "It's this way, just past that music-hall exhibit."

In the Indian Room, designed for the Marquess of Longview by Sir Arthur Zollverein, the lighting was a mélange of subtle yellows, emanating from lamp globes of frosted glass, shaped like half-opened water lilies. Maloney approached the rosewood statue of the wood nymph and touched the concealed button which was her right nipple. Slowly the false wall rolled back, revealing the Correction Chamber. "Oh, my!" said Mary Ann. Timid as a sacrificial vestal in her long white dress, she stepped uncertainly into the center of Carrington's evil dream. As she walked by the flogging horses and punishment racks and paused before a wall hung with every kind of spanking equipment, including hairbrushes, worn slippers, leather belts, birches, rattan canes, thong whips, cat-o'-nine-tails, and an enormous bull's pizzle, Maloney pressed the wood nymph's left nipple. The back wall of the inner chamber creakingly slid back to show the bookshelves of Sadean literature. Vaterman, grinning, pulled down one of the larger illustrated volumes, opened it, and handed it to Mary Ann. Her glossy auburn hair hid her face as she bent over the illustration. There was a swift intake of breath as she stared at a beautiful girl, her knickers down about her ankles, being flogged on the buttocks by a schoolmaster in Holy Orders. A huge member protruded menacingly from the cleric's unbuttoned trousers. Shamed (what will she think of me for dreaming up stuff like that?), Maloney hurried to take the book out of her hands. But failed: she turned away from him, abruptly, as though they were children engaged in some game. "Wait! I haven't seen it yet."

"It's pretty awful stuff."

"No. Look at this." She held up a double-page illustration showing a curious combination: a gentleman in riding breeches sodomizing his housemaid as she horsed a younger girl, whose posteriors he flogged with a thin cane. "Why is he beating her?" she asked.

"Hey!" Vaterman held up a folio of tribadic scourgings. "There's some great stuff here. You know, I should do a follow-up story on this side of your Collection."

At that moment, one of the Securiguard attendants entered the Indian Room. "Professor Maloney, Mr. Brewster says to tell you that one of the experts is here."

"I'd better close up, then," Maloney said to Mary Ann.

"No, you go ahead," Vaterman said. "I'll do it. It's these little buttons on the nipples, right?"

"Yes. Right. Are you sure you want to stay here?"

"Yes. We're having fun. You don't mind, do you?"

"No," he said, and unwillingly withdrew. His last vision of the Indian Room was the sight of their heads together, her auburn mane, Vaterman's porcine, whitish locks bent over a truly erotic first edition of *Une Société de Flagellantes*, Charles Carrington, Paris, with 31 illustrations by Martin Van Maele and A. Lambrecht.

Professor H. F. Clews, who waited in the parlor, was tall, with a port-wine nose and protuberant eyes arrested permanently in a glaucous stare. He was known to Maloney, and, indeed, to all historians of the period, as the author of the *Tractatus of Victorian Chroniclers* and also of many learned monographs.

From the first, Maloney feared him: sensed his implacable enmity. The inquisition began in cold unease and lasted more than an hour. Then, having declined Maloney's offer to act as guide, Professor Clews set off, unaccompanied, to the parking lot. His examination was thorough. At dusk, he sent word that he would need a flashlight. Floodlamps were also set up in the main aisles. The painstaking examination continued.

Sir Alfred Mannings, the second expert, arrived shortly after seven, declaring himself exhausted by his long flight from London. He at first stated that he would go directly to his room, but on learning that Professor Clews was examining the Collection, at once called for a flashlight and went down into the parking lot. He did not bother to interview Maloney. Soon, his flashlight began crisscrossing that of Professor Clews.

The experts did not speak to each other beyond a polite "Good evening." Reporters began to assemble at the entrance to the lot. There was a sense of tension, almost of crisis. As Vaterman and his girl drifted through the lobby, Maloney overheard their whispered conversation.

"Why are they taking so long, Fred?"

"Because they think the stuff is phony."

"But how could they? It's so beautiful."

"Oh, come on! It's just a lot of stuff."

"It's not. It's terrific."

"How do you know? What makes you an expert?" Vaterman said, but at that moment the girl, seeing Maloney in the lobby, nudged Vaterman, warning him to silence. Both smiled falsely as Maloney passed by.

At 10 P.M., Professor Clews came up from the lot. As his professional opinion had been commissioned by *The New York Times,* he first asked for a private meeting with Brewster, promising that he would hold a press conference afterward.

"May I join you?" Maloney asked Brewster.

Professor Clews stared, his glaucous eye forbidding. "Unethical," he said to Brewster.

And so, humiliated, Maloney was forced to wait with the reporters while Brewster and the expert closeted themselves in Brewster's room.

Later, Brewster wrote for his superiors a report on this secret meeting. From the outset, Professor Clews cast doubt on Maloney's qualifications as a historian. "While this young man may have received a doctorate from a *Canadian* university," Professor Clews told Brewster, "there is absolutely no reason to believe that his knowledge of Victoriana is that of an expert. There is, to my mind, something wholly untrustworthy about this young person. Perhaps he is insane. I am not qualified to judge. But, certainly, his claim that he 'dreamed up' this collection is not worthy of serious comment, don't you agree?"

"But what about the Collection itself?" Brewster asked.

"Very skillful fakes. In addition to items from British public collections, it contains what seem to be skillful imitations from private collections, not known to me personally."

"Maloney claims that many of these items have only been written about and that they do not exist in any known collection in their present form. In other words, that they are his own original creations, based on his research."

"I know what he claims," Professor Clews said. "But I would suspect the truth is rather more prosaic. In my view, these copies were created in what is, almost certainly, a fraudulent attempt to lure collectors to purchase them at very inflated prices. Nowadays, as you may know, there is a considerable collecting boom in items of Victoriana."

"So you believe that all these things are fakes?"

"Well, no. Possibly the coin collections and the pinchbeck jewelry collection are genuine. Hard to tell with that sort of thing. But in the majority of cases the things you see out there are copies of well-known originals which I know are stored elsewhere. Ergo, these copies here are just that. Copies. Fakes."

"All right. But don't you think a clever crook would think up a more plausible story?" Brewster asked. "I mean, no one in his right mind could hope to get away with saying he dreamed this stuff up. I've been wondering who's behind Maloney. He doesn't strike me as very smart."

Professor Clews made a small rictus, impersonating a smile. "As a historian, let me comment that such conjecture is dangerous. I can only say that were I you, and were I representing a national newspaper, I would exercise great caution to avoid giving credence to a hoax, exposure of which will certainly discredit you and your publication."

"So you're sure it will be exposed as a hoax?"

"Indubitably."

"Okay. But, as we hired you for an opinion, I'd be obliged if you'd say nothing to the other newspapermen until I have time to check this out with my office in New York."

"Mr. Brewster, my contract does not specify that I must keep silent. Silence, in this case, would imply tacit approval of a probable fraud. I am afraid, if asked, I must tell the truth as I see it. After all, my critical reputation is at stake."

"All right," Brewster said. "In that case, let's get it over with."

But when Brewster and Professor Clews went down to the motel parlor, a press conference was already in progress. The reporters, together with Mary Ann and Maloney, were listening to Sir Alfred Mannings, who delivered himself of the following opinions.

"First of all, I have not interviewed Professor Maloney and, thus, cannot make a judgment on the truth or otherwise of his assertion that these items are supernatural in origin. Alas, I am not qualified to deal with such metaphysical matters. What I am qualified to discuss—and no one is better qualified, may I add—is the authenticity and origins of many items which you can see outside there in that car park. I am Director General of British Imperial Collections with authority over the museums in which a great many of the originals of these items are on exhibit."

A reporter from Reuters interrupted: "You said 'originals,' Sir Alfred. Does that mean you believe these items here to be copies?"

"Let me try to be more precise," Sir Alfred replied. "The extraordinary fact is that every object of which I have first-hand knowledge is here reproduced in a form indistinguishable from its original. Not only that, many items known to me only through book illustrations and other descriptions are here reproduced just as they must once have existed. It is a truly astonishing feat of copying."

Maloney, face flushed, heard himself speak up in protest. "Why do you say they are copies, if you admit there is no original in existence?"

"You would seem to have a point there, young man," Sir Alfred said. "But let's think about it, shall we? Perhaps there is no original in existence. Yet you claim that you 'dreamed' these objects up after reading about them in books, and so on. Now, if you 'dream up' something which you have already read about, I hardly think you can claim it as an original creation."

"Then, in your opinion, Sir Alfred, this collection is *not* original?" the Reuters reporter asked.

Sir Alfred pursed his lips. "No, I do *not* think they are fakes. I believe they are neither original nor fake. Let me give you an example. Tonight, examining these familiar and well-loved British artifacts twelve thousand miles from their true home, I must confess I felt moved to indignation. To see these wonderful treasures laid out in flea-market fashion in an American car park! One's blood boils. And then I came on an object particularly dear to me, because I was its original discoverer. I refer to the Nouds Hop Pickers Tea Urn, which I turned up many years ago, on Colonel Addison's estate near Sittingbourne in Kent. Gentlemen, I dug the original urn out of the earth. I know its lineaments as I know those of my own face. Yet this tea urn here in Carmel not only resembles the original Nouds urn, it is *indistinguishable* from the original. It was as though today I became the first man in the world to look on something which has never been seen before: a unique object which has, mysteriously, become a duality."

"Then it's *not* a fake?" the Reuters man persisted. "You're saying it's sort of a mysterious re-creation, or something?"

"I am not saying it's *not* a fake," Sir Alfred warned. "Nor am I saying it's original. I am saying it may be something which has not been categorized before, an act of homage to a period, perhaps. I'm afraid I'll have to think about it. I simply say we mustn't be too hasty in assigning it a category."

Professor H. F. Clews, who had entered the room with Brewster and had listened to most of Sir Alfred's remarks, now interrupted testily. "A fake is a fake."

"So you believe they are simple fakes, do you, Professor Clews?"

"Surely you are not claiming them as originals, Sir Alfred?"

"No, of course not."

"All right, then. If they are not originals, what is your opinion as to their origin?"

"I have no opinion on that," said Sir Alfred. "Because I don't know where they came from. Do you?"

"Well," said Professor Clews. "I don't for one moment believe they're the result of someone's dream. Do you?"

"Of course not."

"Excuse me, gentlemen," said the Reuters reporter. "Do I take it that both of you reject Professor Maloney's explanation?"

At this point the two experts exchanged glances; then, as though performing some prearranged vaudeville routine, they raised their eyebrows, shrugged, and nodded their heads affirmatively.

Maloney felt his face grow red.

"Well, gentlemen, it's quite late and I've had a very exhausting journey. Good night." Sir Alfred Mannings went toward the door.

"Good night, gentlemen," said Professor Clews, joining his colleague in the walk out. The reporters, including Vaterman, at once rushed for the telephones, leaving Maloney alone in the room with Vaterman's girl, who fidgeted for a moment, then came up to him, her large eyes serious, her manner that of a child preparing a recitation.

"I just want to tell you," she said, "that I think that was awful—just stupid. All that talk about fakes and originals—I mean, they're missing the point. The point is, you dreamed up this stuff and made it all come to life out there. That's got to be sort of genius—right?"

Flushing, a weal of redness going from her cheek to her long elegant neck, she turned and hurried out of the room. He stared after her, moved—*sort of genius*—God bless her! But his anger, heavy and painful, remained as he went to his bedroom. All his life he had wanted to do something out of the ordinary. And now the subject he had studied, the objects he had seen and read about and remembered had suddenly escaped from his subconscious mind and become *real,* here in Carmel. Yet nobody seemed to understand just what had happened. All people talked about was whether these miraculous objects were originals or not. As if anything could be more original than one's dream come true!

And so, weary, worried, angry, Maloney fell asleep on that second night of the Collection's existence. And dreamed. And in the dream, rose from the bed, climbed out of the window, and walked again among the aisles of his Collection, looking with wonderment at the stalls, the stands, the paintings, the books, the furniture, the jewels, the manufactories, all those tangible, visible proofs of Victorian life on earth. In his dream he patrolled his creation, lovingly lingering over its particulars—a Collection unsurpassed by any other assemblage of its kind. He had dreamed it into existence and now he dreamed that he guarded it against all enemies in a world which did not yet realize its true worth. He was its creator and would become its defender. Again he dreamed all night. And, in the morning, woke.

4

"Tony, may I see you, please?"

"Sure, Fred, come on in. Where's Mary Ann? Did she come out with you this morning?"

"No, she's at her own place." Warily, Vaterman sat on Maloney's bed and unfolded a newspaper. "I wanted to explain this story to you. I didn't want you to feel angry at me personally."

Maloney took the newspaper. It was *The Monterey Courier*. On the right-hand side of the front page was a three-column headline.

BRITISH, AMERICAN EXPERTS CONCUR:
CARMEL ''DREAM'' COLLECTION IS
FAKE
Yale professor hints at scheme to
defraud would-be collectors

There was no need to read the story.

"I want you to know I didn't write that," Vaterman

60

said. "I sent in a more favorable version and Yorkin, my editor, had it rewritten. It's not my fault."

"That's all right, Fred."

"And now Yorkin has turned the follow-up story over to the police desk. He wants me to go back to my regular beat. It's awful. I mean, this is the most important story that ever happened in this town and they're trying to ruin it."

Angry, Vaterman tossed the newspaper aside and stood up, his whitish locks forming an aureole around his impassioned face. "Not only that," he said. "These stories are ruining *you*. You've got to clear yourself. You should put out a press release, stating your position. Better—you should call a press conference."

"What about? What can I say?"

"Wait, wait," Vaterman said excitedly. "I've just had a great idea. Why don't we get Mary Ann to come to work as your secretary? I could write your press releases and she could type them. We could really help you."

"But I couldn't ask you to do that."

"Why not? Listen, it would be good for me too. You see, with Mary Ann working right here in the motel, I could keep up with every development of the story."

"I thought you said you'd been taken off the story?"

"But that's it!" Vaterman, agitated, went to the window and pointed dramatically to the aisles and awnings of the Collection. "This is *my* story. I've got to stay with it."

"Look, Fred, there's another point. I can't afford to pay you."

"Don't worry about that. The way we feel, Tony, it will be an honor to help you. Besides, Mary Ann doesn't have any job right now and, between ourselves, the kid is bored sitting at home all day. Look—don't you want to clear your name? Are you going to let these people call you a liar?"

"All right. Well, in that case, thanks. Thanks very much."

"Good. I'll tell Mary Ann. I think she should come over here at once."

"Are you sure she'll want to do it?"

"Of course, I'm sure," Vaterman said. "She wants to help me. And besides she's very excited by this Collection. She talks about nothing else."

"Well, I'll have to make some salary arrangement with her. Maybe I could sell off some item from the Collection."

"Don't sell a thing!" Vaterman said, buttoning up his safari jacket Mao-style, and turning, determined, in the direction of the door. "Just you leave it to us."

On that same afternoon a small hairy man arrived in Carmel by private plane and was brought in at once by Bourget in direct contravention of Maloney's instructions about visitors. "Professor, this is a gentleman who has arrived to see you. It's very important, I took the liberty."

Money had changed hands. Bourget backed out of the room.

"Professor Maloney, my name is Hickman, which may not mean anything to you. The firm of which I happen to be president is Management Incorporated, which you may have heard of."

"Mr. Hickman, this is my secretary, Miss McKelvey. She handles all appointments."

"How are you, dear. Professor, I know how important

your time is. I apologize for bursting in like this. But I felt this matter was important enough for me to make a special trip from New York. So if you will give me a minute? Just one minute?"

"All right. But we have a television interview at four, isn't that so, Mary Ann?"

"Yes, Tony."

Hickman made a small throat-clearing sound. "Thank you. First, let me say that in all my years in this business I've never seen anything so completely mismanaged as your discovery. Why, the way the media has treated you is a crime!"

"What is your business, exactly, Mr. Hickman?"

"Professor, I'll bet people are asking you who represents you?"

"No. Not exactly."

"Well, they will. And let me explain. Management Incorporated is not only an agent, it is a combination of lawyer, business manager, and personal friend. Do you realize the harm already done this collection of yours by allowing the *Times* to send in those experts without proper briefing? *We* would not have handled it that way. We would, first of all, have hired our own experts as a backup. We would have orchestrated the news of each step in this story for maximum effect. In the first place, I hear that the Collection contains one of the world's most fabulous lodes of erotica. Do you realize the audience potential in a discovery of that sort?"

"No, I suppose I don't. The dream aspect, I believe, is by far the most important one."

"Of course, of course. Professor, let me ask you another question. What do you think of the idea of moving this Collection to a more suitable location?"

"I'm afraid that would be very difficult."

"Why? I believe you know Dr. Johannes Fetema, the Amsterdam clairvoyant?"

"Well, we spoke on the telephone."

"Professor, before leaving New York I took the liberty of consulting Dr. Fetema, also by telephone. He gave it as his opinion that now that the items have fully materialized here, the Collection will not be damaged in the slightest by its transit to a new location."

Toy engine. Japanese fake. "He's wrong. It mustn't be moved."

"Is that a creative decision?"

"Yes."

"Very well. Will you let me get back to Dr. Fetema with a further question? I'll only be a few minutes."

"Tony, it's nearly four," Mary Ann warned.

"Your interview. Fine, go ahead. I'll contact you when you're through with your taping."

Maloney and Mary Ann then went across the corridor, where a television mobile unit had been set up. Half an hour later, when they emerged from the interview, Hickman was waiting in the corridor, a triumphant smile on his face. "Suggestion. What if you leave the Collection here in Carmel, but you yourself travel and lecture on it? Dr. Fetema thinks that would be possible. And I can set up a truly substantial set of bookings, if we move now, while this story is hot, so to speak. You could make one hundred thousand dollars in six weeks."

"One hundred thousand dollars?"

"That is correct, yes."

"And Dr. Fetema thinks the Collection won't disappear if I go away and leave it, under guard, here in Carmel?"

64

"That is his judgment, yes."

Maloney turned to Mary Ann. "You know, that means I could go back to Montreal. I could get my old job back."

"Why would you do that?" Hickman said. "There are thousands of history professors. But, as the creator of this Collection, you're unique."

"Look, I trained all my life to be a history professor."

"That's no longer the point, if you don't mind my saying so. The point is, did you or did you not dream up this Collection. Your credibility is the issue, don't you realize that?"

"He's right," Mary Ann whispered.

"Of course I'm right," Hickman said. "And when I suggest a lecture tour to put your point of view across, I assume you'll want to take your own people along. Like your secretary. Remember, it will be first class for you and your party all the way."

"Well, I don't know. I'd have to think about it."

"All right, why don't you do that. Tell you what. I have to go into Monterey for an hour. I'll come back and check with you before I leave for New York. All right?" Hickman produced, like a tip, a sudden, broad smile. He turned and went out of the front door. A Lincoln Continental waited. He waved to them as he got in.

Maloney and Mary Ann went back to the motel room. "Tell me," he said, watching her for reaction. "Would you like to go on a lecture tour?"

"Oh, gosh, I don't know. I'd have to ask Fred. But I do think you should get all the publicity you can."

"It's all very well for Dr. Fetema to say the Collection won't disappear if I go away from here. But what if he's wrong?"

She looked at him, her large, luminous eyes clouded with sudden fear. "Do you mean, if you leave, it might vanish, or something?"

"It might."

"Then you'd better not risk it." She went to the window and looked out. "It's—it's just the most perfect thing. It would be terrible if you lost it."

"Tell you what. Why don't I try an experiment, a sort of trial run?"

She turned from the window, her face questioning.

"I mean, I could get in the car and drive, say, twenty miles down the coast. You'd stay here and watch the Collection. I could phone back and check with you to see if it's still all right. Is Fred around?"

"Yes, he just came in. He's writing a press release in the parlor."

"All right. Let's tell him our plan."

"Well . . ." she murmured and hung her head.

"What's the matter?"

"Couldn't I come with you? We could leave Fred to watch the Collection."

"Why do you want to come with me?"

"I don't know. I just would like to come, that's all."

"All right," Maloney said. "Let's go tell Fred."

Mary Ann wore a blue silk shawl over her long white dress. The sun shone as their car moved past the sightseers outside the parking lot, turning south in the direction of Big Sur. Maloney drove in silence, and as they passed the rich villas on the outskirts of Carmel and came to a bare, bleak vista of cliffs and cold turbulent ocean, he was filled with a panicky sensation, like the one he experienced in an airplane when he heard a

66

strange noise, the lowering of the undercarriage or the changing tempo of an engine. Within moments he had slowed to a pace so dilatory that other drivers began to sound their horns and move past, giving him angry looks.

"What's wrong, Tony?"

"Supposing it disappears?"

"It won't. And, like you said, you have to find out sometime."

"That's true. Yes, that's true."

"Would you like me to drive?"

"No."

"Then I think you could go a little faster. We're holding up traffic."

"Maybe we should stop and phone?"

"But, Tony, we've only gone eight miles."

He accelerated slightly and, as he did, felt her move closer to him on the car seat, her body from shoulder to long, elegant thigh reassuring him by the most subtle of contacts. Her voice, that increasingly familiar, diffident whisper, repeated, "It won't disappear. It *won't.*"

He felt calmed. He began to drive faster. I've been under a constant strain, he told himself. I've needed someone to talk to. He felt grateful to her. He was glad she had come with him.

"Tell me?" he said, glancing at her. "Are you and Fred sort of engaged?"

Abruptly, she shook her head, her mane of auburn falling over her features. She moved still closer, peered at the odometer, then delicately moved away. "We've done just about twenty miles. There's a phone booth up there. You could pull in past that Mobil sign."

Obedient, he turned the car off the road, left the engine running, and entered the phone booth. Unease caught him again as he began to dial. And Vaterman's voice, answering, confirmed it.

"Thank God you called, Tony. I think you'd better come back at once."

"What happened?"

"Well, about ten minutes after you left, it began to rain. Heavy rain. Mr. Bourget says he's never seen rain like it at this time of year. Many items are threatened with water damage."

"I'll come at once."

"We're covering up stuff with plastic drop sheets. I think we've saved most of it. But I'd hurry, if I were you."

Maloney ran back to the car.

"What happened, Tony?"

"Let's go."

He drove out of the gas station. She huddled close to him, shivering. "What *happened?*" she whispered.

"It's raining on the Collection."

"But it can't be. Look, you can see Carmel across the bay. The sun is shining."

"Fred says it's raining."

He felt her tremble. "It's my fault," she whispered. "I never should have let you do this."

They drove on. He leaned forward, staring at the wet ribbon of road ahead. "Look, it *has* been raining. Do you realize what this means? If I can make it rain just by driving out of Carmel, people are going to have to believe me."

"That's right." She seemed cheered. She touched his arm, her fingers tightening on his wrist. "Of course, they'll believe you. This Collection is going to be very, very important. And I want to be part of it."

68

He looked at her. What did she mean? But, suddenly, he was himself too shy to ask.

Vaterman waited for them in the street outside the motel. "Do you want to see the damage? And, listen, can I file a story on this rain development?"

"Yes, all right."

Maloney and Mary Ann went down the central aisle. The damage seemed minor. Plastic drop sheets were draped everywhere, giving the Collection the look of a shut-up market. As they turned into one of the side aisles, Hickman came bustling up behind them.

"Hi. How do you like the drop sheets? I rushed them over here for you. Bought out the entire stock in Carmel."

"Thank you."

"I'm here to help. By the way, have you made any decision on representation?"

"Yes, I suppose I'm interested."

"Good," Hickman said briskly. "Then let's you and I have a word in private. Let's go sit in your car. That way, nobody will disturb us."

Hickman smiled at Mary Ann. "See you later, dear."

In the car, Hickman consulted his wristwatch, which was set in a twenty-dollar gold piece. "I've got to get back to New York tonight. So, let me outline, briefly, what Management Incorporated can do for you. First of all, I take it the lecture tour is out?"

"For the moment. Unfortunately."

"In that case, Carmel becomes more important, as the site of presentation, so to speak."

"Look, I don't want the Collection turned into some sort of Disneyland."

"Absolutely. I entirely agree. The first thing is for me to have a meeting with my people in New York. Then we'll go out and talk to some money and as soon as we can line up a suitable funding proposal we'll get back to you and make you an offer which will take care of the guards and the other expenses, including salaries for your staff. In the meantime, we'll make sure that you and this story are promoted in the proper manner. Oh, apropos of that, Tony—mind if I call you Tony?"

"Not at all."

"This young fellow Wasserman says he's your director of publicity. He's got to be kidding, right?"

"No. I appointed him."

"Nothing in writing?"

"I gave him my word. I can't go back on it."

"Well, we'll work something out. You just worry about the creative end, Tony. By the way, may I ask if you have another dream in the works?"

"No, not yet."

"May I say something which might be out of line?"

"Of course."

"Well, this Collection is terrific, but apart from the erotic stuff, the kinky room with the whips and the brothel parlor and so on, most of it's a bit over the heads of the general public. I keep thinking, what if you could have another dream, a different dream?"

"I've thought of that, too. But perhaps a person can only dream the sort of thing he knows. And what I know is Victoriana."

"How can anyone tell what he's capable of until he gives it a try?" Hickman said. "Don't underestimate your potential. There are many exciting dreams you could dream."

"Like what, Mr. Hickman?"

70

"Call me Bernard, okay? Well, the first thing that comes to mind is how interesting it would be if your next dream had people in it. Imagine if you could materialize real people. That would be a major breakthrough."

"I should say it would. I would be known as God."

"Ha, ha. I must tell that to my associates. Well, I have a plane waiting. I think the best thing for me to do now is talk to the money and get back to you. And in the meantime we're going to get *our* side of this story before the public. You can expect to see our experts here tomorrow. And they'll be good ones."

"When will I hear from you about the funding?"

Hickman got out of the car. "We'll be in touch. Coming back to the motel now?"

"No. I think I'll just sit here a while."

"Well, pleasant dreams, Tony. See you soon."

And walked away, Bernard Byron Hickman, short and hairy, his expensive navy-blue blazer flung over his right shoulder like a tournament cape, opening to reveal a lining of rich crimson silk. Beyond, in the parking lot, a security guard placed stones on the loose edges of one of the plastic drop sheets which flapped in the wind with a sound like distant gunfire. Alone in the car, Maloney stared out at Bluff Road, where sightseers filed by in constant procession, peering in at the Collection as though it were a palace where, at any moment, Royalty might appear among the shrouded stalls. And there, in the middle of the road, was the madman he had seen this morning: a tall unkempt figure, barefoot, wearing a greasy black suit jacket and stained white duck trousers, holding aloft a hand-lettered sign which read:

71

As the madman, lips moving in a silent babble, walked purposefully along the crown of the road, a cab almost ran him down. The cab, veering sharply, drove in at the motel entrance, was signaled down by the highway patrolman on duty, and after examination of some document, was allowed to enter the motel grounds. When it stopped outside the front door, a woman got out and began to fuss with her handbag in a way which Maloney found instantly familiar. His mother. His mother, who, as soon as she had paid the driver, turned to stare distrustfully at the shrouded stalls of the Collection; she, who had created him, peering at these things which he had created. His mother and the Collection. Even and odd. True and false.

And in that moment, staring at his mother, Maloney thought of his dead father, his father whom he now remembered not as a person but as a figure in a photograph. His father, an amateur photographer, had rarely been photographed: he had insisted in taking all the family snapshots himself. In that one remaining picture, he stood with a group of fellow editors and reporters in the city room of the *Toronto Picture Sun,* shirtsleeved, a Leica around his neck, celebrating some long-ago circulation triumph by drinking rye whiskey out of a paper cup. His father, who had spent his life arranging newspaper layouts, lived on only in one fading group portrait. As the Collection, were it now to disappear, might continue to exist only as a set of photographs taken for *The New York Times.*

Maloney's mother, bending down, picked up her bag and went into the motel. Predictably, in less than five minutes, Bourget and Mary Ann were out, hunting him among the shrouded stalls. He waited in his car, until Mary Ann came close.

"Hey."

"Oh, there you are. Your mother's here."

He got out of the car. "I know."

"You don't look pleased."

"Would you be?"

"My mother's dead," she whispered. "I only have a father."

Together they went in at the front entrance of the motel. The ground floor, including the lobby, was the original frame house around which the Sea Winds Motel had grown. On their left was a lifeless parlor, its cretonne-covered armchairs, unused fireplace, and maple side table with green silk runner, artificial as a furnished room in a folk museum, a relic of that private life the Bourgets had permanently forsaken the day they nailed the shields of credit cards on what had been the front door of their home. In these drear surroundings, fretting and pale, Maloney's mother waited.

"Hello, Mother. So you came after all."

His mother smiled nervously, like a child expecting to be rebuked.

"This is Mary Ann McKelvey, my temporary assistant."

"Yes, we've met."

"Maybe you'd like some coffee, Mrs. Maloney?"

"No, thank you. If I could just have a few minutes alone with my son?"

"Of course." Squirming, embarrassed, Mary Ann fled the room.

"*Cherchez la fille*," Maloney's mother said.

"Don't be ridiculous, Mother. That was very rude."

"Was it?"

"You know it was. Now why did you come here, when I told you not to?"

"Well, for one thing, I never heard from you again. And, for another, an hour after I called you I found out that Reggie Morse is definitely planning to get rid of you. Dear, listen to me. You must come home at once."

"What do you mean, 'get rid of' me? That's crazy."

"It's not crazy. They *are* trying to get rid of you. Susan says unless you're back at your classes by the beginning of the week, the Dean has agreed to look around for someone to replace you."

"To *replace* me?" he said. He walked across the parlor and sat on a cretonne-covered armchair, staring at the flower pattern in the rug, his mind moving gingerly around what it had just been told. He was twenty-nine years old. He had been a student until he was twenty-six. He had been lucky to find a university appointment in his home town. Very lucky. He had often said it himself, had had it said to him by former classmates, now exiled to academic Siberias in western Canada and the United States. To be a professor was to be respected, even if the money wasn't big. There were long vacations, there was a chance to do your own writing, there was advancement and, eventually, tenure. This rubble of facts, often chewed over in his mind as a hedge against dissatisfaction with present achievements and future prospects, now regurgitated with strange new intensity. Unless he was back in his classroom by next

74

week, he would be fired. His career would be ruined: he would not find another university post.

"Tony, can I say something? What if you were to come out now and tell them this is a practical joke? Tell them you made a bet with a friend in Montreal. Say you bet him that people would believe this story—now don't interrupt, please listen! If you own up now, it might just pass off as a sort of joke."

"Own up to what, Mother? Where do you think this stuff came from? Do you realize there's no earthly way I could have bought or borrowed even a fraction of what's outside there? You haven't even seen it yet. It's beautiful, Mother. It's wonderful and valuable and unique. And it's appeared here like a miracle. What do you want me to do? Go back and tell some stupid lie about it?"

"I'm not asking you to tell a lie, Tony. Oh, all right, I suppose I am. The point is, if I can't make myself believe in your story, then who *will* believe it? Nobody I've spoken to at home believes it for one single moment."

"All right, Mother, what do you suggest I do? Burn this stuff? Have somebody cart it away to the local dump? Give it to the Salvation Army? And supposing I do that, suppose I then get on a plane and go back to Montreal and next week I wake up one morning and find I've dreamed another dream and there's a whole new lot of stuff outside the window on Mountain Street?"

"That's ridiculous and you know it."

"Why is it ridiculous? Are you so sure I'll never have another dream?"

"Well, all right, I'm not sure. But I'm your mother. And I know that on both sides of the family there never

75

was anything odd, nothing like spiritualism or anything like that. I tell you the honest truth, at the back of my mind I have an idea of what's behind all this. But I'm not going to mention it."

"No, mention it."

"It will only make you angry."

"No, go on, tell me."

"I think it has something to do with Barbara. I think you borrowed this stuff from someone here and you worked up this really crazy story so that it will get a lot of attention and you can stay on out here and not go back to Barbara."

Maloney, despite himself, began to laugh in angry fashion.

"Well, isn't it true she asked you if she could come back?"

"Who told you that?"

"Never mind who told me, it's true, isn't it?"

"Yes. We were supposed to have dinner this week and talk about getting back together."

"Hah!" said his mother, and shook her head angrily, as though on the rim of tears. "I knew it. You don't *have* to take her back. I bet she talked you into it."

"She didn't talk me into it. I didn't even speak to her, I spoke to her sister. Oh, Mother, why do you relate every single thing that happens to me to my trouble with Barbara? You should hear yourself."

"I'm sorry," his mother said. "I told you I'd only make you angry."

"I'm not angry. But you're dead wrong."

"All right, dear. I didn't come all this way to fight with you. No matter what you decide to do, remember I want to help. Now, listen. I have some savings put away. I want you to have them."

"What for? What's all this about?"

"Well, if you don't go home, you're going to lose your job. And meantime, who's going to pay for all this? Who's paying for those guards out there? This must be costing you a fortune."

He stared at her. His mother who could not believe he would do anything extraordinary, because he was her son. Who offered him her life savings. His mother who sat opposite him in tears in this strange parlor, her hair, as usual, hidden behind a kerchief because there was so little left of it. He knew that. He knew that she felt guilty about the slacks she was wearing because they had cost sixty dollars. He knew that, in compensation, she had bought her blouse in a thrift shop for four dollars. He knew these things because they were the things his mother worried about. She was not equipped to face a twenty-nine-year-old son who had made his dream come true.

And so, going to her, he put his arms around her. "Now, don't worry," he told her. "Look, come outside and I'll show you the Collection. When you see it, you'll realize it isn't just some stunt to avoid taking Barbara back."

It was the right decision. When they went outside, she dried her tears. The Collection was the sort of display she, of all people, would normally enjoy. For the next hour, carefully skirting the pornographic sections, he led her up and down the aisles, watching her particular delight in the exhibits of embroidery, the silverware assemblies, the ceramics and decorated glass. The great crystal fountain by F. & C. Osler sent her into a special gush of praise as he, with some show of erudition, explained how Victoria and Prince Albert had admired it on the opening day of the Great Exhibition of 1851. "Never before," said he, quoting from memory, "had a piece of glasswork been executed involving the treatment in casting, cutting, and polishing of blocks of glass of a size so large and of a purity so uniformly faultless."

"But, Tony, it must be worth a fortune! You must have *several* fortunes here. Why, if you sold off even a little part of this Collection, you'd be as rich as Croesus."

"The police and the American government are now trying to decide whether the stuff is mine to sell."

"It's so gorgeous," his mother said, staring up at the fountain. "Imagine, if the fountain itself were working."

"It works," he said, and pressed a lever. Feathery plumes of water jetted out over the incomparable glitter of glass. The pilasters shimmered wetly, in a kaleidoscope of rainbow prisms.

"Oh, Tony! It's the most beautiful thing I've ever seen!"

Vaterman approached, coming from Bluff Road with a large package of mail. "Hey, Tony? Are you busy?"

"Hello, Fred."

"Lots more press clippings. I was just looking at some German ones. Here—from Oberammergau, even! My father's village."

"Mother, this is Fred Vaterman, who was the first reporter to write a story about the Collection."

His mother, surprisingly, adjusted her kerchief to a more rakish angle and smiled on Vaterman. "How do you do? Did Tony tell you his father was a newspaperman?"

"No, Mrs. Maloney, he didn't. Nice to meet you."

"Very nice to meet *you*, Mr. Vaterman. So you were the young man who wrote the first story about this?"

"Yes."

"It must have been so exciting, finding these treasures! I've never seen anything like them. Don't you think this is amazing?"

"Indeed it is, Mrs. Maloney."

"But, there you were, you just went right ahead and wrote about it. And I always thought newspapermen were so skeptical. My husband certainly was. He'd have been sure it was some sort of practical joke, or something."

Vaterman's eyes became wide, unblinking circles. "Practical joke?"

"Yes. You know. A prank."

"Your son is a practical joker?"

"Oh, no, not at all. It was just that, before I saw the Collection myself, I wouldn't have guessed that Tony could dream up something like this. I just wouldn't *believe* it. But now, of course, seeing's believing, as they say."

"And should *I* not have believed your son?"

"Look, Mother, don't go around giving people the impression I'm some practical joker."

"*Are* you a practical joker?" Vaterman said.

"You see? You see what you've done?"

"I'm sorry," his mother said. "Don't pay any attention to me, Mr. Vaterman. I'm always thinking of silly questions and then blurting them out. By the way, Tony, that reminds me, I promised to phone Les as soon as I got here. I want to ask his advice about this."

"Why don't we leave Uncle Les out of it?"

"No. What a thing to say! Look, I saw a phone booth

79

in the lobby. Let me just give him a buzz, I've lots of change here."

"Mother, I wish you wouldn't."

"I'll only be a minute," his mother said. She went off. Vaterman stared at her departing back.

"If this is a practical joke, then what can be the point of the joke?"

"Fred, it's not a joke. Look, I have to go and shave now. I have an interview coming up."

"But you used to play practical jokes?"

"Never."

In the motel lobby he caught up with his mother as she entered the phone booth. "Mother, I don't want you to mention the words 'practical joke' to anybody else here, do you understand? What are you trying to do, ruin me?"

"What's your room number, dear?"

"Nine."

"I'll come and see you after I talk to Les."

"Did you hear what I said about the practical joke?"

"Yes, I heard you, dear."

In the bedroom he stripped off his shirt and went into the bathroom to shave. The telephone rang in the bedroom. It rang again. Someone picked it up. He heard Mary Ann in the bedroom speaking to the caller. He began to shave. He became aware Mary Ann was standing at the bathroom door. "Tony, can I speak to you for a moment?" she whispered.

"Yes, sure."

"Fred's kind of upset."

"I know. But that's silly."

"Well, Fred worries about people making fun of him. You know—being German and all."

Maloney turned and looked at her. At once, embarrassed, she averted her eyes. "Tell me," he said. "How long have you known Fred?"

"Oh, ever since I got in a hassle with my father."

"When was that?"

"Oh, it's been a while. It's kind of a complicated story, I don't want to bore you with it."

"You won't bore me."

"Well, my father was in the army. He's retired now. Oh, hello, Mrs. Maloney. Did you make your call?"

"Yes, thank you. Am I interrupting?"

"No, no, I have some letters to mail. See you later, Tony."

Mary Ann went out.

"So your secretary comes with you to the bathroom."

"Oh, knock it off, Mother."

"It's none of my business, I know. I just came to tell you that I've spoken to Les again. He's been making inquiries on the legal side. He tells me that if you refuse to return to your classes within the week, the Board of Governors of the university will have the right to break their contract with you."

"He doesn't know what he's talking about. It's nothing to do with the Board of Governors. It's purely a departmental matter."

"Your Uncle Les is a lawyer. Now, don't tell me he doesn't know about contracts."

"He doesn't know university procedure."

"Maybe so. But he's trying to help. And he's partly responsible for the fact that you ever *got* to university, don't forget."

"I know that. For goodness' sake!"

"There's no need to lose your temper, dear. I came here to help you, not to fight with you."

"All right, Mother, I'll tell you what we're going to do. We're going to have a nice dinner this evening, just the two of us, and then, tomorrow morning, I want you to get on a plane and go home. And, above all, stop worrying."

"That walleyed girl has something to do with your staying on here, hasn't she?"

"What walleyed girl?"

"Mary Ann Whatever-you-call-her."

"She's not walleyed."

"No? Her right eye has a definite strabismus."

"Nonsense!"

"Is it? Twenty years as a grade-school teacher, looking at children's eyes for defects, do you think I can't recognize a strabismic condition? It may have been corrected from a more serious squint, but when she's relaxed, her right pupil shows a slight divergence."

"She has a tiny spacing, *very* slight, of the right eye, now that you mention it. I think it's quite attractive."

"So I was right. You're smitten with this girl."

It was always this way. No one loved him more than she did, no one angered him more surely, no one was, or ever would be, the subject of so many broken resolutions to keep his temper. And so, once again, he resolved that, no matter what, they must not fight. "Mother, I have to go for my interview. I'm late. If you ask Mary Ann, she'll arrange a room for you here. I'll come by later to pick you up for dinner. I want us to have a nice evening. And, please, let's not fight."

"I'm not fighting, Tony. You are."

82

They dined at eight. And, inevitably, they fought. They fought about a second phone call which his mother had received from her brother, the ubiquitous Uncle Les. In Uncle Les's opinion, Maloney's story of how the Collection came into being would not stand up in any court of law. Therefore, he would be denied title to the Collection. As for the supposition that the Collection was valuable, Uncle Les disagreed. No collector, in Uncle Les's opinion, would purchase items which, at any moment, might disappear into thin air.

"So you see, Tony, that changes everything, doesn't it? It doesn't matter any more whether the stuff *seems* valuable. In Les's opinion, its value is zero in the resale market. As he says, it would be like buying a card in a three-card trick."

"Oh, forget about Uncle Les."

"I'm just telling you what he said. If you're counting on this Collection to secure your financial future, you're living in a dream world."

"Mother, will you stop it? Will you please shut up? Will you go home, for God's sake! I wish you'd never come."

"I won't say another word," his mother said. "I will hold my tongue and I'll leave first thing in the morning. I'm sorry I'm such a nuisance to you. I really am."

And so, in tears, leaving her veal parmigiana untasted, his mother left the motel parlor and went to her room. Later he knocked on her door. There was no answer.

Next morning he was awakened, at seven, by the telephone ringing at his bedside. "Tony, I'm sorry to disturb you, I know the man at the desk said you don't like to be disturbed. But I just phoned Air Canada and the only direct flight to Toronto leaves at noon. So if I'm going to go home, as you want me to, I'll have to drive to San Francisco at once. I'm going to call a taxi now, and I'll stop by your room to say goodbye. In about ten minutes, all right?"

"I'll get dressed," he said. "Don't call a taxi, Mother, we'll find a car for you. I'd drive you myself, but, as I told you, if I leave here it rains."

"I don't want to be any more trouble."

"It's no trouble."

He found the home phone number which Mary Ann had left with him in case of an emergency.

"Sure, Tony, I understand. I'll be glad to drive her. I'll take her up now and I'll be back by this afternoon."

"Listen, when you get back, maybe you and Fred would like to eat supper with me tonight?"

"Fine, I guess. I'd better check with Fred."

Twenty minutes later Mary Ann arrived and picked up the keys of his rented car. He went down to the lobby to find his mother and, as he did, saw her come out of her bedroom carrying her suitcase, wearing a kerchief, slacks, and the old mink-collared coat of which she had once been so proud. She had not seen him, and as he stood watching her, she turned and walked on toward the front door. Suddenly moved, he went up behind her and caught hold of her, as though to stop her leaving.

"Tony, dear, what's the matter? Wait, let me put my suitcase down."

He held her. He did not speak.

"Are you all right? What's happened?"

"Nothing, nothing. I've got a car for you."

"You shouldn't have bothered."

He kissed her on the brow. "It's no bother."

Arm in arm they began their walk to the car. "Mother, I'm sorry about last night. Really sorry."

"I'm sorry too, dear. I shouldn't have mentioned Les."

"Listen, we'll keep in touch," he told her. "Phone me tonight, when you get home. And don't worry. I'll get it all sorted out somehow."

"I hope so, dear. I hope so."

He put her bag in the back of the car.

"Good morning, Miss McKelvey."

"Good morning, Mrs. Maloney."

"It's very good of you to drive me. It's a terrible imposition, I'm afraid."

"Oh, no. It's no bother."

He stood, facing his mother. "Well . . ." he began. But what could he say? She had come so long a way on such a hopeless journey. He had said he did not want her here.

As he stood silent, his mother stared up at him as though he were some impenetrable stranger whose language she did not speak. "Listen," she said, at last. "No matter what happens, don't worry, dear. Remember, there's always a place for you. Remember that, won't you?"

"A place?" he said, stupidly.

"Yes, of course, a place. I mean at home. I can always make up a bed for you in the spare room."

5

On the day of his mother's departure, Maloney faced a new and significant influx of experts. For, on that morning, the Vanderbilt University research group, under the direction of Dr. I. S. Spector, began a series of taped and filmed tests and interviews which, later, became the original source material for all other scholars and reporters investigating the creation of the Collection. In addition, there arrived that same afternoon Henry Prouse, Regius Professor of History at the University of Saskatchewan, and Charles Hendron, Keeper of the Dulwich Memorial Trust. Both were eminent Victorian scholars and had collaborated on a two-volume work entitled *The Lodging Houses of Victorian London*.

Management Incorporated possessed an excellent research department. Some years before, *The Lodging Houses of Victorian London* had been reviewed unfavorably in *The Times Literary Supplement*. The unsigned review was written by Professor H. F. Clews of Yale.

Within three hours of their arrival, following inspection of the main facets of the Collection, the new experts called a press conference.

"Contrary to some recent reports in the popular press," Hendron began, "it is our opinion, after a preliminary examination, that this Collection contains many original items, previously seen only in illustration or described in writings of the Victorian and Edwardian eras. For this reason alone, the Carmel Collection is, without doubt, the greatest single collection of Victoriana to have been uncovered in this century."

Professor Prouse, concurring in this opinion, made a further point. "The fact that Sir Alfred Mannings, Director General of British Imperial Collections, has admitted that even he cannot distinguish certain well-known items shown here from the originals in his possession implies that, indeed, this Collection may have come into being in a way never before known to man. I am, myself, no believer in the occult. I am a liberal humanist, agnostic in temperament. Yet I sincerely believe that today, in that parking lot, I was in the presence of what may be, perhaps, the first wholly secular miracle in the history of mankind."

The reporters in attendance at once hurried to their typewriters. Vaterman, who led the pack, wrote an enthusiastic press release which he headlined:

FURTHER EXAMINATION BY EXPERTS
REVEALS GREAT VICTORIAN COLLEC-
TION TO BE A ''SECULAR MIRACLE''

Later that afternoon Brewster announced, "New York is very impressed with this new development. They're going to give the story a full page next Monday, with a piece by me, a side bar by Professor Prouse, and a layout of pictures. That should help."

There were other encouragements. Two television networks called to request interviews. Bourget received calls from reporters asking if he had rooms to rent. A new air of optimism was apparent in the Sea Winds Motel.

Shortly after five, Maloney was taking his daily tour of the Collection when he saw Vaterman and Mary Ann come into the parking lot.

"Hi, there. How was the trip, Mary Ann? Did my mother get off all right?"

"Fine. She's *such* a nice woman."

"Humph," Vaterman said sourly.

"What's the matter, Fred?"

"Fred's still worried about the things your mother said," Mary Ann explained.

"Fred, on my word of honor, my mother doesn't know what she's talking about. Now, why don't we all have supper together tonight? Seven, all right?"

Vaterman sighed, heavily. "If you wish." He turned to Mary Ann. "I want to talk to you. Privately."

"Sure, Fred. Tony, if you'll excuse us?"

"Of course."

They went off together.

Seven o'clock came and went, but there was no sign of them. Maloney waited, disconsolate, in the lobby until half past eight. At that point, Brewster asked him to join him for dinner. Distracted, furious at Mary Ann and Vaterman, indifferent to his present company, Maloney dined in a large group which eventually included Dr. Spector and two editors from a Japanese publishing house. Twice he sent messages to Mary Ann's room in the motel and twice was told that she had not come in yet. At ten, he telephoned *The Monterey Courier* and

88

was told Vaterman had left for the evening. He then phoned Vaterman's apartment in Monterey, reaching only the answering service.

Then where were they? At ten-thirty, weary of Dr. Spector's questions and Brewster's journalistic anecdotes, Maloney asked to be excused. Dr. Spector, a tall man with a heron's stoop, leaned close. "Are you sleepy? You look sleepy."

"Yes, I am, a bit."

"Then we mustn't keep you. You must not tamper with the dream process. Pleasant dreams, and we will resume our discussion in the morning."

Maloney went to his room. As was his habit on retiring, he locked the door. At that moment, sensing something was wrong, he switched off the room light and ran to the window. Below, in the parking lot, the yellow orb of a watchman's flashlight came into view, dancing down an aisle. It was transected by the beam of a second guard's flashlight. Both lights spun in an idle arc as the guards met, stopped, and lit cigarettes. At that point, furtive, although he did not know why, Maloney removed his shoes, hoisted himself on the windowsill, and climbed down. Stealthily he went toward Aisle III, Shed IV, the placement of which rendered its contents invisible to exterior scrutiny, keeping an eye on the distant flashlights as he ducked into the shed, at the door of which stood a work by Matthew Cotes Wyatt, a marble and bronze statue of a large Newfoundland retriever treading nobly on a squirming serpent. The inscription on the plinth of this statue read: BASHAW: THE FAITHFUL FRIEND OF MAN TRAMPLING UNDERFOOT HIS MOST INSIDIOUS ENEMY. Passing Bashaw, who appeared to guard the entrance, he moved from exterior darkness into the faint golden glow of an oil lamp turned low. The shed contained a bedroom exhibit, the centerpiece of which was an ornate, canopied double bedstead. Built in Birmingham, circa 1851, the bed was of japanned metal with papier-mâché panels, painted and gilt, its canopy adorned with tassels bound in silk. Sitting on the edge of the bed was Mary Ann. She wore a Victorian evening dress of plum velvet, with flared skirt and leg-of-mutton sleeves, black silk stockings, and black velvet pumps. On a chair, in semi-darkness at the other end of the exhibit, Vaterman perched, wary and suspicious.

"Hello, Tony," she said.

Silent, he stared at her. She turned to Vaterman. "I didn't even light the lamp until he was coming down the aisle. So he couldn't have seen us from his bedroom."

Vaterman shrugged slightly, as though unconvinced.

Mary Ann turned to Maloney. "You *sensed* we were here, didn't you?"

"No, not exactly. When I went into my room tonight, something seemed to be wrong outside. I concentrated and something told me that some items of women's clothing had been moved from the Jane A. Wooten Trust Collection and brought here, to this bedroom exhibit in Shed IV."

"Clothing. Was that all?"

"Yes. That dress, stockings, shoes, a corset, underwear."

"But you didn't know that I was here and was wearing them?"

"No."

She blushed. "Maybe that's just as well. I wouldn't like to think you have X-ray eyes."

It was his turn to redden. "No, nothing like that."

"Anyway, aren't these clothes really something?" she said. "Like the corset. How did they manage? I'm not fat, far from it, but I can't even get it to close."

"Ladies' maids laced them up. Tiny waists were prized in those days. Wasp waists, they were called."

"Oh? And the panties are really strange, too."

"Knickers. They called them knickers." He looked uneasily at Vaterman, who sat, silent as a jury.

"But they don't seem to do up behind?"

"They, ah, they open in the rear. There are buttons to, ah, to button them up behind."

"Oh?" To his sudden excitement, she lifted the hem of her plum-colored dress, exposing perfect legs in black silk stockings and mauve garters. She felt under the hem of the dress. "Oh, yes, yes, I've found them. Buttons. Wait."

She knelt on the bed, kneeling up straight as though she were in a pew, her hands fumbling behind under her dress. "There, that's it. Good." She let her skirt drop back into place and sat back on the bed. "I felt so bare—behind."

Hoarse, Maloney cleared his throat. "Well, you're certainly what this Collection has needed. A live Victorian girl. You look like a figure in a Pre-Raphaelite painting."

Suddenly, squirming in a return of her habitual shyness, she colored and hung her head. Maloney turned to Vaterman. "Didn't you remember you were to have dinner with me tonight?"

"I'm sorry about that," Vaterman said. "We had to deceive you in order to carry out this experiment."

"What experiment?"

"Tell him about it," Vaterman said to Mary Ann.

"No, you tell him."

"*You* tell him," Vaterman said, loudly. "It was your idea."

"Well," Mary Ann began, in her low, urgent voice. "What we did is, we hid here just after six when the day guards went off duty. We planned to move this clothing I'm wearing back to my apartment after midnight, when the night guards break for their meal. I told Fred that when you dreamed tonight, you would know in your dream that these clothes were missing. And I was right. It's like that magazine article said. You're clairvoyant."

"Maybe he is and maybe he's not," Vaterman said. "He could have noticed some movement down here tonight when he looked out of his window."

"Are you calling me a liar?" Maloney asked.

"No. But you have forgotten something. There are other objects missing. You have not mentioned them. They, also, have been removed from their stall."

What objects? Maloney looked at Vaterman and at once, as in a trance, heard himself say, "You have two glass paperweights in your left-hand pocket. And you have hidden an ivory-backed hairbrush of Indian design under your shirt."

"You see!" Mary Ann, triumphant, sat up in the bed and clapped her hands. "I was right. He knows. There's no mistake about it."

"I'm sorry." Vaterman began to take the objects from his pockets. "And also very pleased. I misjudged you, Tony. You *are* a genius."

"All right, now. Don't anybody move. Easy there."

A security guard, his revolver drawn, stood covering them from the rear of the exhibit. "Oh, excuse me, Professor. I didn't know it was you."

"That's all right," Maloney said. "We're just leaving."

"Didn't see you come in, sir. Thought we'd run into our first bit of trouble."

"That's all right, Hollis. Good night."

"Good night, sir."

The guard withdrew, holstering his gun.

"Well, I suppose we might as well go to bed," Vaterman said.

Maloney went to the lamp. "Ready? I'll just put this out."

"Oh, wait." Mary Ann stood up. "I'd better get out of these clothes. Maybe you'd wait outside for a minute?"

"Oh, come on," Vaterman said, "what's the big deal? We won't look."

And so Maloney found himself facing a mahogany chest of drawers, built in 1838, while, behind him, he heard a rustling as Mary Ann began to remove items K to R in the Jane A. Wooten Trust Collection.

"By the way," Vaterman said. "New York phoned this afternoon and said Radiodiffusion Française wants to do a TV interview next Monday. Will that be all right?"

"Monday? Yes," Maloney said, hoarsely.

To the left, near the oil lamp, stood a Victorian dressing table with two drawers, on top of which was a tray dressing glass tilted at an angle of thirty degrees. Maloney, moving slightly, caught sight of Mary Ann removing blue satin stays, those stays she had been unable to fasten.

"You know about Dr. Spector and the Vanderbilt interviews in the morning? That's at ten in the parlor."

Now she stood, her back to them, wearing long cotton knickers, black silk stockings, frilled moiré garters, and silver-buckled black velvet pumps. As Maloney muttered an affirmative to Vaterman's question, she moved into full mirror view, unbuttoning the back panel of the knickers.

"By the way," Vaterman said, "when I was writing that story today, I turned up the fact that it was Duke University, not Vanderbilt, who was first in this extrasensory-perception field."

For a moment, the white globes of her pretty behind transfixed Maloney's attention. Then she moved out of sight.

"Yes," he said. "Dr. J. B. Rhine at Duke."

He heard the soft fall of a garment. He tried to maneuver himself to a different angle, closer to the mirror.

"Experiments on the laws of chance, weren't they?" Vaterman asked.

"Yes, with cards and dice."

Knickerless, she sat and removed the moiré garters, rolling down the tight black stockings. Naked, she rose and reached for her own long purple dress. At that moment Vaterman turned to her, casually, and asked: "Nearly ready?"

"Yes, just a moment."

Vaterman was looking at her. *He* could look. In that moment a primal jealousy overcame Maloney and he lowered the oil lamp to a guttering matchlight.

"Oh, where are my shoes?"

"Here they are," Vaterman said.

"Tony, could you turn up the lamp a moment? What will I do with these clothes?"

"I'll put them back."

"No, let me. I took them, after all."

"I know where they go," Maloney said, turning, look-

94

ing at her, then, kneeling, gathering up the garments still warm from her body.

Vaterman took her arm. "I will take you home."

"Okay. Thanks. Good night, Tony."

"Good night, Mary Ann."

They went out ahead of him. He followed them into the warm Pacific moonlight and stood, holding her garments, listening until the sound of their footsteps diminished. Then, sudden, furtive, animal, he buried his nose in these, her silks.

6

The following letter was written to Dr. James What-more, a psychiatrist, by Dr. I. S. Spector, ten days after the start of the Vanderbilt University experiments.

Dear Jim,

Thank you for your letter. I was particularly interested in your comments and queries on how the subject is bearing up under the strain of constantly dreaming the same dream. It is, I quite agree, crucial to the precognitive aspect and is also related, as I've noted, to difficulties experienced in the Dement-Fisher experiments some years ago. I think you will be interested in the transcript of an interview which follows, but first, before I attempt to answer your question about unconscious, or dream, stress, let me mention some of the conscious stresses which now occupy the subject's waking hours.

In the first place, he worries about losing his position

as a professor of history at McGill University. Subsequent to his failure to return to his classes last week, the chairman of his department placed him on suspension. He fears that his academic enemies have laid undue stress on the erotic elements of the Collection and have cast doubt on his account of its conception. This, of course, is part of his overall problem in making people accept this incredible happening. As yet, his account of how the Collection came into existence has not been widely believed. While some mass-circulation newspapers, particularly in Europe, have written uncritically of the event, more serious media reporting has tended to be guarded, even skeptical. This irritates him. Indeed, there is a paranoiac tendency evidenced in his reaction to adverse criticism.

Then there is the problem of the Collection's inaccessibility. Because it is not yet open for public viewing, many people suspect some trick. The guards inform me that more than two hundred people are turned away every day. A number of these disappointed sightseers utter insults and abuse which is heard by Maloney as he sits in his motel room.

Lastly, there is the police inquiry into his story, an inquiry which he claims does not bother him in the slightest, as it will uncover no trace of any wrongdoing. Nevertheless, even an innocent man will feel harassed and vaguely guilty when, for the first time in his life, he becomes the subject of a criminal investigation.

I have digressed, I know. You asked me to describe a typical day in the subject's present life.

The day (for all of us here) begins when Maloney wakes each morning. Usually this is between 8 and 9 A.M. It is his custom, he tells me, to get out of bed as soon as he wakes and walk to the bedroom window to make

97

a visual check that the Collection still stands. He complains that he invariably wakes in a tense and irritable state because "it's exhausting to dream that same dream night after night." Shortly after nine his temporary secretary, a Miss McKelvey, arrives, bringing him coffee, his morning mail, and the newspapers. At ten, he comes to our suite and submits to one or another of our daily series of tests and interviews. This continues until noon when he breaks for a light lunch, which he usually eats in the motel parlor with Miss McKelvey and a young man named Vaterman who handles publicity matters for the Collection. He seems most at home with these two young people, who, like himself, are, in their conversation, undistinguished from the norm of their generation.

After lunch, Maloney usually devotes an hour to meetings with lawyers and publishers on business concerned with future plans for the exhibition and funding of the Collection. This is being arranged through a firm called Management Incorporated and has assumed considerable importance for him in view of his possible dismissal from his university post.

From 3 to 5 P.M. he holds interviews with newspapermen and other media people who have requested interviews. From five to six, he visits the Collection, often in the company of scholars and other experts who have obtained permission to meet him and view the exhibits. This is, undoubtedly, his happiest hour. He delights in pointing out details, and in recalling in what museum, in which book, or set of illustrations, he saw those objects which have not yet been discovered in other Collections. Sometimes he will activate the water pump of the central crystal fountain, or climb into the cab of the South Eastern Railway Company locomotive "Folkstone," a great favorite of his. At other times he will lecture on specific collections, set a spinning loom in motion, or demonstrate the workings of some moving object, such as an invalid's recumbent chair.

At 6 P.M. he reports to our suite for a further hour's session with members of my team. Usually, these involve testing his precognitive, telepathic, or clairvoyant powers through parakinetic and psychokinetic methods and involving dice, cards, and other stimuli. EEG studies are also carried on in some of these sessions. So far, however, he has shown no evidence of heightened ability in obtaining extrachance scores, nor has he entered trance states normally associated with sensitives.

Shortly after seven his public day ends. At first he ate in the motel, but now he walks to his secretary's apartment, which he and Vaterman are helping her redecorate. Thus, for the past five evenings he has eaten there in the company of the girl and Vaterman. He tells me that when he returns to his motel room he gets into bed and watches television for about an hour, putting out his light about 11 P.M. And each night he has dreamed the dream described in my first letter, the one in which he guards, admires, and patrols his Collection.

I have outlined a typical day. I would emphasize that at no time since I have known him has Maloney, like other sensitives we have studied, withdrawn into any trance or fantasy state. Nevertheless, as you will see from the following transcript of a taping, the idea of a new fantasy does obsess him.

Q. What do you feel when you waken each morning and discover that the Collection is still there?

MALONEY. At first, I feel a sense of relief and pleasure. Maybe *reassurance* is a better word. But then, as the morning wears on, I begin to feel depressed.

Q. Perhaps you are now sorry that you created the Collection?

MALONEY. No, I wouldn't say that. I get great pleasure out of knowing that I did it. But it's got to be accepted, seriously, I mean, by serious people. The answer is, of course, for me to bring another dream of mine to life. That would solve all my problems. It's the one way to make people believe in this present dream.

Q. Have you ever thought of this: Supposing, the moment you dream a new dream and bring it to life, the old dream—the Collection—vanishes? Wouldn't you feel you'd somehow "betrayed" your original dream?

MALONEY. Yes, that's possible. But I'm already "betraying" the Collection.

Q. Why is that? I don't understand.

MALONEY. Well, I've sold an option on it to a consortium of businessmen headed by my agent. They're paying all my operating expenses for six months in exchange for first refusal on exhibition rights.

Q. Why did you do that?

MALONEY. Because it's too big for me to look after myself. These guards cost a lot of money. And there are salaries, my secretary's and Vaterman's, and my own expenses. Besides, if the Collection is to be opened to the public, it will cost a lot to set up ticket facilities and so on. And now I have a court case on my hands. I had to hire lawyers.

Q. A court case?

MALONEY. The State of California has gone to court to argue that, because it appeared here, the Collection is the property of the state.

Q. But there's every chance the court will rule in your favor, surely?

MALONEY. I hope so. But I wonder if it's worth it.

Q. What do you mean?

MALONEY. I mean, I wonder is any one thing of this sort worth devoting one's whole life to it? Frankly, my instinct right now is to go home, forget the Collection, and try to get my old job back.

Q. And forget about dreaming up a new dream?

MALONEY. Let me ask *you* a question. Would you give up your present career as a scientist if you could dream some dream and make it come to life?

Q. Well, I might, if I could dream of a cure for some major disease. Or of broaching some new frontier of the mind.

MALONEY. Right. But those dreams are impossible for me. A man can only dream what he knows. And my field is the Victorians.

Q. Theoretically, through study, it might be possible to alter one's power to dream. As you, by your studies of Victoriana, were enabled to dream up the Collection.

MALONEY. Yes, I've thought about that.

Q. Is there something you've considered studying in order to dream a new dream?

MALONEY (agitated). Let's take a break. I think I've said enough for one day.

7

The telephone, ringing early, roused him from the order of his dream to the confusions of reality, bringing him in off his long night's patrol to a voice, distorted, yet instantly familiar.

"Tony? Is that you?"

"Who is it?" he asked, unnecessarily.

"It's Barbara. Were you asleep?"

He did not answer.

"Well, aren't you surprised to hear from me?"

"I hadn't thought about it."

"I'm calling about our so-called date. It was supposed to be Wednesday, right?"

"It was," he said. "I should have written. I'm sorry."

"I see. I'm told you've given up your job at McGill."

"The job seems to be giving me up."

"And I'm also told you want to sublet the apartment."

"Well, I haven't decided yet. I haven't decided anything. This is a completely abnormal situation, you know. I mean, this thing that's happened to me."

"Never mind what's happened to you," she said. "I'm calling to know what's going to happen to us. And I seem to have my answer, don't I?"

He did not speak. He had not spoken to her since the Sunday morning, a year ago, when she left him. They had been in bed at the time, having a stupid, ordinary row. He had said that the bottle of Château Latour was too good to have for dinner with the Comptons. Jack Compton wouldn't know a bottle of Château Latour from a bottle of Molson's Ale, he said. The Comptons were *her* friends. She got up out of bed, naked, a tall girl with titian-red hair and a mole the size of a quarter on her left shoulder blade. She didn't put on any under-clothes, just pulled on a dress and put her feet into a pair of pumps. Then she went into the dining room of the apartment, took the bottle of Château Latour out of the sideboard, put it under her arm, threw her sheep-skin overcoat over her shoulder, and walked out.

She did not come back. Two days later her sister came and took her clothes away. Later he heard she'd taken a six-months lease on a flat on Sherbrooke Street. She could afford it. She was a talks producer for the Canadian Broadcasting Corporation and earned as much as he. She did not phone him or try to get in touch with him. For a long time after she walked out, he had been lonely and angry and had missed her. But now, hearing her voice after a year of not hearing it, he was shocked by a surge of resentment.

"You amuse me," he said, bitterly, to that voice far away in Montreal. "You walk out, you don't get in touch for a year, and now you want an instant decision on what's supposed to happen to us."

"I don't want an answer, Tony. I think I have the answer. I think we've given it plenty of time and now we should get a divorce. Right?"

"Right," he said, furious. "Whatever you like."

"It's not whatever I like, it's something we should have discussed months ago. I know that's partly my fault. Still, I must say I find it strange that you never tried to come after me."

"You do, do you?"

"Is that all you have to say?"

"Is that all *you* have to say, Barbara?"

"All I have to say is, I thought we were civilized human beings."

"Well, we're not, it seems. So tell your lawyer to write to me, if that's what you want."

"If that's what *you* want," she said. "It's Harry Crenshaw, you remember him?"

"Yes."

"I'll tell him to contact you, then. Is your furniture and stuff still in the apartment?"

"Yes, why?"

"Well, there's the furniture and the silverware and things that were mine before I met you. I could send you a list and we could make a fair division of the stuff, including the wedding presents."

"Fuck the wedding presents."

"What's that supposed to mean?"

"Take them. Take anything you want."

"Well, if that's the way you feel, you'd better send me authorization to go into the apartment and take what I need."

"I'll mail you the key. Goodbye."

He put the phone down. To think he had waited a

104

year and worried himself sick about not being back in time. To hell with her!

At once, he felt much better. Ten minutes later, Mary Ann knocked on the door. "Ready for your breakfast?"

"I'm getting a divorce."

"Oh," she said, and hung her head. "Is that good or bad?"

"Good. Very good. Where's Fred, is he around?"

"No, he's at the *Courier*. He said he'd be over around lunchtime."

"Okay, let's all have lunch together. Or do I have an appointment?"

"No."

"So, at one o'clock, then?"

"I'll ask Fred."

From the back seat of Vaterman's battered Mustang, en route to the restaurant, he watched as Mary Ann massaged Vaterman's neck. At once an odd, painful jealousy suffused him. He remembered her, half naked, moving around behind the ornate, canopied bed, then pulling down her drawers. Of course, she and Vaterman were sleeping together.

Or were they? And what business was it of his?

Yet, in the Konditorei Karmel, as the three of them stood in line for smorgasbord, hoarsely casual, he put a question. "Tell me, you two. What do you think of having children? What's your attitude?"

Saw Vaterman exchange a glance with her. "Well, I guess Mary Ann and I feel no children, at least not now."

"And what do you feel about marriage? Or do you think people should live together first?"

Vaterman seemed embarrassed. Uneasy, he indicated the food table. "Oh, they have red cabbage today," he said. "It's excellent. So are the dumplings."

Maloney looked at Mary Ann. Her habitual blush moved in an arc from her cheek to the long line of her neck, but for once she did not flinch under his gaze. This time it was he who found himself unable to meet her stare. Guiltily, he spooned dumplings. Better not ask any more questions. Yes. Better not ask.

But some things cannot be avoided. A few evenings later, Vaterman, declaring that they both needed exercise, suggested they play a game of Frisbee on the beach.

"What about Mary Ann?"

"She's taking her recorder class in Monterey from seven-thirty to eight-thirty. We could meet here afterwards and go out to supper."

"Right, Fred. Good idea."

The sands of Carmel are ash gray, the beach swept clean of trash, protected by local ordinance. Long breakers curl and whiten hundreds of yards from shore. Dunes, perennially covered by thick green banana clusters of ice plant, screen the roadside. In the distance, tall groves of Monterey pines hide the houses of the rich who live above the sweep of the bay on this rim of land and sea. In the vermilion backwash of a Pacific evening, Vaterman's bright yellow plastic Frisbee turned black against the sky, spinning like a dish plate from hand to hand.

"Hey, great!"

"It's what we need."

"There you go."

Vaterman, who had removed his safari jacket and shoes, ran angularly about, skidding in the sands, energetically fielding and returning the disk. But Maloney, though out of condition, was more adept than this former European at the basic American game of catch. And so, as play continued, distances grew greater and returns were speeded up until, suddenly out of breath from his undisciplined running, Vaterman collapsed on the sands, panting, his long hair spilling into his eyes. Maloney held the Frisbee in reserve and walked toward Vaterman. In a few minutes it would be dark.

"You all right, Fred?"

"Yes." Vaterman sat up, attempting a smile. Then, as though he heard a noise, he looked back over his shoulder, narrowing his eyes to peer at the dune.

"What's wrong?"

"The father," Vaterman said, as though beginning the Lord's Prayer.

"What father?"

"Mary Ann's. What's he doing here? When we separate, he follows *her*."

Maloney turned to look.

"He's over there by the path leading down to the road."

There was no one on the darkening dune. No one stood on the steps of the path which led up to the roadway. "I can't see him," Maloney said.

"He just ducked down behind that bench."

"But why does he follow you and Mary Ann?"

"He wants to catch us in bed together. When he does, he's going to kill me."

107

"You're joking."

"No. He's dangerous. He was an instructor in un-armed combat."

"Oh, come on."

"He's warned me. I tell you it's made my love life quite difficult. I mean, if I try to lay her, I worry in case he's lurking about, ready to rush in on us."

"But doesn't he have a job? He can't follow you *all* the time."

"He's on an army pension. Listen, do you remember the night Mary Ann and I hid in the Collection?"

"Yes."

"Well, between you and me, one of the reasons I agreed to that stunt of hers was I thought I might be able to lay her in that shed. I mean, with the guards around, I was sure he would stay out in the street. But, do you know something?"

"No. What?"

"When we left the shed that night and said good night to you, I saw him in there, hiding behind a booth. It was a good thing you showed up when you did. I was just about to try and lay her on that antique bed."

Maloney felt himself flush. He looked up at the dunes, but saw no one. "Shall we go back now?" he asked.

"May as well."

Together they climbed the steps to Sea View Drive. Street lamps had been lit and lights shone from the picture windows of houses that fronted on the beach. An elderly couple peered out of a passing car. There was no sign of the father.

"Has he gone?"

"No, he's down below there on the beach."

Maloney turned and walked quickly to the beach wall. Below, the ash-gray sands were deserted. Vaterman fell in beside him and they walked in step, the matched tread of their footsteps loud in the silence. "You see, he's an expert at hiding himself," Vaterman said.

In silence, they covered the last blocks to the motel.

"Is he still following us?"

Vaterman turned and looked back. "Yes."

"I remember Mary Ann once mentioned some hassle with him. What was that?"

"You don't know?" Vaterman lowered his voice. "He's sick. I mean mentally sick. Mary Ann's mother died when she was very little. When she was fifteen her father was still giving her baths. Can you imagine?"

Footsteps sounded behind them in the street. Maloney whirled around. A boy ran past, accompanied by a boxer dog.

"When she was seventeen she ran away to San Francisco. And he found her. He told the police she'd stolen money from him. He said she was on drugs. He brought her back to Monterey. That's when I met her. A year later I helped her run away again. She went to Big Sur and hid there with a girlfriend. But he found her. So I helped her move to Carmel and at the same time I wrote him a letter saying if he bothered her any more, we'd go to court and say he'd been messing around with her. Ever since then, he's wanted to kill me."

They went into the motel. No, Bourget told them, Mary Ann had not returned yet.

An hour later, as they sat drinking from a six-pack of beer in the motel parlor, she came in carrying a large white cardboard box. She unbuttoned a long, frayed cardigan and, sitting down, showed her long, elegant, coltish legs in red suède boots. "I got some stuff from the deli," she said, in her low, urgent tone. "Sandwiches and strudel. I hope that's all right?"

"Fine," Maloney said. "How was your class?"

"Okay. How was the Frisbee?"

"Something very unusual happened tonight," Vaterman told her. "The father followed *us*."

She rose, took off her cardigan, and went to the window. She stood, for a long moment, looking out at the street lamps. "Did Tony see him?"

"He kept out of sight," Vaterman said.

She turned, looked at Vaterman, then went and opened the large cardboard box, took the box and stood before Maloney. "I got pastrami on rye and lox with cream cheese on rolls. Which would you like?"

"Pastrami, thanks."

"You can have one of each, if you want."

"Well, I'll start with pastrami, thanks."

"He has gray hair," she said. "And he has kind of a red tanned face. And he walks with a limp sometimes when his leg hurts. I mean, my father."

Maloney accepted the pickle she offered.

"You *didn't* see him, did you?"

"No."

"He's outside right now, I'm sure of it," Vaterman said. He rose and went to the sandwich box. "I want lox and cream cheese."

Mary Ann ignored the request, not offering the box, letting Vaterman pick out the sandwich himself. Instead, she knelt on the rug, facing Maloney. She looked up at him, like a penitent in the confessional. "He has gray hair, red tanned face, and sometimes a limp. If you *do* see him, will you tell me?"

"Of course."

"He'll see him all right," Vaterman said loudly. "He may decide to kill Tony too."

8

Exactly two weeks after the Collection's appearance in Carmel, the winds of Maloney's fortune swept into a strange upturn. It was a time of omens. On that morning, when, as usual, he looked out of his window to check on the Collection, he glanced over at Bluff Road to see if the madman had come yet. For eleven days, the madman had arrived each morning on the stroke of nine, walking up and down until dusk, a tall, unkempt figure, barefoot, shirtless, wearing a greasy black suit jacket and white duck trousers, holding aloft a hand-lettered sign:

GOD ALONE CAN CREATE
Do Not Believe This Lie

Today there was no sign of him. Unaccountably cheered, Maloney began to whistle.

That afternoon, he toured the Collection with Lord Rennishawe, a Hellenist of stature and also proprietor of Creechmore Castle in Wales, a repository of Victorian treasures which Maloney had visited four years ago, during the period of his doctoral studies. A tiny, frail figure with shoulder-length hair, Lord Rennishawe was sometimes mistaken by shortsighted persons for a ten-year-old girl. This lack of height ran in the family, he told Maloney, and indeed, in Victorian times Lord John Russell, when Prime Minister, had said of the Rennishawes: "If we Russells are members of the race of Great Dwarfs, the Rennishawes are midgets *manqués*."

Lord Rennishawe was eighty-one years old. In his letter requesting permission to view the Collection, he cited a report by Sir Alfred Mannings that certain items of drawing-room furniture in the Collection appeared to be copies of originals in the Glamis Wing of Creechmore Castle.

This proved to be so, and, like other experts who had seen known treasures duplicated in the Collection, Lord Rennishawe confessed that he was unable to distinguish the furniture here in Carmel from the originals in Wales. This, of course, was the sort of confirmation Maloney desired. He was on the point of asking Lord Rennishawe if he would write a letter confirming this opinion, when the tiny old man ducked under the portico of a large model of Heidelberg Castle, execrably executed in cork, and like a child scurried across the model courtyard, opened a cork door, and emerged in the next aisle. "Come here!" he called in his imperious falsetto. "Come here at once, young man!"

Maloney, unable to pass through the model castle, ran down to the end of his aisle, turned a corner, and ran up the parallel aisle. Lord Rennishawe was standing outside one of the furniture exhibits, a room with three walls like those in department-store showrooms. Each item here was reduced to about two-thirds size, giving it the look of a room in a giant dollhouse. The wall paint, silks, and velvet coverings all were of a peculiar shade of pale green, ornamented in some cases with a subtle phallic motif. The furniture in this green room consisted of a half tester bed, with a chaise longue at its foot, four Eastlake nursery chairs, a tray dressing table with a tray dressing glass on top of it, and a washstand decorated with erotic motifs and executed in the Gothic style in the manner of William Burges.

"*Where* did you see this?" Lord Rennishawe cried, in a quavering, breaking tone.

"Where did I see what?"

"This—this room!"

"I believe it was—yes, this was also at your family seat, Lord Rennishawe. Creechmore Castle."

"When?"

"Well, I was there one afternoon about four years ago, as I told you."

"My God," said Lord Rennishawe. He went to the chaise longue and lay on it. He tested the nursery chairs and, finally, sat on the bed. "Extraordinary. It fits me. It was made for my grandfather. But *you* didn't see it, young man. Nor did you read about it, because nothing, absolutely nothing, has ever been written about it. Very few people ever did see it, excepting a few of the servant class. This room was my grandfather's secret. It was concealed behind a dummy wall in an old summerhouse in the small wood below the south lawn at Creechmore. I know that my father and brothers never saw it. But I did. Yes. It was the midterm holiday and I went down from school to stay with my grandparents. I remember I was about ten at the time, so it would have been nineteen-oh-two. Yes, one afternoon I was flying a kite on the south lawn. The kite got away, floated up over the wood, and got stuck in a treetop. I went into the wood and climbed up the tree to extricate my kite. While I was up there I heard the sound of footsteps. I looked down and there, below me, running as though frightened out of her wits, was a young servant girl, an under-parlormaid, I think. Her dress was open, unbuttoned all the way down, and I saw that she was naked underneath. I remember I was very excited. When she reached the edge of the wood, she gathered her dress together, holding it modestly closed over her bosom, and went around the edge of the south lawn to the servants' quarters, which are just behind the main house.

"I collected my kite and climbed down, in great haste. I wondered where she'd come from. I turned and went back a little way along the path and came to the old summerhouse in the clearing. I'd been forbidden to play there, because, my grandmother said, it was dangerous, and ready to collapse. Well! There was the summerhouse, all right, and standing in the doorway, smoking a cheroot and holding a brandy glass in his hand, was my grandfather. In some disarray!" Here Lord Rennishawe uttered a high, childish giggle. "No trousers, you see. In his undershirt. And behind him I saw, like a stage room in the foreground, the old summerhouse with moldy rattan chairs and table, and behind it, where the wall had been, this more intimate room. The green room. This very room. Well!

"And at that moment my grandfather looked up and saw me. I remember I was quite afraid. I was very young, but I knew I'd rather walked into something. Well! He had great panache, my grandfather. He greeted me quite casually, invited me to step inside, and then told me this was his secret place, where he came sometimes to read or have a nap. Then he put on his trousers, quite unconcerned, and took me into the secret room and showed me how the wall rolled back, and so on. And as I stood there, by this very bed that you see, I noticed the young maid's chemise and white cotton drawers lying on the floor. I can remember them to this day. Well, my grandfather slid the wall back into place and then swore me to secrecy, made me give him my word of honor that I wouldn't tell it to a living soul. I was quite afraid of him, you know. Well! A few days later, when I went back to school, he slipped me a little change purse as a present and in it were five sovereigns. Another secret, he said. So there it was. I didn't tell anyone. And a few years later I heard that my grandmother had gone down to the old summerhouse one night and had an accident with a lamp there and that the place had burned to the ground. Of course I knew why. Oh yes. And, a few years after that, I decided to tell my sister Antonia. We were very close at the time. But she was shocked and made me promise not to tell anyone else. She said it would hurt Mamma if it got out. Well! And here it is. The selfsame room. Look, that was his special color, that shade of green. And d'you see these little touches, the phalli on the embroidery of the coverlet, the little lascivious cupids there on the iron-work of the washstand. Extraordinary! Oh, there's no doubt about it. You could not possibly have had access to any documents describing this room. There *are* no such documents. You are a necromancer, a wizard! This Collection of yours is undoubtedly one of the most astonishing events of the century!"

Lord Rennishawe's excitement was such that he could not contain it. Before the day was out, he had repeated his conviction in several newspaper interviews and had agreed to appear on a network television talk show on his way home to Wales, via New York. He proved, by virtue of his great age, his clear diction, and his minuscule size, to be a memorable television guest. As he told his story, television cameras probed the contents of the secret chamber, and this story, more than the original story of the Collection itself, at once piqued public fancy and resulted in a rash of publicity, all of it in a tone markedly less skeptical than that which had greeted Maloney's original announcement.

The upturn continued. Within a week, Maloney was notified by letter that the F.B.I. investigation had been dropped, for lack of evidence of any criminal intent or connection. Lieutenant Polita of the sheriff's office was still keeping his options open, it seemed, but, for the moment, had been temporarily transferred to a more urgent case. In the same period, a federal judge handed down a verdict in Maloney's favor, stating that the Collection would seem to be his property and that the State of California could claim a share of the revenues from its public exhibition only were it to be exhibited exclusively within the state.

Perhaps the most significant of all these reactions was the way Lord Rennishawe's statement was received in Maloney's native city. Again, in that same euphoric week, as he was leaving the motel one evening to dine at Mary Ann's apartment, he received a call from Montreal. The caller was John Palliser, a friend since high-school days and now a member of the history department at McGill.

"Tony, is that you?"

"Hey, John. Good to hear from you."

"I didn't wake you up, did I?"

"No, it's early here."

"Well, it's just after midnight here and I'm still so wound up, I had to call you. You know what happened tonight? There was a great big meeting in the Union. All about you, Tony my boy. It was really something."

"About me?"

"Yes, in protest about what the department's done to you. The response has been terrific. It started with that story, day before yesterday, by that English lord, saying your Collection was one of the great events of the century. Frankly, that really switched a lot of votes in your favor. Nobody can accuse Lord Rennishawe of being a phony, now can they?"

"No."

"Anyway, suddenly everybody began talking about the injustice of it, the university suspending you and so on. And then all over campus we began to see these posters, protesting on your behalf. Students did it. Amazing. And then some of us in the department got together and tonight we held this protest meeting. You should have seen the crowd. First I spoke, then Jack Monsey, he's the head of the student council, then Lise Roy, and, anyway, after the meeting we got signatures from graduate assistants and teaching staff. I tell you, Tony, we can close down the whole damn history department unless they reinstate you at once."

"Reinstate me?"

"They fired you, didn't they?"

"Yes, they did, but I can't blame them, really. After all, they have to have somebody to teach my classes."

"Come on, Tony, what are you talking about? The rest of the staff could have divvied up your classes and handled the extra load. We weren't even consulted. Listen, how long are you going to be out there?"

"I'm not exactly sure."

"Well, what are your plans? I mean, we only know what we read in the papers, but my understanding of the situation is, you're trying to arrange some funding to permit the Collection to be exhibited out there, right?"

"Yes, that's right."

"And once that's arranged, I assume you'd want to come back here and get on with your own work."

"Well, you know the situation's very complicated."

"You haven't been offered another teaching job, have you?"

"No."

"Then they had no right to fire you."

At that moment, as in a dream, staring out at the darkened aisles of the Collection, Maloney seemed to see an audience of faculty and students sitting in the great darkness of the Union while the opening speaker, John Palliser, adjusted the microphone, turning it up to emit its usual harsh shriek. Then John's voice, booming out—"no right to fire this man"—a call for justice there in that familiar atmosphere of cigarette smoke and the damp of winter woolens.

"Tony, are you there? Look, as I said tonight in my speech, we can all talk about scholarship and so on, but what more creative scholarship can anyone imagine than to re-create the artifacts of a period simply through an act of the imagination? Any university but dear old McGill, my God, they'd be so proud of what you've done. But we Canadians, we never recognize originality, because we have no real use for it. We *fire* the man who thinks up something new. My God, think of it. This is the academic scandal of the century!"

A scandal. John's voice crying scandal, as hundreds

rise to their feet, applauding, cheering, calling for a demonstration. From now on he, Anthony Maloney, would be a campus hero, controversial, whispered about in the faculty club, pointed out to outsiders as he crossed the campus on his way to class. All he had to do was go home.

"John, listen, I'm very grateful to you. It was damn good of you to organize all this for me."

"Nonsense. It's not just your friends, Tony. After that Rennishawe story, *everybody's* beginning to have second thoughts, believe me. We're going to win this one. We don't want to lose you to the United States. You've got to come back, dammit. We're proud of you."

Proud of him. Emotion overcame him, hearing these words.

"Anyway," John was saying, "this is long distance and it's late. I'll write to you tomorrow and give you the battle plan. Take care, Tony. And good night."

"Good night, John. And thanks."

Excitement, as if he had just drawn an outstanding hand at cards, filled him as he replaced the receiver. A full house of people assembled back there in Montreal, a flush of students, faces blooming upward. A campus hero. A hero who gave up fame in the States for the cause of academic justice. I am a historian who was witness to that first moment in history when a man's dream literally came true. I could work up a course, say, on the Victorian era as a factor in modern man's historical consciousness, an extension of my Ph.D. thesis. I'd be an outstanding lecturer, unique in my field.

He went into the bathroom to brush his teeth. Brushing vigorously, bending toward the white concavity of the washbasin, he saw, in the porcelain, white snows, snows which covered the lawns at McGill, saw the path, brushed clear, leading up to the library, saw himself walking up the path. Students paused to stare and whisper, breath pluming from their mouths in the cold morning air, as he moved on, an academic hero, the man who had dreamed up the world-famous Great Victorian Collection in faraway Carmel.

He put down his toothbrush and stared at himself in the mirror. Now there, he told his mirror self, there is a fine dream for you. If I could go to bed tonight and dream that I will return to Montreal in triumph, with all this behind me.

He shut off the bathroom light, returned to the bedroom and sat, pensive, on the bed. To dream myself into some happier future, to dream the thing I want most and make that dream come true: that would be ideal, wouldn't it? Of course it would.

But to dream oneself into the future would be to obliterate the present. If his dream succeeded, would the Collection simply vanish in the miasma of his future?

Remorse, totally unexpected, totally affecting, suffused him. How crass to even think of erasing his dream! He rose, went to the bedroom window, climbed out, and dropped to the ground below. He began to walk down the center aisle, staring up for a moment at Osler's crystal fountain, seeing the myriad panes of glass glisten in the stark Pacific moonlight. Turning into Aisle IV, he came to one of his favorite exhibits, the paintings by Victorian Royal Academicians. His hand, as though guided, reached out and found a small kerosene lamp, which he lit, adjusting the wick to a modest flame. Raising the lamp to look around, he was at once confronted by a circular oil painting executed by Charles Baxter, entitled *The Sisters*. Pubescent, soft garments spilling about snowy shoulders, liquid eyes wide in what waves of childish innocence, or wise in what hidden schoolroom depravities, *The Sisters* silently reproached him for his faithlessness in wishing to abandon them. Faithless, he turned away to be met by Sir Edwin Landseer's monument to fidelity, *The Old Shepherd's Chief Mourner,* a highland collie on his last lonely guard duty, his nose across his master's coffin. Rebuked, Maloney moved out of the shed, still carrying the oil lamp. Opposite him now was one of the most peculiar rooms in the Collection, a room which experts said did not exist, a room he had read about in an obscure volume only available from the Reserved Shelf in the British Museum. This was the receiving room of Mrs. Beauchamp's bordello in the Strand, a musty parlor adorned with obscene wall panels, its furniture heavy and serviceable, many horsehair poufs, large tête-à-tête sofas in stuffed plum velvet, chaise longues plumped up with blue swansdown pillows, brass spittoons, and small brass side tables of Turkish design. A smell of long-ago cigars, patchouli, and cheap scent lingered still: on these very chairs and sofas, mustachioed males had lolled, regardant, as Mrs. Beauchamp clapped her hands and the parade began: the girls, young, working class, awkward, sauntering across the room in an attempt at grace, plump naked thighs peeping from beribboned drawers, hair cascading about their white shoulders, chemises with cherry draw-string ribbons undone to reveal erect nipples; shy half smiles directed at the fuddled male stares. And later, what scenes of cruelty and vice would be enacted in the curtained alcoves, under the infamous series of paintings depicting *The Lion in Sinful Love* and showing the King of Beasts engaged in bestial dalliance with three terrified nymphs. Maloney stood at the threshold of this room, his lamp highlighting these very solid objects, objects which today existed only because he had dreamed them into life. How could anyone abandon such things? It would be worse than neglect: it would be a crime.

But as he put the lamp down on one of the brass tables and sat, like one of those Victorian dandies, on the buttoned, tufted, tête-à-tête sofa, a new thought came into his mind. *This room is empty.* No seventeen-year-old whores parade here before waistcoated gentry and Piccadilly swells. There is no life in my creation. There are no living figures. How can I give up my future happiness for a series of empty rooms?

He went out, going down Aisle II, passing the Ross telescope, the 1842 model of Liverpool docks, the Coalbrook Dale Dome and two casts of Arabian horses, "in most spirited attitudes," owned by the King of Württemberg. He lingered briefly by John Bell's statue of Andromeda exposed to a sea monster, staring at her buttery breasts, the full cornucopia of female belly, the pupil-less eyes. And as he looked into those blank Grecian orbs there came to his mind Mary Ann's vivid, unusual features, her lips lit by a smile, her sudden, shy blush, her awkward, coltish movements, her long, elegant legs in their red leather boots.

But how could he go on living with a set of statues? A man must live with a real woman. How could anyone spend his life wandering up and down the aisles of a museum, night after night dreaming the same dream? After six months, after a year, he would no longer be able to look at all this. He would grow to hate it.

He lifted the kerosene lamp and blew into the glass funnel, extinguishing the flame. Retracing his steps, he left the lamp where he had found it, under the painting of *The Sisters.* Then, reaching his window, he climbed up, re-entering the motel room. He closed the blind and suddenly, as though decided, undressed and got into bed.

He would make himself dream that he was back in Montreal, reinstated, promoted, with all his troubles behind him. He would dream of his future, a year from now.

But as soon as he had decided this, for a moment, like a thief, the Collection slipped back into his mind. If he now dreamed of that future life, he might never see the Collection again. By dreaming of leaving it here, in the past, he would be willing its destruction.

Fear gripped him. But I mustn't give in, he thought. I must renounce the Collection. I will renounce the Collection. I renounce the Collection!

He closed his eyes. After a moment his panic subsided and, as in a dream, unbidden, an image, reflected in a tray dressing glass, came to him: the memory of Mary Ann as he had seen her that night she changed her clothes in the bedroom exhibit. As in a dream, he watched her unfasten the blue satin stays, revealing long white cotton knickers, black silk stockings, frilled moiré garters, and silver-buckled black velvet pumps. She bent slightly, unbuttoning the back panel of the knickers. The panel fell away. As the white globes of her pretty bottom filled his mind, he sank into a hot, drowsy doze.

For a long moment he dozed, luxuriant, watching the movements of her naked behind. And then, as she had that night, she moved out of mirror range. The looking glass went blank. He tried to turn to find her, but his head seemed caught in some terrible vise. He was forced to remain staring at the blank tray dressing glass. It

124

blurred, then changed. Now he saw that it was no longer a Victorian looking glass but a television screen, the screen of one of those surveillance monitors one sees in supermarkets. In dream, he stared at this screen, hoping to see her reappear. Instead, he was presented with a long view of one of the aisles of the Collection. For thirty seconds the scene remained stationary. Then, with a flick of the picture, the camera eye moved on to scrutinize another aisle. Maloney lay in his bed, forced to monitor this dream monitor.

The new dream was infinitely more exhausting than his former patrol dream. In the earlier dream, he had moved about the Collection at will, often in a state of wonder and delight, pausing to examine and admire the many facets of his Collection. But now he was shown only an overall, distant view of each aisle, the camera holding on yet another dreary passageway. And where, formerly, he had seen the Collection, in dream, in all its wonderment of shades and colors, now each aisle appeared to him only in the fuzzy blue-gray hues of black-and-white television. Trapped, unable to deflect his gaze or turn off the monitor, he lay for eight hours, a prisoner of this banal and terrible spectacle.

He woke. It was morning. At once he looked over to the corner of the room. There was no television set on the wall. He sat up, swung his legs to the floor and stood, trembling, sweating, filled with the panic of a man who tries to escape from a burning building. But when he moved forward, he fell, his limbs like deflating balloons. He lay, face down, on the floor.

Someone knocked.

"Tony, are you awake?"

Dr. Spector's voice.

"Yes," he called, in a voice weak as his limbs.

"Just to remind you our interview's at nine. See you then."

He heard the footsteps retreat. Bracing himself like a man attempting a pushup, he tried to stand, but lacked the strength. He lay, his heart pounding, his face on the polyester carpet, abandoning himself to a nameless, hopeless panic. After a time he heard a second knock. That would be Mary Ann. The door was locked from inside. With a tottering lurch he gained his feet, moved two steps to the door, scrabbled with the key, and, when it turned, fell, exhausted, to his knees. She entered, carrying his morning coffee.

"What's wrong, Tony? Are you sick?"

He looked up at her, unable to speak. At once, putting down the coffee, she knelt beside him. "Tony, answer me? Are you all right?"

With a gasp he sucked in breath and then, bowing his head, rested it on her shoulder. "I've got to get away from here," he whispered. "I've got to get away at once."

"Wait." She helped him to his feet. He stumbled to the bed and sat heavily on it. "I have to go. I must go now."

"But you're not able to go anywhere. You're sick."

"If I can get in the car, I'll be all right."

"Where do you want to go?"

"Please. Just help me."

"Of course I will. But first I've got to speak to Fred."

He sat in trembling unease as she went to the phone. He heard her ask Vaterman to come over at once. When

126

she had finished, she came and sat on the bed beside him. "Now tell me. What happened?"

He caught his breath again. "Is the Collection still out there?"

She walked to the window. "Yes, it's there. Nothing's changed."

"What color is it?"

"What do you mean? It's all colors."

"Not just gray?"

"No. Tony, what happened?"

"I don't know," he said. He put his head between his knees as if he would be sick. "Last night something went wrong with my dream. I can't go through it again. I can't."

"Can't what? What is it you can't do?"

"I can't stay here. I want to go to some other place, some city, Los Angeles, maybe. I could get to Los Angeles by tonight, couldn't I?"

"By car? Sure."

"All right, then, will you help me get out to my car?"

"Fred will be here any minute. Here, try some coffee."

"No, thanks. Please, I want to go now."

But she shook her head, her mane of hair hiding her face. "Wait. I promised Fred."

"Promised what?"

"Nothing."

He turned from her and lay back on the bed. His trembling increased. He heard someone come into the room. He heard her whisper, then heard Vaterman's voice, whispering in reply. He could not distinguish what they were saying. He summoned his strength and said loudly, "Will someone help me get up?"

Vaterman loomed over him, distorted, at an angle. "Why do you want to go to L.A.?"

He shut his eyes. They were worried about what would happen to the Collection if he left it. He would have to tell them something.

"Tony?" Her voice, murmurous, low, very near. He opened his eyes and looked into her face. "Tony, I'm going to call a doctor."

"No," he said. And at once it came to him. "No, don't do that," he said. "I'm going to dream a new dream. But I have to get away from here to do it."

"A new dream?" Vaterman said, excited. "Well, why didn't you say so in the first place. Listen, I'll drive you to L.A. I mean, if you have a new dream come true, I want to be first with the story. Right?"

"But what if it rains while he's gone?" Mary Ann asked.

Maloney, with a great effort, raised himself in the bed. "Nothing's going to happen. I promise you."

"How do you know?" Vaterman said.

"I know. Now, let's go."

"First," Vaterman said, "I had better call my paper and tell them what I'm up to."

"No, don't tell anyone. I don't want Dr. Spector or anyone else following me. We're going to sneak out through that window."

"Right." Vaterman seemed excited. "We will use my car. And Mary Ann can stay here and watch the Collection in case there are changes."

"Oh, please, Tony," Mary Ann said. "Please, let me come with you."

Maloney stood and, with an effort, walked toward the window. "All right," he said. "Yes, let her come."

Red blurs appeared before his eyes. He staggered. Vaterman took his arm and whispered, "Mary Ann, go and bring my car around to the parking-lot entrance. We'll meet you there. Steady, Tony."

Buzz Harvey, the senior Securigard officer on duty that morning, later reported that about 9:15 A.M. he saw Professor Maloney climb down from his bedroom window and come, stumbling, along the main aisle of the Collection. He was followed by Mr. Vaterman, who carried a small bag of the overnight type. When Maloney rose, he seemed shaky. He put his hand over his eyes.

"Are you okay?" Vaterman called out.

"Yes. Where's your car?"

"This way."

Harvey reported that he went up to Maloney at that point and asked if he could be of assistance. Maloney shook his head and, following Vaterman, went toward the entrance to the parking lot. The usual crowd of would-be sightseers was peering in from the roadway. Maloney, Harvey reported later, "walked real slow, like an old man. He looked very sick."

A few minutes later, Vaterman's car drove up to the entrance to the parking lot. Miss McKelvey was at the wheel. Harvey and Vaterman helped Maloney cross the aisle and get into the car.

"Goodbye, Buzz," Vaterman said.

"Goodbye, sir. Going for a drive?"

"Yes."

As Harvey went to close the back door of the car, Maloney, sitting in the back seat, put his head between his knees. "Hurry, hurry!" Harvey heard him tell Miss McKelvey.

The red Mustang eased its way past the usual double line of parked tourist cars, which extended for two or three blocks up Bluff Road. After turning onto Sea View Drive, it stopped outside Mary Ann's apartment.

"Don't stop," Maloney called out.

"Only be a minute," Mary Ann said. She ran inside. Vaterman took the wheel. A few minutes later she ran out wearing a long yellow dress, sandals, and a sheepskin cape. She carried an airlines flight bag.

"And away we go," Vaterman said, putting the car in gear and swinging out suddenly into traffic. "Los Angeles, here we come."

"I love L.A.," Mary Ann said. "Fred, remember last time, when we went dancing on the Strip and stayed up all night?"

Maloney lay back on the seat, staring through the window at the metallic California sky. At Salinas, they turned south. The red Mustang roared on, past row on row of lettuce fields, moving onto an eight-lane highway, among a rush of traffic flowing southward. Vaterman drove with total concentration, rarely taking his eyes off the road. Mary Ann occasionally looked back to check if Maloney was all right. He did not speak to them. He remained slack on the seat, staring up at the harsh sky.

Time passed. At Pismo Beach, where they stopped for coffee and sandwiches, Maloney refused to leave the car. And when Mary Ann suggested phoning Carmel to find out if the Collection was still all right, for the first time, ever, he shouted at her. "Don't phone, dammit! I don't want a whole lot of people following me."

"I'm sorry." She went off with Vaterman to the restaurant. Alone in the car, Maloney closed his eyes and inadvertently found himself drifting toward the rim of sleep. But panic floated back. He sat up straight, remembering the surveillance dream.

After what seemed a long time they returned to the car, Mary Ann carrying three boxes of Cracker Jack. "I phoned Carmel," Vaterman said. "And you'll be interested to know that your prediction is correct. It is not raining in Carmel. The Collection is okay."

"I told you not to call Carmel."

"And I am telling *you* I am not your servant!" Vaterman shouted.

"Anyway, Fred didn't say where he was calling from," Mary Ann said. "He didn't tell them a thing."

They drove on. Mary Ann munched Cracker Jack. In late afternoon they merged with the giant snakes-and-ladders scramble of the Los Angeles freeways.

"Where do you want to stay, Tony?"

"Any place. I don't know."

"Let's stay at that hotel on the Strip," Mary Ann said. "Same as last time."

At once, Vaterman slowed the car to about forty miles an hour. "You mean the Sunset Plaza?"

"Yes. It's okay, isn't it?"

Vaterman did not answer. A moment later, he turned the car onto the San Diego Freeway ramp. "We have company."

Maloney sat up straight, in new panic. "Who?"

"Mary Ann's father. See that green Chevy that's been following us, over there in the left lane?"

Maloney looked through the rear window. There was

a Chevy in the left lane. Its driver was a stout matron wearing a red and yellow bandanna kerchief. "Are you sure? There's a woman driving."

"She is probably some friend of his. He is crouching down in the back seat."

Maloney looked over at Mary Ann. "What do you think?"

"I wish I had more Cracker Jack."

"It's not a time for jokes," Vaterman said crossly. "This means separate rooms."

She stared ahead obliquely. "Whatever you say."

Minutes later, the Mustang left the concrete anonymity of the freeway, moving into the sad, billboard-blighted streets of Hollywood as though crossing the frontier from an advanced to a backward country. Maloney saw the green Chevy move past, going on down the freeway toward San Diego.

"You seem to have lost him."

Vaterman shook his head. "He will come off at the next exit."

"But how will he find us? We'll be miles away by then."

"He will find us," Vaterman said.

The Mustang went up Doheny Drive, turning onto a hilly street lined with buildings resembling huge blocks of multiflavored ice cream. Vaterman pulled into a driveway which read SUNSET PLAZA HOTEL & APTS. It seemed to Maloney not appreciably different from the motel he had fled. "It's nice," Mary Ann whispered. "And it has a great pool."

"I don't want a room overlooking the pool," Maloney said. "I want to look out at the street. Or, better still, at a blank wall."

"Why's that?"

"I just do, that's all."

The room clerk to whom Maloney later made this request was a young man of considerable sophistication. "Agoraphobia," he said. "Yes. You'd be surprised how many people are hung up on that. Let's see. I can give you 14A, which has one small window facing a blank wall about twenty feet away."

"Good. And I want the television set taken out of the room before I go up there."

"Right. If you'll just wait a minute."

A sixteen-year-old bellhop, dressed in blue jeans and pink-and-white-flowered shirt was sent upstairs to remove the television set. Later, he escorted Maloney to a small second-floor room. A single bed faced the window with its promised view of a nearby wall. After the bellhop had accepted money and left the room, Maloney moved the bed so that it faced away from the window. He then went to the window and looked out. The window gave on a narrow alley in which a row of cars was parked. The wall, some twenty feet away, was blank, windowless brick.

There was a knock on the door.

"Come in."

Mary Ann entered, tentative, almost furtive. "Can I see you for a moment?"

"Of course."

"I just wanted to apologize about Fred. You see, he gets real cranky if he feels people are ordering him around. If you don't mind, please try not to make him mad. Okay?"

"Fine," Maloney said. "I was a bit cranky myself today."

She smiled her shy, awkward smile and tossed her mane of auburn hair. "Anyway, Fred doesn't like L.A. Last time we were here, I kept him up dancing all night."

"You like to dance?"

"I love it. But, I mean, we won't be doing any of that this time. With your dream, and all."

"Never mind my dream. Let's go dancing tonight."

"Oh no." She laughed, embarrassed. "No, really. Besides, you need to rest. You look tired."

"I don't want to rest. I'd like to go dancing. Let's go dancing."

"Are you sure?"

"I'm sure."

At that moment, inadvertently, he saw the window and the blank brick wall. "First, I want a drink," he said. "I want a drink right now. Let's go out to some bar, okay?"

"Okay."

There was a knock on the door.

"Who is it?"

"Me. Fred."

She went to open.

"Ah, so here you are. I was wondering where you were, Mary Ann."

"We were just going to go out. Tony wants a drink."

"He's found us," Vaterman said. "I told you he'd find us. I have a room that looks on the street. I looked out and a green Chevy went past, very, very slow. I went downstairs just now to check. It is parked at the end of the street."

"All right, let's go out. Tony wants to go to a bar."

"Tony?" Vaterman said. "Before we start off, I want to ask you something. When do you think I can file a story back to the *Courier*? I mean, they don't even know I've left Carmel."

Maloney ignored this. "Let's go."

"We could go to J.J.'s," Mary Ann suggested. "They have drinks and food too, if anyone's hungry."

"Just a minute," Vaterman said. "Tony hasn't answered my question."

But Maloney was staring at the blank wall outside. "It's not night yet," he said.

"What do you mean?"

Red blurs came before his eyes. His head throbbed.

"I said, what do you mean."

"I mean I'm not sleepy. I want to have some drinks. And then I want to dance. Mary Ann, you want to go dancing, don't you?"

"Well . . ." She looked to Vaterman for guidance.

"What's this about dancing?" Vaterman said. "I thought you came here to have a new dream? How can you have a new dream if you're out drinking and dancing?"

"Let's get that drink," Maloney said, loudly.

"Fred," Mary Ann whispered. "Please? Get the car."

Hours later, in a club like a barn, vast, windowless, strobe lights prismatically piercing the gloom, rendering all vision a simulacrum of drunkenness, sound a cacophony so total that no other noise could penetrate the iron heartbeat of the music: in this place, her feet now bare and black with dirt, Mary Ann danced, a creature transformed, possessed, her shyness vanished like a stammer, pausing between sets only to drink another Coca-Cola, her feet still moving restlessly to remembered music, her hand beckoning Maloney once again onto the dance floor as he, coatless, disheveled, drunk, reeled and whirled in parody to her virtuosity. While at their table, weary, nodding with sleep, Vaterman sat like an old man in an asylum, forgotten in this great screaming throat of sound.

"I want to talk to you," Vaterman shouted, raising his voice in a rare moment of silence.

"Fred wants to go home," Mary Ann said.

Vaterman turned on her. "Oh, shut up! Listen, Tony, I have a story to file. I did not come to L.A. to sit in a goddam dance hall. You said you were going to dream a new dream. How can you dream a new dream when you're drunk?"

"I'm not sleepy yet," Maloney said, and held out his hand, beckoning Mary Ann onto the dance floor, walking away from Vaterman's shouted complaints. When they returned from the set, the table was empty. A note was propped up against the lamp.

> *Gone home*
> *Careful: The father is outside.*
> FXV

Mary Ann read the note and crumpled it into a ball. "That means he's mad at me."

"Who? Your father?"

"No. Fred."

"Tell me something," Maloney said. "Why would your father drive all the way to Los Angeles and yet never speak to you? It doesn't make sense."

The cymbals clashed. The lead guitar player screamed into the mikes. All speech died in the train wail of the music. Again he led her to the floor, his drunken vision kaleidoscopically fragmenting her moving torso in the flicker of the strobes. The question he had asked blurred and was lost, as in these several hours of spastic movement he seemed to have lost the reason for his panic and flight. Yet the panic, dulled by uncounted Scotches, waited to surface again.

At last, a great crash of sound and, suddenly, strobe lights were shut off, music died, and the barnlike ceiling of the dance hall was revealed in electric whiteness. The performance was over. The stage, an empty tangle of wires, mikes, amplifiers, stood in trashy confusion, silent as a carnival midway when the crowd has gone home. Mary Ann still gyrated, lonely on the dusty floorboards. "What happened? It's not over, is it?"

"Yes, it's over. Band's gone."

"What time is it?"

"I don't know," he said. "Let's go some place. There must be other places."

But the teenaged troglodyte who guarded the cloakroom offered no hope. "It's after four. You won't find no place. Maybe some bar with music, or something."

"Then let's go to a bar. Okay, Mary Ann?"

"Okay." She took his arm and led him toward the door. "You know," she said suddenly. "You're fun. Did you know that? Fred isn't fun, you know."

"I know. Let's find a bar. I think I need another drink."

A yellow cab, lonely American survivor among the late moving shoals of foreign cars in Beverly Hills, found them and removed them to a go-go bar. Naked girls undulated to recorded music in a cage high above the dance floor.

"Hey, good music," Mary Ann said.

He stood, staring at the jukebox, suddenly remembering the television dream. His panic surfaced.

"What's the matter?" she asked.

"Nothing. Let's dance."

They danced. He drank. An hour passed. By now, the go-go girls had gone. There were four other customers in the bar, none sober.

"Do you think your father's still hanging about?"

She shrugged.

"Do you really think he followed you down here?"

"Fred says he did."

"But *you* didn't see him?"

"No."

"Do you ever see him?"

"Oh, sure. At least I used to. He used to come up and talk to me in the street."

"What did he say?"

"Oh, he'd ask if I was being a good girl. Stuff like that. Hey, what's happened to the music?"

"We can put quarters in that jukebox. I'll get some."

But, going toward the bar, Maloney tripped and fell. She helped him up. "You're really high tonight, aren't you?"

He looked at her, her face now close, her luminous eyes concerned for him, her auburn hair tumbling about her cheeks. All at once, he felt as though he would weep. "You know," he said, "my life is going to be lonely from now on."

"What do you mean, Tony?"

"Nothing. Let's dance some more."

"Are you sure? Maybe you want to call it a night?"

"Not yet. Let's dance."

But, minutes later, suddenly, unmistakably ill,

Maloney sought the men's room. A wrong turning led him out into a back alley. There he retched and, sobered, raised his head and saw bright sunlight on the pastel alley wall. The night had passed. He went back into the club.

Alone on the tiny dance floor, she moved in response to those intricate rhythms which had animated her through the night. The three remaining customers, all male, focused on her with blurry concentration as, feet bare, her long hair damp, her white dress clinging to her elegant, coltish legs, she gyrated in trance, her large luminous eyes dreaming of some unending rhythmic paradise.

"Mary Ann? Mary Ann?"

The music ended abruptly with a sudden scud of drums.

"Mary Ann, it's morning."

"Yes, and I'm going to close the place," the bartender told the room. "You can get yourself some breakfast at the pancake place up the street."

"Good idea. Hey, Tony, let's get some breakfast."

At the House of Pancakes, she ate a double order of eggs and blueberry pancakes, with a side dish of pistachio ice cream. Maloney drank black coffee.

"That was really fun tonight, wasn't it? You know, that was the best fun I've had in a long time. What's Montreal like?"

"It's nice. You'd like it."

"We should go there sometime."

"What would Fred say?"

She looked at him oddly. "What do you mean?"

"I mean, you're Fred's girl, aren't you?"

She looked away. "I'm not anybody's girl," she whispered. "That's the truth."

The middle-aged waitress who had served them breakfast came up, with a small prefatory cough.

"Excuse me, folks."

Two younger waitresses materialized behind the first waitress. All wore uncertain smiles.

"The check," Maloney said, dutifully.

"We have sort of a bet going," the older waitress said. "I wonder, can I ask you a question?"

"What is it?"

"Are you the gentleman we saw on television, the one with that collection up in Carmel?"

"Yes, I am."

"I win," the younger waitress said.

"Thank you," said the older waitress. "And it certainly is an honor meeting you."

When the waitresses had gone, Mary Ann suddenly said, "I just thought of something. You didn't sleep at all last night. Yet, when you sleep, it's to guard the Collection. Supposing something's happened to it?"

"Let me worry about that."

She blushed. "I'm sorry. It's just that sometimes I feel like I'm a part of the Collection. I don't know how to explain it. It's silly."

"No, it's not," he said. "Maybe you *have* something to do with it. But supposing it did vanish last night. Supposing I have to go home to Montreal and take up the life I had before this happened. Would you just forget about me, in that case?"

She shook her head, her auburn mane hiding her

features. "Anyway, nothing's going to happen to the Collection, right?"

"Right," he said.

In the taxi, going down Sunset Boulevard, he said: "I'm serious. Would you come to Montreal with me if I asked you?"

She put her hand on his knee. "Shh!"

"Would you?"

"I really had a nice time last night," she said. "Didn't you?"

"I'd get my job back. I'm hoping to be made an associate professor soon. Then I'll have tenure."

"What you need now is a good sleep."

"Sleep?" His panic floated upward for a moment.

"Sunset Plaza, was it?" the driver asked.

"Right," Mary Ann said.

"I don't want to sleep. I wish we could go on to Montreal right now."

Mary Ann was silent.

"I mean it."

The cab entered the hotel driveway. Mary Ann got out first. Maloney, following her, fumbled with a fistful of bills, overtipping the driver, spilling money on the asphalt walk. As he bent over to pick up the bills, he became aware that his drunkenness had worn off. His hands trembled. His panic floated up, full-blown.

As they went through the lobby to get their keys, red blurs came before his eyes. He took his room key. 14A. The bed; the blank wall. His head throbbed. The hues of black-and-white television came down like a screen over his vision, and endless, monotonous as rows of cells in a prison corridor, the aisles of the Collection held in the unblinking scrutiny of the television monitor, unmoving, grim, strangely terrifying as though, like some maze, once entered, its labyrinthine silences would imprison him forever. He began to tremble. And then, as though he were regaining consciousness after an anesthetic, the red blurs returned. His head cleared.

In front of him stood Mary Ann, key in hand, waiting for the elevator. "Could I stay with you?" he heard himself say. "I don't mean sleep with you, but could we just lie down together?"

He saw her flinch. A red welt of embarrassment laid itself like a stripe across her cheek. "Why?"

"Because I'm afraid to be alone."

She turned away, as though to hide herself from his eyes. The elevator came. The doors shut on them and the elevator began its climb. It reached her floor. Suddenly, in awkward haste, she took his arm. "Come on."

He began to tremble.

She came from the bathroom, toweling her long dark hair. She wore a white cotton nightgown with Mexican white-flower embroidery at the collar and shoulders. She looked at him.

"Take your clothes off and take a shower," she said. "It'll make you feel better."

Obedient, he went toward the bathroom. As he passed, she lay down, languorous, in the narrow bed.

In the shower his panic was such he stood for a long time unable to move from under the jet of water. To sleep and not to dream. Not to dream. He said it over and over like a prayer. When at last he came from the bathroom, still trembling, wearing only shorts, Mary Ann had already dozed off. As he crossed the room, he stumbled against the bed table. A Gideon Bible fell with a slap on the floor. She woke.

"Pull the blind down before you come to bed," she said.

In the new darkness of the room, he lay beside her, trembling. She turned to him and stroked his chest with long, delicate fingers. "Now go to sleep," she told him. "Everything's going to be okay. And when we wake up we're going to have a nice day."

He nodded. Within moments, she was asleep again. He closed his eyes, waiting for the appearance of the television monitor in some corner of the bedroom.

After a while he opened his eyes. In the maw of his panic, he steadied himself and, leaning on one elbow, looked down at the girl who lay asleep beside him, her dark hair tousled like a child's, the sheet kicked aside by her long, naked legs, her white cotton nightdress rucked up to show the delicate oval of her buttock. For one tantalizing instant she became a Victorian servant girl asleep in an attic bed while he, the young master of the house, looked on her nakedness, possessed of the *droit du seigneur* to her sleeping charms. But in that one giddy flush of desire, panic returned like an attack of nausea, to float him down a new and vertiginous slope. She slept now, but could he? What if, away from Carmel, *all* sleep would be denied him?

Trembling, sweating, catatonic, he lay, open-eyed, for the next two hours. It ended with a knock on the door.

"Mary Ann? It's Fred."

She sat up, startled, in the confusion of a person wakened from deep sleep.

"Mary Ann?"

Her finger went to her lips, then pointed to the bathroom. An instant conspirator, Maloney rose and tiptoed across the room. As he closed the bathroom door behind him, he heard her call: "All right. Just a minute."

He stood by the tub, trembling, hastily putting on his clothes. He heard her open the bedroom door.

"What time did you get home?"

"Around eight."

"Eight? So you were out all night with him."

"Yes, we were dancing."

"Your father is going to kill him. You know that, don't you?"

"Oh, come on."

"I am serious. When I left the club, he did not follow me. He must have stayed there all night, watching you and Tony."

"Well, *we* didn't see him."

"Where is Tony?"

"In bed, I guess."

"He's not in bed. I have been three times to his room. A few minutes ago I got the bellhop to use the passkey. The bed is not even slept in. Perhaps he has run off again?"

"Oh, he'll turn up."

"Did he say anything to you before you left him?"

"I think he said something about phoning Carmel. Why don't you go down to the desk and check if anybody saw him go out?"

"Good idea. I'll see you in a few minutes."

The door shut. She came into the bathroom.

"Hurry. Go to your room before he gets back. Did you sleep?"

"No."

"Oh, poor Tony. Listen, I'll talk to you very soon."
She leaned toward him, kissed his cheek and, at the same
time giving him a little push, bundled him out into the
corridor. He went toward the elevator and pressed the
button. The elevator was slow in coming. When it did,
Vaterman was in it.

"Tony, I've been looking for you everywhere. How
are you?"

"Tired."

"I've just talked to Carmel. They tell me it was on
television last night that you've disappeared."

Television. A familiar unease filled him. "How is the
Collection?"

"What?"

"The Collection. Is it all right?"

Vaterman seemed nonplused. "I suppose so. I didn't
ask."

"You didn't ask?"

He rushed past Vaterman, stepped into the elevator,
went up to his room and, agitated, his hands trembling,
put in a call to the Sea Winds Motel. Bourget answered.
"Oh, it's you, Professor. Listen, Mr. Hickman just flew
in, he wants to talk to you."

"No. Get me Dr. Spector."

"Hold on."

"Spector speaking."

"It's Tony Maloney, Doctor."

"Tony, where are you? Are you all right? Why did
you go off like that?"

"It's an experiment, Doctor. I'm sorry, I couldn't tell
you about it beforehand. Did you look at the Collection
this morning?"

"As a matter of fact, I did."

"Was there any change in it?"

"No. I didn't look very closely, mind you."

"Well, please go and look now."

"All right, but what do I look for?"

"Some kind of damage. I'm not sure what."

"Hold the line," Dr. Spector said. "I'll be right back."

While Maloney waited, Hickman came on. "Ah, so there you are. What are you doing in L.A.? All right, don't answer, I don't want to make waves. Frankly, I'd have appreciated it if you'd been able to let me know your schedule. Just when we're right in the middle of the franchise negotiations, just when public opinion is beginning to *buy* the idea of the Collection, you disappear."

"I had to. It was an experiment."

"Okay, so it was an experiment. So the Collection is still here. So that stuff you told me last week about it raining if you leave Carmel isn't true. Tony, if *I* can't be sure you're telling the truth, who can? You understand this isn't a criticism."

"If it isn't a criticism, then what is it?"

"Okay, okay. I'm sorry. Tony, I just wish you'd take me into your confidence, that's all. I want to help. Listen, how long are you going to stay in L.A.?"

"I don't know. It depends."

"Well, try to get back as soon as you can, will you? We've got a lot riding on this deal."

"All right."

"Okay, then," Hickman said. "Take care."

Alone again, Maloney began to tremble as he waited for Dr. Spector to return to the phone.

"Tony?"

"Yes, Doctor. What happened?"

146

"Well, what can I tell you? Of course, I'm not an expert on Victoriana, so my observations are without scientific merit. So, when I say I detect some change, it's nothing I can put my finger on. It's as if the objects I examined just now were a little—shall I say—a little more worn than before. I am sorry I can't be more definite. It could also be because there's some coastal fog here this morning and the quality of light is not as strong as it has been on other occasions."

"They've faded," Maloney said.

"Excuse me?"

"They seem faded, don't they?"

"Yes. Yes, that's how I would describe it. Tony, do you realize this is an excellent example of precognition. This is one of the few times in which your experience parallels that of other sensitives. I wonder if you would sit down now and try to write out a full description of your feelings?"

"I'm sorry, Doctor, I can't at the moment. I'll talk to you later."

After replacing the receiver, Maloney called the desk and told the clerk he was not to be disturbed. He locked the bedroom door, pulled down the blind, and lay on the bed, trembling, facing the wall. When had the deterioration begun? What had caused it? Was it the television dream, or was it his absence? Or was it the fact that he had not slept at all? He did not know, he no longer knew anything and so, in alcoholic malaise, he lay, nodding toward sleep as might a person driving a car late at night, desiring it, yet fearing what it might bring, a limbo in which he passed an hour, then another, trembling, exhausted yet always and ineluctably awake.

Shortly after noon he rose, shaved, dressed, and went to her room. He knocked. Vaterman admitted him.

"Ah, so there you are. We were told you were sleeping and that you mustn't be disturbed."

Behind Vaterman was Mary Ann, still in her short nightgown, sitting at the dressing table, carefully combing her long hair. On another table were paper cartons containing Chinese food.

"Any luck with the new dream?" Vaterman asked.

"No."

"So, what are you going to do? Go back to Carmel?"

"No, I'm staying here, at least for one more night."

"But that is irresponsible," Vaterman objected. "I have been talking to Hickman about the franchise negotiation. He wants you back in Carmel."

Maloney did not answer. He did not answer because, at that moment, vomit rose in his throat. He hurried into the bathroom, kicking the door shut behind him as he bent over, retching into the toilet bowl.

"Tony, are you all right?" Mary Ann's voice outside, soft, worried.

"Please, go away. Go shopping or something. Give me a couple of hours."

"Are you sure you'll be all right?"

"Yes."

Again, he retched. After a while he heard her call out a goodbye, heard Vaterman say something he did not catch. He stood up and washed his face and hands in the washbasin, then went back into the bedroom. Vomiting had purged him of yet another defense against sleep and now, as he sat on her bed, he no longer seemed able to maintain his balance. He fell like a rag doll face down on her pillows, smelling her strange girlish scent.

So it had not been destroyed by his flight. No floods or rainstorms had come to sweep it away. Instead, it was fading, cracking, deteriorating. All those strange and wonderful things were becoming damaged. The longer he stayed away, the more they would diminish, like invalids suffering some wasting disease.

He had thought he could destroy it at will. All he had to do was run away. But now he knew there would be no easy escape. The destruction of the Collection would take years. It would die a lingering death, in continuing reproach to his neglect and indifference. Better not to think about that. But, in his desire to reverse this frightening thought, his panic dropped into the opposite fatal chamber. What if he could dream no dream at all, away from Carmel? What if he could not even fall asleep, away from Carmel?

He sat up, stiff with tension. Nausea rose again. On his way, hurrying to the bathroom, he stumbled and fell, knocking over a table which held the remains of the Chinese meal. Cardboard cartons of fried rice and almond chicken fell about him on the rug. He did not get up, but lay prone, his hands pressing into the rug's pile in an effort to control his uncontrollable tremor. Sooner or later, everyone must sleep. Sleep was life's other half. Without it, a person would collapse into madness and death.

After some minutes, he got up off the floor and telephoned down to the hotel desk. Later, pale and sweating but filled with desperate determination, he got out of a cab and went into an office building off the Sunset Strip. There a doctor recommended by the hotel clerk examined him, told him he had a temperature and a high pulse rate and, grudgingly, wrote a prescription for a small amount of Nembutal tablets. Shortly afterward, Maloney returned to his hotel, having filled the prescription at a nearby drugstore. He went to his room and left instructions that on no account was he to be disturbed. He locked his door, swallowed three pills, pulled the blind down, and lay on the bed, face toward the wall.

At eight o'clock that evening, Mary Ann came to his room and knocked on the door. His voice, drained, weak, called out at once. "Come in."

She found him lying half dressed on the bed, trembling, sweating like a man in a high fever and pathetically glad to see her.

"Oh, poor Tony, what's happened? Hadn't I better get a doctor?"

"No, no, just stay with me. I thought nobody would ever come."

"We were told you were asleep. In fact, Fred's downstairs waiting for the result of your new dream. He'd be mad at me if he knew I came up here."

"I can't sleep. I took pills but I can't sleep. Mary Ann, stay with me, will you? I don't want to be alone."

"Of course I'll stay. Should I order up some food?"

"No, let's go out. Yes, that's a good idea. Let's go out. Let's go dancing again. When I'm dancing I don't think about anything. Yes, let's go dancing."

"But you're sick."

"No, I'll be all right. Honestly."

She hesitated. "Are you sure?"

"Yes, I'm sure."

He sat up in the bed and, unsteady, got to his feet. He went into the bathroom and toweled his face and neck. With shaking fingers he knotted his tie and put on a jacket. "I'm ready," he said. "Do you want to check with Fred?"

She looked at him and suddenly shook her head. "No. Come on. Let's go."

9

But Vaterman was waiting in the lobby.

"No dream?"

"No," Maloney said. "We're going dancing. Want to come?"

"Oh, for Christ sake. All right, that is the end of it. I am going back to Carmel first thing in the morning."

"Suit yourself."

"And if you are not ready to come back with me by eight o'clock, both of you will have to find your own transport."

"Fine by me," Mary Ann said. "Now, are you coming dancing, or aren't you?"

Vaterman stared at her. "Goddamn you," he said.

Yet, at four in the morning, he was still with them, driving the battered red Mustang along Santa Monica Boulevard in search of the Big Bomb Club, a place which the parking attendant in their last spot had assured them stayed in session until dawn. Maloney, who had danced or reeled about constantly for the past six hours, sat slack on the back seat. He had drunk a great deal of bourbon and had been sick twice in men's rooms. He looked abject.

Vaterman, more out of temper than ever, peered from time to time into his rear-view mirror. At last he announced, "I thought so. Here he comes again."

"Who?"

"The father."

"Where?" Maloney asked.

"See the green Chevy coming up behind us?"

" 'S not green."

"It is green," Vaterman said. "You are too drunk to know the difference."

The neon sign of the Big Bomb Club loomed on their left. The Mustang pulled in under a dusty porte-cochere. Long-haired boys and girls, coming out of the club, stood about in the parking lot, eyes dulled, waiting for carhops to find their cars.

"Pretty," one of the boys said, as Mary Ann got out of the Mustang. "Hi there, pretty girl."

Vaterman caught Maloney's sleeve. "Listen, I warn you, the father hates long-hairs. Let's get out of here." He leaned forward and called from the car. "Mary Ann, get back in. We're leaving."

She turned, flushing, and then, suddenly, leaned into the car and whispered to Maloney: "Come on, let's go inside."

"Don't listen to her," Vaterman said. "If you do, when you come out of here you'll find that maniac waiting to murder you in the parking lot."

Flushing, Mary Ann waited. Maloney opened the car door and got out. At once, Vaterman leaned across the front seat, slammed the door shut, gunned the engine, and, with a roar, the Mustang shot out of the club entrance as though escaping from a bank robbery. Maloney looked around. There was no sign of any Chevy. Mary Ann, walking ahead of him, went in at the club entrance. In the tunnel gloom inside, a long-haired youth stood behind a ticket counter. "That will be six dollars each," he warned. Sound eddied over and around his voice, diminishing it to a whisper. They walked toward electronic furor and within moments were again on a dance floor, she moving in synchromesh to the beat; he, clownish, reeling, out of step, in a poor mime of his fellow dancer.

Between sets, he stood at a long bar, drinking a brown liquid the barman said was wine.

"Mary Ann?"

"Yes, what?"

"Fred's going to be pretty angry, isn't he?"

The music started up.

"What?" He screamed the question.

"I don't know. Let's dance."

Two hours later, on the stroke of six, the Big Bomb fizzled to silence. As the few remaining patrons emptied out into the parking lot in search of their cars, Mary Ann and Maloney, hand in hand, walked unsteadily along Santa Monica Boulevard.

"See any green Chevrolets back there?"

"Don't worry," Mary Ann said. "Hey, I really had fun. Didn't you?"

"Yes."

"I mean, I feel we kind of got to know each other on this trip, didn't we?"

"Yes, didn't we."

"It was like a vacation. And now it's ending. I mean, for me. You had a bad time, I know."

"Listen," he said. "It would have been worse if you hadn't been here. You're an angel, do you know that?"

She looked away, embarrassed. They walked, searching the sparse dawn traffic for a taxi.

"What are we going to do?" she said after a while. "Are we going back to Carmel?"

His head throbbed. Suddenly, imposed on his vision, the monitor screen with its television gray-blue image panning past the "Folkstone" railway engine to hold on an aisle of the Collection displaying a range of William Morris furniture. Panic, the trapped panic of a prisoner waiting a dawn summons to judgment, filled him. Red blurs came before his eyes. His vision cleared, revealing pale stucco buildings and ugly advertising hoardings in silhouette against a pale pink Pacific sunrise.

"No," he said. "I want to go on."

"Where?"

"I don't know. Montreal. Maybe I can have a new dream there."

She looked at him and, suddenly, smiled. "All right. Why don't we go, then?"

"Now?"

"Yes."

"Do you mean it? What about Fred?"

"I don't have to ask Fred. I'm not married to him."

"That's right, you're not."

"Hey, there's a taxi."

"There's someone in it."

They walked on. It was after seven when, still walking, they reached their hotel. They crossed the lobby, hand in hand. The desk clerk, a knowing type, reached around behind him and, in silence, handed them the key to Mary Ann's room.

"I'd like my key as well," Maloney said.

The desk clerk smiled. "Whatever you say."

Hand in hand, they went into the elevator. There were no other passengers. As they went up, she leaned over and kissed him, clumsily, on the cheek. Tears came to his eyes. She likes me. She wants to be with me. I'm no longer all alone. "Listen," he said. "I'm going to go to my room and try to sleep for an hour or two. Then we'll go on to Montreal."

"All right. Will you tell Fred?"

"Okay."

When Maloney reached his own room he at once phoned Vaterman. "Fred, I'm going on to Montreal this afternoon."

"Montreal?"

"It's part of the experiment."

"What's Hickman going to say? You are supposed to go back to Carmel."

Maloney felt himself begin to tremble. "And, by the way, Mary Ann wants to come with me."

"I do not think that's wise, Tony."

"What do you mean, Fred?"

"Mary Ann is a minor. The father is following you. If

156

you transport her to another country, there may be all sorts of legal actions he can take."

"Surely he wouldn't follow us all the way to Canada?"

"Why not? Anyway, it is your funeral. I am going back to Carmel."

"All right. Listen, I'll phone you from Montreal."

"As you wish," Vaterman said coldly.

"And I'll take good care of Mary Ann. Don't worry."

"Why should I worry?" Vaterman said. "She is your problem now. Don't say I didn't warn you."

The phone clicked.

For a moment Maloney pondered ringing Vaterman back and trying to end on some more friendly note. But was it possible, considering the circumstances? He thought not. He went into the bathroom, removed his shirt, and washed his head and torso in warm water. Then he swallowed three Nembutals, pulled the blind, and lay down on the bed. Nembutals, drink, exhaustion: it had to work.

But it did not.

At ten he phoned Air Canada, then shaved and packed his overnight bag. He sat in a chair until eleven. At eleven-ten he rang Mary Ann and asked her to get ready. There was a flight for Montreal at one.

"Did you talk to Fred?"

"Yes, he's going back to Carmel."

There was a silence. Then she said, "All right, I'll meet you in the lobby in half an hour. Did you get to sleep?"

"Yes," he lied.

The plane climbed. The captain spoke: "Today our route will take us over Las Vegas, Nevada; Salt Lake City, Utah; and, moving on, to Omaha, Nebraska. Then into Chicago and across Lake Michigan to Toronto and Montreal, Canada."

He sought Mary Ann's hand and held it. The captain continued: "Our flying time will be four hours and forty-eight minutes and we expect to land in Toronto at eight-fifty local time. Weather conditions are excellent, but while we don't anticipate any turbulence, we recommend that you keep your seat belts fastened, as a precaution. Thank you. Relax and enjoy your trip."

She turned to him, her dark eyes widening in alarm. "What's the matter? You look terrible."

"I feel sick."

"Why don't you try to get some sleep? Rest your head on this pillow and I'll make sure nobody disturbs you."

Gratefully, he accepted the little pillow and closed his eyes. Perhaps on a jet, thirty thousand feet above the world, he would be freed from the dream, or freed to dream? But, as always on this odyssey, sleep refused him. Dazed, he lolled in the anesthetic drone of the engines. Guilt, the continuing guilt of his abandonment of the Collection, came up in strong panic waves. Would the fading increase as he distanced himself from Carmel? Or did the fading depend on the amount of time he remained away from the Collection? He resolved to call Dr. Spector as soon as he reached Montreal.

In Toronto they were told they must disembark to clear Canadian customs and immigration. In the vast terminal, slack-kneed, erratic in his walk, he followed her down corridors to the customs desk. The officer who took his passport singled him out instantly.

"Say, didn't I see you on television? Aren't you the man who says he 'dreamed up' all that furniture and stuff out in California?"

"Yes."

The customs officer turned to tell his fellow officers. Three of them stopped work to stare. "Well," said the first officer, "no point asking you if you have anything to declare. You could have a whole warehouse full of stuff hidden away in your head."

Two of the officers laughed immoderately. The third whispered something to the first officer.

"Oh, yes. Seriously, sir. You're sure you don't have any forbidden items? Pornographic books or pictures?"

"No, no."

"There were a number of items of that nature turned up in Carmel," one of the other officers said loudly.

"All right, sir. Will you just open these bags?"

The search was thorough; the manner cordial.

"The young lady is with you?"

"Yes."

"No liquor or gifts, have you, miss?"

"No."

"All right then, you can both go ahead."

Weary, his head aching, Maloney went back with Mary Ann to reboard for Montreal. But now things had changed. No sooner were they in the air with the seat-belts sign turned off than a woman passenger carrying a Polaroid camera came down the aisle. "May I take your picture, Professor Maloney?"

Mary Ann began to comb her hair.

Flashcubes flared. Suddenly the aisles were filled with passengers. Some asked for autographs, some merely stood about, watching, whispering, giggling. A stewardess forced her way through. "Dr. Maloney, if you and the young lady wouldn't mind, I think you'd have more privacy in first class."

In Montreal, the airline provided a "complimentary" limousine to bring them into town. As it glided away from the airport, the driver respectfully requested a destination. Maloney sat silent. He did not know where to go. Barbara had been up to his apartment. He had been told she had stripped it, taking all the sheets and blankets, the silverware, and most of the furniture. No one, not even his mother, knew he was here. And, as he gave the driver the address of a downtown hotel, it came to him that for the first time in his life he was entering his own city as a stranger.

A stranger, but not unknown: when their bags were brought in from the limousine, an assistant manager, magically apprised of their presence, appeared to show them to a special suite. Within the hour, two newspapers had called to ask how long he planned to stay in Montreal. Was it true he was planning to take the Collection on tour? Was he, perhaps, planning a permanent home for his Collection in Canada?

At nine-thirty he saw his photograph flash on the television screen. The announcer said he was traveling with his secretary and staying at a downtown hotel. Against his better judgment, he then made a telephone call.

"Mother?"

"I just saw you on TV! Where are you? What are you doing staying at a hotel, you could stay here, is it because of having that girl with you, listen, I could make some arrangement and put her up too. I'm not *that* narrow-minded."

"Mother, it was very sudden. I just called you tonight to say hello, because I want to get some sleep now. I'll speak to you tomorrow."

"Can I tell John Palliser you're here? He's very anxious to see you. It's wonderful what he and the others have done for you at McGill, isn't it? Such a nice boy, John."

"Mother, I'll call John tomorrow. I'm dead beat. And promise you won't tell anyone else where I am."

"Well, I think you should at least say hello to Les tonight. He's going to feel hurt."

"No, Mother. I'll do it in the morning. Now, good night. Talk to you tomorrow."

He ordered the hotel switchboard to hold all further calls. He went to the window and looked out at the great dominoes of lighted windows, tall office blocks abandoned to night cleaners. Beyond was the long sprawl of the city's east end and, far away, across that black band of night which was the St. Lawrence River, the firefly glimmer of dwelling lights on the farther shore. Here he had been born twenty-nine years ago in a hospital room in Notre Dame de Grâce; here, a child in a Red River coat, he had skated in Westmount Park; here, in the ugly classrooms of Verdun High School, he had begun the metamorphoses of an ordinary life: a schoolboy, overeager, quickly discouraged; a university undergraduate who would one day become a university professor; a son who would become a husband; a lover who would again be alone. In all these years he had moved anonymous in the veins of these streets, a microcosm of his city. But tonight he had lost that anonymity and, in losing it, had become estranged.

He turned from the window and as in confirmation of his changed status saw the unfamiliar elegance of the suite. He sat on a Biedermeier sofa in the sitting room and looked at the shut Empire doors of the adjoining bedrooms. At that moment a drowsiness overcame him. His head lolled forward and he closed his swollen eyelids. At once, as if caught in a vise, his neck stiffened and his eyes again saw the gray-blue image moving slowly past the "Folkstone" railway engine to hold on that aisle of the Collection which contained a display of William Morris furniture. But this time, even in the blurred hues of television, the stalls gave off an air of decay, a sense of abandonment, the stillness of a burial ground. Red blurs came before his eyes. His vision cleared. He awoke, calling out her name.

She came at once from the bathroom, wrapping a large white towel around her. "Tony? Are you all right?"

"Yes," he said. "Let's go out."

"Are you sure? Aren't you pooped?"

"No," he said. "I want to take you some place. You want to see Montreal, don't you?"

"Well, yes. Whatever you like."

"All right, then. Hurry and get dressed."

She ran back into the bathroom. Within moments, like an obedient child, she reappeared wearing her long yellow caftan. "Ready," she said.

He looked at her, longing, with the hangdog stare of love.

André's Grande Allée was a student rendezvous. In it, Maloney had first been introduced to his wife. Before and after that event he had spent uncounted evenings there with friends, drinking beer, dancing, making it a night with a supper of André's pizza special. Even the graffiti scratched on the walls of the men's room were so familiar that, unintentionally, he had memorized most of them. To walk into André's was, in a sense, to come home. Home is where the expected is ordinary. In all these ordinary evenings, no famous, dangerous, or outrageous events had occurred within these walls.

Until that night. For, when Maloney and Mary Ann entered, they found themselves the cynosure of the room, focus of a wall of unremitting stares. Momentarily he thought it was because of Mary Ann, a girl unlike any other he had ever escorted to this place. But when René Turcotte, the manager, led them at once to the choice reserved tables by the dance floor, sweeping off a "Reserved" sign as he seated them, and ordering a round of beer on the house, the evening became as no evening at André's within Maloney's memory. Students he knew, and scores he did not, began pointing him out, granting him that total attention he had sought from them in vain in all his classroom hours. Seeming to want to touch him, they pressed close: "You're Dr. Maloney, aren't you?" or, "Hi, sir, remember me?" while others simply bobbed their heads in uncharacteristically humble nods of recognition, muttering half sentences like prayerful ejaculations: "Fantastic, I tell you!" — "Really far out."

Far out. At last, like a dream come true, he had been granted instant canonization as a patron saint of youth. "I hope they reinstate you right away, sir, I surely don't want to miss your class," a pretty American girl told him, respectfully laying her hand on his sleeve. "Yes, they'd better get their heads straight in that history department," a red-haired basketball giant warned. "Right on!" cried the giant's outriders.

The music struck up. Mary Ann, ignored by his fans, smiled at him hopefully across the table. Rising, he led her onto the dance floor. And now, as in a scene from an old film, when, clumsily, he began to orbit his lissome partner, the other dancers stopped dancing and crowded around to watch. For a few moments he and Mary Ann were the only couple moving on the floor. Then, respectfully, the rest of the dancers resumed their dance.

"It felt like we were on show there," she said, blushing furiously. "I nearly died, didn't you?"

They danced. As soon as they returned to their seats, they were again the center of a crowd of admirers. Strategists of his reinstatement offered questions and advice. It became more difficult to get back to the dance floor. Beer did not lift him into the requisite state of drunkenness. The questions and conversations made his head spin. Shortly after midnight, watching him shuffle his feet on the floor, pretending to dance but scarcely moving from one spot, Mary Ann whispered: "Why don't we go home? I'm dead tired and so are you."

But it was not easy. When he tried to pay his bill, new friends and eager strangers protested his departure, then offered to drive them to some other place. Outside in the street, more students materialized in the guise of autograph hunters, and when, at last, they found a taxi and drove back to their hotel, a young man waiting in a white station wagon across the street jumped out and ran up to Maloney. "Mr. Maloney, I'm from CKHL's Nightwatch program. You wouldn't care to come along to our studios and talk with our Nightwatch host, Don Ireland? He's waiting for you right now."

"No, thank you."

"Well, perhaps in that case we could set up something for tomorrow night?"

"I'm not sure where I'm going to be tomorrow night."

They entered the hotel lobby. The elevator came. As it climbed to the fifteenth floor, Maloney, suddenly dizzy, put his arm out to steady himself and caught hold of her in what must have seemed like an embrace. At once, she moved close, her breasts pressing against his chest. As his vision cleared, he found himself staring into her dark eyes, eyes like those of the older of the pubescent sisters in Baxter's Victorian portrait, and for a moment it seemed to him that he held that innocence, that long-ago girlishness re-created as flesh and blood. Lust stiffened him, lifting him from his drunken exhaustion. He ran his hands down her long back to fondle soft buttocks, his lips seeking the cleft of her throat.

"Let's go to my room," she whispered.

Her voice broke the spell. It was her voice, American, not that long-ago English lisp. He remembered that he had not called Dr. Spector. He had gone through the entire evening without one thought of those treasures wilting away in Carmel. *The Sisters.* Perhaps, even at this moment, the canvas was cracking, obscuring those dark, liquid stares.

When they went into the living room, she threw down her cape and shyly put up her face to be kissed. Trembling, he turned his head away. For one electric moment she stared at him, her cheeks red, then, snatching up the cape, ran into her bedroom. He ran after her and caught hold of the bedroom door.

"Mary Ann, I'm sorry."

"Nothing to be sorry about. You're tired, that's all. See you tomorrow."

He heard her lock her bedroom door. He stood trembling for a moment and then in sudden panic went to the telephone and called Carmel. "Mr. Bourget, this is Tony Maloney. Can I speak to Dr. Spector?"

"No way."

"Is he asleep?"

"He and his team pulled out last night. Left me with six rooms not rented."

"But I thought they were going to stay another two weeks."

"They went to New York to do some TV show. Educational television, I think he said."

"But aren't they coming back?"

"He didn't say. New York called this afternoon and they went after dinner."

"Is the Collection still all right?"

"I guess so. It's still out there, is all I know."

"It hasn't rained, has it?"

"No."

"All right, Mr. Bourget. I'll call again tomorrow. Good night."

It was two o'clock in the morning. The city slept. As he stood in the silence of the hotel sitting room, it came to him that all that he had fled and all that he sought was at one and the same time inescapable, unattainable, incapable of change. His manner of falling in love with Mary Ann was another symptom of his curious fate. There could no longer be any real life for him—no life at all apart from the Collection. There would be no new dream, here or elsewhere. Even sleep might be impossible, away from Carmel. And so, sensing some ultimate defeat, he did not even go into his bedroom, but, as

166

though willing his worst fate, stripped to his under-shorts, turned on the television set to a series of silent images and, like a prizefighter awaiting the bell, sat down in an armchair, arms slack, facing the set.

And so, he who had feared the television dream, who had fled across a continent to escape it, now sought to reinstate it in the city of his birth. He fixed his eyes on the soundless flow of images of a late-night movie, willing them to disappear and be replaced by the gray, televised booths and stalls, by the monitor camera's unremitting scrutiny of the Great Victorian Collection.

It did not happen.

Far away, a siren cried in the night as an ambulance rushed across the city. He heard it like a knell. Sleepless, his body abused by drugs and alcohol, would he, like others who could no longer dream the dreams which had made them famous, end his days in a madhouse or lie in a suicide's grave?

At 4 A.M., while he was still sitting staring at television, the images were replaced by a test pattern. He stood, went to the set, and turned it off. He was the prisoner of what he had wrought.

Better to go back at once.

At seven, wearing trousers and a shirt, he knocked on her door.

"Mary Ann?"

She opened to him, looking sleepy and touching in her white cotton nightgown. "What's wrong?"

"Can I come in for a minute?"

"Sure."

Blinds had been drawn in her bedroom. She had switched on a bed lamp on awakening. Now, in the small pool of lamplight, she moved toward the bed and got in, pulling the sheet up to cover her body. "What time is it, Tony?" she whispered.

"About seven. We'll have to go back to Carmel."

"Oh? Why?"

"I didn't tell you before," he said, "but I haven't slept since I left. I've been awake more than sixty hours."

"But you slept in L.A."

"I lied to you."

"So you weren't even sleepy," she said. It was a statement, not a question.

"I tried pills, booze, everything. But it's no use. It's as though I can't sleep when I'm away from the Collection."

Coloring suddenly, she said, "What about sex?"

"What?"

"Sex. It makes people sleepy."

"Oh? Yes, I suppose so."

"Well, then?" Tossing her mane of hair, she stared at him, intent, expectant. Uneasy, he hesitated, studying the backs of his hands.

"Tony, there's something wrong with me, isn't there?"

"Wrong with *you?* What gave you that idea?"

"First Fred and now you. Why don't you want to sleep with me?"

"Fred?"

"Oh, sure. Why do you think he pretends my father is following us all the time? It makes it easy for him to stay away from me."

"So that's it," Maloney said. "Mary Ann, listen to me. You're beautiful. I think I've wanted to go to bed with you ever since I saw you that night—remember, when you wore those Victorian clothes?"

"Listen, you don't have to make speeches. It's like when a person has bad breath. Nobody wants to tell them."

"Oh, please," he said. "Don't cry. You're wrong. Of course I want to sleep with you."

"Honestly?"

"Honestly."

Clumsily she jerked back the sheet and began to lift the hem of her nightgown.

"Wait," he said. "Let me take your nightdress off."

Obedient, she lay back in the bed. He went to her and bent over her, arranging the ribboned, embroidered collar of the nightdress to present an image of Victorian innocence. Then stood back, looking down at her. Exhausted, trembling, at the end of his forces, he summoned up those first erotic memories of her, recasting her in the rooms of the Collection where he had seen her naked, reliving his fantasy of her as a serving girl—innocent, gentle, frail—lying now on her attic bed, obedient to her employer's lust. Slowly, like an actor playing a role, he dropped his trousers and pulled his shirt over his head. Naked, he bent over her and, his confused, weary brain heating to his imaginings, undid the collar strings of her nightgown and drew it down about her shoulders, revealing her splendid breasts, the nipples erect, hard to his touch. Slowly, almost reverentially, he stripped the nightgown down to her ankles and turned her on her side, his hands caressing her from neck to thigh. And, as he did this, trembling, excited, suddenly she reached out and took hold of his penis. She

169

was real, no dream, she was Mary Ann, awkward in her youth, urgent in her desire, who now began to jerk his penis up and down as though warning him of desperate needs. And so, as he was and always would be, a dreamer, this reality undid him. No longer a man and maid in those far-off wicked times, they were now equals, contestants, almost enemies. In silence they grappled on the bed and in silence, perfunctorily, preliminary, he experienced a brief moment of release. An onanistic moment, he was sure: his awkward partner seemed barely to have begun. Guiltily, he attempted to give her pleasure, but, as if by his untimely climax he had confirmed her worst self-doubts, she pushed him away and sat up, shaking her auburn hair over her face as though it were a veil of chastity. He felt his eyeballs twitch with tears of pity. She rose and, naked, went abject into the bathroom. The shower ran. He listened. The shower stopped. After a moment, he sensed her return. "If we're going to California," her voice whispered, "let's get ready."

He sat up. "Mary Ann, I'm very sorry. Next time it will be a lot better."

"I'll be ready in half an hour. Better go to your own room and get dressed."

"Maybe we could have some breakfast together?"

"No, thanks, I'm not hungry."

He returned to his own bedroom, dressed, and packed. When he came out into the sitting room her small bag sat by the door, with a note on its handle.

Please bring this down when you come.
I'll meet you in the lobby at nine.

170

He looked at the bag, and then, as a person might who fears he has forgotten something, went back into her bedroom and stood, staring at the rumpled bed, remembering her tears.

After a while he came out and went to the sitting-room windows, which looked down on Sherbrooke Street. Far below, morning traffic moved in silence behind the Thermopane glass. A gray haze, dirty as a tenement curtain, screened out the sun's rays. He thought of Mary Ann, who had loved the Collection, who had wanted, she said, to be part of it. And, suddenly, he too, wept.

At ten minutes to nine he went down to the lobby. Mary Ann was waiting. In silence they boarded the bus, and sat, silent, as it departed. On the plane, she pretended to sleep.

Vaterman met them in Monterey. Mary Ann ran to him and hugged him. Wary, Maloney offered his hand. "Hello, Fred, how have you been?"

"Busy, busy," Vaterman announced. "Hickman is arranging a fantastic franchise setup, very important for Carmel and the entire region. Yorkin is really excited about it. I have been told to write the story and we will front-page it the minute the agreement is signed. Really, it is a very big deal."

He had not, Maloney noticed, responded to Mary Ann's enthusiastic hug. But neither did he seem angry with her. They drove at high speed to Carmel. No questions were asked about Montreal.

"So, you're back." Hickman, in salmon-pink shirt,

stood framed in the motel entrance, surrounded by strangers. The strangers were of middle age. They wore their hair long in the latest style, but without conviction, as though it were a guise of conformity. Similarly, they affected the florid modes of dress currently in vogue. Hickman, beckoning like a tour guide, gathered them about him. "Gentlemen, this is my friend and client, Professor Maloney, creator of this magnificent Collection. Tony, these gentlemen are members of the board of directors of our business consortium."

The strangers, cordial yet distant in the manner of senior executives, came forward with set smiles, hands proffered in greeting. Hands shook his. Almost subliminally, he saw Mary Ann and Vaterman move around the edge of the group and disappear into the lobby.

"Tony, now that you're back, perhaps you can help us. The directors have been looking over some of the items here, but they haven't yet seen the erotic collections, the secret rooms and so on. I wonder if, perhaps, you could take us on a little tour?"

"I'm sorry. Maybe later? I just got in from Montreal and I'm very tired. If you'll excuse me, for now?"

"You do look a bit bushed," one of the strangers agreed. "Rough trip?"

"Yes, it was."

"Okay, you get some rest, Tony," Hickman said. "We're going to have meetings right through tomorrow, so we'll have lots of time to work up a little tour when you're in better shape. Right, gentlemen?"

"Of course."

"Nice meeting you, Professor."

"Great pleasure, Dr. Maloney."

They stood in a semicircle, watching him go, surprised when he walked, not toward the motel lobby, but down into the parking lot, moving along the main aisle of the Collection.

Yes, there was fading. But it was not, as he had at first hoped, a fading one might attribute to aging, the patina which can make a time-scarred Romanesque statue of the Virgin more beautiful than a similar statue which has survived unharmed. No, there was deterioration: but there was something worse. When, at the end of the main aisle he reached Osler's great fountain, he stared at the large polished blocks of glass shaped in myriad curlicues and pilasters. He turned on the illumination and set the water pump in motion. Water jetted and shimmered over the glass. He was gripped by a sudden unease. He switched off the water and, leaning over the rim of the fountain, stared at some of the lower pilasters. He removed his shoes and socks and waded into the fountain for a closer look. These blocks of glass, real and beautiful, had now, among them, some which did not look real. Eerily, certain of the blocks seemed to have the plastic lightness of Lucite, a substance unknown in Victorian times. Yet they were glass. It seemed to him that these false-looking blocks now stood out as obvious imitations, blatant shams, marring the perfection of the others.

He put on his shoes and socks and went back toward Aisle III, and an exhibit which, he was certain, he had examined closely in the past. This was an ornamental clock, much admired by Mary Ann, on which its maker, Jacob Loudan, had labored thirty-four years. On a smaller scale, but rivaling in ingenuity the great clock in Strasbourg's cathedral, its intricate movements included a scenic panorama of day and night, a perpetual almanac, a belfry with ringers, and a bird organ. Maloney hurried to it because his watch told him he was within a minute of the hour. He stood, waiting.

Yes, it seemed to be normal. The hour sounded, the bird organ trilled, the almanac appeared to be properly set, the registers of the tides, of the moon, of the date and month—all these indices were functioning. Yet, when the little bell ringers came forth from their belfry, something was wrong. The clock, which had performed perfectly, now worked as though a few parts of the mechanism had worn away. The bell ringers slipped as they approached the bell, their hammers striking wild. The little cock on the belfry which flew up at the last chime staggered up, then sank back, as though his ratchet was worn away. At the end of the striking, the bell ringers did not retreat completely but remained half in and half out of their little stable.

He moved on. He stopped by one of a set of pianofortes by Collard and Collard, lifted the lid and played a scale. The piano had been perfectly in tune, but now its pitch was slightly off and the tones muffled, as though the felt on the hammers were in need of replacement. He turned away and saw, high above the parking lot wall, a hand-lettered sign:

GOD ALONE CAN CREATE
Do Not Believe This Lie

The madman was back.

Like a prisoner returning to his cell, Maloney went up toward the motel entrance. Hickman and the members of the consortium were getting into several limousines. There was no sign of Vaterman or of Mary Ann. Weary and sick, Maloney entered the familiar lobby, where Bourget sat like a warder at his desk. He handed Maloney his key. Maloney asked that he not be disturbed, then went to his room.

He locked the door. He stripped off his clothes, put on pajamas, and lay on the bed. He did not even bother to pull down the blind. Had one single night of dreaming the television dream caused this deterioration? Or was it the three sleepless nights of his absence in Los Angeles and Montreal? There was only one way to find out. Through sleep; if he could still sleep.

He closed his eyes. At once, the television screen came onto the retina of his eye just as he had seen it before, hung high in a corner of the room. The camera scrutinized an aisle of the Collection. For thirty seconds it remained stationary; then, with a flick of the blue-gray picture, it passed to another aisle. He lay trapped, monitoring the monitor, forced to watch each aisle until the camera moved on. And so, returned to Carmel, he slept at last. And dreamed, again, the television dream.

Next morning he awoke. The sun shone. He rose and went to the window. The Collection stood. He opened the window, climbed down to the main aisle, and went at once to Osler's fountain. Stepping into the water in his bare feet, he went up to the lower tier of glass pilasters, a tier he had examined carefully the day before. The third pilaster from the left, which yesterday had not suffered from the Lucite look, now had the new, slightly dulled, plastic-appearing surface. He climbed out of the fountain, went at once to the Collard and Collard pianoforte, and played the same scale he had played yesterday. The notes jangled now, still more out of tune, the sounds still more muffled.

The guards were watching him. He realized he was still in his pajamas. Nodding to them, he retraced his steps, climbed back through his window, and then stood in his room staring down at the Collection. Those tin roofs, those wooden sheds, those gray and green tarpaulin awnings, that hodgepodge of aisles and entrances which, yesterday, had seemed prosaic and arbitrary as a transit camp put up for migrant workers, glittered in this morning's sunlight, remote and mysterious as the minarets of Samarkand. And, looking at it now, he saw it for the first time as it really was: a faëry place, ringed around by spells and enchantments, a web of artifice as different from the reality it sought to commemorate as is a poem about spring from spring itself.

He felt cold. A strange chill emanated from these roofs and sheds. In that moment he passed the bar into a new sea of uncertainty. Until then, he had believed that, by his actions, his inattention, his unworthiness, he could destroy this Collection he had so miraculously and fortuitously wrought. But what if the Collection, singular, faëry, false, had, with true artifice, begun to destroy him?

He looked over at Bluff Road. There were few sightseers. A sheriff's car came slowly down the road and turned in at the motel entrance. Lieutenant Polita got out.

And on the crown of the road there appeared a large hand-lettered sign. Carrying it, eyes dulled, lips moving in a silent prating, came its bearer: the madman.

10

That same morning, when Maloney stepped out from the seclusion of his bedroom, it was as though the world waited his rising. There were the businesslike strangers he had seen yesterday, Dr. Spector and his team of researchers newly returned from New York, Vaterman with a reporter in tow, Lieutenant Polita with a complaint from a citizens' group that the Collection contained depraved items detrimental to the community, Mrs. Bourget to ask what he would like for breakfast.

There was no sign of Mary Ann.

"Where is she?" he asked Vaterman.

"Mary Ann? I don't think she'll be coming in."

"Is she sick?"

"Can we talk about it later, Tony? This is Harold Greenfeld from United Press International. He's interested in doing a story on the reasons for your trip to Los Angeles and Montreal."

"I said, is she sick?"

"She told me yesterday that she doesn't want to work for you any more."

"Ah, there you are, at last!" Hickman, small, hairy, decisive, pushed through the crowded lobby, followed by two men who carried large leather portfolios. "Come on, Tony, you're just in time for our meeting."

"Excuse me a moment," Maloney turned to Vaterman. "Look, could you ask her if she'll have lunch with me?"

"If I do it, will you speak to my friend Greenfeld?"

"Yes."

Hickman seized his arm. "Tony, if we can go into the parlor right away? We've been waiting for you. My associates are just starting our major session, we want to have your views on it."

"Just a minute." Maloney turned back to Vaterman. "Call her now. If you do that for me, I'll do the interview with Greenfeld as soon as possible."

In Bourget's funereal front parlor the businesslike strangers sat grouped uncomfortably close to each other, briefcases open on their knees, some thumbing pocket computers as they compared blueprints and conversed in low, boardroom tones. The two men who followed Hickman and Maloney into the room opened large leather portfolios and placed pencil sketches on an easel. Then the younger of the two took up a pointer and nodded to indicate that he was ready to begin.

"Gentlemen," Hickman said. "Let me introduce Robert Athelston and his assistant Billy Longworth. Mr. Athelston, as most of you know, has designed and built some of the largest shopping complexes and the most important recreational facilities in the country. Bob?"

Robert Athelston smiled in acknowledgment of this tribute. "Good morning," he said. His pointer tapped against the top sketch. "Gentlemen, some of you may recognize this. Certainly Professor Maloney will know it. Professor?"

Maloney, who had been standing near the door, went up and looked closely at the drawing. "It's an altered version of the south portico of the Crystal Palace."

"Exactly. And the Crystal Palace, gentlemen, was the great Victorian exhibition hall, a marvel of its time, erected by the order of Prince Albert, Queen Victoria's consort, to house the Great Exhibition of 1851. Right, Professor?"

At that moment Mrs. Bourget entered with Maloney's breakfast tray. One of the strangers at once leaped up, vacating his seat. "Sit here, Professor."

"Thank you very much."

As Maloney, balancing the tray, sat in the empty seat, Athelston tapped his pointer on the edge of the easel. There was silence in the room. "Now, what I propose, gentlemen, is that we make this portico the trademark by which the Collection will be known all over the world. We would begin by building a replica of this façade at the entrance to what we shall call the Great Victorian Village. From then on, all our print advertising, television commercials, bumper stickers, key rings, or whatever, will feature this portico. It will be the insignia, the trademark by which the Collection is known."

"Excuse me," one of the strangers said. "But I'm not quite clear on one point. Are you going to erect this gate outside the Collection, or outside the Great Victorian Village?"

"That's a good question, Mr. Stewart. The Great

Victorian Village will *not* be at the site of the Collection. Our survey shows that in order to maximize the facilities we plan for the Village, it will have to be close to the freeway system. It will be erected on a commercial site which can be acquired on advantageous terms."

"But how will we tie it in with admission fees at the site of the actual exhibit?"

Athelston glanced nervously in Maloney's direction. "Well, in point of fact, Mr. Stewart, the restaurants, boutiques, motel units, and so on, do not necessarily have to be right beside the original concept or exhibit."

Another of the strangers put up his hand. "May I ask Professor Maloney a question? Wouldn't it be possible to move the Collection from that parking lot out there to some more convenient location, near the proposed new site and close to a major highway?"

"No," Maloney said. "I don't think so. Would you excuse me for a moment? I have to make a telephone call."

Hickman bounded to his feet. "Tony, we don't want to keep you any longer than necessary, but there *is* one big question we'd like to put to you right now. It's a question which was raised in our initial meeting last night."

"All right. What is the question, then?" Maloney said. He should have called her himself. It had been a mistake to let Vaterman telephone on his behalf.

"Well, naturally, the Village itself will be a commercial proposition. But this portico which Bob Athelston has shown us would be a work of art, similar to the stuff you dreamed up. Yet if *we* build it, it will only be a copy, not like the genuine antiques in the Collection. And, in addition, it would be very expensive, right, Bob?"

"Right."

"Now, is there any chance, Tony, that just this once you could dream us up this portico? I've told these gentlemen that, based on my previous conversations with you, I doubt that you'd want to do it. But still, I'm throwing it out as a suggestion."

"Are you joking?"

"Tony, we're just trying to explore every avenue."

They were waiting. He was now in their employ. Sarcasm or anger would merely antagonize them, disqualifying him in their minds as the sort of temperamental idiot they imagined people like himself to be.

"So you're planning a sort of town, gentlemen?"

"No, no, it will be more on the order of a shopping center, a mall with adjoining motels, fountains, restaurants, and a plaza."

"Well, then," Maloney said, "I think you, Mr. Athelston, as an architect, will understand what I mean. All I can do is be faithful to what I know. So if I dreamed this I would almost certainly bring the original structure to life. The south portico alone extended for, I would say, seven city blocks. If I could dream it up, you'd be forced to buy land on a very large scale to accommodate it. And land near a freeway comes pretty high nowadays, I'm told."

"I see," said Athelston. "Of course, we didn't do any on-location surveys at this preliminary stage. We merely worked from drawings and so forth. So, naturally, we had no way of telling that the original structure was that large."

The boardroom murmurs intensified in volume. Heads went this way and that.

"So," Hickman said, "if Tony dreams it up, it would have to be a really big structure, right?"

"Not practical," said one of the businesslike strangers.

"That leads to a further point," said the one called Stewart. "The possible question of censorship. As I understand it, there are things in this Collection which, while they may appeal to a certain audience, nevertheless are not what one would call family-trade items. For that reason alone, it might be better if the commercial investment were minimized, so to speak, at the site of the actual Collection. I mean, in case of censorship action."

"Good point, Mr. Stewart."

Maloney stood. "Well, if you'll excuse me, gentlemen?"

The strangers nodded distractedly. The discussion continued as he left the room.

In the lobby, Vaterman and the man from UPI were nowhere in sight. But Dr. Spector was. "Tony, I have the full team standing by now to tape and film what we hope will be the concluding section."

"Excuse me, Doctor, but I have to make a phone call."

"When I say it is the concluding section, I don't want you to think we're losing interest."

"No, no. Excuse me. Be right back."

She was at home.

"Mary Ann?"

There was a long moment of silence at the other end of the line.

"Yes."

"Did Fred talk to you about lunch?"

"Fred?"

"He didn't phone you?"

"No."

"Well, will you have lunch with me?"

There was another silence. Then she asked: "Did you get to sleep yet?"

"Yes. Finally. Mary Ann, that's what I want to talk to you about. I know I was terrible in bed yesterday, but I hope I'm back to normal now. I want to see you. Please, let's have lunch."

"No," she whispered. "Besides, my dad's coming over."

"Well, what about later?"

"I think I'd better hang up. Goodbye, Tony."

"Wait. Even if you don't want to go out with me any more, won't you stay on as my secretary?"

"I'm sorry. But thanks for everything, okay? And listen, it wasn't your fault."

"Look, why can't we just meet and talk. You said once that you wanted to be part of the Collection. Don't you still want that?"

"Oh, Tony," she whispered, "that's over, don't you see? But, look. Good luck. And good luck with your new dream and everything."

"Couldn't we just meet for half an hour?"

But she had hung up.

In the doorway, Vaterman waited, the United Press reporter at his heels. "Ah, there you are. Ready now?"

"Why didn't you phone Mary Ann?"

"I did phone her. She will come here for lunch with you. I did my part. Now it's up to you to do yours. This friend of mine must talk to you."

"You say you *did* phone her?"

"Absolutely."

"Then she—look, I can't do the interview yet. Sorry."

He pushed past them. In the lobby, Dr. Spector waited, standing on one leg, then on another, like a heron on cold ground. "Ready now? Did you make your phone call all right?"

"Can I borrow your car? It's an emergency."

"Of course. But will you be long?"

"I'll telephone you, Doctor. Which one is it?"

"The Oldsmobile on the far side of the street. It would be good if we could have our session before lunch. My people are getting restless."

"I'll do my best, Doctor. And thanks for the car."

Her apartment was six streets away, the upper flat in a four-unit bungalow which was reached by an outdoor staircase leading up to a long outside deck. He and Vaterman had helped her move in. He had repainted the small, impersonal living room and hung curtains on the bedroom windows. Now, as Maloney parked the Oldsmobile in the parking lot and went up the staircase, he noticed that something had changed. There were no curtains. The deck chair was missing; the door to her apartment was ajar. He knocked, then entered. The meager furnishings provided by the management remained: all her gear was gone.

"Mary Ann?"

An empty bedroom, the bed stripped, a Kleenex box in the wastebasket. The closet doors were open, the dress racks a cat's cradle of wire hangers. In the pullman kitchen, all was tidy as never during her occupancy. He touched the gas ring: it was still warm. He went back into the living room, looking for a note. There was no note.

He picked up the telephone. It was still working, but whom could he phone? Holding the receiver, he stared at the wall, searching for the nail on which he had hung a Peter Max print. Yes, that was the place. He was not in the wrong apartment. The receiver continued to give off the dial tone. He replaced it on its cradle, remembering that the woman who owned the building lived on the ground floor. Maybe Mary Ann had given her some forwarding address? He went out onto the sun deck. The sun, warm and seasonless, made the concrete wall hot to his touch. He went down the outside staircase and rang the bell, peering through the glass side panel of the woman's apartment to see if anyone was home. With dismay, he saw several days' mail piled up in the hallway inside the door.

A car door slammed behind him in the parking lot and footsteps crossed the lot. He turned, saw a man's shoes moving on the outside staircase above him, and went outside to look. A red-faced man with a brush cut of gray spiky hair was walking along the upper sun deck. The man dragged his left leg with a pronounced limp. As Maloney watched, he went into Mary Ann's apartment. Two at a time, Maloney went up the stairs and stealthily moved along the sun deck to the open apartment door. The man was in her kitchen. He took a cardboard box from a closet, opened the refrigerator, and began to put pickle jars, a milk carton, butter, and a package of hamburger patties into the box. When he had finished, the man pulled the plug out of the wall and left the door open. Maloney drew back from the entrance, moving out of sight as the man came out of the apartment and put down his cardboard box. From his trouser pocket, the man produced a key and locked the door. Then, as though he had known all along that Maloney was there, he turned, smiled, and winked sociably. "Hi, Professor, how are you today?"

"Are you her father?"

"I'm the father."

"Mr. McKelvey, I must talk to her, it's very important."

The father bent and picked up his carton. "I'll bet it is."

"No, listen . . ." Maloney began, and stopped, unable to say it. The father, red-faced, grizzled, peered at him like some old Alaskan bear, weary but capable of delivering a sudden, wounding clout. "I'm listening," the father said.

"I miss her terribly."

The father shook his head, as though to clear it. "Let's go downstairs and have a snort. I have a bottle in my car."

In the parking lot, a green Chevy sat directly opposite Dr. Spector's Oldsmobile. The father opened the Chevy's front door and took a bottle from the glove compartment. He held it up to the light, revealing only a finger of Scotch. "Son of a gun. Thought there was more. Tell you what. Let's go and pick up a crock and go to your place. I imagine you'll want to have a talk."

"All right," Maloney said. If he got this old man drunk, he might loosen him up on her whereabouts.

"You take your car and I'll follow in mine. Okay, Professor?"

Maloney got into the Oldsmobile and drove back to the Sea Winds Motel. The Chevy, wavering a little, followed him uncertainly. As Maloney drove in at the motel entrance, Hickman and his associates were installing themselves in their limousines. "Hello there,

Tony," Hickman called out. "We're just going off to look at a couple of sites. Why don't you join us?"

Maloney declined. Dr. Spector came out from the lobby, anxious, but polite as always. "Ah, you're back. I hope everything's all right?"

At that moment the green Chevy moved through the front gate, cutting perilously close to the limousines. The father leaned out of the window. "Hey, we forgot the bottle."

"I'm sorry," Maloney said.

"It's okay, I'll go down to Ocean and get one. Be right back."

"Perhaps we can start the taping session now?" Dr. Spector suggested.

"We could start, I suppose," Maloney said. "But I have to see that man when he comes back."

"Well, if we can get started, it will be a great help. If you'll come with me?"

As they went toward Dr. Spector's suite, Maloney saw Vaterman closeted in the public phone booth. Angrily, Vaterman jerked the door open. "You really screwed me up, didn't you! You ask me to do publicity for you and then you treat a top wire-service reporter as if he was dirt. That is one hell of a lousy thing to do to me."

"Mary Ann has gone," Maloney said.

"Mary Ann, Mary Ann! That's all you ever talk about. She is *my* girl. Let us get that straight, right now."

"She's nobody's girl," Maloney said. "She's disappeared. Her apartment's been cleaned out."

"Nonsense."

"Go and see for yourself."

"*If* you please, Tony," Dr. Spector said, nervously. "We're ready now."

"Right," Maloney said. He went into the suite, leaving Vaterman outside.

A man with an Arriflex camera moved up to face him. Tape machines whirred. "Interview 8. Subject and Spector. Take 1," Dr. Spector declaimed. The camera turned.

Ten minutes later, during a break to load new film, Maloney looked out of the window and saw the green Chevy parked at the front entrance. "I'm sorry," he told Dr. Spector. "I have to speak to that man. I'll come back as soon as I can."

"Not too long, I hope?"

"I hope not," Maloney said.

He went out to the front where the father, his gaze somewhat unfocused, sat in the Chevy, an opened bottle of liquor in his hand. "They told me you were busy with an interview or something. So I've had a couple of snorts. I got you Canadian Club, is that okay? You *are* Canadian, aren't you?"

"Let's go into my room, then," Maloney said.

"I think about things like what brand to buy," the father said, "because I was a supply sergeant. I managed PX stores. Mostly overseas. Twenty years in the service but, like they say, I never fired a shot in anger."

They went to Maloney's room. "Did Mary Ann travel with you, overseas?"

"Some. Her mother died when Mary was just a baby. I had to be father and mother to her. Do you have kids yourself, Professor?"

"No. Do you want water?"

"I take it straight." The father sat heavily on

Maloney's bed and poured. "It's not easy, let me tell you. A girl who looks like that, you've got to keep tabs on her."

"Did you follow us to Los Angeles?"

"Vaterman said I did, didn't he?" The father began to laugh, but the laughter collapsed in a fit of coughing.

"I just want to talk to her. Surely you've no objection to my just having a talk."

"You're too late."

"Why?"

"Because she's free now. Free from all of us."

"Oh, my God," Maloney said, suddenly afraid. "What's happened to her?"

"Have a drink."

"I don't want a drink. What have you done to her?"

"Now, don't get a dirty mouth on you," the father said. "That other sonofabitch, trying to make out there was something between me and Mary. Mess with my own daughter. Jesus Christ! I'm her father and I love her like a father. That's why I'm helping her now."

"How are you helping her?"

The father filled their glasses. "I let her go," the father said. "I put her in a cab to the airport. She's gone."

"She took a flight. Where? Overseas? Back East?"

"Yes, she took a flight. But that's all I'm going to tell you, Professor. So don't ask any more."

"I miss her," Maloney said. Suddenly he felt he would weep. "I don't know what I'm going to do without her."

"You'll get over it. Fellows like you must be in love with yourselves. Otherwise, why would you dream up things to make the world take notice of you?"

"Mr. McKelvey, my dream was an accident. Believe

me, there's nothing I'd like more right now than to go back to being an ordinary teacher."

"But you can't, can you? Besides, I don't think you'd ever have been right for my Mary."

"But she liked me. And she admired the Collection."

The father sighed and stood. "I'd better be moving along."

"Look, if I give you a letter addressed to her, will you deliver it?"

"No."

"Why not? Just one letter?"

"Listen to me," the father said. "Yesterday I went to the bank and signed a note for Mary. Ten thousand dollars. And when I gave her the money I didn't ask her where she's going or what she's going to do. I'm helping her get away on her own. That's a father's love. You wouldn't know anything about that."

"So you don't know where to reach her?"

"Correct. I don't know what plane she took this morning. And I don't want to know."

"But she might write to you?"

"She might."

"Well, if she does, will you forward a letter for me? Please?"

"Better keep the bottle," the father said. He turned toward the door. "The bottle helps. For a while."

"It will take me two minutes to write a letter. Just a short note? Please?"

"Have a nice day," the father said. The door shut.

Maloney rose to go after him, but staggered as the ground, at first very far away, came suddenly close. He sat down, clumsily, on his bed. He was not a drinker, not at all, but in his eagerness and excitement he had drunk down a huge glass of whiskey as though it were

Coke. His head seemed to expand as the whiskey assailed his senses. He sat, staring at the floor.

Someone knocked. Then a second, urgent knock.

"I'm coming," he called, rising unsteadily.

The visitor was Vaterman.

"You're right, Tony, she *has* gone. I have been all over Monterey, I spoke to Mona, her girlfriend, I checked at her flat and with the rental company that leases her car. She gave up the car this morning. Nobody knows anything. It has got to be the father. He has taken her some place. Maybe against her will."

"It's not the father," Maloney said, with slurred deliberation.

"You don't know him. He is tricky."

"He was here a few minutes ago."

"He was here? You *saw* him?"

"He brought this whiskey. Do you want a drink?"

"What did he say?"

Maloney told him.

"He gave her *ten thousand dollars?* Do you mean to tell me you believe that?"

Maloney rose, rinsed out the father's glass in the bathroom, and poured two whiskeys. "Here. You'd better believe it too."

Vaterman took the glass but suddenly put it down untasted. "This is all your fault," he said in a high, angry voice. "I never should have got mixed up with you. I always knew there was something phony about your story. If I had been a better reporter, I'd have kept on digging until I got to the bottom of it. You didn't fool very many people, you know. Even now, most newspapermen believe you are a phony. Phony Maloney. I remember that remark your mother made about you being a practical joker, don't think I've forgotten that. I am too trusting, that is my problem. What a fool I was, letting the pair of you go on to Montreal. I lost my girl because of it."

"I'm sorry. I know how you feel."

"No, you don't. Trouble with you is, you have no idea what other people feel. All you think of is that damn Collection. What a joke! The Great Victorian Collection. Never mind whether you dreamed it up or not, have you ever listened to what serious people say about it? Why, they say it isn't relevant, it's completely out of date, it has nothing to do with our contemporary reality. That's what they say and they are right."

"Who says?"

"People who know. People who are not taken in like I was. And, my God, was I taken in. Do you know what you are, you're a fraud, you are not a dreamer at all, all you are interested in is stealing other people's girls, getting her to go to Montreal with you under false pretenses, and then making passes at her, you pig—"

Suddenly beside himself, he turned on Maloney, who sat on the bed, a drink in his hand. Vaterman's claw fingers struck out at Maloney's face. Whiskey spilled on the rug. "What did you do to her? She came back completely changed!"

"Wait, wait," Maloney said dully, putting his arms over his head to protect himself as Vaterman, standing above him, let loose with further blows. "Listen, Fred. She wants to get away from all of us."

"Don't you dare talk about her, you pig!" Vaterman shouted. "I am through with you. You can take your lousy job and stick it. Great Victorian Collection! It is a flop, a bust, a collection of old junk nobody cares about, out of date before it's even shown. Imagine asking the public to pay to see this crap. And what about those other dreams you were supposed to have? Listen, you. You think you got away with it, but you didn't. Deep down, nobody ever did believe it. And now, by God, if it's the last thing I do, I'm going to show you up to the whole world for the damned fraud you really are!"

"Fred, look, just a minute—"

"Don't 'Fred' me! You go to hell!"

The door slammed shut. Maloney got to his feet, dizzily. It was as though the shouting and the blows had emptied his mind, leaving him too weary for anger or disgust. Instead, a drowsiness came upon him, a noon drowsiness which at once overwhelmed him. He felt his eyelids droop. If he fell asleep now, in the daytime, he might not even dream.

Yawning, almost asleep, he went to the telephone.

"Mr. Bourget. Maloney here. I don't want to be disturbed by anyone until further notice."

"But what about Dr. Spector? He's waiting for you."

"Not even by Dr. Spector."

He lay down. Without any warning, he fell into a stuporous slumber. He slept on into the afternoon, in heavy, narcotic, dreamless ease, until, sometime before dark, he shifted in his sleep and began to dream.

It was not a new dream. It was the television dream. But he dreamed it as a drunk man dreams, disconnectedly, unaware, in the stopped clock of intoxication, of those inexorable waits before the camera shifted surveillance from aisle to aisle. He guarded the Collection as a drunk guard might, surrealistically irresponsible, the camera dancing up and down those gray aisles. And so, for the first time, the television dream became a fitful, inconsequential fantasy. He slept on into the night and woke before dawn, dry-mouthed, hung-over, but still drunk.

At 5 A.M. he fell asleep again. But now, as his drunkenness decreased, the television dream righted itself. The camera held long and steady on each aisle. For the last two hours of his sleep, he suffered the familiar torments of the surveillance dream.

He woke at seven. At eight, Dr. Spector called. An hour later, the final interview in the Vanderbilt Series was filmed and taped. In the *Journal of Parapsychology*, Vol. XX, No. IV, this note occurs in Dr. Spector's summation of that interview:

A discernible difference was evident in the subject's behavior in this final filmed interview. Agitation which had been remarked on previous occasions and which had been particularly evidenced in the three preceding sessions was markedly absent. Toward the end of the interview, on being questioned about the apparent change in his attitude, the subject made the following observations.

MALONEY. Well, I suppose I've accepted it. I've faced up to what's happened to me. There's a certain calm in knowing the worst.

Q. The worst? Could you explain that, a little?

MALONEY. Well, I used to think that, because I dreamed up the Collection, it belonged to me. I was responsible for it. But now I'm beginning to think it's the other way around.

Q. I'm sorry. I don't quite understand.

MALONEY. Well, if something you dream up comes

to life, it stands to reason that it develops a life of its own. And now it's taken me over.

Q. In what way?

MALONEY. It's cut me off from my former life, from my job and so on. I can't even plan any future. I'm a prisoner. The only way I could leave, I suppose, would be if I could dream a new dream. And then I'd probably become the prisoner of the new dream.

Q. You mentioned earlier that you find it exhausting to dream the same dream night after night. Have you ever considered some mind-altering process? Perhaps the use of an hallucinogenic drug might induce a new dream?

MALONEY. I don't believe it would work. Those things don't produce real dreams.

Q. What about a sedative? Something which would plunge you into a deep, dreamless sleep, blocking your current dream out?

MALONEY. I tried barbiturates in Los Angeles. They didn't even put me to sleep.

Q. Then, in your judgment, there's nothing which will ease for you the nightly ordeal of this dream?

MALONEY. Whiskey seems to help.

Q. You've tried whiskey?

MALONEY. Yes. Look, are there any more questions?

Q. Would you like to stop now?

MALONEY. Yes.

Q. Fine. Well, this was our final interview. Thank you, Tony.

MALONEY. Thank you, Doctor.

11

Six months later, a traveler on the highways of California approaching Los Angeles, San Francisco, the gambling cities of the desert, or remote national monuments such as Joshua Tree or Death Valley, could not fail to see a sign, positioned at fifty-mile intervals. Beneath a simplified drawing of the south portico of the Crystal Palace was the legend:

VISIT CARMEL-BY-THE-SEA
Home of
THE GREAT VICTORIAN COLLECTION

There was no need for further information. Hickman had copied this form of advertising from Disneyland. Disneyland is known. It is not necessary to explain what it is in billboard advertising. Similarly, as Hickman had foreseen, the Collection was becoming known. However, it began its life as a public exhibit in an atmosphere of confusion concerning its claims. Dr. Spector's team continued its guarded inquiry without, as yet, having published any conclusions. Other kinds of experts—historians, antiquarians, collectors—remained interested but tended to ignore its supernatural aspects. As for the general public, most people visiting the Collection accepted with a mixture of embarrassment and amusement the explanation that it had been dreamed into life. Some, a definite minority, were filled with envy and curiosity and wanted to meet Maloney and discuss dreams of their own. As for the news media, they had long since passed on to other stories, leaving coverage of the exhibition to popular weeklies and Sunday supplements, which, starved for marvels, tended to write almost uncritically of the dream aspect.

Initially, it seemed that the Collection would be a great success as a public exhibition. Advance requests for tickets were impressive. However, following public announcement by the State of California that the Correction Chamber, the bordello parlor, the erotic library and collection of pedophilic photographs, would remain closed to the general public, ticket sales dropped sharply. Hickman's consortium at first protested this decision, claiming that they, as co-exhibitors, had been robbed of the Collection's greatest drawing card. This protest was dropped abruptly when the consortium learned that diminished attendance at the Collection itself had actually resulted in a gain of admissions to the Great Victorian Village, three miles east of the Collection. The Village, an impressive construction wholly owned by the consortium, comprised three hundred motel units and two shopping plazas which housed a number of emporia decorated in the Victorian manner. The prurient were wooed in Mrs. Beauchamp's Parlour, a nightclub decorated in a bowdlerized version of the

Collection's bordello, which had been closed to the public because of its bestial wall decorations. In Mrs. Beauchamp's Parlour, young California girls wearing black lisle stockings and white cotton knickers with panels which opened to expose their behinds moved among the patrons, serving drinks and flaunting their breasts in provocative deshabille. There was also the Penny Gaff, an imitation Victorian music hall, with low comedians, topless can-can dancers, and three nude girls in red silk stockings who sailed over the heads of the audience in red velvet swings, their bare bottoms elegantly cushioned on white swansdown seats.

There were, in addition, two large family restaurants, the General Gordon and the Gladstone; a food market named Covent Garden; and a number of shops, including the Olde Curiosity Shoppe, the Florence Nightingale Tea Room, Oscar Wilde Way Out (a men's-wear boutique) , and, finally, a large warehouse supermarket filled with cheap reproductions of Victoriana and misleadingly named the Great Victorian Collection. The whole was fronted by an altered scale reproduction roughly corresponding to the south portico of the Crystal Palace.

Indeed, as the months passed, it became apparent that, of the thousands of tourists who came to Carmel to view the Collection, a surprising number spent most, if not all, of their time in this Village, and, as Maloney was to discover, many of them believed that the warehouse supermarket in the Village itself *was* the Great Victorian Collection.

Maloney rarely visited this Village. He continued to reside, close to the original Collection, in his motel room in the Sea Winds Motel. Responsibility for maintenance and upkeep of the Collection, including guard patrols and guide duties, had been assumed by the California Parks Service. In conjunction with the Hickman consortium, the Parks Service had erected here a second, still smaller replica of the Crystal Palace south portico. This modest entrance facility contained ticket booths, toilets, and a lounge in which tourists assembled for guided visits.

These visits were conducted by Parks Service rangers, wearing their regular khaki uniforms, polished riding boots, and scout-type campaign hats. Hickman referred to them as "Smokey Bears," a disparaging reference to the cartoon bears in ranger uniform used on fire-warning posters. But Maloney liked them. They were, after all, people he saw every day. They frequently sought his advice in answering questions put to them by their tour groups. Trained as rangers, they were invariably courteous and respectful and were in the habit of saluting when their paths crossed his.

After the first few weeks of the Collection's exhibition, Maloney laid down a rule that he was not to be pointed out to the tourists. The small gratification of being recognized by strangers quickly evaporated when this became a daily occurrence and when the tourists, in the manner of tourists everywhere, pestered him with requests for information and autographs, and asked him to pose for photographs with their group. But when news of his decision reached Hickman and the director of the California Parks Service, efforts were made to have him change his mind. A survey carried out by the Service had indicated that the most frequent request made by visitors was to be shown the room in which the original dream had taken place. The second most frequent request was to be allowed to meet, or at least to catch sight of, the creator of the Collection.

"Just four times a day for as little as five minutes, and revenues would triple, I guarantee you," the director said.

"But this isn't a circus. I'm not a freak, I'm an ordinary person. It's what I've done that's extraordinary. The Collection is what counts. If you carried this thing to its ultimate conclusion the public would lose all interest in the Collection itself."

"Exactly right," Hickman said. "That's what's happening here. Face it, once the Parks Department closed off the hot parts, how many people do you think still want to come down here to look at the rest of the stuff? Don't misunderstand me, Tony, I'm not knocking your Collection. It's just that very few people are interested in art works of any kind. What they want is a show, something spicy and interesting. That's what we're giving them down at the Village. The one thing we can't give them down there is you. Everybody would like to meet a guy who made his dream come true. You're what people will come here to see."

"All right, but what will they think when they do see me? I'm not an interesting person. In fact, it's probably because I'm not interesting that I became a dreamer and dreamed this stuff."

"Well, of course, ultimately it's up to you," the director said. "If your privacy is that important to you, I withdraw my suggestion."

"Just a minute," Hickman said. "Let's not abandon the plan altogether. Why don't we review it two months from now? And, in the meantime, I've got an idea. All these motel rooms look much the same, so let's furnish one of them with some books and stuff and exhibit it as

Tony's dream room. That way we can at least add *something* to this setup."

This was done. But the question of Maloney's making personal appearances was not raised again. For, by the time two months had passed, his condition had deteriorated to the point that the tour guides, if they saw him approach, would turn their groups into another aisle.

It was about this time that Maloney began the intimate journal from which Dr. Spector later published excerpts, as an appendix to Spector's long article: "Psychokinetic Elements in the Manifestation of Dreams: The Carmel Experiments," which appeared in the *Journal of Parapsychology,* Vol. XX, No. V.

In his preface to this appendix, Dr. Spector notes: "At first, the diary would seem to have been compiled for the subject's private use, as a listing of certain tasks which he had been able to accomplish. Entries consist of a few lines written after each date, viz.:

APRIL 21.
TV dream three hours? Wrote Mother A.M.
Answered Smithsonian catalogue inquiry.
Night: Exercised on beach, midnight to 3 A.M.

"But, two days before the anniversary of the Collection's appearance, the style changes. As will be seen, the subject now seems to be trying to communicate his experience to some eventual reader of these lines."

MAY 8.
I have been reading about nightmares. Doctors say a dream is a nightmare when it is so unbearable that the

dreamer is forced to wake from it. That is what happens to me. I wake, every night, from the television dream, screaming, my throat raw.

When that happens, I get out of bed, go to the middle of the room, and stand there, hour after hour, until other people wake up. As long as I remain standing, I don't fall asleep and so am spared the dream. This morning I stood until 8 A.M., when I heard Mrs. Bourget's clock radio down the hall. Then I went to the bathroom and took a shower. I stood in the shower thinking of people I'd known as a child, trying to remember the look of certain streets and the furniture in certain rooms. When the shower ran cold, I realized that, once again, I'd been standing for a long time doing nothing. I no longer worry about wasting time like this. At least, I hadn't fallen asleep again. So I counted it a victory. The morning, I mean.

But then I made a mistake. When I had shaved, I went back into the bedroom to get dressed. I passed near the window and was not on guard and so looked out. Weeks ago, I don't remember exactly when, I woke up with a hangover and for some reason went until about four in the afternoon without doing what I usually do as soon as I wake, which is go to the window and look out to make sure the Collection is still there. But that morning I forgot. And so for some hours I remained in the state of mind I used to know long ago. I was not in a state of anxiety. I did not think about Mary Ann. I did not think about my former life. And, most of all, I did not think about what is happening to the Collection. And so I have begun to want that state of forgetfulness as I never wanted any other sensation. Sometimes I manage to drift through a few hours each morning without thinking of the Collection. But, as soon as I do,

I am drawn to the window. And when I look out and see it there, in the parking lot, I behave like a sleepwalker, in a trance. I open the window, climb out, and go down to wander in and out of the aisles and booths. And then I am undone. My day falls down about me.

For something terrible is happening to the Collection. Several terrible things, in fact. There are the cases where the original materials now seem false. And other cases where actual damage has clearly occurred. The fountain, for instance, Osler's great crystal fountain: those perfect blocks of polished glass are now mostly dull, light in weight, dead as plastic. They may not be Lucite, they may still be made of glass. But they feel and look like Lucite, not glass. It's the same with the silverware. The hallmarks have faded completely, so that I can't tell any more whether it's silver, or silver plate. The Staffordshire pottery has lost its glaze: it looks imitation. But in most cases it's not change but simple damage, though where it comes from, I don't know. The Parks Service has erected very sensible overall roofing which completely protects the aisles and booths from rain and sun. Yet, the machinery either warps or breaks down, the canvas cracks, the furniture stuffing appears, the toys don't wind, the dolls' eyes no longer move, the damask and linen have brown stains, I don't know where they come from. I won't try to describe the deterioration of the marquetry furniture, bookcases, and escritoires. Let's just say that doors don't close, the wood has swollen, the drawers stick. The statuary has developed cracks, even in the cast-iron pieces. The musical instruments all give out false notes, there are mysterious bare patches on the collection of sables and ermines, the Ross telescope lens is misted, I've polished it a dozen times, but it does no good. The Folkstone locomotive has one wheel badly buckled, making the whole engine tilt as though it's been in an accident. Why go on, the simplest way to put it is to say that nowadays, if I stop and examine any item in any collection within the Collection, chances are that there's something wrong with it, some breakage or other defect that definitely wasn't there six months ago. The Collection is deteriorating, and the deterioration is getting worse.

You might ask why I care? I mean, didn't I do my best to get rid of the Collection, didn't I try to run away from it, don't I suffer nightmares every night because of it? All that is true. I know this deterioration is not my fault. I've done my best. I gave up my job, Mary Ann, everything, to stay here and look after it.

So it's not my fault if it's deteriorating; is it?

MAY 15.

I feel sick, most of the time. I drink to get through the day. I have taken to hiding from other people. When I wander the aisles of the Collection and see a tour group coming, I at once hurry into one of the prohibited rooms like Mrs. Beauchamp's Parlour, or the Correction Chamber. Sometimes I spend hours in the Correction Chamber, not because I am particularly interested in cruelties, but because it is so private, so hidden away from the rest of the Collection.

Of course, it is becoming as painful to linger there as it is anywhere in the Collection. The wooden benches have warped, the whips and hairbrushes are losing their thongs and bristles, the flogging-horse padding is moldy and limp, the punishment costumes are mildewed and eaten by moths. In the flagellation library, the books suffer continuing damage. Spines have loosened, the edges of the pages wilt, the bindings have weakened and lost their glue, so that, when I handled a beautiful volume of Villiot's La Flagellation Amoureuse *the other morning, its pages scattered like confetti and I spent an exhausting two hours picking up and rearranging text and illustrations.*

Still, I seem to suffer less from anxiety in this room. I think it's because very few people have seen it as it was before its deterioration. This is not true of the rest of the Collection. I suspect that the tourists know what is happening. From my hiding places I peer out at them as they come along the aisles. First comes the guide, who stops, waits for them to assemble in a semicircle around him, lectures, then moves on. The tourists follow, straggling, gossiping, to reassemble again at the next lecture point. I study their bored faces. I know that, like tourists everywhere, they know nothing of what is being told to them. But I would guess that even the most mindless of mobs can sense the difference between those things which have endured for centuries and those which will not last out a lifetime. Unlike the great places of antiquity, the Collection does not stand aloof, indifferent to philistine scrutiny. Rather, these objects which I love seem to entreat the tourists' attention and respect. And fail. I can foresee a time, not far away, when very few tourists will bother to leave the Great Victorian Village to come up the road and look at my Collection.

MAY 19.
There is an armchair in the Correction Chamber which, at the touch of a concealed spring, suddenly sprouts iron bands which bind the unsuspecting victim hand and foot. It was designed as a "seducer's chair" by Charles

Everett, a notorious London rake. The other day, touching the spring, I saw that the mechanism had rusted and no longer works. Since then, I have taken to sitting in this chair. It is very comfortable. Last night, having drunk more than was good for me, I came down here with the idea of trying to sleep in it. I had some confused notion that if I fell asleep inside the Collection, I might not dream the television dream.

The experiment did not succeed. I did not sleep a wink. In addition, I felt more anxiety than if I were standing shaking in the middle of my motel room. So, after a few hours, I left and went back to my own room. I lay down and, as usual, dreamed the television dream.

MAY 22.

I have not spoken to Hickman in two months. As my agent, he used to call every other day. And I have not seen Vaterman since the day he left here, shouting out that the Collection was a flop. Strange, I wouldn't mind seeing Fred again. I wonder what has happened to him? Is he still on the Monterey paper? I could phone. But I suppose I won't.

MAY 26.

Maybe Fred has had news of Mary Ann? I might call him tomorrow, if I feel better.

JUNE 13.

Ten days ago I was wandering around drunk among some garden furniture designed by William Robinson and Gertrude Jekyll. I bumped into a terra-cotta urn, fell down, and sprained my ankle. A doctor was called in, and in the course of examining me, he told me I am suffering from hypertension and described my condition as "one of exhaustion." I was struck by the phrase. I tried to explain to him, guardedly of course, about my sleeping problems.

"What about sleeping pills?" he said.

At first I resisted, explaining that I am trying to create a new dream and I suspect it will not come to me under the influence of drugs.

"Then why do you drink?" the doctor asked. "Alcohol is a drug, and a dangerous one."

I had no answer to that. I did say that I drink to get through the day.

"Tranquilizers would be better," the doctor said. "The way you're going now, you're simply killing yourself. Also, if you don't mind my saying so, you spend too much time in this room. You need other interests besides this work of yours. Do you have a girl?"

I felt tears come into my eyes when he said this and, to conceal them, pretended to blow my nose. But the doctor was not deceived. "You see," he said gently. "You're under a strain. You're emotional and easily upset. I'm sorry, but I do feel it's urgent that you make some effort to get yourself together again."

"Maybe I'm Humpty Dumpty," I said.

"What did you say?"

"Sorry. Nothing."

The doctor then wrote on his pad and tore off a sheet of paper. "Well, here you are, then. Get this filled. Better for you than all that schnapps."

I mention this visit from the doctor because it brought me to my senses, so to speak. Although I had the prescription filled, the bottle of pills stands unopened by my bed table. I have reduced my drinking to *one Scotch before lunch and two before going to sleep. I make it a point to answer my mail and to assist those scholars who are writing papers on various aspects of the Collection. I have again begun to read. At the moment, you might say, my life is devoted to improving my life. It is, I find, a full-time occupation.*

Three weeks later, there is a further entry.

J U L Y 3 .
Perhaps this is a good time to make a progress report. Although I've had a few relapses, I no longer suffer nightmares. I dream the television dream, but somehow I seem able to bear it. I sleep all night, so I am feeling less exhausted. During my first relapse I made my one and only use of the sleeping pills the doctor prescribed. They didn't help and I am not tempted to continue with them. I find that I cannot be "tranquilized" simply by taking pills.

J U L Y 9 .
Progress report. I try not to visit the Collection. I have not gone out there once in the past three days. I tell myself that its deterioration is something that cannot be stopped. There is no point in my becoming upset about it. It is, perhaps, an intermediate step in my development. Now I must work toward a new dream, a dream which will be more permanent than the Collection. I understand what is needed. All I have to do is cut down on my drinking, avoid nightmares and, above all, concentrate. I must prepare my mind to break through to a new threshold of dream.

A week later, there is a one-word entry.

JULY 16.
Nightmare.

Four days later, there is this entry.

JULY 20.
*Today I found myself forced to return to the Collection.
I sat for hours in the Correction Chamber.*

*Perhaps I will not be able to dream a new dream
until the Collection has deteriorated completely and is
carted off as rubbish?*

JULY 21.
The television dream again. I woke, screaming.
I have made no progress. I must face that truth.

On the afternoon of July 25, Park Ranger William
Hutton, who was conducting a group of tourists
through the Collection, came to the booth containing
the W. Hunt & Son exhibit of double damask linen
manufactured for Queen Victoria for her use in the
Highlands. Kneeling before the damask display, fanning
it with a lighted sheet of newspaper, was the creator of
the Collection. He was attempting to set the booth on
fire. "He was drunk," Ranger Hutton later told Dr.
Spector. "He kept waving the flame about over the
damask, the frames, the whole stall. 'Look at that,' he
said. 'It's not flammable, none of it is flammable. It
should be flammable, but it's not. It's not permitted, do
you see?' "
Hutton telephoned the main gate. Two rangers were
dispatched to the booth, where they extinguished the
flames and assisted Maloney back to his motel room. He
was incoherent and appeared intoxicated. He did not

209

order dinner that night or leave his room until the following morning.

Two days later, there is a brief entry.

JULY 27.
Having tried fire, this morning I attempted force. I used a hammer, but was unable to shatter a single fragile piece of the Staffordshire.

On July 31, at four in the morning, Paul Bourget, the nineteen-year-old son of the motel owner, who was visiting his parents on vacation from college, wakened and heard a noise outside his room. He looked out of the window and saw Maloney, wearing only pajama trousers, standing in the center aisle of the Collection. He had just switched on the illumination for the Osler fountain and now he waded into the fountain pool and attempted to set the water mechanism in motion. It did not work. Maloney tugged at the levers for a moment, then, abandoning his efforts, stood dejected in the fountain pool, not moving, staring up at the imposing, brightly lit tiers of glass. The temperature was in the low forties and there was a fog coming in from the ocean. Young Bourget, remembering his father's worry about Maloney's recent drunkenness, dressed and went down into the parking lot.

In his report to Dr. Spector, young Bourget said: "He was standing like a soldier at attention, shivering, and he looked right at me and didn't see me."

The young man asked, "Are you all right, Professor?"

"Yes," Maloney said. He did not seem drunk.

"Kind of chilly, isn't it?"

"The way I feel, I'd welcome a chill," Maloney said. "In fact, I'd prefer pneumonia."

Young Bourget, not knowing what to make of this, took cover in laughter.

"I'm serious," Maloney said.

Young Bourget did not reply but, guided by some innate tact, helped Maloney out of the fountain and led him back to the motel. In his own bedroom, Maloney refused to sit down. Young Bourget said that he left Maloney standing in the center of the bedroom, staring in the same sightless way as before.

On the following Sunday, this notation was scrawled in the diary in a large, loose hand, unlike Maloney's small, careful script.

AUGUST 4.
Perhaps the way to break through is through unconsciousness itself?

On that day, a normal Sunday, usually a slack time, as most tourist groups leave after lunch in order to return home by Monday morning, Maloney was not seen in the lobby or on the grounds. Nor did he order any meals to be sent to his room. On the following day, Monday, he did not call the switchboard to order breakfast. At 10 A.M. there was a long-distance phone call from Hickman in New York. When Maloney failed to answer his telephone, Hickman gave instructions that he was to be awakened.

The elder Bourget went to Maloney's room. The door was locked. Using a passkey, he entered the room.

The blind was not drawn. Maloney was sitting in an upright position on his bed, fully clothed, his head resting against the headboard, staring out the window. "He looked as if he'd just seen something," Bourget said. "Matter of fact, I went and looked out the window myself, thinking maybe something was wrong. But it was just the usual. The guides had three tour groups going the rounds. I looked back at the Professor—I was going to speak to him—and all of a sudden I knew he was dead. There was a bottle of bourbon on the bed table, pretty near empty, and a pill bottle with some pills spilled across the bed. I picked up the phone and called the doctor."

Within the hour, the news that Maloney was dead and that the Collection still stood was on news wires around the world. The press descended again on Carmel and for twenty-four hours the event was of front-page importance. Dr. Spector flew in from Vanderbilt University that same afternoon. At the inquest, which was held on the following day, the Salinas County Coroner announced that the deceased had died of an overdose of barbiturates mixed with alcohol. Time of death was put at about ten hours previous to the discovery of the body, which would make it shortly after midnight on that Monday morning.

Dr. Spector at once called in Professor H. F. Clews, of Yale University, for an expert opinion on the condition of the Collection. The Collection, in Dr. Clews's opinion, had suffered some deterioration since he had last examined it, probably as a result of having stood for more than a year in a semi-outdoors, subtropical location. But it was still, essentially, intact.

At the request of Maloney's mother, the body was flown to Montreal, where, after a private funeral, it was buried in the family plot in Mount Royal Cemetery. Mrs. Maloney refused to make the body available for medical research. Maloney died intestate, but royalties from the Collection are now being paid to his mother, who is his only surviving relative. The royalties in question have greatly diminished since his death. For, while tour groups continue to patronize the nearby Great Victorian Village, paid admissions to the Collection itself are now minimal. The number of guides has been reduced to two. As Dr. Spector wrote in the afterword to his final report in the *Journal of Parapsychology,* Vol. XX, No. V:

"Later, as is often the case in such matters, fewer and fewer people seemed to believe in the veracity of Maloney's account of the circumstances of the Collection's creation. Nevertheless, as our researches have shown, there seems no reason to doubt that this Collection, a duality which exactly reproduces the originals it commemorates, will continue to exist as a minor marvel in Carmel-by-the-Sea, California. The extent to which it will outlive the man who created it, or its interest to succeeding generations, is, of course, beyond the range of our predictions."